Nate concentrated on threading among the trees with the same skill as his Indian companions. The chase continued, and Nate and the Flatheads were goaded on by distant war whoops. When the forest gave way, Running Elk took the lead, skirting a hill and, hemmed in on both sides by high rock walls, entering a ravine. The rest promptly followed.

Nate didn't like being boxed in. Should the Utes gain the rim, he and his companions would be easy to pick off. Nate avoided a boulder in his path and saw Running Elk bear right as the ravine curved. Seconds later he galloped around the turn and was stunned to discover the Flatheads bunched together at the base of another stone wall. The ravine was a dead end.

DEATH HUNT

Exercising extreme caution, Nate moved closer to the rim of the drop-off. He heard a guttural cough, then the distinct whine of an infant. The baby was down there! Eager to save the child, Nate dashed forward and took in the scene twelve feet below.

The mountain lion stood in the middle of a secluded gully. At its huge feet rested the cradleboard. The lion was eyeing the baby hungrily and might tear into it at any moment.

Nate took a hasty bead on the cat's head, hoping to end the menace with one shot. He began to steady his rifle when he felt his left foot slip out from under him. Startled, he realized he was going over the bank....

Other *Wilderness* Double Editions:
KING OF THE MOUNTAIN/
    LURE OF THE WILD
SAVAGE RENDEZVOUS/BLOOD FURY
TOMAHAWK REVENGE/
    BLACK POWDER JUSTICE

WILDERNESS

VENGEANCE TRAIL
DEATH HUNT

DAVID THOMPSON

LEISURE BOOKS   NEW YORK CITY

LEISURE BOOK®

August 1997

Published by

Dorchester Publishing Co., Inc.
276 Fifth Avenue
New York, NY 10001

If you purchased this book without a cover you should be aware
that this book is stolen property. It was reported as "unsold and
destroyed" to the publisher and neither the author nor the publisher has received any payment for this "stripped book."

VENGEANCE TRAIL Copyright © 1991 by David L. Robbins
DEATH HUNT Copyright © 1992 by David L. Robbins

All rights reserved. No part of this book may be reproduced or
transmitted in any form or by any electronic or mechanical means,
including photocopying, recording or by any information storage
and retrieval system, without the written permission of the
Publisher, except where permitted by law.

The name "Leisure Books" and the stylized "L" with design are
trademarks of Dorchester Publishing Co., Inc.

Printed in the United States of America.

Dedicated to
Judy, Joshua, and Shane.
And to Scott Kendall,
a great guy.

VENGEANCE TRAIL

Chapter One

The lone rider reined up on the crest of a rise and surveyed the pristine landscape below. He was a tall, muscular man, not yet twenty years of age, as hard as iron and radiating vitality. Buckskins and moccasins clothed his powerful frame. On his head perched a brown beaver hat. Jutting from under the hat, at the rear, was the tip of a white eagle feather securely tied to his shoulder-length black hair. His green eyes noted every detail of the terrain with delight.

A February thaw had transformed the Rocky Mountains from a snow shrouded wilderness into a prematurely glorious, spring-like wonderland. Temperatures in the fifties and sixties over the past week and a half had melted most of the white mantle, causing the rivers and streams to run full and tinged the brown grass with a dash of green. A few deciduous trees, fooled by the unseasonal warmth, had started to bud. The perennial evergreens, smarter and hardier, had only to lose their heavy, hoary blankets of wet, packed flakes to present the illusion of springtime.

Nodding in satisfaction, the young man urged his big black stallion down the slope. Had anyone been watching, they would have noticed that he appeared armed as if for a war. Slanted across his chest were a powder horn and a bullet pouch. Two flintlocks were nestled under his wide brown leather belt, one on each side of the buckle. A butcher knife with a 12-inch blade rested in a beaded sheath on his right hip. Angled under his belt above his left hip was a tomahawk. And resting across his thighs, his left hand loosely holding it in place, was a Hawken rifle. A Mackinaw coat and a bedroll were positioned snugly behind the saddle, and dangling from the saddle horn was a water bag.

He picked his way with care down the slippery slope and breathed a sigh of relief when he reached the valley floor below. Scanning the land ahead, he searched for any sign of smoke that might be drifting skyward from the cabin he'd traveled twenty-five miles to reach. The azure heavens, however, were crystal clear.

Cradling the Hawken in the crook of his left elbow, he pressed onward. Although he saw no hint of habitation, he felt certain he was in the right valley. His best friend and mentor, Shakespeare McNair, lived in this remote nook of the world near the top of the Rockies. He was eager to find the grizzled mountaineer and ask his advice on two important matters.

A gurgling stream bisected the valley and he took the west bank, riding northward, seeing wildlife or signs of wildlife everywhere. Sparrows and chickadees chirped and frolicked in the undergrowth. Ravens and jays occupied the tall trees. Rabbits bounded from his path. Once he flushed an elk, and twice he saw black-tailed deer in the distance. Along the stream, imprinted in the dark soil, were the tracks of countless creatures that had quenched their thirst at the water's edge. There were tiny chipmunk tracks and huge bear tracks, panther tracks and bobcat tracks, wolf tracks and fox tracks. He saw them all as he traveled a half-mile, and then he saw the cabin.

He almost missed it, so cleverly was the log structure blended into the surrounding forest. Shakespeare had constructed it at the base of a knoll fifty yards from the stream. Enormous pines ringed it, affording shade and protection from the elements. There was a pen for horses on the north side and a small shed to the south. A narrow strip of ground near the front door had been cleared of all brush, but otherwise the undergrowth was undisturbed. It was as if Shakespeare had deliberately built the cabin so it wouldn't disrupt the natural flow of things, just like an Indian would do.

Turning the stallion, he rode toward his friend's home. He noticed that no smoke curled from the sturdy stone chimney. Either Shakespeare wasn't in, he reasoned, or the grizzled mountaineer was forgoing a fire because of the warm weather. Suddenly he realized the front door was hanging open several inches and his eyes narrowed suspiciously.

Shakespeare would never go off and leave the door open knowing that a wandering bear or some other critter might waltz on in and help itself to the food supply and whatever else appeared tasty. He approached the cabin cautiously. Nothing stirred inside or out.

When the stallion was only ten feet from the door, he stopped. Gripping the Hawken in both hands, he slid to the ground and cocked the hammer. The loud click made him frown. Anyone or anything inside was bound to have heard it.

He advanced quickly and moved to the left of the

doorway, leaning against the jamb so he could peer within. The sight he beheld chilled the blood in his veins.

The interior of the cabin was in a shambles. Furniture had been upended, personal effects strewn about, and various items smashed to bits. Clothing lay in disarray. Broken dishes littered one corner.

Stark fear coursed through the young man's body. All he could think of was that his mentor had been slain, and in his mind's eye he envisioned Shakespeare being tomahawked or scalped. His heart beat wildly and his temples pounded. For a moment he felt dizzy. "Get a grip on yourself, Nate King," he said sternly.

Somewhere nearby a bird chirped.

The innocent sound served to snap Nate out of his anxious daze. He shook his head to clear his thoughts and stepped inside. Relief flared when he realized his friend's body was nowhere in the cabin. Perhaps, he told himself hopefully, Shakespeare was still alive. But if so, who had done this to the cabin and where was McNair?

He pivoted, scouring the room. Abruptly, he spied the large book lying on the floor next to an overturned table and stepped over to it. The title was easily discernible, and he read it with acute trepidation: THE COMPLETE WORKS OF WILLIAM SHAKESPEARE.

Nate's stomach muscles constricted. His friend would never go anywhere without that book. The volume had been Shakespeare's pride and joy, his constant companion on the trail or at home, going wherever he went to be read at any hour of the day or night. It was part of the reason McNair had long ago acquired the nickname 'Shakespeare'; that, and the fact McNair could quote countless passages from memory and did so with a striking eloquence.

If the book was there, Nate concluded, then his friend must be dead. He picked up the volume, righted the table, and gently placed the heavy book on top. Next he searched the cabin for traces of blood but found none. Mystified, he went outdoors and halted in consternation.

There were signs of Indians all over the place, clearly marked in the spongy soil. If not for the melted snow, the ground would have been too hard to bear many prints. He examined them at length and concluded the Indians had visited the cabin within the previous twenty-four hours and departed within the past twelve.

Chiding himself for not noticing the signs before, Nate bent at the waist and did the best he could reading the tracks. He wasn't as skilled as his mentor —yet—but he knew enough to deduce that ten mounted warriors had ridden up and eleven men had departed. He saw footprints he felt certain had been made by Shakespeare, leading to the inescapable conclusion that his friend had ridden off with the warriors.

Or been forced to accompany them.

Why else was the cabin a shambles? Nate mused. He turned, more perplexed now than ever. If hostile Indians had been responsible, they would have burned the building to the ground. Then again, while some of Shakespeare's things had been broken, most were undamaged. The clothes weren't torn to ribbons and the furniture was still intact. Hostiles would have taken particular delight in totally destroying both.

Nate let the hammer down on his rifle and thoughtfully scratched his chin. This made no sense, he noted. Friendly Indians wouldn't have committed such an outrage and hostiles would have skinned Shakespeare alive on the spot.

Strange.

He began executing a wide circle around the dwelling, seeking more signs. The trail the Indians had taken was as clear as the nose on his face; they'd ridden northward. If they had been a band of blood-thirsty Utes, who frequented the territory regularly, they would have ridden south toward one of the Ute villages. Due north lay land frequented by several tribes, not all of them friendly.

Now he had a decision to make, and he didn't like it one bit. He could mount up and follow the trail while it was still fresh, or he could forget the notion and do nothing. But if he didn't go after his friend, Shakespeare might well die and the death would be on his conscience for the rest of his born days.

So he should go.

But, Nate realized, if he rode off in pursuit, there was no way of determining when he would be able to return to his own cabin and his beloved wife. His beloved, *pregnant* wife who was due to deliver their baby in two moons. How could he desert her to go after Shakespeare?

Damn. What a fine pickle this was.

Maybe he should compromise, he decided. He could follow the trail for a short distance and try to ascertain if Shakespeare was with the Indians of his own free will or whether Shakespeare was a captive. The idea appealed to him. He swiftly closed the door to secure the cabin against animal invasion, then swung onto the stallion and took up the chase.

Since the sun was only a few hours above the eastern horizon, he would have plenty of time for tracking the band and still be able to turn back well before dark. He could spend the night in the cabin and head for home in the morning. With his mind made up, he goaded the stallion into a canter, eager to learn more.

The party had continued up the valley, then passed

between two lofty mountains. Another verdant valley stretched before Nate's admiring gaze, and he made a beeline across it as he stuck to the tracks. From the depth of the hoof prints and the long strides the horses had taken, he surmised the Indians were in a hurry to get somewhere. But where?

The band had come on a game trail and promptly changed direction. They were now moving to the northwest, still pushing their mounts.

Nate rode easily, his body flowing in rhythmic motion with the gait of his stallion. He tried not to think of the extra distance he was putting between his wife, Winona, and himself. Surely she would understand if for some reason he came back a day later than anticipated.

Thick woodland hemmed him in on both sides. He idly listened to the cries of animals and the songs of birds, his concentration focused on the trail. Dimly, he recalled Shakespeare advising him time and again to always be aware of the surrounding countryside, to always be alert for movement in all directions. But in his concern and haste he dispelled the memory and simply kept going.

The tracks climbed a gradual slope to a ridge, then went down the other side toward a small, shimmering lake. Nate spotted elk on the shore but they bolted as he drew closer. In the dank earth bordering the lake he found where the Indians had halted to allow their animals to drink. He did the same. Kneeling while the stallion gulped, he touched his fingers to several of the tracks, trying to gauge how far behind the band he was. The manner in which his fingers speared into the earth without making the dirt crumble convinced him he was not more than ten hours or so behind. Good. If he kept pushing, he could probably overtake them within the next day or so.

Nate mounted and resumed the pursuit, traveling

along the west shore of the lake, then entering a thick track of forest that seemed to stretch on forever. It was well past noon when he emerged from the vegetation into a high country meadow. A badger saw him and took flight. So did a doe.

He barely paid any attention to them. Preoccupied with his quest, he soon left the meadow behind and found himself in a region dotted with boulders the size of wagons. The tracks beckoned him ever onward, tantalizing him with the mystery of what lay at the end of the trail. He saw no evidence to indicate Shakespeare had been harmed. Because the mountain man's white mare, like Indian mounts, went unshod, it was difficult to tell which tracks had been made by Shakespeare's horse. Difficult, but not impossible.

The trail skirted another mountain. On the opposite side the direction of travel once more became northwest. Nate racked his brain, trying to remember which tribes dwelt in the land that lay ahead. The Shoshones, of course, the tribe into which he had been adopted by virtue of his marriage to Winona, herself a Shoshone. There were also Bannocks up that way, a tribe as ruthless in its extermination of whites as the widely dreaded Blackfeet. And, if he recollected Shakespeare's teachings correctly, the Nez Perce and the Flathead Indians also staked a claim to some of the land farther to the northwest.

He wound along a sparsely forested valley to a series of hills. The band had gone straight up one and he imitated their example. From the top a wondrous vista unfolded before his appreciative gaze. He could see for many miles no matter which way he turned. His pulse quickened when he spied a group of horsemen far, far to the northwest, crossing a plain. He squinted in the bright sunlight, striving to distinguish details, but the attempt was futile.

Then he heard a faint drumming noise.

For a moment Nate couldn't identify the sound. He cocked his head, listening intently, and belatedly realized the drumming was caused by horses moving at a full gallop—*to his rear*. Twisting, he gasped in surprise at discovering three Indians several hundred yards away, riding hard to overtake him. He recognized their style of dress instantly and goaded the stallion down the hill at a reckless pace, aware that his life hung in the balance if he failed to elude his pursuers.

They were Utes eager for his scalp.

Chapter Two

The big stallion's muscles rippled as it raced to the bottom of the hill and galloped between two others. Nate glanced over his right shoulder at the crest he had just vacated and saw the three Utes appear. One of them vented a savage whoop and the trio surged over the rim.

Facing front, Nate surveyed the terrain, trying to think of a way to shake the warriors. All three carried bows, and he knew from bitter experience that most Indian men were exceptionally adept archers. Warriors were trained from childhood in the use of the bow, and by the time they reached adulthood many could hit a target the size of an apple at fifty yards with consummate ease.

He held his body close to the stallion, trying to make as small a target of himself as possible. The feel of the Hawken in his left hand reassured him a bit. If he could get far enough ahead, he might be able to discourage the three warriors by slaying one.

Beyond the hills lay a grassy meadow. He made a beeline for the forest on the other side, and he was halfway across when he glimpsed the network of earthen burrows in his path. With a start he realized they were prairie dog holes, dozens and dozens of them, and he vividly recalled all the terrible stories he'd heard about careless riders who ventured into prairie dog towns and wound up being unhorsed when their mounts broke a leg and went down.

Nate's mouth went dry at the prospect. He was already among the low mounds. To try to stop would court disaster since slowing the stallion would more likely cause him to step full into a hole. He saw scores of the white-tailed rodents diving for cover, vanishing into their burrows with a flick of their tails while uttering shrill barks.

He did his best to avoid the larger mounds where the holes were obvious, but some holes were in flat ground where they were partially concealed by grass. A prairie dog abruptly darted in front of the stallion and the horse veered sharply to the left. A large mound lay right in their path.

Nate hauled on the reins in a frantic bid to avert catastrophe, but his efforts were in vain. The stallion started to go over the mound when one of its front legs caught in a burrow and it toppled forward. Nate threw himself from the saddle, leaping to the right, clutching the Hawken for dear life. He landed hard on his right shoulder and rolled to his knees, fearing the worst.

The stallion had also hit and rolled, and now the horse lay on its side, dazed, waving its legs and wheezing.

Shoving upright, Nate ran to his animal, fearing one of its legs had sustained a break. He moved around to its head and gripped the bridle, intending to help the horse rise. Then he heard a hateful screech and spun.

Charging toward him were the three Utes, who had fanned out to give themselves room to maneuver and to make it more difficult for him to slay them. They were slightly over one hundred yards off and each warrior already had a shaft nocked to his bowstring.

Nate knew there was no time to try and get the stallion up and ride off. If he attempted the feat, he'd be a pincushion before he traveled a dozen feet. His sole recourse was to fight and hope for the best.

He whipped the Hawken to his right shoulder, cocked the hammer, and took a bead on the centermost Ute. The warrior saw him aim and began swerving from side to side. Stubbornly, he tracked the rider, and when he felt certain he couldn't miss, he fired. At the booming retort lead streaked from the barrel accompanied by a cloud of acrid smoke.

Ninety yards out the middle warrior flung his arms into the air and pitched from his mount.

Nate quickly placed the rifle stock on the ground and went to work reloading, his fingers flying. He didn't want to rely on the pistols just yet. Move! his mind screamed. They're getting closer! He swiftly poured the proper quantity of black powder from his horn into the muzzle, using a crease in his palm as the mark to determine how much powder was sufficient. Then his fingers flew to the ammo pouch and removed a ball and patch. It took all of his self-control to prevent panic from overcoming him. He wrapped the ball in the patch and shoved both into the barrel using his thumb. With a wrenching motion he extracted the ramrod, glancing at his foes as he did.

The Ute on the right let an arrow fly.

Nate saw it coming, saw the glittering tip and the spinning feathers, saw that it had been aimed unerringly. All this he noticed in the span of a second, and even as the shaft arced down toward his chest he nimbly stepped to the right. The arrow thudded into the earth several feet past the spot where he had stood.

He glimpsed the other warrior about to fire and shoved the ramrod down the barrel. Don't stop! he urged himself. Stay calm and keep going. The ramrod tamped the ball home and he yanked the long rod out, let it fall, and pressed the stock to his shoulder once more.

Out of the blue flashed a whizzing arrow.

Acute pain flared in Nate's left shoulder. He looked down to find he'd been hit, creased by the shaft, his shirt and skin torn open. Ignoring the wound, he sighted on the warrior on the right, pulled back the hammer, and squeezed the trigger when the man was sixty yards distant.

The second Ute jerked when struck, then soundlessly toppled.

Only one left, Nate told himself, placing the rifle at his feet. He drew the twin flintlocks, pivoting to confront the last attacker. The Ute had a shaft ready to fly, and as Nate laid eyes on him he did just that.

Darting to the left, Nate extended both pistols. The shaft sped harmlessly past him. He couldn't fire yet, though. Pistols had a limited range and the final Ute was fifty yards away. He had to get closer, and instead of waiting for the warrior to come to him, he charged.

The Ute appeared surprised by the tactic. He was nocking yet another arrow, riding straight for the young mountaineer. In a smooth motion he brought the bow level.

Nate still couldn't fire. Both of his pistols were smoothbore single-shot .55 caliber flintlocks, powerful man-stoppers under thirty yards and forty yards still separated him from his enemy. He ran faster, hoping to shoot before the Ute let the arrow go. But the very next instant, the warrior fired.

Taking one more stride, Nate dived, landing on his
elbows and knees, pain jarring his limbs. He was
barely aware the shaft had passed harmlessly over his
head. All that mattered was ending the battle then and
there. From his prone position he held the pistols
steady, angled the barrels upward, and when the
onrushing Ute materialized in front of both sights,
about to loose another arrow, he squeezed both triggers.

The twin balls struck the warrior high in the chest,
smacking into his body and lifting him from his horse.
He grimaced as he fell, landing flat on his back and
not moving again.

Nate lay equally still, catching his breath, trying to
calm his nerves. He looked at each Ute; none displayed any hint of life. Then he remembered a crucial
lesson he'd learned the hard way, namely to never
leave his weapons unloaded for any longer than necessary. A mountaineer could never tell when a new
danger might crop up, sometimes immediately on the
heels of another.

He rose to his knees and proceeded to reload both
flintlocks. Once done, he hurried to retrieve the
Hawken and loaded it. As he slid the ramrod back into
its housing he looked around for the stallion. To his
delight, the horse was not more than fifteen yards to
the south, standing still. He ran to the grazing animal
and bent down to examine its legs. To his immense
relief, none were broken.

Nate straightened and saw the Ute mounts running
off to the southwest. He let them go. They were of no
use to him and he had more urgent business to attend
to. Mounting, he glanced at the corpses. A year ago he
would have given them a proper burial. But he'd
learned a great deal since coming West, and one of the
lessons had been that carrion eaters existed for a

reason. Who was he to deprive the coyotes and the buzzards of their food? The good Lord had put such critters on the Earth for a reason, and he wasn't about to buck divine foresight.

Shrugging, still ignoring his flesh-wound, Nate rode hard to the northwest. He eyed the nearby mountains excitedly, seeking the ideal spot. A deer trail leading up the slope of a high peak to his left attracted his attention. He estimated he could climb hundreds of feet before he would need to turn the stallion around, and from such a height he might be able to see the distant party on the far plain.

Up the slope he went, the stallion responding to his guidance. There were trees and high weeds on both sides until he rose above the vegetation and reined up. The plain was visible, but the party was nowhere in sight. Frustrated, he squinted, and at the extreme limit of his vision he spied them, a cluster of riders still bearing to the northwest. For a moment he thought he saw a white horse among the group, and then they were too indistinct for him to note any details at all.

Had he really seen Shakespeare's mare, or had his eyes played tricks on him? Nate frowned, debating what to do next. If he pressed the stallion to its limit, he might overtake that party by tomorrow afternoon at the very latest. It meant another day's delay in returning to Winona, but if Shakespeare was indeed in trouble, then he owed it to his best friend to make a rescue attempt.

The decision sparked prompt action. He turned the stallion and went to the bottom of the mountain, then headed toward the plain. Now that he had a definite destination in mind, he stuck to as straight a route as possible given the ruggedness of the terrain.

Slowly the day waned, the golden sun climbing ever

higher in the blue sky and dipping toward the western horizon. The shadows lengthened. As evening approached, deer and elk came out to feed in larger numbers.

Nate ignored them. He was too concerned over Shakespeare to think about food. Reaching that plain before nightfall became his singular goal. His thoughts strayed as he rode, dwelling on the beautiful woman he proudly called his wife and his anxiety over the impending birth. He'd never been a father, but he knew that childbirth could be dangerous for a woman, knew that many women died in delivery. The idea of such a fate befalling Winona was too horrible to contemplate, but contemplate it he had, which was one of the reasons he'd gone to visit Shakespeare.

The mountain man had been married before and must know all about the act of giving birth, Nate reasoned. He figured he could ask his mentor for advice on how best to guarantee Winona's delivery went without a hitch. There must be something he could do. When he'd broached the subject with Winona, she had bestowed one of her enigmatic wifely smiles on him and advised him not to worry, that she knew what to do and everything would be fine. So he'd bluntly asked her how she intended to deliver the baby by herself, and her answer had shocked him to his core.

"Indian women have been giving birth since the dawn of time," Winona had explained in the manner she might adopt to instruct a six-year old child. "I will go outside when the baby is ready, find a quiet spot in the woods, squat, and the baby will be born."

Nate had mistakenly believed she was joking and laughed. Her eyes had flashed in the manner they often did when he made a fool of himself, and he'd realized she was serious. "Dear God. You don't mean it?" he'd blurted.

"Is something wrong?" Winona had responded rather indignantly.

"Are you telling me that Shoshone women always go off by themselves to have babies? They must have help of some kind."

"Well, yes, we do."

"I knew it."

"We usually squat next to a sapling so we can grip the tree as tight as we want. It helps us when we push the baby from our womb."

"A tree?" Nate had repeated in amazement.

"Yes. How do white women give birth?"

"They lie in bed, as any sensible person would, and they have a doctor come to help them. If a doctor isn't available, then they get a midwife or a friend or two to help out."

Winona had stared at him in evident confusion. "White women give birth on their *backs?*"

"Certainly. Why?"

"But a baby must come out from between a woman's legs. It is so much easier if the woman is upright. Then the baby's own weight helps to bring it into this world. Why, the way you describe it, the woman must push and push to get the baby out," Winona had said, and then blinked as if in sudden comprehension. "Perhaps that is the reason white women need so much help."

"I'd be a lot more comfortable if *we* had some help," Nate had said.

Winona had laughed. "Since when does a Shoshone woman need help in using her body in the manner in which the Great Mystery intended it?"

Nate's cheeks flushed with embarrassment at the memory of that conversation. He hadn't been able to come up with a good answer for her, and now she was intent on delivering the baby alone. Why did women have to be so obstinate all the time? If there was one other lesson he'd learned since setting off on his own, it was an observation most men seemed to share: Women were damned peculiar.

He chuckled at the notion and absently scanned the forest ahead. By his reckoning he should reach the plain within an hour. He went around a thicket, over a knoll, and along a stream. Birds were chirping nearby and a squirrel chattered at him from a high tree. The tranquility lulled him into complacency, so he didn't notice the creature eyeing him hungrily until a bestial snarl rent the air and he glanced to his left to behold the terror of the Rocky Mountains, the scourge of every Indian and white man alike.

Lumbering toward him was a mighty grizzly bear.

Chapter Three

Nate urged the stallion into a race for its life, watching the bear charge and dreading the consequences should the horse falter. He'd tangled with grizzlies before and knew from firsthand experience why they were so formidable. Adult males weighed 1400 pounds or more and possessed five long claws on each paw that could be used to slash flesh to ribbons with a single swipe. And although grizzlies walked with a slow, clumsy gait, when necessary they could run as fast as a horse.

Now Nate found that out the hard way. He saw the grizzly gaining and goaded the stallion to greater speed. Since trying to shoot the grizzly while galloping on horseback would be a waste of the ball, unless by some miracle he hit an eye or the heart, he didn't bother to fire. He knew its thick skull protected the bear's brain from all but shots fired at very close range.

He could see the bear's sides heaving as the brute

ran. A pronounced hump above its shoulders distinguished the terrible beast from its lesser cousin, the black bear. The concave face, enormous in its own right, was set in feral determination.

Not this time! Nate thought, hunching over in the saddle.

On three prior occasions he'd been forced to fight grizzlies; once, while en route from St. Louis to the Rockies with his Uncle Zeke; again, when on the way to the 1828 rendezvous just last summer; and the third time while off with Shakespeare learning how to trap beaver. All three times he'd barely survived the encounters.

Thinking of those attacks brought to mind the Indian name bestowed on him by a Cheyenne warrior who witnessed the first scrape. 'Grizzly Killer,' the Indians now called him in honor of his prowess. Although, if it had been up to him, he would gladly have avoided each run-in with the fierce beasts. Having an Indian name was fine, but gaining it had nearly cost his life.

The grizzly vented a furious roar.

Nate looked back, elated to find the stallion had pulled out well ahead of the bear. Grizzlies weren't able to sustain their top speed for any great distance, so the stallion's stamina would prove the determining factor. He stared anxiously down at the ground, afraid there might be more prairie dog burrows in his path, but the ground was level and clear.

After a minute the grizzly gave up the chase and slowed to a disgruntled walk. It glared at the departing horse as if indignant that any animal would decline the privilege of being its main course.

Laughing in delight, Nate straightened and continued toward the plain. But he was more alert, constantly scanning the countryside for bears. Grizzlies were everywhere in the Rockies and the Plains, and their aggressive temperaments made them the most dangerous creatures in the wilderness.

The sun sank below the horizon and twilight enveloped the landscape. Still Nate pressed ahead, and the shadows had merged into an inky blanket by the time he ultimately reached his destination.

At the southern edge of the plain he halted, planning to make camp right there, but the stallion raised its head and sniffed loudly, then tapped one hoof on the ground, seemingly eager to keep going. He gave it a free rein and the horse cut to the right, traveled fifteen yards, and stopped beside a small spring.

Nate patted the stallion's neck in gratitude. "Always trust your horse's instincts," Shakespeare had once advised him, and the admonition had proven remarkably beneficial. He climbed down and let the stallion drink.

Should he make a fire or not? Nate mused, and decided against the notion. Campfires stood out like sore thumbs in the vast sea of benighted forest, and for all he knew the party he'd seen might spot his. He had plenty of jerked venison in his saddlebags and fresh water to drink. A fire wasn't necessary, although he was tempted to start one just so he could spend a few hours reading his copy of James Fenimore Cooper's latest book. He'd already read *THE LAST OF THE MOHICANS* once and liked it so much he'd begun reading it again.

He stripped off the saddlebags and the saddle, then tied the stallion to a nearby tree using a twenty-foot length of rope so the horse could graze at its leisure. Not tying a horse in Indian country was downright foolish, since the animal might wander off or Indians might steal it. The trappers had a saying along those lines: "It's better to count ribs than to count tracks."

Which meant it was wiser to let a horse go a little hungry by limiting its grazing space rather than let it loose to roam and not have it in the morning.

He took a handful of venison from the saddlebags, spread his blanket near the water, and settled down for the night. From near and far arose the sounds of animals; the deep coughs of panthers, the hoots of owls, the howling of wolves, and the yipping of coyotes. Stars filled the heavens, more than he had ever seen at any one time in New York City, and he propped his head on his left hand to admire the celestial spectacle.

Nate wondered about Winona, hoping she was well. He felt slightly guilty over leaving her to visit Shakespeare, but the trip had to be made. Besides her upcoming delivery, there was the matter of the guns to discuss.

Recently three men had tried to trade crates of rifles to the Utes in exchange for prime beaver pelts. Had they been successful, the Utes would have acquired the firepower necessary to become the dominant tribe in the Rockies. Only through sheer chance had Nate discovered their greedy scheme and thwarted it. Now all three were dead and he had the crates safely buried near his cabin. He hoped Shakespeare could give him advice on what to do with the guns.

He finished the jerked meat and drank heartily from the spring. He could hear the stallion munching on grass, and deep in the forest an animal shrieked in pain, perhaps under attack by a predator. Laying down again, he pondered his predicament and debated whether to turn around by tomorrow night if he failed to overtake the riders he'd spotted. Gradually his eyelids drooped and he entered the realm of dreams, although in his case they were nightmares. Once he imagined Shakespeare being hacked to bits by a band of hostiles wielding butcher knives, and later he dreamed that Winona had fallen and hurt herself and was calling his name over and over in vain.

The chirping and raucous cries of countless birds roused him from slumber before the sun rose. He sat up, listening to them greet the dawn in their own cheery manner, then rose and stretched. The stallion eyed him expectantly. He led it to the spring, chewed on a piece of venison while it drank, then saddled up. Twenty minutes after opening his eyes he was on the way again.

Nate found the tracks left by the band and followed them. Crossing the plain took hours; the sun was high by the time he reached a tract of woodland and found where the band had paralleled a stream for a spell. In a spacious clearing he came on the warm embers of a dying fire, the site where the band had camped for the night. The find encouraged him. It meant he was closer to them than expected.

He pressed onward, noting the riders were continuing to bear generally to the northwest. Unfortunately, the mystery party left no clues behind as to their identity beyond the obvious fact they were Indians.

At noon he was deep in mountains again. He halted for a brief break, eating more jerky and allowing the stallion to rest. Then he mounted and headed out.

After he covered two more miles, a high ridge appeared. The trail wound along its base, bearing westward because the riders skirted it, but he altered direction and rode to the top of the ridge in the hope of seeing them. No sooner did he rein up than his persistence was rewarded.

Eleven men were less than a quarter of a mile away, camped at the edge of a meadow. He spied a white horse that might or might not be Shakespeare's. Grinning, he retraced his path to the bottom. The Indians, not expecting pursuit, had stopped for an extended midday rest. Now he would find out what was going on.

He rode to the west end of the ridge, then warily moved into dense woodland beyond. The meadow wasn't more than a couple of hundred yards off and he exercised the utmost caution as he drew within half that distance and dismounted. After tying the stallion to a low limb, he hefted the Hawken and stealthily advanced until he could see figures moving through the trees.

Nate crouched, going from trunk to trunk, studiously avoiding all twigs and branches in his path. Twenty yards from the band he eased onto his stomach and proceeded to crawl. He glimpsed Indians whose style of dress seemed oddly familiar, although try as he might he couldn't place them. Then he spotted Shakespeare.

He halted in surprise, his eyes narrowing. The mountain man was conversing with two warriors. Shakespeare's hands weren't tied, but Nate noticed something odd. His friend wasn't carrying any weapons, not even a knife. Since no mountaineer in his right mind would go anywhere unarmed, Nate concluded the Indians had taken his mentor's firearms and butcher knife. But if so, and acting on the logical assumption Shakespeare was their prisoner, why had the warriors not bound him? At the very least Nate expected to find his friend's wrists bound.

It made no sense.

Perplexed, Nate inched nearer until he was within ten feet of the band, lying partially concealed under the low limbs of a small pine tree. Another fact struck him as strange. Previously, the warriors had been heading northwest at a rapid clip. Yet now they were idly conversing as if they didn't have a care in the world and weren't in any great hurry to reach their destination.

Nate scanned the entire group, striving to piece together some rhyme or reason to their behavior. His brain abruptly shrieked a warning and he felt that something was very, very wrong, but he couldn't isolate the cause. He studied the Indians, even more closely.

And then he saw it.

With a start Nate realized there were only eight warriors present now, not ten. Where were the other two? He looked right and left and saw no indication of them. Between the time he'd spotted the whole band from the ridge and his arrival at the meadow, the pair had disappeared. He figured they must be in the woods hunting for game.

Thank goodness he hadn't blundered into them!

He saw Shakespeare peer into the forest and frown. Why? The idea of signaling his friend occurred to him but he discarded the notion as too dangerous. One of the Indians might see him. He crossed his forearms and rested his chin on them, the Hawken at his right side.

A tall Indian approached McNair. He wore fine buckskins and had long, dark, braided hair flecked with spots of gray and adorned with four eagle feathers. Instead of a bow, which was far more common among warriors of all tribes, he cradled a flintlock rifle in his arms.

Nate figured the warrior must be a prominent member of the tribe. The man stopped and addressed Shakespeare, and to Nate's utter amazement the warrior spoke English.

"It will not be long now, Carcajou."

The name was familiar to Nate. It was the French word for the wolverine, a denizen of the Rockies reputed to be every bit as fierce as the grizzly, and the name by which several of the tribes referred to the white-haired mountain man. He saw Shakespeare glare at the speaker, then respond bitterly.

"May all your male children become women."

One of the other warriors laughed.

The tall Indian took the insult in stride. He sighed and gazed into the distance. "How long will you be mad at me, my brother?"

"For as long as the sun shines," Shakespeare replied. "And don't call me your brother, Buffalo Horn. You are the lowest, meanest son of a bitch who ever lived and I hope the Blackfeet take your hair real soon."

Nate was astounded his friend would use such language. Indian men adhered to a strong unwritten code of honor and dignity, and they rarely tolerated personal insults. Then, to compound his confusion, the tall warrior and the same one who had laughed before both did so.

This other warrior, a lean man with a hooked nose and a pointed chin, wagged the war club he held and said, "You know a man must be true to his word. Whether white or Indian, a man's word is a measure of his worth as a human being."

Shakespeare bristled. "If I wasn't so outnumbered I'd teach you about worth, Running Elk, you polecat."

Buffalo Horn made a gesture as if to say that talking with McNair was a waste of time. "We have been through that once."

"Don't remind me," Shakespeare said.

"I never thought I would live to see the day when *you* would turn your back on your word," Buffalo Horn declared. "And after all that happened."

"It happened twenty years ago, damn your hide," Shakespeare snapped. "You can't expect to hold me to it after so much time has passed."

"It is out of my hands," Buffalo Horn said solemnly.

"I'll remember you for this," Shakespeare promised. "Some day, some way, I'll get even."

Nate wished one of them would drop a clue as to the topic of their discussion. He had no idea what was going on. Sliding forward several inches, he cocked his head to listen better. So well that he distinctly heard the click of a hammer being cocked. A heartbeat later he felt the barrel of a gun jab into the nape of his neck.

Chapter Four

Nate froze, knowing the slightest move would prove fatal. He heard someone snicker, and then a pair of moccasin covered feet stepped into view. The gun barrel, however, never moved, which indicated there were two of them. The two missing warriors, he figured.

A young warrior squatted in front of him. Smiling, he wagged a tomahawk he held in his right hand, then motioned for Nate to rise.

Bewildered, Nate complied. The pressure on his neck disappeared, and a second warrior moved around in front of him. This one held a cocked fusee, one of the inferior trade rifles the Indians received from the fur companies in exchange for prime pelts. While fusees lacked the range of conventional long guns, they were every bit as lethal pinned in one's neck.

The warrior with the tomahawk leaned forward and picked up the Hawken. Rising, he removed both of

Nate's pistols, the butcher knife, and Nate's tomahawk. He admired the weapons for a bit, then jerked his thumb toward the camp.

Incensed at himself for being taken so easily, Nate walked forward. The other Indians heard him coming, as did Shakespeare, and they turned to regard him with a mixture of curiosity and amusement, but no hostility.

The mountain man placed his hands on his hips and declared testily, "I thought I taught you better than this. How could you let yourself be taken by these half-wits?"

"I was about to ask the same thing of you," Nate retorted, annoyed at the brusque greeting. After all the trouble he had gone to, he felt a friendly smile at the very least was in order.

A hearty laugh burst from Buffalo Horn. "The cub has a point, Carcajou. What is your answer?"

Shakespeare snorted indignantly. "I have a valid excuse. You curs sneaked into my cabin while I was reading and got the drop on me. Otherwise, I wouldn't be here."

Running Elk grinned. "And we should thank you for leaving your door open. Otherwise, we could never have sneaked in."

"Grind a man's face in it, why don't you?" Shakespeare snapped, and glancing at Nate he encompassed all of the band in a single sweep of his arm. "Go, bind thou up yon dangling apricots, which, like unruly children, make their sire stoop with oppression of their prodigal weight: Give some supportance to the bending twigs. Go thou, and like an executioner, cut off the heads of too fast growing sprays, that look too lofty in our commonwealth."

Nate knew his mentor had quoted William Shakespeare again, although he had no idea from which play the quote stemmed. He saw Buffalo Horn and Running Elk exchange grins and shook his head in confusion.

The warrior who had confiscated Nate's weapons stepped forward and placed them at Buffalo Horn's feet. A short discussion in their native tongue ensued, after which the two warriors responsible for his capture hastened back into the forest.

"They will find your horse and bring it here," Buffalo Horn addressed Nate. "You will need it on the long ride ahead."

"What long ride?" Nate asked, and faced his mentor. "Do you mind telling me what in blazes is going on?"

"What's to explain?" Shakespeare rejoined. "It should be obvious. We're in the clutches of savages who will likely take our hair."

Buffalo Horn hissed like an angry viper. "That is not true and you well know it, McNair. We will not harm a hair on either of you." He paused and smirked. "Unless you try to escape, of course."

"Heathen devil," Shakespeare muttered, and walked a few yards to the west, turning his back on the Indians.

Stepping to his friend's side, Nate placed a hand on Shakespeare's shoulder. "None of this makes any sense to me. You seem to know these Indians. Who are they?"

"Flatheads," Shakespeare snapped distastefully.

Suddenly Nate recollected where he had seen such Indians before; at the last rendezvous. Various tribes attended the rowdy annual event to trade, sell women, or participate in the contests of marksmanship, horse riding, and other skills. "The same ones who were at the rendezvous?" he inquired, studying them.

"No, a different bunch," Shakespeare said. "Buffalo

Horn and these others are from another village. They weren't at the rendezvous because they're afraid to travel so near to Blackfoot country."

Nate glanced at Buffalo Horn, who had overheard the remark, and saw the Indian scowl.

"Again you lie, McNair," the warrior declared. "We have been at the rendezvous every year except last year, when we could not come because of a council we were holding with the Nez Perce. Why must you keep trying to make me mad?"

"Because I'm hoping you'll take a swing at me so I can break your jaw," Shakespeare responded.

Buffalo Horn looked at Nate. "Please forgive his manners, Mr. King. Most men would not treat their brother-in-law with such disrespect."

"Brother-in-law?" Nate said in astonishment, then realized the Flathead had called him by name. "Wait a minute. How is it that you know me?"

"Shakespeare has told us much about you," Buffalo Horn said. "He told us you are not like most whites. You respect our way of life and the earth on which all men must live. He says you are a mighty warrior and generations to come will remember you."

"He did?" Nate blurted in surprise.

"I was exaggerating," Shakespeare said defensively. "I was trying to convince them to let me go. Told them you'd be after them if they didn't." He snorted again. "I had no idea you'd practically walk into their hands."

"They found me by accident," Nate said.

"Accident, hell. Running Elk saw you on that ridge back yonder," Shakespeare stated. "They deliberately dawdled here to give you a chance to make a fool of yourself. And you accommodated them."

"They set a trap for me?"

The mountain man nodded. "Buffalo Horn sent

two men into the trees to wait for you to show up. He told them to take you alive, otherwise you'd be bald right about now."

Nate felt like a prize dunderhead. He glanced at the forest to discover his two captors returning with his black stallion, then at Buffalo Horn, the man who claimed to be McNair's brother-in-law. The thought jogged his memory. "Didn't you once tell me that you were married to a Flathead woman a long time ago?"

"I may have."

"Was the woman Buffalo Horn's sister?"

"Unfortunately."

Nate's confusion doubled. When a white man married an Indian woman, the tribe usually adopted the groom as one of their own, just as the Shoshones had done with him. If the Flatheads had done likewise with Shakespeare, why were they taking him against his will? And to where? He posed the question to Buffalo Horn.

"We are on our way to our village," the warrior answered. "You are welcome to come, if you like. If not, and if you give your word that you will not interfere with what must be done, we will give you back your weapons and allow you to ride off."

"Just like that?"

"My people have never taken the life of a white man and there is no reason for us to take yours," Buffalo Horn said. "We have always been friendly to all whites. When trappers come to our village, we feed them and let them stay in our lodges. Even though many of them treat us as inferiors, we know that all men are brothers."

Nate didn't know what to say.

"My people are as friendly to whites as your wife's people, the Shoshones," Buffalo Horn went on.

"You know about my wife, then?"

"Carcajou told us."

Shifting, Nate regarded his mentor critically. "Is there anything you *didn't* tell them?"

Shakespeare made a show of placing a palm to his forehead and feigning hurt feelings. "Thy wit is a very bitter sweeting. It is a most sharp sauce."

Buffalo Horn took a step toward Nate. "Do you understand him when he talks like that?"

"Sometimes," Nate said.

"I never do," the Flathead said. "I think he does it just to upset other people."

"Probably," Nate agreed, and added, "You speak excellent English, though. Where did you learn it so well?"

"Carcajou taught me during the years he lived in our village."

"And me," Running Elk chimed in.

The grizzled mountain man sighed. "That's what I get for being so blamed considerate. I taught them the language, and now they use it to mock me and treat me like buffalo *crap.*"

"We do no such thing," Buffalo Horn said, and looked at Nate. "Now, what about you, Grizzly Killer? Do we have your promise you will not try to stop us from taking McNair to our village?"

"Are you fixing to harm him?"

"No."

Shakespeare pivoted and jabbed a finger at the warrior. "Now who is lying? You have the most horrible fate any man can face lined up for me. Why, I'd rather be skinned alive or eaten by a grizzly."

"You exaggerate again," Buffalo Horn said.

Nate couldn't take the suspense any longer. "What *is* the fate in store for him? Just what the hell is going on, anyway?"

Buffalo Horn went to answer when another brave

called out in the Flathead tongue and pointed to the southeast. Every warrior whirled.

Glancing in the same direction, Nate felt his breath catch in his throat at seeing over two dozen riders on the very same ridge he'd been on when he first spied the Flatheads. He could tell they were Indians and hoped they were friendly, but a single word uttered by Running Elk proved otherwise.

"Utes."

The Flatheads scrambled for their mounts even as the band of Utes vented war whoops and surged down the ridge toward them. Shakespeare ran to his white horse and swiftly mounted.

Nate found himself standing alone, not a yard from his weapons, the only one still on foot. He glanced at his rifle, wondering if the Flatheads would stop him if he made a grab for it.

Buffalo Horn moved his horse closer. "Pick up your guns. If those Utes catch us, they will torture us to death."

In a stride Nate was bending down to hastily reclaim all of his arms. In seconds the pistols, knife, and tomahawk were again around his waist and the Hawken in his left hand. He swung onto the stallion and noted with surprise that every Flathead had waited for him.

Barking words in the Flathead tongue, Buffalo Horn led the band to the northwest at a gallop.

Nate fell in beside Shakespeare, his stallion easily keeping pace. He was glad he'd opted to bring the big black instead of his mare. Recently acquired from the same trappers who had tried to trade rifles to the Utes, the stallion possessed remarkable strength and endurance.

The Flatheads quickly crossed the meadow and entered woodland on the far side, staying clustered together, each warrior riding with an air of grim resolve about him.

Glancing at his mentor, Nate saw the same expression on his friend. He knew from prior experience that Indians were capable of perpetrating atrocities every bit as grisly as any ever practiced by white men, especially where warring tribes were concerned. Buffalo Horn had understated the situation. Any Flathead who fell behind or was captured would die a horrible death.

He wondered why the Utes were at least a day's ride north of their normal range, and an answer occurred to him that made him stiffen in surprise. He might be the reason. If those three Utes he'd slain were part of a larger war party, when the other Utes found the bodies they would have set out to track the culprit down. They had tracked him to the top of the ridge and spied the Flatheads.

Damn. It was all his fault.

Nate concentrated on the task at hand, threading among the trees with the same skill as his Indian companions. He saw Buffalo Horn look back at him two or three times. Why? And what would the Flathead do once they eluded the Utes? Try to take his weapons again? He wasn't going to permit it, no matter what.

As the chase continued, the Flatheads were goaded on by the distant whoops of their fierce mortal enemies. When the forest gave way to a series of hills, Running Elk took the lead in winding among them.

Looking over his shoulder, Nate was startled to find four of the Utes had pulled out well ahead of the rest and were closing the gap rapidly.

Running Elk skirted a hill and, hemmed in on both sides by high rock walls, entered a ravine. The rest promptly followed.

Nate didn't like being boxed in. Should the Utes gain the rim, the Flatheads would be easy to pick off. So, for that matter, would Shakespeare and he. Nate avoided a boulder in his path and saw Running Elk bear to the right as the ravine curved. Seconds later he galloped around the turn and was stunned to discover the Flatheads bunched together at the base of another stone wall.

The ravine was a dead end.

Chapter Five

Nate hauled sharply on the reins to avoid colliding with the Flatheads in front of him. The black stopped almost instantly, jerking its head up within inches of another animal's rump. He heard thundering hooves to his rear and glanced back to see one of the warriors stop almost on top of him. For a few moments confusion reigned. The Flatheads were talking excitedly in their own tongue, some pointing at the high walls.

All Nate could think of was the Ute war party rapidly drawing closer. He brought the stallion around, motioning for the nearest warriors to move their animals so he could accomplish the feat, and glanced at his friend.

Shakespeare had done the same. "We've got to get out of here," he stated somberly.

Nate nodded. He felt the same sense of dire urgency. The Utes would reach the mouth of the ravine soon, if they hadn't already, and he wasn't too fond of the notion of fighting his way through them in the

cramped confines of the rocky defile. Thank goodness
he had the pistols; they would give him a slight edge.
He started to move past the milling Flatheads, glancing over his shoulder at Buffalo Horn. "I'll take the
lead," he offered. "Have your people ride hard on my
heels."

"Wait for me," Shakespeare said, and looked at the
tall warrior. "I want my weapons, damn you, and I
want them now."

Buffalo Horn frowned and hesitated.

"I need a chance to defend myself, don't I?" Shakespeare demanded angrily.

Demonstrating marked reluctance, Buffalo Horn
snapped instructions at another warrior, who then
moved his horse over beside Shakespeare's and
handed over the mountain man's rifle, pistol, and
knife.

Shakespeare beamed as he reclaimed his weapons.
"I should thank the Utes for this," he said in delight.

"Ready?" Nate asked impatiently, eager to be off
before the Utes had them trapped.

Nodding, Shakespeare hefted his rifle and gripped
his reins tightly. "Advance our standards, set upon
our foes. Our ancient word of courage, fair Saint
George, inspire us with the spleen of fiery dragons!
Upon them! Victory sits on our helms," he roared,
and grinned. "King Richard III."

Nate shook his head and goaded the stallion into a
gallop. Sometimes he wondered if his good friend had
been struck on the head as a child. He discarded the
train of thought to concentrate on the critical matter
at hand. Behind him came Shakespeare and the
Flatheads, the pounding of their horses echoing off the
stone walls.

Had the Utes reached the ravine? That was the
crucial factor. Nate tensed as he came to the turn and

raced around it to see his worst fears realized.

The four Utes who had pulled ahead of their fellows were just entering the narrow chasm. They spied the onrushing frontiersman immediately and voiced strident cries. A hundred yards to their rear, coming on strong, was the rest of the war party.

Nate never let the stallion break stride. He leaned forward, a fiery resolve fueling his being, and tucked the Hawken's stock into his right shoulder. Aiming on horseback was difficult under the best of circumstances, and Nate found the task harder while weaving among the boulders scattered in his path. He saw the Utes stop as three of the warriors frantically tried to nock shafts to their bow strings and the fourth wagged a war club overhead. Good. The Flatheads would have momentum working in their favor when they crashed into their foes.

He took a bouncing bead on the foremost Ute, a stocky man armed with a bow, and when only ten feet from the quartet he fired. His ball bored into the Ute's face just as the warrior raised a bow, catapulting the stocky figure off his horse. Nate sped onward, holding the rifle and the reins in one hand while he drew a pistol with the other.

From behind him came the blast of Shakespeare's rifle and a second Ute toppled.

Nate was on the remaining twosome before he could so much as blink. A war club swooped at his head and he ducked under the blow, extending his pistol at the same instant and sending a ball into the Ute's forehead. And then he was past the ravine mouth, temporarily in the clear. Temporarily, because he was now hemmed in by hills on each side and charging toward him was the rest of the war party, in the same gap, not seventy yards away.

Going straight would be certain suicide. Nate cut to

the right, heading up the slope, his body held low over the stallion's back as the animal's powerful legs drove them upward. A backward glance showed Shakespeare and the Flatheads following his example. Lying in the ravine were the bodies of the four Utes. Not one Flathead had been slain . . . yet.

Nate looked at the Utes. They were galloping up the hill on an intercept course, but the steep slope was slowing them down, just as it impeded his stallion. He wedged the spent pistol under his belt and kept going. The top of the hill was fifty feet off, yet seemed to be a mile. Focusing on the rim, he rode like a madman.

The Utes were shrieking loud enough to be heard clear back in Missouri.

In less than half a minute the black stallion attained the crest, and Nate paused to mark the progress of his friends and his foes. Shakespeare and the Flatheads were right behind him, the Utes thirty feet below. He whipped out the second pistol, tilted the barrel to compensate for the distance and the elevation, and fired, not really expecting to score a hit but to deter the war party.

One of the foremost riders threw out his arms and fell with a scream.

Five down, Nate mentally noted, but the Utes still outnumbered his allies. Jamming the flintlock underneath his belt, he spun the stallion and headed for the far side. Shakespeare and several of the Flatheads were ahead of him, and the mountain man sped over the rim a heartbeat later. He found himself riding beside Running Elk, and the two of them rode even with one another as they left the top and galloped down the opposite slope. Even steeper on this side, Nate had to dig his feet into his stirrups to keep from being unhorsed.

At the bottom lay a plain, and Nate breathed a sigh

of relief as the stallion hit the level ground and went all out, passing several of the Flatheads. In short order he was again next to his mentor.

Shakespeare grinned at him, as if enjoying every second of their harrowing ordeal. "This is the life!" he shouted.

Nate didn't bother responding. As far as he was concerned, he much preferred a quiet evening home alone with Winona to racing pell-mell through the wilderness with bloodthirsty Utes on his tail.

For minutes the chase continued, the Utes not more than thirty yards behind. The plain ended, replaced by verdant forest, which in turn gave way to an arid tract of dusty red earth marred by deep ruts.

Twisting in his saddle, Nate was overjoyed to find the Utes had fallen even farther behind. He faced front as Shakespeare changed direction slightly, making to the northwest where high peaks dominated the landscape, and emulated him. The prospect of finding themselves in another ravine or box canyon caused his stomach muscles to tighten, and he prayed that Shakespeare knew what he was doing.

They attained the mountains without mishap. By now all the animals were tiring and the pace had flagged considerably. Skirting the base of the first peak in the range, Shakespeare swung into a wide gully.

Nate got the impression his friend was heading for a specific destination. Even so, he gazed nervously at the stone walls. To his relief, when only halfway into the gully the mountain man suddenly reined to the right toward a narrow opening. He was forced to ride directly behind Shakespeare as they entered since there wasn't room for both of them. A rocky trail led from the gully floor to the top of the north wall, and once up there he looked toward the entrance where the Utes had yet to appear.

Shakespeare swung off his mount and motioned for Nate to do the same. "Don't just sit there! Reload!"

Insight dawned, and Nate promptly dismounted and hastily commenced reloading all three of his weapons.

The Flatheads joined them, swinging down and moving to the lip of the wall where they crouched and nocked arrows in preparation for the ambush.

As Buffalo Horn went to walk past Shakespeare, the mountain man grabbed the warrior's arm. "Where the blazes are my powder horn and ammo pouch? I need to reload my rifle."

The tall Flathead pointed at another warrior, who had Shakespeare's items slanted across his slim chest, and motioned for them to be returned to their rightful owner.

All this Nate absently took in as he reloaded, his fingers flying. He finished with the Hawken and reached for a flintlock when the drumming hooves of their enemies heralded the arrival of the Utes in the gully. With no time to lose, he dashed to the lip and knelt, staying low to avoid detection.

The Utes were pushing their mounts to the limit. Having lost ground during the last few miles, they were apparently trying to make it up. They galloped down the gully without once gazing up at the top of the walls.

Nate tingled in nervous expectation. He cocked the hammer, his gaze glued to the war party, watching the lead riders. Dust kicked into the air by the Flatheads' mounts still hung in small clouds, rendering it difficult for the Utes to see tracks. A few were trying to do just that, bending down as they rode.

The Flatheads had their bows ready, except for two men who held fusees and Buffalo Horn with his rifle.

When the Utes were almost to the side opening, a warrior in the lead glanced in that direction, saw it, and shouted. The Utes were now twenty feet away and fifteen feet below the rim.

Rising, Buffalo Horn took aim and fired. It was the signal for the other Flatheads to do the same. A shower of arrows and lead poured down onto the hapless Utes, piercing torsos, spearing through necks, or striking limbs.

Nate sighted on the Ute who appeared to be in charge of the war party, the one who had spotted the opening. He took his time, wanting to be sure, holding his breath so he could keep the rifle steady, and fired as the Ute went to turn. The man clutched at his face, then pitched to the ground.

Eight of the Utes were lying in the dirt now. Shakespeare's Hawken cracked and a ninth fell. The survivors were desperately striving to flee, bumping into one another, their mounts spooked by the gunfire, the bodies underfoot, and the dust rising to choke the gully.

Shakespeare cackled in delight.

More and more arrows streaked into the disorganized Utes, their razor barbs slicing through flesh as readily as a Bowie through butter. Three more warriors were sprawled in the dirt before the rest finally got underway, racing for the entrance to the gully in stark fear for their lives, jostling each other in their anxious haste to be the first to escape the slaughter.

Nate didn't fire again. He'd wanted to stop the Utes as much as anyone there, but the one-sided massacre disgusted him. Shakespeare's rifle cracked almost in his very ear and yet another Ute hit the dirt. He shifted to see the Flatheads dashing to their mounts so they could give chase. Let them, he reflected. He had no craving for more killing. Instead, he reloaded the Hawken and both pistols, observing the next stage in the drama from where he knelt.

He saw the Flatheads burst from the side opening

and ride to the fallen Utes. To his surprise, the Flatheads stopped and jumped down. They weren't going to chase the rest of the war party, after all. Aghast, he observed them draw their knives and tomahawks and set to work on the dead and injured with a vengeance. Every body was repeatedly stabbed or hacked. Fingers were chopped from hands; noses and ears from heads; abdomens were ripped open and the entrails strewn about; and scalps were taken with the most savage joy imaginable. The Flatheads became spattered with blood and gore from their own grisly handiwork. Nate felt his stomach flutter and feared he might be sick.

"Not a pretty sight, is it?"

Nate started and turned to find his mentor regarding him carefully. "Revolting is more like it," he said, and stood, adjusting the flintlocks on either side of his belt buckle, the Hawken in his left hand.

"I figured you would be accustomed to this by now," Shakespeare said.

"I doubt I ever will."

"Then there's hope for you yet," the mountain man said with a snicker.

Nate wasn't sure if he'd been insulted or not. "And what about you?" he retorted. "You seemed to think this was all great fun. Weren't you in the least bit afraid for your life?"

Shakespeare launched into another quote from his favorite author. "My lord, wise men ne'er sit and wail their woes, but presently prevent the ways to wail. To fear the foe, since fear oppresseth strength, gives in your weakness strength unto your foe, and so your follies fight against yourself. Fear, and be slain; no worse can come to fight. And fight and die is death destroying death; where fearing dying pays death servile breadth."

"I don't have the foggiest notion what you're babbling about," Nate said testily.

Sighing, Shakespeare stared at the butchery transpiring in the gully. "When you've lived as many years as I have, Nate, you'll learn to take each moment as it comes and to fully appreciate whatever that moment brings."

"Oh? I seem to recall you're not very appreciative of the fact the Flatheads want to take you to their village."

"That's different."

"How so?"

Shakespeare looked Nate in the eyes. "They're taking me there to get married."

Chapter Six

"Get married!" Nate blurted in amazement.

A shadow seemed to descend over Shakespeare's weathered features. He nodded and said softly, "Oh, I am fortune's fool."

Bewildered, Nate idly gazed into the gully and saw Buffalo Horn decapitating one of the Utes. He watched the Flathead chop at the vanquished warrior's neck for a moment, then looked at his mentor. "You have some explaining to do."

Shakespeare stared off into the distance, his lips compressed, his brow knit in contemplation.

"When I found your cabin in a shambles, I figured you were in mortal danger," Nate went on. "I came all this way just to rescue you. You have no idea what I went through, and now you tell me that you're only going off to get married?"

"Unless I mount up and run," Shakespeare said, shifting to survey the mutilation taking place below them.

Nate realized that his friend was serious, and it shocked him. He'd never imagined Shakespeare would run from anything. There must be more to the situation. He realized both of them could slip away if they wanted since the Flatheads were totally preoccupied. "I'll go if you do," he said.

Shakespeare gazed at their horses, then back into the gully. He hefted his rifle, took a stride toward his mount, and abruptly halted. "Damn!" he snapped, and angrily slapped his thigh.

"What is the matter with you?" Nate asked, completely mystified. He'd never seen the mountain man behave in such a peculiar fashion, never known McNair to be the least bit indecisive.

"I can't cut out," Shakespeare said.

"Why not?"

"Because Buffalo Horn and Running Elk are right. A man must keep his word or he isn't much of a man."

"And you gave your word to marry someone?"

"About twenty years ago."

Nate cradled the Hawken in his arms and scrutinized his friend's tormented countenance. "Why don't you start at the beginning and tell me the whole story? The Flatheads will be busy for a while."

Sighing, Shakespeare stepped to a low boulder and sat down. He placed his rifle stock on the ground and gripped the barrel with both hands, his shoulders slumped in dejection. "You know I was once married to a Flathead called Rainbow Woman."

"You never mentioned her name."

"I don't like to talk about her much. Some memories are just too painful to bring out in the open," Shakespeare said, his voice lowering. "She was the most beautiful woman who ever walked this earth and I loved her with all of my soul."

"The Blackfeet killed her, didn't they?" Nate

brought up, and promptly regretted his stupidity when he saw Shakespeare wince as if from a physical blow.

"Yep. The stinking vermin hit the village one day at dawn. I told her to stay in our lodge while I went out to help the Flathead warriors fight them off." Shakespeare paused, inner pain twisting his face. "But of course she didn't listen. Women never do. She came out with a bow and was covering my back. I didn't even know it until she shouted a warning when a Blackfoot came at me from behind." He stopped and bowed his head, his shaggy mane of hair falling down over his eyes.

"What happened next?" Nate asked.

"I shot the Blackfoot, but while I was taking care of him another of the murdering sons of bitches put an arrow in Rainbow Woman."

Nate made no comment, his heart going out to the profoundly sad man seated in front of him, in perfect sympathy with his friend because he knew all too well how he would feel if the same fate were to befall his precious Winona.

"I left the Flatheads shortly after that terrible day," Shakespeare said.

"But what does all this have to do with Buffalo Horn taking you back for another marriage?" Nate inquired, hoping the change of topic would cheer McNair up.

Shakespeare straightened, the corners of his eyes slightly moist. "Rainbow Woman had two brothers, Buffalo Horn and Spotted Owl. I was good friends with them and spent a lot of time with Spotted Owl. One night, about a year before she was killed, we were sitting in his lodge and got around to discussing what would happen to our wives if either of us ever died. Indian men have a much shorter life expectancy than their women, you see. Well, we didn't want our wives to be forced to fend for themselves, and we damn sure didn't want them to take up with just any warrior who was interested in them so they'd have food to eat and a lodge to live in. So we took a vow."

"A vow?"

"Yes. Spotted Owl promised that if something ever happened to me, he would look after his sister. And I gave my word that if Spotted Owl should die, I would take his wife, Blue Water Woman, into my lodge."

Shakespeare fell silent, and suddenly Nate understood. "Spotted Owl has died?" he probed.

The mountain man nodded. "About six months ago. Buffalo Horn offered to take Blue Water Woman into his lodge, but she insisted that he find me and make me honor my vow."

"What?" Nate said in surprise. "After so many years have gone by since you made the promise? Why?"

"If I knew the answer to that I'd be a happy man," Shakespeare said, his tone conveying sheer misery. "Apparently, Buffalo Horn has been searching for me since then. Then he ran into a trapper from Canada, Frenchy D'Arnot, he's called, and that rascal Frenchy told him exactly where my cabin was. Even drew a map with all the major landmarks." Shakespeare's eyes acquired a flinty cast. "And here I thought Frenchy was a friend. Wait until I get my hands on him."

"If he's a friend, why did he do such a thing?"

"Because Frenchy is the biggest practical joker who ever wore pants. He's always pulling a trick on someone. Giving Buffalo Horn directions to my cabin was his way of having a laugh at my expense."

"Speaking of your cabin, why was it in such a mess?"

Shakespeare brightened somewhat. "Because I was determined not to go with Buffalo Horn and he was determined to take me. It took all ten of them to get me onto my horse."

"So you were never in any real danger?"

The mountain man bestowed a critical glance on his protege. "I keep forgetting that you've only been married a short while."

"So?"

"You still have romance in your blood. All Winona has to do is flutter her eyes and give you a kiss and you think you're on top of the world," Shakespeare said. "You won't begin to appreciate the true nature of marriage until after your first child is born. Then it will sink in."

"You're exaggerating again."

"Think so, do you?" Shakespeare responded, and laughed. "Nate, marriage is the most dangerous fate that can befall a man. Dangerous, because it's also the most glorious, and glorious because our passion overrides our wisdom and transforms us into doting idolaters at the altar of sweet Venus."

"You've lost me. Is that more Shakespeare?"

"No, I'm not quoting old William S. this time. I'm speaking from experience."

"Are you saying that the state of marriage is bad, that all marriages are wrong?"

"Never in a million years. Every man should get married. It's one of the reasons the good Lord put us here. If He had meant for men to be with men, He never would have created women."

"Then what's your point?"

"I'm simply saying that marriage is a heady nectar better sipped than gulped."

Nate shook his head in exasperation. "Do you know what would make *me* a happy man?"

"No. What?"

"Just once I'd like to know what the blazes you're talking about."

The mountain man threw back his head and cackled. Then he stood and slowly walked to the rim. "I reckon I'll have to face her, after all. I'll never be able to live with myself if I don't."

"Do you mean Blue Water Woman?" Nate asked.

Shakespeare nodded. "Running from a problem never does any good. The problem only comes back later, worse than before."

Why, Nate wondered, did he intuitively sense there was more to the situation—something Shakespeare wasn't revealing? He had the feeling his friend was holding back, but he decided to respect his mentor's privacy and not pry.

"You haven't told me," Shakespeare said. "What were you doing at my cabin?"

Nate shrugged. Now wasn't the proper time or place to bring up his own problems. "I was out hunting and wound up in the area."

"Are you pulling my leg?"

"What makes you say that?"

Shakespeare snickered. "Oh, just the fact that there's more game in the Rockies than there are fleas on a mangy mongrel. Still, you couldn't find anything to shoot at in the twenty-five mile stretch of virgin wilderness between your cabin and mine." His eyes narrowed. "Do you reckon I was born yesterday?"

"Of course not," Nate said defensively. He wanted to tell the truth, but he suddenly felt quite silly about bothering his friend over Winona's delivery. Shakespeare had just made fun of his knowledge of the marital state; bringing up the birth would only compound the mountain man's low assessment of his knowledge.

"Suit yourself," Shakespeare said. "Just remember old William S. had a few words to say on the subject."

"He did?"

"This above all; to thine own self be true, and it must follow, as the night the day, thou canst not then be false to any man," Shakespeare quoted.

"I seem to recall you told me that once before," Nate noted.

"Some words of wisdom bear repeating as often as necessary," Shakespeare responded.

"At least I understood you this time," Nate said, slightly miffed. "And I should think it works both ways."

"How's that?"

Nate locked his eyes on his mentor's. "I thought only those without sin are supposed to cast stones."

A look of sheer incredulity rippled over Shakespeare's face, then he laughed. "It's good to see that you know the Bible."

Suddenly, from the gully, arose a tremendous chorus of exultant whoops and screeches.

Gazing down, Nate saw that four of the Utes had been decapitated, their heads impaled on lances, and now the Flatheads were venting their delight while the gory trophies were hoisted high into the air. He noticed blood dripping from one of the heads onto Buffalo Horn's shoulders and felt sick again.

"So noble one minute, so savage the next," Shakespeare commented thoughtfully. "Nature's children are a paradox in themselves."

"Do you want me to go with you to their village?" Nate inquired.

"The choice is yours," Shakespeare replied. "I don't need looking after at my age." He scratched his chin. "And I should think you'd want to return to Winona as soon as possible. She's well along in the family way, as I recollect."

"In two moons the baby is due."

"Then you'd better skedaddle for your cabin or she'll greet you with a pan in her hand."

"What about you?"

"I'll be fine," Shakespeare said. "I haven't gotten all these white hairs by being careless."

Nate smiled, but his emotions were in turmoil. By all rights he should return to Winona immediately, yet he didn't want to simply ride off and leave Shakespeare, to abandon his friend at a time when Shakespeare might need him to be around. He owed the old-timer more than he could ever hope to repay, and here was an opportunity, however slight, to make good on part of the debt.

The barbaric celebration in the gully took over five minutes to wind down. Only a few Flatheads were still cutting Utes to pieces when Buffalo Horn and Running Elk mounted their horses and rode up the trail to the top.

"Shakespeare, my friend!" Buffalo Horn declared as he jumped to the ground. "You are as clever as a fox and as dangerous as the wolverine you are named after." He walked up to the mountain man and slapped McNair on the back. "Our people will hold a great celebration a few days after we return to honor this victory."

"Glad I could help," Shakespeare said.

Running Elk, still on his horse, vented a triumphant shriek, then said, "I am glad I lived to see this day. Utes killed my brother years ago, and now I have avenged his death." He looked at McNair. "Did you deliberately lead the band into the gully?"

"Yes," Shakespeare said. "I remembered being in this neck of the woods some time back, beaver hunting. I knew about the opening in the wall and figured we could stop them cold."

"As usual, your judgment has won the day,"

Buffalo Horn said. His eyes drifted to the mountain man's weapons and he frowned. "But now we have another matter to talk about. Will you agree to come with us or not? If so, we won't try to take your guns from you or tie you onto your horse. If not, then everything is as before."

Shakespeare expelled a long breath, then nodded. "I've thought it over and decided to go to the village and settle this personally."

Buffalo Horn beamed. "You have made my heart happy." He turned to Nate. "And what of you, Grizzly Killer? Will you come with us also?"

Nate became aware of Shakespeare's eyes boring into him. He deliberately ignored him and asked, "How far is it to your village?"

"We will be there by late tomorrow afternoon," Buffalo Horn disclosed.

Just one more day. Nate felt a twinge of guilt in the depths of his conscience as he forced his lips to form his next words. "Yes, I'll tag along if you don't mind."

"You are more than welcome," Buffalo Horn said. "My people will greet you with open arms."

Nate gazed down at his moccasins, thinking *I just hope Winona does the same when I get back to our cabin.* He gripped the Hawken in his left hand, studiously avoided looking at Shakespeare, and walked to his stallion.

Chapter Seven

The Flathead village was nestled in a picturesque valley at the juncture of Beaverhead Creek and Stinking Creek, as they were known. Composed of 180 lodges stretched out on the south side of the junction, the village teemed with life; warriors working on their weapons, engaged in games of chance or conducting horse races; women curing buffalo hides, doing bead work or cooking; and children everywhere, playing and laughing in delighted abandon.

Nate first surveyed the sprawling village from the crest of a hill to the southwest. Buffalo Horn and Running Elk led the warriors, eager to see their loved ones again, down the slope at a canter. He was with Shakespeare, bringing up the rear.

"How times do change," the mountain man remarked philosophically.

"Why do you say that?" Nate asked.

Shakespeare nodded at the village. "When I lived among the Flatheads, things were a lot different. In the summer they lived in lodges consisting of cottonwood frames covered with thick bullrush mats. In the winter they lived in earth houses that were partly underground." He sighed. "Then they started trading with the fur companies and with other tribes. They took to imitating the tribes east of the Rockies, living like the Blackfeet and the Cheyenne. Now you can hardly tell the difference."

"Is that so bad?" Nate inquired in mild surprise. He'd grown to admire certain aspects of the Indian way of life quite highly, including their rugged independence, their appreciation of Nature, their close-knit families, and, in the case of tribes like the Flatheads and Shoshones, their innate friendliness.

"No, I reckon not," Shakespeare said. "At least the Flatheads never got around to flattening heads like some of the tribes off to the northwest do."

Nate wasn't certain he'd heard correctly. "Flattening heads? Are you telling another tall tale?"

"This is plain fact," Shakespeare said. "Tribes that live out near the Pacific Ocean have this custom of flattening the heads of their babies by tying a board over the skull until it becomes the right shape."

"Why in the world would they want to do that?"

"I guess they figure it makes them more attractive. Some even pierce their noses and stick small bones and rings in the holes."

"Now I know you're pulling my leg."

Shakespeare snorted in indignation. "Ignorance and blindfolds have a lot in common." He looked at Nate. "Have you ever been to the Pacific Ocean?"

"You know I haven't."

"Then until you do, don't go around implying that someone who has is a liar."

"I didn't mean to offend you," Nate said, not knowing what to make of his friend's unusual testy behavior.

The corners of Shakespeare's mouth curled down

and he turned his head to gaze to the west. "No, I suppose you didn't. Sorry."

Nate rode in silence to the bottom of the hill. Already Buffalo Horn and the rest were dozens of yards ahead. He studied the people in the village for a moment, then said, "There's something I don't understand. These Indians have heads shaped just like ours, normal in every respect. So why are they called Flatheads if they don't flatten their heads?"

Shakespeare chuckled. "Observant cuss, aren't you?" He reached up and tapped his brow. "Yes, the Flatheads have normal heads. They have flat foreheads just like ours, not peaked ones like the tribes I was telling you about."

"Why would anyone call a tribe with normal heads the Flatheads? Shouldn't it be the other way around?"

"You'd think so," Shakespeare said. "Blame the French for the confusion. It was some of their early trappers who got the names all backwards."

Nate laughed lightly. His mentor's store of knowledge never ceased to amaze him, and he wondered if he would ever be as wise in the ways of the people and wildlife of the Rockies as was Shakespeare.

The return of Buffalo Horn's party had caused a widespread stir in the village. People were coming from all directions, the warriors dressed in buckskin shirts, pants, and moccasins, the women in beaded dresses. Buffalo Horn and the other returning braves were relating their adventures to groups of intent listeners.

Nate noticed Shakespeare craning his neck to scan the crowd. "Do you see her yet?" he asked.

"Who?"

"Lady Godiva."

"I'm not looking for anyone special."

"If you say so," Nate said dryly. He saw many Flatheads turning to regard Shakespeare and him with intense interest, and he straightened in the saddle and held his Hawken firmly across his thighs. When Shakespeare reined up a moment later, he did the same.

A number of tribe members detached themselves from different groups and came over to the mountain man. Cheerful greetings were exchanged, and Shakespeare dismounted to give several warm bear hugs.

Nate listened to their conversation, conducted in the Flathead tongue, and wished he spoke the language. He felt a bit like a bump on a log. A few smiles were displayed his way, but no one stepped forward to talk to him until a young warrior boldly moved up to his side and addressed him in the Flathead language. He shook his head and used his hands to reply in sign language, "I am sorry. I do not know your tongue."

The warrior grinned, his own fingers flying as he said, "And I do not know yours. I am Wind In The Grass."

"I am called Grizzly Killer," Nate signed.

Wind In The Grass cocked his head to one side. "The same one who helped the Shoshones defeat Mad Dog?"

"Yes," Nate responded, slightly embarrassed by his notoriety. Bitter memories of the conflict between his adopted tribe and Mad Dog, a brutal Blackfoot who had led a war party in a raid into Shoshone territory, filtered through his mind. Winona's father and mother had lost their lives during the deciding battle that resulted in Mad Dog's death and a bloody, costly victory over the Blackfeet.

"I heard about you from some white trappers who stopped at our village," Wind In The Grass revealed.

"Some men talk too much," Nate signed, grinning.

Wind In The Grass smiled. "I would be honored if you would stay with my family while you are here."

Nate glanced at Shakespeare, who was busily greeting old friends, unsure of what to do. He knew to refuse such unselfish hospitality would be construed as an insult, and he certainly didn't want to offend anyone, in addition to which, sleeping in a lodge was vastly preferable to sleeping on the hard ground. "I will be happy to stay with you," he responded.

"Good," Wind In The Grass signed, and motioned northward. "Come, and I will show you where my lodge is."

Dismounting, Nate held the stallion's reins in one hand, his rifle in the other, and walked alongside his new acquaintance, threading among the Flatheads and the teepees until they came to a small lodge not far from Stinking Creek. Only twelve feet high and patched in two spots with newer pieces of hide, the plain dwelling indicated an important fact to Nate: His friendly host was a poor man. Just as in white society, there were wealthy and poverty-stricken Indians. The lodge of a well-to-do warrior might be fifteen to twenty feet high, the hides would be in perfect condition, and the exterior would be gaily adorned with symbols important to the owner.

For confirmation of his hunch, Nate had only to gaze at the four horses grazing nearby. Three were mares well past their prime. The fourth was a stallion that also showed its age and undoubtedly served as Wind In The Grass's war and buffalo mount. Since a warrior's prowess could be measured by the number of animals he had stolen from other tribes, it meant that Wind In The Grass had yet to fully prove himself.

The flap to the lodge was down. Wind In The Grass turned to Nate and signed, "Wait here while I tell my wife the news." He went inside.

Nate became aware of other Flatheads staring at him and did his best to stand in a dignified but appropriately humble manner. Suddenly, from within, arose loud voices, that of a woman and Wind In The Grass arguing heatedly. He suspected the wife was objecting to his surprise stay and debated whether to simply walk off. But to do so would greatly humiliate Wind In The Grass. He decided to wait and see if the warrior would change his mind about the offer.

A second later the flap opened and a sheepish Wind In The Grass signed, "Come in, Grizzly Killer. My wife is very pleased that our lodge will be honored with your presence."

Feeling uncomfortable, Nate ground-hitched the stallion and entered, racking his brain to recall the lodge etiquette rules Shakespeare had previously imparted to him. He remembered that when a male visitor entered a lodge, he should always step to the right and wait for the owner to seat him. So he promptly did so, his eyes adjusting to the reduced illumination.

Standing beside a buffalo paunch cooking pot situated in the center of the teepee, directly under the ventilation opening at the top, was a skinny young woman with long dark hair and a pointed nose. She mustered a wan smile and gave a deferential bow.

"Grizzly Killer, this is Flower Woman," Wind In The Grass introduced his wife.

"I am happy to meet you," Nate signed, the Hawken tucked in the crook of his left arm. He heard a peculiar cooing noise and glanced to his right to find a baby in a cradle board that was propped against the lodge wall. Most Indian tribes used such devices in one form or another. Consisting of a skin pouch laced around a wooden frame, the cradleboard constituted an infant's tiny home until the child was capable of walking. Every tribe had a different style that was typically used, and in this instance the cradleboard flared out at the top to provide a soft leather cushion for the child's head to rest on. He noticed the outer skin had been artistically decorated with elaborate bead work.

Wind In The Grass walked over to the cradleboard and gestured proudly. "This is my son, Roaring Mountain, who will one day grow up to be a mighty warrior in the Flathead nation."

"I am certain he will," Nate signed, and looked at the wife. "The cradleboard you made is one of the nicest I have ever seen," he complimented her, not bothering to mention that he'd only viewed two or three up close during his brief time in the Rockies. His statement had the desired effect.

Flower Woman beamed happily and moved her thin fingers in a grateful answer. "Thank you. I worked very hard to give our son the best cradleboard I could."

Nate gave the cradleboard another appreciative appraisal. "Such a fine cradleboard is worth saving for your son's children to use. They will remember your kindness always."

"I had not thought of that," Flower Woman replied, even more pleased. "It is a good idea."

"Where are my manners?" Wind In The Grass signed, and motioned for Nate to take the seat of honor located to the rear of the cooking fire and to the left of the spot where the warrior would himself sit. "You must want to rest after so much riding."

"We did come a long way," Nate noted, and walked to the proper spot. He sank down with a sigh, sitting cross-legged as warriors customarily did. Women, however, were prohibited from ever doing so. Any female who did was branded as possessing lax morals. "And that fight with the Utes did tire me out a bit."

"I heard Running Elk speak of it," Wind In The

Grass mentioned. "In a few days there will be a celebration and all the warriors who took part will tell of the battle." He paused. "But we would enjoy hearing your story now, if you wish."

Nate obliged, giving them a brief account of the chase and the battle in the gully. By the time he was done his arms were tired. He noticed that Wind In The Grass hung on every sign and detected an enthusiastic gleam in the young warrior's eyes, leading him to suspect that his host had been in very few life or death conflicts. If he was right, Wind In The Grass couldn't wait to prove himself on a raid and earn the respect of the entire tribe.

At the conclusion of the report, Flower Woman devoted herself to the meal she had been preparing before their arrival. She walked to a rawhide parfleche, one of several artistically decorated carrying bags lying against the south side, and removed a handful of wild onions.

"We are having buffalo stew tonight," Wind In The Grass signed. "I hope that will be all right."

"I enjoy stew," Nate assured him. He observed Flower Woman pause, then reach into the parfleche for more onions. They must have meager food stores, he deduced, and decided to eat sparingly but praise her cooking to high heaven. As he watched her chop the onions into pieces, he reflected that coming to the village had been a bad idea. Shakespeare obviously didn't need him around. Tomorrow morning, first thing, he would head for home.

A patter of rushing footsteps sounded outside, and suddenly a voice called out urgently in the Flathead language.

Wind In The Grass promptly answered, and in poked the head of another young warrior who immediately launched into an excited narrative. Wind In

The Grass then turned in alarm to Nate and signed, "You should go to Carcajou right away."

"What is wrong?" Nate asked, beginning to rise, trying to guess what sort of trouble Shakespeare could have gotten into in such a short time in a village where he obviously had a great many friends. The answer was totally unexpected.

"He is fighting one of our warriors."

Chapter Eight

Nate raced out of the lodge with his rifle in hand. Without a word the young warrior who had brought the report turned and raced to the south, and Nate sped along on his flying heels. Behind him came Wind In The Grass. Apparently news of the fight was spreading rapidly because there were other Flatheads hastening in the same direction.

He heard the commotion moments before he saw it, heard men and women shouting and children shrieking in their high-pitched voices, and then he rounded a lodge to discover a wide circle of boisterous Flatheads surroundings two grappling figures in the center. The crowd was already three and four deep. In his concern for Shakespeare's safety he didn't bother with polite niceties; instead of requesting those blocking his path to move aside he simply barreled into them and shoved his way through with his broad shoulders.

Nate glimpsed faces registering surprise turning his way. One warrior barked an angry exclamation. In moments he was on the inside, and before him were the struggling combatants.

Shakespeare and a prodigiously muscled warrior were wrestling furiously, rolling over and over, each striving to get the better hold, each red in the face from his strenuous exertions.

Nate looked around. Off to the right stood Buffalo Horn and Running Elk, both apprehensively watching the contest. Off to the left were three warriors Nate didn't know, one a burly Flathead whose features were twisted in a perpetual scowl. Even as he laid eyes on them, they closed in on the fighters.

Buffalo Horn shouted something in his own tongue.

The burly warrior snapped an answer and gestured, as if telling Buffalo Horn to mind his own business.

Confusion gripped Nate. He had no idea what had started the fight, and he didn't know if the threesome approaching his mentor were friends or foes. For all he knew, they were allies of the Indian Shakespeare was battling.

In a swirl of motion the elderly mountain man wound up on top of his adversary, pinning the Flat-head's shoulders to the ground with his knees and holding the warrior's hands flat on the grass.

Suddenly the trio darted forward and two of them seized McNair from behind, hauling him off the pinned warrior.

Nate had witnessed enough. He wasn't about to let them or anyone else manhandle his friend. In four bounds he was there, swinging the stock of the Hawken up and around and clipping one of the men holding Shakespeare on the temple. The man fell on the spot.

Bellowing angrily, the burly warrior leaped with outstretched arms.

Nate pivoted, rammed the rifle's heavy barrel into

the Flathead's stomach, doubling him over, then whipped the stock into the wheezing warrior's forehead, dropping him also.

The third Flathead let go of McNair and sprang, his left hand grasping Nate's shoulder.

All it took was a slight twist and Nate buried the stock in the man's abdomen. The warrior staggered backwards, sputtering. Out of the corner of his right eye Nate saw the muscular Flathead on the ground going for a hip knife, and he instantly swung around to train the Hawken on the man's forehead as his thumb pulled the hammer back with an audible click. He touched the trigger, his every nerve on edge, ready to fire if the Flathead drew the blade.

Several things happened then.

The warrior froze, his hand just touching the hilt, his dark eyes burning with rage.

A hush promptly descended on the assembled Flatheads. Many gasped.

And Shakespeare took a frantic step forward to grasp the rifle barrel and pull it upward. "Don't shoot!" he cried.

Nate glanced at his friend, then at the ring of Indians. Most were staring at him in nonplused amazement, a few in outright resentment of his interference. He slowly lowered the gun and eased the hammer down.

Buffalo Horn and Running Elk came running over as the muscular warrior stood. From the throng walked a stately individual with gray hair who carried a war club and wore a buckskin shirt on which had been drawn the likeness of a large bird of prey.

Shakespeare rubbed his left side, his hard gaze on his opponent. "Thanks for the assist, Nate, but you shouldn't have interfered. This was between Standing Bear and myself."

"Do you mind telling me what's going on?" Nate requested.

"In a bit," Shakespeare responded, and nodded at the approaching gray-haired warrior. "We might be in for it now. That's White Eagle, their chief. If he's mad, there's no telling what will happen. Whatever he says is law. The Flatheads put more stock in their chiefs than most tribes, and obey their every word."

Stepping back so he could cover Standing Bear and the three he had struck in case they turned hostile, Nate glanced at the stately warrior just as the man reached them.

If ever there was a face that reflected wisdom, this was it. White Eagle held himself with dignity, his severely weathered visage and penetrating eyes reflecting the soul of a man of vast experience. He betrayed neither anger nor condemnation as he looked at each of them in turn, his gaze lingering on Nate, and finally settled on Buffalo Horn. In softly spoken words he addressed the tall Flathead in their mutual language.

A lengthy conversation ensued, with all the Indians in the middle of the circle participating. Standing Bear growled his words and motioned angrily at Shakespeare and Nate. The three Nate had bested chimed in with harsh statements of their own. Finally Shakespeare interjected comments that caused White Eagle to grunt and nod knowingly.

Nate waited impatiently for an explanation. As near as he could tell, Buffalo Horn and Running Elk had sided with Shakespeare in the dispute. Standing Bear seemed to be trying to convince the chief to take some sort of action, but White Eagle evidently refused. After a heated argument, Standing Bear stalked off with the three other warriors in tow.

White Eagle then talked to Shakespeare for several minutes. When they were done the chief smiled, then turned to survey the tribe. He gave a short speech that started the crowd to murmuring, and walked off.

"*Now* will you tell me what's going on?" Nate asked. He saw the people beginning to disperse, conversing in hushed tones with repeated glances at McNair.

"I reckon I should," Shakespeare said.

Buffalo Horn frowned and shook his head. "This is bad, very bad. There will be blood shed before too long and it might well be yours, old friend."

"I'll watch out for myself," Shakespeare promised.

Running Elk made a clucking sound of disapproval. "This is all her fault. She should tell Standing Bear she wants nothing to do with him and there would be no problem."

Shakespeare started slapping dust and bits of grass from his buckskins. "She has her reasons, no doubt."

"Perhaps," Buffalo Horn said, "but I want you to know that I had no idea this would take place. I did not know Standing Bear had an interest in her. Had I, I would never have let her convince me to bring you to our village."

"I understand," Shakespeare said.

Nate's patience had reached its limit. He stepped forward and demanded in an irate tone, "Tell me what the blazes is going on."

"Oh. Sorry," Shakespeare said, continuing to dust himself off. He paused to stare after Standing Bear. "It seems I have a rival for Blue Water Woman's affection."

"The two of you were fighting over her?" Nate asked in astonishment. He found the notion of someone Shakespeare's age brawling over a woman almost ridiculous.

Shakespeare nodded. "Sort of. One minute I was talking to several old friends and the next Standing

Bear walked up and demanded to know if it was true that I intended to take Blue Water Woman for my wife."

"What did you tell him?"

"I said it was more like the other way around. He informed me that she was going to be his wife, no one else's, and gave me a shove to emphasize his point."

"And you shoved back."

"Naturally. So we wound up rolling around in the grass until you arrived and turned a minor disagreement into a life or death dispute," Shakespeare said. Neither his eyes or his tone betrayed any hint of reproach.

"I didn't mean to," Nate said, aware the two Flatheads were regarding him critically. "I thought you were in trouble."

"I know," Shakespeare said, and chuckled. "I must admit you handled them better than I could have done myself."

"It is not funny," Buffalo Horn interjected. "Now Standing Bear, Bad Face, Smoke, and Wolf Ribs have been insulted. They will try to restore their honor by humiliating Nate as badly as they were shamed."

Running Elk nodded. "In front of the entire tribe, no less." He focused on Nate. "I know those men well. They are not the kind to forgive and forget, particularly Bad Face. You must be on your guard here every minute."

Nate didn't need to ask which one of the threesome had been Bad Face. It had to be the burly warrior with the perpetual scowl.

Shakespeare placed a friendly hand on Nate's shoulder. "I know you meant well, son, but you've put yourself in a dangerous situation. The best thing for you to do would be to mount up at dawn and head for your cabin."

"You want me to run?" Nate inquired in disbelief.

"I wouldn't put it in those words," Shakespeare said.

"It sounds like running to me," Nate declared. "And I'm not about to let Bad Face and the rest think I'm a yellow belly."

"The wise man knows when to fight and when to make tracks, and knows the difference between causes worth fighting for and those that are just a matter of personal pride."

"Are you leaving?"

"I can't."

"Then neither am I."

The mountain man was clearly displeased. He walked a few yards to the west and leaned down to retrieve his Hawken, which was lying in the grass, then straightened. "How about if I ask you to leave as a personal favor to me?"

"Ask me anything else and I'd do it," Nate said. "But I'm not about to turn tail for you or anyone else." He was peeved his friend would even suggest such a degrading act. During his long trip out from St. Louis with his Uncle Zeke, he'd learned the hard way that in the wilderness a man was invariably measured by the bravery he exhibited. Cowards were generally disdained by whites and Indians alike. Several tribes went so far as to force men who had attained a certain age and still not displayed the courage expected of them by counting coup or stealing horses to perform the jobs of women. The Crows, in fact, made such men the slaves of the women; they were compelled to obey every order a woman gave, to carry wood, fetch water, and do every menial job imaginable. It was widely known that braves who fell into the ranks of the women became supremely eager to prove themselves and thus overcome the terrible stigma.

Shakespeare gave him a strange look. "No, I guess you're not. Very well. We'll just have to wait for them to make the next move." He paused. "I apologize for not paying much attention to you when we arrived. I had other things on my mind."

"I know."

McNair smiled. "Now we need to find you a place to stay. I've been invited to hang my moccasins in Buffalo Horn's lodge. Maybe Running Elk would—."

"I already have somewhere to stay," Nate interrupted.

"You do? Where?"

Before Nate could reply, Wind In The Grass stepped forward and rather nervously said "With me, Carcajou. I invited Grizzly Killer to share my lodge for as long as he is in our village."

Nate noticed both Buffalo Horn and Running Elk frown as if severely displeased by the disclosure.

"Do I know you?" Shakespeare said in return.

"I am Wind In The Grass," the young warrior revealed. "I was only two years old when last you were in our village, or so I was once told by my father. You knew him well, I believe."

"Who is he?" Shakespeare inquired.

"Little Hawk."

The mountain man grinned. "Yes, indeed. He and I go back a long ways. Where is he? I would like to see him again."

"The Blackfeet killed him," Wind In The Grass said slowly.

"Oh. Sorry to hear it. Your father was a good man, a brave warrior."

Buffalo Horn nodded, then said, "In truth he was. Now if only his son would demonstrate the same courage, it would make everyone in the tribe very happy."

"What are you talking about?" Nate inquired.

"It is best for Wind In The Grass to tell you himself," Buffalo Horn answered.

"Yes, if he can stand the shame," added Running Elk.

Nate glanced at his host and detected the hurt in his eyes. He felt the two older warriors were being unduly harsh and determined to get to the bottom of it later, when Wind In The Grass could relate the details in private. For now there was a much more important matter to discuss. "I'll be glad to hear the details some other time," he said, turning to Shakespeare. "I'm more interested in hearing what you plan to do about this contrary female who might wind up getting you killed."

"Perhaps it would help if we got her side of the story," Shakespeare suggested.

"When?" Nate asked, eager to get the matter settled so he could return to Winona.

"Right now, if you want," Shakespeare said, and gazed over Nate's shoulder. "She's standing right behind you."

Chapter Nine

Nate had seldom been as embarrassed as he was at that very moment. He hesitated before turning, trying to compose his face so he wouldn't betray his feelings. Then he slowly pivoted, not knowing what to expect but certainly not expecting the sight that befell his surprised gaze.

Blue Water Woman stood three feet away, attired in a beautiful beaded dress that barely did her justice. Raven hair fell to the small of her back, framing an oval face remarkable for its smooth complexion and deep, dark eyes. Her lips were full, her nostrils thin. Her teeth, when she smiled, were small and white.

"Hello," Nate blurted, and mentally berated himself for being an idiot. She might not even speak English. He had to admit she was one of the loveliest woman he'd ever seen, perhaps even second to Winona. She betrayed no sign of her age, yet he knew she must be nearly as old as Shakespeare.

"Hello, Grizzly Killer," she replied, her pronunciation crisp and precise. "This contrary female is very pleased to meet the famous man she had heard so much about."

Nate wished he could shrivel up like a dry plant and disappear. Either that, or beat his head against a tree. He mustered the friendliest smile of which he was capable and said, "You must be Blue Water Woman. I've heard a lot about you, too."

"Have you, now?" she responded, and looked at McNair.

"He thinks he has," Shakespeare said quickly, "but he doesn't know the bare bones."

Blue Water Woman nodded. "That is nice to hear." She held out her right hand toward Nate. "I believe this is the customary way whites greet each other."

"Sure is," Nate said, shaking. He got the impression there had been a hidden meaning to his mentor's words, but for the life of him he couldn't figure out what it might be. "I'm pleased to make your acquaintance."

Buffalo Horn stepped forward. "Did you see the fight between Carcajou and Standing Bear?" he asked angrily.

"I saw," Blue Water Woman answered, letting go of Nate's hand.

"What do you have to say for yourself?" Buffalo Horn demanded.

"I have no control over Standing Bear," she said.

"Did you know he was interested in you before you begged me to go after Shakespeare?"

"Yes," Blue Water Woman stated calmly, then added, "And I did not *beg* you to go find Shakespeare. I asked you."

The tall Flathead's features became iron. "And you did not think to warn me so I could warn him?"

Blue Water Woman refused to be intimidated. She

replied in an even tone, "I have told Standing Bear many times that I have no interest in sharing his lodge. He refuses to accept me at my word."

"Has he courted you?"

"He sent Wolf Ribs with four fine horses. I sent them back. He also sent Smoke over with a deer he had killed, but I sent it back, too."

"This is bad," Running Elk commented.

"I will tell you what my heart feels," Buffalo Horn said to Blue Water Woman. "I believe you deliberately did not tell me because you knew I would not want to involve my brother Shakespeare in a fight with Standing Bear. I believe you deceived me."

Blue Water Woman stiffened indignantly. "I have never deceived you in all the years we have known each other. I did not expect Standing Bear to challenge Carcajou."

"Before this is over, there might be blood spilled," Buffalo Horn said. "And it will be on your shoulders." He turned on his heels and walked off, Running Elk dogging his heels.

Nate detected profound sadness in the woman's eyes and felt sorry for her. He suddenly realized that Shakespeare would probably like to be alone with her and turned. "Well, I'd better be getting along myself."

"I'll look you up later," Shakespeare said, his eyes on Blue Water Woman.

"No rush," Nate said, heading northward. Wind In The Grass fell in beside him. He glanced back once to see his friend holding her hand. Neither was saying a word; they simply stood and stared into each other's eyes. And here he thought Shakespeare had been upset with her.

They walked for a dozen yards when Wind In The Grass turned and asked in sign, "How did you learn to be so brave?"

"I'm no braver than most," Nate replied absently, still thinking about Shakespeare and the strange manner in which his mentor had been behaving.

"That is not true," Wind In The Grass said. "I was there. I saw you go up against the four worst men in our village, and you never hesitated." He laughed lightly. "You beat all of them in the time it takes to blink."

"You take after the Wolverine," Nate signed. "Both of you exaggerate stories."

"This is a very serious matter to me," Wind In The Grass noted. "I would not make light of it."

"I did not mean to insult you," Nate signed.

Wind In The Grass sighed and gazed toward Stinking Creek. "Did you see the way the older warriors treated me?"

"What do you mean?" Nate responded, feigning innocence.

"Buffalo Horn and Running Elk do not think I am much of a man. Many other men in our tribe feel the same way."

"Do they have a reason?"

"They think they do," Wind In The Grass signed.

"Want to talk about it?" Nate inquired, certain the young warrior had broached the subject for that very reason.

"If you do not mind."

"Why would I mind? Go ahead."

Wind In The Grass moved his arms and fingers in a fluid flow. "It all started eight moons ago when I took part in a raid on a Blackfoot village. It was the first such raid I had been on. Buffalo Horn was in charge, and he left me in a gully to watch the horses while he and the others snuck up on the Blackfeet. All went well at first. They gathered nine Blackfoot animals and started back to where I waited." He stopped, his expression forlorn.

"What happened next?" Nate prompted.

"I was sitting there on my horse when three Blackfeet came out of nowhere. They had been off hunting because one had a small antelope slung over his shoulder. Two had bows, one a rifle. The moment they saw me they shouted and charged. I put an arrow in the first one, then the brave with the rifle fired." He lowered his arms for a moment. "The shot missed me but scared several of the horses and they bolted along the gully. The rest followed. I had a choice to make. Either I could stay and fight the two Blackfeet, who had taken cover, or I could go after the horses and retrieve them so my friends could make their escape. I went after the horses."

Nate nodded. "I think I would have done the same," he signed.

"Thank you," Wind In The Grass said. "But there is more. The Blackfeet in the village heard the shot and rushed out to investigate. They spied Buffalo Horn and the others and gave chase, forcing our warriors to let go of the horses they had stolen. Buffalo Horn led our warriors to the gully, but I was not there. They took shelter in nearby woods and fought a running battle for many miles before the Blackfeet turned around and returned to their village. Two of our warriors were killed."

"And they blame you?"

"I gathered the horses as quickly as I could, but they had scattered over several miles," Wind In The Grass related. "By the time I tracked Buffalo Horn and the rest down, they were far into the forest. Some of them accused me of running off. I explained about the three Blackfeet, but it seemed to make little difference."

"Surely Buffalo Horn saw the two Blackfeet who were still in the gully when you rode off?"

"No," Wind In The Grass signed. "The pair must have seen our warriors coming and hid, or else they had gone after me and were not there when Buffalo Horn and the others got back."

Nate pursed his lips, pondering the tale. Small wonder that Buffalo Horn and Running Elk had treated his host so coldly. Wind In The Grass bore the worst stigma any Indian warrior could ever have; that of being a coward. The young warrior was branded unless he could prove them all wrong.

Wind In The Grass cleared his throat. "I will understand if you want to move out of our lodge and stay with someone else."

The poor man practically radiated anguish, and Nate wasn't about to add insult to injury. "Are you throwing me out?" he signed.

"No, of course not," Wind In The Grass replied. "I just—."

"Then why bring it up?" Nate cut him off. "I certainly do not believe you ran away on purpose."

Wind In The Grass looked at him. "You do not?"

"I always take a man at his word unless he gives me cause to think otherwise," Nate explained. "And I think I know you well enough to say that you are the kind of man who would stick by his friends through the worst possible danger. You are definitely not a coward." He smiled, hoping his words had cheered the warrior up. To his astonishment, tears welled in the man's eyes.

"Thank you, Grizzly Killer," Wind In The Grass signed.

"Be patient," Nate advised. "You will get your chance to prove yourself to their satisfaction." He chuckled. "In a way, you remind me of myself a year ago."

"I do?"

"Yes. I had a lot to prove when I first came to the wilderness. If it had not been for a grizzly that tried to take its own life by throwing itself on my knife, I still might have a lot to prove."

Wind In The Grass tossed back his head and laughed in delight. "Thank you for those kind words," he then signed. "But I may not be able to prove myself if no one will take me on a raid."

"No one?"

"Buffalo Horn has been out twice since that terrible time. Running Elk and several others have also led raids against different enemies. None have invited me along, and no one will go with me should I try to lead one."

The man had a problem, Nate reflected. Wind In The Grass needed witnesses when he demonstrated his bravery to refute those who accused him of cowardice. But if none of the other warriors would associate with him, Wind In The Grass had no way of clearing his reputation.

Suddenly, from their rear, a gruff voice barked out a string of words in the Flathead tongue.

Nate turned, and was shocked to see his four newly made enemies advancing toward him. They were still a dozen feet off. He raised the Hawken, covering them, and they immediately halted.

Standing Bear addressed Wind In The Grass, who gave a brief answer. The muscular warrior grunted, then resorted to sign. "This coward tells me you are fluent in sign language."

Other Flatheads had stopped their activities to view the confrontation, including two gawking boys nearby.

Averse to lowering the rifle, Nate nonetheless did. He couldn't use sign with his hands full, and he wasn't about to let the quartet think he was afraid of them. After tucking the Hawken in the crook of his left elbow, he glared at them and replied, "Call my friend a coward again and we will finish what you started earlier."

Bad Face hissed and made as if to attack, but a word from Standing Bear froze him in place.

"We have no quarrel with you, Grizzly Killer," the muscular warrior signed. "I came to apologize for what happened."

Surprise delayed Nate's response. Could it be he had misjudged Standing Bear's character? No, he doubted it. Still, he had to exercise proper Indian protocol. "Your apology is accepted."

"I also want you to talk to Carcajou," Standing Bear said.

"About what?"

"Tell him to leave our village at first light. Tell him Blue Water Woman is going to be my woman and no one else's. Tell him no one will take her from me."

Nate felt his temper flare. The gall of the man, he mused, and signed emphatically, "Tell him yourself unless *you* are a coward."

Standing Bear took a pace forward, his hand straying toward his knife. He glanced at the Hawken and the pistols, scowled, and dropped the notion. "I can see words are wasted on you. You are as stubborn as your friend, Carcajou. It will be fitting for the two of you to die together."

"A lot of men have tried to kill us," Nate signed "and their corpses are feeding the worms."

The muscular warrior snorted. "How did a cub like you ever get the name Grizzly Killer?"

"The hard way," Nate replied. "How is it the four of you are strutting around like men when you should be mending hides with the women?"

Again Bad Face made as if to leap. The other two grabbed his arms and held him fast.

"This is not the end of it," Standing Bear signed.

"You will regret the day you insulted us." Wheeling, he stalked off with his three friends in tow. Bad Face kept glancing back and glaring.

Nate heard Wind In The Grass expel a long breath. He cradled the Hawken and resumed walking toward his host's lodge. "Now what were we discussing?"

"Bravery," the warrior answered. "And I will tell you here and now that you are either the bravest man I have ever met, or else the biggest fool who ever lived. Those men will not rest until you are dead."

"Then maybe I should move out of your lodge. It might be safer for your family."

"Nonsense. You may stay as long as you want. Your enemies are my enemies."

They looked at each other, and a genuine friendship was born.

Chapter Ten

Nate awoke before sunrise and glanced at the peacefully slumbering family on the other side of the small lodge. Wind In The Grass snored lightly, while Flower Woman and Roaring Mountain were both breathing deeply. The parents were a foot apart, each with a hand resting on the other, while snugly nestled between them was the infant. He smiled, thinking of Winona and the addition they would have to their own family in a relatively short time, and imagined them sleeping in the same intimate fashion. It warmed his heart.

He slid out from under his blanket, wedged both flintlocks under his belt, and stepped outside for some fresh air, leaving the Hawken by his bedding. As he straightened he was shocked to see his mentor seated cross-legged not six feet away, facing the lodge. To the east a pale rosy light indicated the sun would soon peek above the horizon.

"Good morning," Shakespeare said quietly.

Nate walked over and squatted. "What are you

doing here so early? Is something wrong?"

"Terribly wrong," Shakespeare said, and gazed east-ward, his features reflecting fatigue and a strange melancholy.

"What is it?" Nate asked, certain Standing Bear must be somehow involved. "Were you attacked?"

Shakespeare looked at him and grinned. "Not in the way you think. I came here to talk to you. I've been up all night wrestling with a personal problem, and I thought I'd ask your advice.

"*You* want *my* advice?"

"What's so unusual about that?"

"Nothing," Nate said struggling to prevent his amazement from showing. He regarded Shakespeare as the wisest man he'd ever known, as someone capable of handling anything and everything that came along; supremely self-confident and self-reliant. The notion that Shakespeare needed help with a problem was incredible.

"I spent most of the night with Blue Water Wom-an," Shakespeare disclosed. "We walked and talked about the old days, about how it was when I lived among the Flatheads." He paused. "They were fine times."

"I gather you're not mad at her."

"Mad?" Shakespeare repeated, and snorted. "Nate, I think I'm in love with the woman, just like before."

"Before?" Nate said, bewildered. He promptly sat down, stunned. This made two astounding revelations in a row, and he didn't feel he was alert enough to handle them. He shook his head, dispelling lingering tendrils of sleep from his mind.

"I reckon I should start at the beginning," Shakespeare said, bowing his head.

"Whatever is best," Nate replied, hearing a camp dog yip to the west.

"It all began before I even met Rainbow Woman," Shakespeare said, "and before Blue Water Woman was married to Spotted Owl. We knew each other. In fact, we were quite fond of one another. I made every excuse I could to see her, and we talked about maybe becoming man and wife one day."

"But you wound up marrying Rainbow Woman instead?" Nate asked in confusion.

"Let me explain," Shakespeare said. "You see, Blue Water Woman's father didn't like me. I suspect he was a bigoted son of a bitch who didn't like whites, period. So when our romance became serious and we started to think about living together, he put his foot down and forbade me to see her."

"Did you stop?"

Inner pain was briefly visible on the mountain man's weathered countenance. "Yes. Only because I had no choice. Indian culture is a lot different from ours in some respects. It's unthinkable, for instance, for a young woman to go against her father's wishes. His word was law."

"So you went your separate ways?"

Shakespeare nodded slowly. "I don't mind admitting I was half out of my mind with grief. I even climbed a cliff, figuring I would throw myself off and end the misery."

"*You* did?"

"Yep. Fortunately I came to my senses when I looked down at the bottom and thought of all those big boulders smashing me to a pulp. I also realized I'd be playing into her father's hands by showing I was too weak to confront life's problems head-on, proving I was unfit to be his daughter's husband."

"What did you do next?"

"I got on with my life. What else could I do?" Shakespeare answered. "I spent a lot of time trapping and hunting. Before long I heard that Blue Water's father had arranged her marriage to a warrior named Spotted Owl."

"Wait a minute," Nate interrupted. "Her father set the whole thing up? Didn't she have a say in it?"

"No," Shakespeare said. "It's a common practice in some tribes for the parents to arrange marriages. Sometimes the daughter doesn't even know the man she's going to wed."

"How can they do such a thing?" Nate wondered, appalled. It seemed to him that a woman should have a say in who she wanted to spend the rest of her life with, and he was glad his romance with Winona had developed naturally, based on the strong affections of both of them rather than the wishes of others.

"Easily," Shakespeare said. "You see, sometimes a father will set up a marriage to a warrior from a prominent family, one that has scores of horses and whose men are noted for their bravery. It's the father's way of moving up in the world, so to speak."

"At his daughter's expense," Nate stated in disapproval. He knew that many white women deliberately courted wealthy men so they would marry into money, and that white parents often pressured their daughters into rejecting the man the daughters loved and tying the knot with someone who had a fatter bank account. It was upsetting to learn that some Indians indulged in the same distasteful social practice.

"Well, what's done is done," Shakespeare said with an air of resignation. "Blue Water Woman married Spotted Owl and I saw nothing of her for two years or more. Then one day I met Buffalo Horn, who introduced me to his brother. Surprisingly, I found I liked Spotted Owl a lot. We became close friends."

"How did Blue Water Woman react?"

"She was friendly, nothing more. I figured any feelings she had for me were long gone. Then Spotted

Owl let me know that his older sister, Rainbow Woman, whose husband had died on a buffalo hunt, was quite fond of me." Shakespeare chuckled. "I'd seen her around and admired her appearance, but I never gave any thought to courting her until I learned she was interested in me."

"And you fell in love with her," Nate said, smiling.

"Love, love, nothing but love, still more!" Shakespeare quoted. "For, O, love's bow shoots buck and doe. The shaft confounds, not that it wounds, but tickles still the sore." He laughed. "Yes, I grew to love her more than I had ever loved anyone, including Blue Water Woman."

Trying to be philosophical, Nate commented, "All's well that ends well."

"Not quite, I'm afraid. Because a year and a half after I took Rainbow Woman as my wife, Blue Water Woman came up to me one day and confided that she still loved me with all her heart, that she liked Spotted Owl but he could never claim her devotion as I had."

"What did you say?" Nate inquired, intrigued by the tale. He couldn't imagine what it would be like to be loved by two women at the same time.

"I told her I was sorry to hear it because our relationship was over. I loved Rainbow Woman," Shakespeare related. "Blue Water Woman accepted the fact, but told me she would always care for me no matter what happened. Then she walked off."

"And now she's back in your life," Nate said.

"Which brings me to the reason I came to see you. Do you think I should marry her?"

Nate blinked in surprise. "That's a decision you must make on your own."

"At least give me your opinion," Shakespeare urged. "It's important to me." He reached up and scratched his beard. "I'm getting on in years, as you well know. I'm also sort of set in my ways. Taking Blue

Water Woman as my wife could be the biggest mistake I've ever made, and I've made some whoppers in my time."

Nate detected uncertainty in his friend's eyes, a sight he never thought he would see. "If you're asking my approval, I say go ahead. Unless, of course, you'd rather spend your last years alone, talking to yourself and spending your idle days dreaming about the grand old times."

Shakespeare thoughtfully nodded. "You don't hold back, do you?"

"You wanted to know."

"Thanks," Shakespeare said, and shoved upright. "You've hit the nail on the head. I'd much rather wake up in the morning lying beside a woman who cares for me, all warm and cozy, rather than wake up alone and cold and hugging my Hawken."

Nate laughed lightly.

"I'd better get a little sleep," Shakespeare said, yawning. "I want to be alert when Standing Bear makes his move."

"What do you think he'll do?"

"There's no telling. When a man has a powerful hankering for a woman, his body and mind stop working right. All he can think of is her. Standing Bear will do whatever he must to eliminate me as a rival." Shakespeare nodded and started to walk off. "I'll look you up after I'm rested."

"I'll be here," Nate said. He watched his friend depart, noticing the sun had partially risen. Standing, he moved off to find a spot where he could relieve himself. Two dozen yards downstream on Stinking Creek he found a stand of trees that adequately served his purpose. Once done, he strolled back to the lodge, enjoying the dawn; the happy chirping of the many birds, the growing warmth in the air, the sight of fish leaping in the creek. At times the wilderness resembled his ideal of Paradise on Earth, and he marveled that he had wasted so many years living among the brick and stone canyons of New York City, where the only wildlife he'd observed, other than birds, had been squirrels; the nearest thing to virgin forest had been overused parks.

He saw smoke curling upward from the lodge as he neared it. At the flap he paused and coughed loudly to let them know he was returning. He didn't want to barge in and accidentally catch Flower Woman changing clothes or doing something equally private. After several seconds he carefully parted the flap and peered within.

Flower Woman was breast feeding her baby. She smiled and continued, not the least bit concerned about exposing her breasts.

Wind In The Grass was seated by the fire, feeding small limbs to the flames. He glanced at the entrance, beamed, and signed, "You were up early. Did you sleep well?"

"Never slept better," Nate replied, entering. "I took a short walk." He went to his bedding and rolled up the blankets, then placed them to one side.

"Flower Woman will make breakfast as soon as Roaring Mountain is full," Wind In The Grass signed.

"There is no hurry," Nate responded.

"What would you like to do today?"

"Other than keeping an eye on Carcajou, I have nothing planned," Nate signed.

"We could go hunting," Wind In The Grass proposed.

Nate liked the idea. The family could use fresh game, and bagging a deer or an elk would be a fine way of repaying them for their hospitality. "I would like that," he noted.

They made small talk until Flower Woman finished

feeding the baby. She was just sorting through the parfleches for their food when everyone distinctly heard the sound of rushing feet and a second later a voice called out in the Flathead tongue. Nate tensed, recalling yesterday when the warrior brought news of Shakespeare's fight. He heard Wind In The Grass answer, and in popped a familiar face.

"Good morning, Grizzly Killer," Running Elk said. "I am sorry to bother you but something important has come up and we thought you would be interested."

Nate couldn't help but notice that Running Elk had completely ignored Wind In The Grass, a terrible breach of etiquette. "What is it?" he asked.

"Several of our men went out yesterday after buffalo. They found a war party of Blackfeet camped ten miles north of our village and came back to warn us. Buffalo Horn is leading some of our men against them. Would you like to come?"

"Is Shakespeare going along?"

"I asked, but he said he was too tired from being awake all night," Running Elk said.

Nate hesitated, reluctant to leave his mentor at the mercy of Standing Bear and the others.

"Twenty warriors are going," Running Elk went on. "Standing Bear, Bad Face, Wolf Ribs, and Smoke are among them."

"Oh?" Nate said, his interest piqued. Perhaps going would be a good idea. It would enable him to keep an eye on those four, and accomplish something else just as important. Without glancing at his host, he said, "What about Wind In The Grass? Has he been invited?"

Running Elk frowned and looked at the young warrior. "Buffalo Horn did not ask him."

"I'll go only if he does," Nate bluntly declared.

The statement made Running Elk's brow knit in deep thought. After a bit he sighed and nodded. "Very well. I am sure Buffalo Horn will agree. We will come get the two of you soon."

"We'll be ready," Nate promised.

Withdrawing from view, Running Elk ran off, his footsteps diminishing with the distance.

Wind In The Grass looked at Nate. "What was that all about?" he signed.

Nate explained, studying his host's face as he did. He saw hope flare in the warrior's eyes and knew he had made the right decision.

"Thank you," Wind In The Grass responded. "This is a chance for me to prove myself to the rest of the tribe."

"You will do fine," Nate assured him, while in the back of his mind he prayed that both of them would make it back in one piece. The Blackfeet were the scourge of the Rockies, the most warlike tribe in existence and justifiably noted for their fighting prowess. On top of all that, they positively loathed whites. If nothing else, he reflected wryly, the day was getting off to a rousing start.

Just so he lived to see the night.

Chapter Eleven

Nate had the stallion saddled and was standing outside the lodge talking to Wind In The Grass when the party of twenty warriors approached from the south, Buffalo Horn and Running Elk at the front. He glanced at the riders, tensing when he spied Standing Bear and the three other troublemakers riding near the middle of the group.

"Good morning, Grizzly Killer," Buffalo Horn greeted him with a friendly grin. "Are you ready to take Blackfeet scalps?"

"I'm ready to help you defend your territory," Nate amended, and swung into the saddle. It bothered him that Buffalo Horn didn't say a word to Wind In The Grass, who was now mounted beside him.

"We do not know how many Blackfeet there are, so we must be very careful," Buffalo Horn said.

"Why not be on the safe side and take more warriors along?" Nate proposed.

"And what if a large Blackfoot force attacks our

village while we are gone?" Buffalo Horn rejoined.
"No, the rest of our warriors must stay here to defend
our loved ones."

Nate nodded in understanding and hefted the
Hawken. "Well, I'm ready. Let's hit the trail."

"I would be honored if you would ride at my side,"
Buffalo Horn said, and motioned to his left.

"My friend and I will be glad to," Nate said,
indicating Wind In The Grass with a jerk of his
thumb.

Buffalo Horn glanced at the young warrior, disapproval plainly etched in his face. "As you wish," he
said coldly, with the same enthusiasm as a man who
had been asked to keep company with a carrier of the
plague. He jabbed his horse with his heels, moving
out.

Nate turned the stallion, falling in with the group,
glancing over his shoulder at Standing Bear and Bad
Face, both of whom glared. He didn't like having his
back to them, but he doubted they would do anything
when there were so many others around. They certainly wouldn't shoot him in the back; such a cowardly act
would get them expelled from the tribe.

Buffalo Horn led them to Stinking Creek, crossed it
at a shallow point, and continued northward into a
narrow valley that wound among foothills.

As always, Nate reveled in the abundant wildlife.
He spotted a herd of deer, four elk, and a large hawk
circling high overhead, all within the first mile. Looking to his left, he found Wind In The Grass riding
proudly, head held high, and he hoped he hadn't made
a mistake by having the young warrior brought along.
If Wind In The Grass should be killed, he'd never
forgive himself for sticking his big nose in and trying
to set things straight.

At the end of the valley they passed through a gap
between two hills, crossed a meadow, and skirted a

snow crowned mountain by traveling along its base to the west.

"We are about half the distance to the Blackfoot camp," Buffalo Horn said to Nate. "Our hunters saw their fort near Still Lake."

Nate had seen such "forts" before. Of all the tribes with which he was familiar, only the Blackfeet used them, perhaps because they preferred to conduct their raids on foot instead of on horseback, and were therefore more vulnerable to attack. When a Blackfoot war party was in enemy country and made camp at night, or when they were set upon by those they intended to raid, the Blackfeet constructed large conical forts of stout limbs, or brush forts if there wasn't the time, and defended themselves with habitual vigor.

"I doubt they are still there," Buffalo Horn remarked. "They were probably staying near the lake for the night. We might run into them somewhere along the way."

"Do you think they know where your village is?" Nate asked.

"If not, you can be sure they are looking for it very hard. At least once every three or four moons they raid us, stealing some of our horses and killing a few of our warriors. This time we will give them a surprise."

"Have you ever raided them?"

"Two summers ago we did."

"That's the only time in recent years?"

Buffalo Horn's features seemed to cloud over. "Their territory is far to the northeast. They have many, many villages, and their warriors are everywhere. Few tribes ever send raiding parties into the country of the Blackfeet because most never come back."

Nate thoughtfully pursed his lips. Quite obviously the Flatheads, like the majority of other tribes, lived in fear of the Blackfeet. Buffalo Horn would never admit as much, but Nate suspected that was the real reason the Flatheads had rarely given the Blackfeet a taste of their own medicine.

They went around another mountain and slanted up the gradually tapering slope of the next one, following a well-worn game trail. The narrow track of dirt and flattened grass forced them to ride in single file.

Nate stayed alert, scanning the forest below and the landscape in all directions. There was nothing to indicate the Blackfeet were anywhere around. They climbed several hundred feet, then halted when Buffalo Horn reigned up. "Is something wrong?" Nate inquired.

The Flathead pointed northward. "We are close now. I hoped we would see the smoke from their fire."

Only clear, azure sky dominated the horizon beyond.

Winding down the trail, they entered dense forest consisting of various kinds of pine trees. Squirrels scampered from limb to limb and startled rabbits bounded off into the brush. After traveling over a mile, Buffalo Horn halted once more. "From here we should walk," he declared, and went to swing down.

"Why not let Wind In The Grass watch our horses?" Nate suggested.

Buffalo Horn paused. "Why him?"

"Why not?"

"I would like another warrior to watch them."

"Wind In The Grass will do just fine."

"Do not ask me to do this," Buffalo Horn said, scowling.

"I must. Please. For me," Nate asked.

The Flathead glanced at the young warrior, then at Running Elk. "What do you say?"

"Grizzly Killer is Carcajou's close friend," Running Elk replied.

Perturbed but trying hard not to show it, Buffalo Horn gave a curt nod and dismounted. "Very well. Wind In The Grass will tend our animals."

"Thank you," Nate said, sliding to the ground. He heard Running Elk translate for the benefit of Wind In The Grass, who then beamed and gazed gratefully at him. He smiled, winked, and joined the flow of warriors who were following Buffalo Horn deeper into the forest. As luck would have it, he was only a yard in front of Standing Bear, who was carrying a bow. An odd itch developed between his shoulder blades as he walked ahead of the embittered warrior, and he was glad when they came to a clearing and stopped so he could pass other Flatheads and catch up with Buffalo Horn and Running Elk.

The Flatheads set about preparing themselves; nocking bows, drawing knives, hefting war clubs and lances, and, in the case of the few with firearms, verifying their weapons were loaded.

Buffalo Horn double-checked his rifle, then motioned for them to proceed. The warriors spread out, taking advantage of all available cover, moving from tree to tree and bush to bush. For over a hundred yards they continued in this fashion, and then the forest began to thin out.

Nate spied a body of water ahead and surmised it to be Still Lake. He scanned the shoreline but saw no sign of the Blackfoot forts, no sign of anything moving. Perhaps, he reflected, the Blackfeet had long since departed in another direction. As he neared the water, he moved slower, his thumb curled around the Hawken's hammer.

The deep blue surface of the lake resembled polished glass. Unruffled by even the tiniest wave, it gave the illusion of being solid rather than liquid. There was no evidence of fish, and a complete lack of waterfowl.

The observation struck Nate as strange. Every mountain lake he knew of teemed with life. Why not this one? He wondered if there might be a substance in the water that the animals didn't like.

Glancing to his left, he finally spotted the conical forts. There were three of them aligned in a row on the west shore, at the edge of the trees so they would blend in from a distance. Not a soul was around. He angled toward them, Buffalo Horn and Running Elk a few yards ahead.

Several warriors who were off on the left increased their pace and warily approached the makeshift structures. They were studies in nervous energy, gazing every which way, treading lightly and ready to bolt at the first hint of hostility.

Buffalo Horn and Running Elk stopped. So did the rest.

Nate followed their example. He figured they had more experience in Indian warfare than he did, and relied on their discretion. Apprehensively, he watched four braves move from concealment and dash to the forts. The warriors quickly searched each one, then emerged, relieved and all smiles, and beckoned for their fellows to join them. Almost as one, the Flatheads rose and walked forward.

Reluctantly, Nate stood. He scoured the woods behind the forts and saw nothing move, but he felt uneasy about waltzing into the open without having conducted a thorough check of the woodland around Still Lake. Consequently, he trailed behind the rest of the Flatheads, deliberately dawdling.

The warriors conversed loudly, discussing the situation, Buffalo Horn doing most of the talking.

Nate halted after walking only fifteen feet. His mind was shrieking a warning that things were not as they seemed, that they should all get out of there before something terrible happened. But he was loathe to say anything for fear of coming across as a fool if there was no danger.

What should he do?

Then he remembered advice once dispensed by Shakespeare: "Always rely on your gut feelings, your intuition. The Great Mystery gave it to you for a reason. If more folks used theirs on a regular basis, they would be a lot better off."

The Flatheads were inspecting the forts. A few were searching the ground for tracks.

"Buffalo Horn," Nate called out, finally making up his mind.

Both Buffalo Horn and Running Elk turned. "What is it, Grizzly Killer?" the former asked.

"Get the warriors away from there," Nate said urgently.

"Why? What is wrong?"

"I'm not sure," Nate admitted, his eyes roving over the wall of vegetation to the rear of the forts. Suddenly he saw a flicker of motion, then another, motions that resolved themselves into the shadowy figures of stalking Blackfeet. The sight sent a chill rippling down his spine, but he still retained the presence of mind to cry out, "Behind you! It's a trap!"

The Flatheads, startled by the cry, gazed about in confusion. Since most didn't speak English, they had no idea why he had yelled although they fully appreciated the manifest distress in his agitated tone.

All except Buffalo Horn and Running Elk, who both spun in alarm. They saw the danger, but they were too late to prevent the inevitable.

A swarm of arrows streaked out of the vegetation

attended by the blasting of a number of fusees. In the blink of an eye six of the Flatheads were down, dead, and three others were staggering, pierced by shafts or wounded by balls.

Buffalo Horn bellowed and the Flatheads retreated, helping those who were wounded. Harsh whoops erupted in the foliage and another swarm of whizzing arrows cleaved the air. It was a slaughter. Five more Flatheads were slain, two more wounded. Now there were only four untouched Flatheads left; Buffalo Horn, Running Elk, Standing Bear, and Bad Face.

Nate saw a Blackfoot armed with a fusee materialize and point the weapon at the fleeing Flatheads. Snapping the Hawken to his right shoulder, he fired before the Blackfoot could. The warrior fell, the fusee falling from his hands. Back-pedaling, Nate reloaded on the run, reaching the trees well ahead of the Flatheads. He had to provide covering fire or they were all dead.

His fingers flew faster than they ever had before. First he had to pour in the proper amount of powder, then place a patch around the ball and insert it, then use the ramrod to press the ball down to the bottom of the barrel. All the while the Blackfeet were loosing arrows. One of the wounded Flatheads toppled, a shaft jutting from the center of his chest.

Nate spied another Blackfoot at the opposite tree line and took hasty aim. The man was bringing a bow vertical, about to let fly. Not this time, Nate thought, and let the Hawken punctuate his intent.

The ball took the Blackfoot in the head, catapulting him backwards.

Now Buffalo Horn and the other survivors reached the temporary shelter of the woods near Nate. They pressed onward, aware their lives hung in the balance if they failed to reach their mounts.

Nate brought up the rear, reloading yet again. He could see Blackfeet emerging from behind the forts. Eight. Ten. Twelve. They screeched, hefted their various weapons, and raced in pursuit.

The situation was desperate. Nate could scarcely believe that in the span of less than a minute the Flathead force had been decimated. He hoped Wind In The Grass had heard the gunfire and would bring their horses at a gallop. Then, out of the corner of his eye, he spotted running forms, and looking in that direction he beheld a sight that compounded their desperation.

Running along the south shore, apparently planning to reinforce their companions, were more Blackfeet.

Chapter Twelve

Nate pointed at the reinforcements and shouted to Buffalo Horn, "Here come more!"

The Flathead looked, his features betraying his anxiety. He was supporting another warrior wounded in the thigh. Firming his grip, he picked up the pace.

Running Elk shot an arrow that dropped the foremost Blackfoot to their rear.

Another enemy, who was trying to swing to the west to outflank the Flatheads, attracted Nate's attention. He aimed as best he could while on the run and fired, uncertain whether he would score a hit. The Blackfoot pitched forward and was still.

Not bad shooting, Nate complimented himself, reloading. But it hardly slowed the Blackfeet, who were flitting from tree trunk to tree trunk with the agility of antelope. He wished he knew which one was their leader. Shakespeare had mentioned that when battling a war party, always go for the chief or the warrior in charge. When the top man fell, frequently the rest would take the body and fall back to regroup, or they would discontinue the fight if they felt the death of their leader was a bad omen.

Although the Blackfeet were still sending arrows and a few fusee balls after the fleeing Flatheads, most of their shots missed, deflected by the intervening brush or fired in such haste the aim was off.

Nate fared better. Twice he downed Blackfeet, and the deadly retort of his rifle was serving to keep the group to the rear at bay. Those to the south were not yet close enough to justify diverting his attention from the more immediate menace of those dogging the Flatheads' heels.

The running battle continued for another hundred yards. Evidently knowing they had the upper hand and would soon bring the Flatheads at bay, the Blackfeet made no effort to mount a concerted rush, even after the second group of six warriors joined the first.

Reloading feverishly time and again, Nate did his utmost to buy the Flatheads more time. He glanced over his shoulder repeatedly, expecting to see Wind In The Grass bringing the horses, but his friend had yet to show.

The Flatheads came to a knoll and skirted its base on the right. They were beginning to tire, and one of the wounded men was ready to keel over at any second. A ten-foot high boulder in their path became their sanctuary as they all took shelter in its comforting shadow.

Nate halted beside the boulder, his rifle leveled, seeking another target. The crafty Blackfeet had learned their lesson; his marksmanship was forcing them to stay well back and well hidden.

Buffalo Horn deposited the wounded warrior he had been assisting on the ground and turned to Nate. "Go for the horses. We will wait here."

Surprised at the request and disinclined to desert them, Nate shook his head. "I'm not leaving you."

"Our only hope is the horses," Buffalo Horn stressed, gripping Nate's arm. "We can hold them off until you return."

"If the horses are still there," Running Elk interjected bitterly.

Nate opened his mouth to object again when an arrow flashed out of nowhere, missing his face by less than an inch and almost striking Buffalo Horn in the abdomen. The tall Flathead looked into his eyes, pleading silently. He realized he had no choice. Either he retrieved the mounts, or they would be massacred to the last man. "All right," he said, alertly scanning the woods while moving backwards. "I'll go get them."

"Hurry," Buffalo Horn urged.

Whirling, Nate took only four strides when he heard a sound that was more wonderful than any music ever played; the thundering drum of many horses, coming directly toward him. He spotted them the next instant.

Wind In The Grass was riding at a reckless pace, using only his legs to guide his animal, his hands full with the long reins of the animals he was leading, his muscles straining in rippling relief as he pulled them in his wake.

"There!" Nate shouted, elated, and turned to help a wounded Flathead make for their salvation.

The Blackfeet perceived their quarry might escape and intensified their attack, raining down arrows in a steady hail of lethal barbed points. Venting their war whoops, many broke from cover to try and overtake the Flatheads.

Nate saw Wind In The Grass struggling valiantly to keep the horses under control. With ten trailing from either arm, the mounts were bunched together and demonstrating their resentment of the claustrophobic treatment by jerking their heads back and causing no end of trouble.

Wind In The Grass stopped fifteen feet away. He leaned forward, breathing heavily from his strenuous exertion, sweat beading his forehead.

An impetuous Blackfoot, screaming crazily, sprinted straight at the Flatheads.

Pivoting, Nate let go of the wounded warrior, sighted, and squeezed off a shot that hit the Blackfoot between the eyes. The warrior did a complete revolution on one heel, then collapsed as if his legs were made of potter's clay. Without bothering to reload, Nate dashed to the horses.

The wounded Flatheads were being hurriedly assisted onto horses. An arrow smacked into a riderless horse, causing it to neigh in terror and rear back on its hind legs, throwing several other horses into a panic.

Nate swung onto his stallion. He rode a few yards toward the converging Blackfeet, drew a flintlock, and fired the big pistol into the chest of the closest adversary. The man died soundlessly, prompting the rest to scatter, seeking protective cover. In a smooth motion Nate wedged the pistol under his belt and drew the second flintlock. He risked a look back. The eight surviving Flatheads, four of whom were wounded, were now mounted beside Wind In The Grass.

Buffalo Horn motioned and they goaded their animals into a gallop, heading southward. He stayed, waving his arms and shouting to get the riderless animals to scatter.

Comprehending, Nate wheeled the stallion and helped drive the horses off to prevent the Blackfeet from catching them. No sooner had the last horse galloped off than he did the same alongside Buffalo Horn, trailing the ragtag remains of the once proud band of noble avengers.

A few last arrows, parting shots from the infuriated Blackfeet, fell close behind the departing Flatheads, but none of the shafts came close enough to claim additional lives.

Sweet relief coursed through Nate as their escape became apparent. He thought of all the Flatheads who had died because of blatant carelessness and wished he had shouted a warning just a few seconds sooner. Perhaps more would have lived. Then again, he knew he shouldn't blame himself for their own neglect. He'd done all he could to help them when they'd needed help the most.

Buffalo Horn took the lead, riding hard for almost a mile. He abruptly reined up in a clearing and turned, issuing directions to the warriors. In short order the four wounded men were placed on the grass where the gravity of their individual conditions could be adequately gauged.

Nate stayed on his stallion, turned sideways in the saddle so he could watch their back trail. Thankfully, the Blackfeet had been left far behind. Fleet as they were, they were no match for horses. He glanced at Buffalo Horn, who was examining the last injured warrior. "How are they?"

"Not good, I am afraid. Three of them will never make it to our village."

"What will you do?"

"Tend to them the best we can and keep going. It is too dangerous to stay here very long with the Blackfeet on the prowl."

"I'll keep watch," Nate offered, and did just that while reloading his guns.

Running Elk and Standing Bear went into the woods and returned carrying several leaves and a poultice they had prepared from strictly herbal substances. The mixture was applied to the wounds of each warrior, and after allowing the men to rest for a bit, Buffalo Horn gave instructions and mounted again.

Nate brought up the rear as they moved out, constantly scanning the forest, and not until two more miles were behind them was he convinced they had truly escaped. At that point, as they crossed over a low knoll, one of the wounded warriors cried out plaintively and pitched from his animal. The body was draped over the horse and on they went.

He could well imagine the reception they would receive at the village since he'd witnessed such pitiable scenes of mass mourning before among the Shoshones. And he did not envy Buffalo Horn one bit. Warriors who took it upon themselves to lead war parties were held strictly accountable if that war party met disaster, and the debacle at Still Lake might well effect Buffalo Horn's social standing and warrior status in the tribe.

Suddenly he realized Standing Bear was looking at him and wondered why. It was regrettable, he mused, that Shakespeare's rival and Bad Face had both survived the battle. Had they perished, his friend's problem would be solved and there would be nothing to prevent him from returning to Winona.

Nate thought of her often on the return trip, of the loneliness she must be experiencing because of his loyalty to Shakespeare. But he couldn't leave yet, not until Standing Bear and Bad Face were taken care of.

By midafternoon two more of the wounded Flatheads died. Buffalo Horn and the rest barely spoke the entire time. An oppressive atmosphere hovered around them, a pall of death they were unable to shake.

When Nate finally spotted the village, he smiled

happily. Once again a shout went up and Flatheads converged from all directions. Instead of smiling and laughing, though, they were grim and silent. Where twenty-two men had gone off to slay Blackfeet, only seven were coming back, a staggering toll the warrior ranks could ill afford since the women already outnumbered the men by a considerable margin.

He glanced at Wind In The Grass, who had also been unusually quiet, and noted profound sadness in the young warrior's eyes. Both times that Wind In The Grass had gone on raids, the raiding parties had met disaster. Knowing how superstitious the Indians were, he speculated on whether the tribe might decide Wind In The Grass was somehow jinxed, a living bad omen.

Wails arose from a number of women as the party drew nearer and the wives could see who was there and who was missing. The lamentations became more general as Buffalo Horn led the weary warriors in among the lodges. One of the women rushed up to the horse bearing the wounded man and clutched at his leg, sobbing softly. Friends came to help her, and together they took the wounded man off toward his own teepee.

Buffalo Horn turned and gazed at Nate and Wind In The Grass. "I thank both of you for going along. All of us might have been killed if not for the two of you," he said in English, then repeated the words in his own tongue.

Wind In The Grass mustered a wan smile at the news, replied briefly, and wheeled his horse toward Stinking Creek.

About to tag along, Nate paused. His host might like to be alone with Flower Woman for a while. He'd go there later. For now, he faced Buffalo Horn. "I understand Shakespeare is staying with you."

"Yes. Come. We will go there," Buffalo Horn said, heading eastward.

The warrior's dejected expression tugged at Nate's sympathy. "Try to cheer up," he advised. "One day you'll get your revenge on the Blackfeet."

"If I go on a raid again, perhaps."

"You may not?"

"No. My medicine failed me. White men might call it bad luck, but my people know better. My spirit guide did not watch over me this time as in the past and I must find out why."

Nate shrugged. "I think you're being too hard on yourself. It could have happened to anyone."

"You are trying to be kind," Buffalo Horn said. "If you knew our ways better, you would understand how serious this is. It all goes back to when I was sixteen and I went into the mountains by myself on a vision quest. I fasted for seven days and seven nights, and then the vision came to me."

"What kind of vision?" Nate inquired when the warrior stopped, burning with curiosity.

Buffalo Horn's face lit up at the memory. "It was wonderful. A spirit being, a great fiery buffalo with only one bright red horn, appeared to me and offered to be my personal guardian. It taught me a prayer I must say every day and a ritual I must do once a month to keep my charm filled with power."

"Your charm?"

Nodding, Buffalo Horn reached into a pouch hanging on his left hip and extracted the smooth, severed tip of a buffalo horn. "This is my special charm. Without it, I will surely die."

"I see," Nate said, struggling inwardly with acceptance of the notion. Although he keenly admired most aspects of Indian life, he found their extreme fascination with certain superstitions rather bothersome. He had to remind himself that he had never gone on a vision quest, and had no cause to think lightly of a practice most tribes had indulged in for more years than anyone could recollect. "What will you do?" he asked.

"I will try to contact my spirit guide and find out why my charm has lost its power."

"How do you go about doing that?"

"I will go off and not eat until the fiery buffalo appears to me."

"What if it doesn't?"

"Then I die."

Chapter Thirteen

Shakespeare was seated outside of Buffalo Horn's lodge cleaning his rifle when Nate and Buffalo Horn arrived. He took one look and stood, coming out to meet them. "How did it go?" he inquired.

Nate shook his head.

"The Blackfeet were waiting for us," Buffalo Horn said sadly. "We were ambushed and most of our warriors were killed. By now the Blackfeet have taken their scalps and cut their bodies into pieces."

"I'm sorry," Shakespeare said sincerely.

Buffalo Horn halted and dropped to the grass. A heavyset woman emerged from the teepee, hurrying toward him. They spoke in the Flathead language for a bit, then both went inside.

"He's taking it hard," Nate commented, dismounting.

"He has reason to," Shakespeare said, and placed a hand on the younger man's shoulder. "I'm glad nothing happened to you. I wouldn't want to bear the bad tidings to Winona."

"Is that the only reason?"

Shakespeare grinned. "The only one I can think of at the moment." He motioned at the ground. "Sit down and tell me everything that happened."

Keeping to the essential facts, Nate related the day's events, concluding with a mention of Buffalo Horn's intention to try and contact the spirit guide.

"At his age?" Shakespeare said. "Any extended time without food and water could kill him."

"So he said."

"At my age, I'm not too partial to losing old friends. There aren't all that many left in this world."

"Think you can talk him out of it?"

Shakespeare stared at the lodge entrance, his mouth curling downward. "Not very likely. To an Indian, a guardian spirit is as much a part of his life as is breathing and eating. No warrior can be without one. Buffalo Horn will do anything to restore the power to his charm now that he believes it's not effective."

"So there's nothing you can do?" Nate asked.

"Pray for the best."

Nate leaned back on his palms. "Since you have a moment, there's something else I'd like to bring up."

"What?"

"Standing Bear. Now that Smoke and Wolf Ribs are dead, do you figure he'll back down and leave you alone?"

The mountain man chuckled. "Does a grizzly ever run from a scrap of meat? No. And just because two of Standing Bear's best friends are dead won't mean a thing to him. He'll still try to kill me. I just don't know when or how."

"And what about the lady you're fighting over? Have you given her your decision yet?"

"Not yet. I see her this evening. She's living in the same lodge she shared with Spotted Owl, not far from where Wind In The Grass has his teepee."

"Which reminds me," Nate said, rising. "I should go see how he's doing. He didn't seem too happy about the outcome of the raid."

"At least he redeemed himself with the horses," Shakespeare noted, also standing. "The next time a war party goes out, hopefully they won't hesitate to take him along."

Stepping to the stallion, Nate swung up. "Take care of yourself."

A peculiar expression lined Shakespeare's face. "The single and peculiar life is bound with all the strength and armour of the mind to keep itself from noyance. But much more that spirit upon whose weal depends and rest the lives of many," he quoted.

"What?"

"Arm you, I pray you, to this speedy voyage, for we will fetters put about this fear, which now goes too free-footed."

"Be honest with me, Shakespeare," Nate said, smiling. "Do you have any idea what you just said?"

"Certainly," McNair replied indignantly. "I advised you to take good care of yourself."

"You could have fooled me," Nate said, and headed toward the north end of the village. Everywhere there were sad faces, warriors and women walking around in abject depression because of the outcome of the raid. Even the children were subdued now, either with their parents inside their lodges or sitting around outside and conversing in hushed tones. He felt strangely out of place, as if he was witnessing very private grief not meant for outsiders to observe.

When he was only forty yards or so from his destination, he reined up in surprise. Directly ahead, standing in front of a lodge, were Blue Water Woman and Bad Face. They appeared to be arguing, although both were keeping their voices down. Bad Face gestured angrily over and over.

What do I do? Nate asked himself. He didn't want to meddle, but he didn't want to sit there and do nothing while Bad Face berated his mentor's future wife. Compromising, he slanted the Hawken across his thighs and rode boldly up to them, a friendly grin plastered on his lips. "Howdy, Blue Water Woman," he said.

They both glanced up. Bad Face instantly glowered while Blue Water Woman seemed relieved.

"Hello, Grizzly Killer," she greeted him. "I have heard you fought very bravely today."

Nate fixed his eyes on the warrior. "Did Bad Face tell you that? I didn't know he was so considerate. Thank him for me."

Blue Water Woman laughed. "It was someone else who told me. Bad Face does not hold a very high opinion of you."

"I would never have known," Nate said, and bluntly came to the point. "Is he bothering you?"

"He wants me to accompany him to go see Standing Bear, but I have refused."

The burly warrior had taken all the English he was about to. His hands flew in sharp motions as he signed, "Leave us in peace, Grizzly Killer. This does not concern you."

Instead of signing a response, Nate simply shifted so the barrel of the Hawken was trained on Bad Face's chest. He made no move to lift the weapon or overtly threaten the Flathead in any way, but Bad Face understood his meaning. For a moment they locked eyes in a silent battle of wills as each measured up the other.

Bad Face finally spun and stalked off.

"Thank you, Grizzly Killer," Blue Water Woman said. "Standing Bear is becoming more persistent than I thought he would."

"Why did he send Bad Face instead of coming in person?"

"Because Standing Bear is a very proud man and he could never bring himself to beg me to pay his teepee a visit. So he sent Bad Face in his place."

"You'd better stay on your guard," Nate suggested. "I wouldn't put anything past those two."

"They would never harm me. Such an act would get them expelled from the tribe for the rest of their lives."

"In any case, if you need me I'm staying with Wind In The Grass," Nate mentioned, pointing at the appropriate lodge. "Just give a holler and I'll come running."

"You are quite kind. I can see why Carcajou respects you so highly. He thinks of you as the son he never had."

"He does?" Nate said, flattered by the compliment. "He's never told me that."

"Men are not as open with secrets of the heart as are women. I believe the Great Mystery made them inferior in that respect."

"Sounds like something my wife would say," Nate remarked.

Blue Water Woman nodded. "Women are wiser in such matters than men. All men think about is hunting and fighting and making love."

Shocked by her frank assertion, Nate could only mumble, "Well, not all men."

"Most," Blue Water Woman said. "There are a few who look deeper into themselves and discover the true meaning of life, men like Carcajou."

Nate leaned forward, his curiosity aroused. "What is the true meaning of life?"

"You will find it one day."

"That's not much of an answer."

"It is the only answer."

Puzzled, Nate straightened. He was beginning to understand the reason Shakespeare cared for her so much. They were a perfect match; they both spoke in circles. "If you say so," he said, tightening his grip on the reins.

"Time, Grizzly Killer, uncovers all."

"Oh," Nate said, and coughed lightly. "Well, it's about time I went to see Wind In The Grass. Nice talking to you again."

"The same here. Come visit me soon," Blue Water Woman requested, reaching up to run her right hand along her long hair, smoothing it over her shoulder.

"I will," Nate promised, and rode toward his host's lodge, his growling stomach reminding him that he could use some food. He wondered if Flower Woman had more tasty buffalo stew, his mouth watering at the thought.

As Nate drew up in front of the lodge he noticed the flap was tied up. According to Indian etiquette, that meant any friend of the owner could enter without having to announce himself. Consequently, he dismounted, ground-hitched the stallion, and went in with a smile on his face.

Seated at the customary spot, his head held high, was Wind In The Grass. Cradled in his lap was his son. Flower Woman was busily preparing a meal over the crackling fire. She shifted as Nate entered and beamed, her hands moving fluidly. "I am the happiest woman alive this day. My husband has proven himself to the tribe. Now no one will speak badly of him."

"I know," Nate signed in return, and waited for his host to indicate where he should sit, which turned out to be the seat of honor. He walked over and sank down with a sigh.

"Since this is a special day, I am using the last of our

meat to make a special meal," Flower Woman signed. "I hope you will like it."

"I will," Nate assured her, and looked at Wind In The Grass. Despite the joyous occasion, the young warrior's countenance was tinged with melancholy. "Is something wrong?" he inquired.

"I am sad for the lives of all the brave men who died today," Wind In The Grass responded. "Had I brought the horses sooner, some more might have lived."

"I am sure you did the best you could."

Wind In The Grass was still for a moment. "I tried to come at the sound of the first shots, but several of the horses gave me trouble. It took all of my strength to bring them."

"I saw you," Nate reminded him. "We all did. You were doing all any man could do. No one will blame you for anything." He lowered his hands for a second. "You should know that Buffalo Horn is taking all of the blame for the deaths on his shoulders. He says it is because his charm has lost its power."

Flower Woman uttered a loud snort. "I told you," she admonished her husband. "I said that you were being too hard on yourself. Now the whole tribe will know Buffalo Horn is to blame."

"I think they are all to blame," Nate signed.

Both Flatheads fixed perplexed expressions on him.

"Why?" Wind In The Grass asked.

In detail, Nate signed the story of the blunder the Flatheads had committed by walking right up to the Blackfoot forts, exposing themselves to the hidden ambushers. He explained that they should have checked the surrounding area before venturing into the open, and told how his own feeling had saved his life.

"It is true what they say," Wind In The Grass said

when the tale was done. "The Great Mystery is strong in you."

"Who says?" Nate asked.

"Everyone."

Nate wondered just how much talking the Flatheads had been doing behind his back about the exaggerated accounts of his exploits or of his battle with Mad Dog. Sometimes it seemed as if most people had nothing better to do than sit around and gossip like a quilting circle of elderly matrons.

Flower Woman took a step toward him. "How many Blackfeet did you kill, Grizzly Killer?"

"I did not count them," Nate said.

"Was it many?" she persisted.

"No. Six or seven, I believe."

The statement caused Flower Woman to step back again, but this time in astonishment. She gazed at her husband and signed, "Now I understand. Truly this is the highest honor we have ever had."

"What is she talking about?" Nate inquired, looking at his host.

"You have done more for me in the eyes of my people by staying with me than I did today by bringing the horses," Wind In The Grass said, and placed a hand on Nate's shoulder in friendly gratitude. "Among our tribe, a man is not worth anything if he is not brave. And the braver he is, the more enemies he slays in battle, the more courage he demonstrates, and the more honored he becomes. Other warriors always want to have such brave men as guests at their meals, or to have these brave ones visit often."

Nate understood. By associating with a highly regarded warrior, another man could enhance his own social prestige. In certain ways, he reflected, Indian culture was much like white culture, only in the white culture it was those with the most money who were so highly esteemed. Come to think of it, he decided, the Indian way was infinitely better.

"You wait and see," Wind In The Grass signed. "Having you here will make my lodge very popular."

As if in confirmation, a shadow darkened the entrance a heartbeat before a warrior entered, none other than White Eagle, the chief of the village.

Chapter Fourteen

Wind In The Grass, clearly startled, leaped to his feet and warmly greeted the aged warrior in their mutual tongue. Stepping forward, he motioned for White Eagle to take a seat.

Nate had noticed Flower Woman stiffen at the chief's entrance, leading him to deduce this was a singular event. It might well be the very first time White Eagle had paid them a visit. He nodded at the chief and made the sign for a friendly greeting.

White Eagle returned the courtesy as he sat down, then went on in extended sign language while looking at Wind In The Grass. "I am honored to be in the lodge of a man who did so well today. Buffalo Horn has told me that you carefully watched the horses and brought them as soon as you could after the Blackfeet ambushed our war party."

Pride brightened the young warrior's eyes as he replied, "I only did what was expected of me."

"You did well," White Eagle said, then paused to glance at Nate before continuing. "If you do not mind,

Wind In The Grass, we will use sign language to discuss the matter I have come to talk about, out of respect to your other guest."

"Had you not asked, I would have requested that we do so," Wind In The Grass responded. "I would not want to be impolite to Grizzly Killer."

White Eagle nodded. "Very well." He focused on Nate. "Grizzly Killer, if you would be so kind, I would like to hear your version of the events at Still Lake today."

"I would be happy to tell you," Nate replied, although in the back of his mind he wondered why the chief was specifically asking him when any of the surviving warriors could also provide a factual account. Dutifully, he launched into an extended recital of the fiasco, being careful not to attribute blame to anyone, and emphasizing at the end the outstanding job done by Wind In The Grass. Out of the corner of his eye he saw Flower Woman swell with affection for her spouse.

White Eagle bowed his head when Nate finished, his forehead furrowed in deep concentration. Finally he looked up and frowned. "Then it is worse than I thought," he signed.

"What is?" Wind In The Grass inquired.

"Those Blackfeet defeated our band soundly. I suspect they were able to catch some of our scattered horses and are now using them as their own. There is a chance they will mount another attack."

Nate raised his hands. "Surely the Blackfeet are on their way back to their own country now with the horses and the scalps they collected. Why would they stay in the area?"

"To get *more* horses and scalps," White Eagle said. "Blackfeet do not give up easily. I have known them to raid a village one day, then come back the very next day and raid it again."

Clever tactic, Nate reflected, since no one in the village would expect another attack so soon after the first incident.

"And even if they are not planning a raid on the village, they might be hiding out there waiting to ambush one of our hunting parties or hoping to steal some of our women when they go out foraging for food and herbs."

"Post more sentries," Nate proposed. "And do not let any women leave the village unless they are accompanied by warriors."

"Sound suggestions," White Eagle said, "ones I have already put into effect."

"Then all you can do is hope for the best," Nate signed.

"That, and one more thing."

"What?"

White Eagle gave each of them a meaningful stare. "I was thinking of sending out two or three men to see if the Blackfeet have departed our territory."

It took all of Nate's self-control to keep from frowning and thus insulting the chief. He knew who White Eagle had in mind, and it bothered him. Why couldn't they send out several of their own warriors? Why rely on him? The answer, ironically enough, was obvious; he was the great Grizzly Killer.

"I have already asked Carcajou and he has said he will go," White Eagle disclosed. "Would the two of you like to go along with him?"

"Wherever Carcajou goes, I go," Nate signed.

"And I would be glad to accompany them," Wind In The Grass answered.

"Good," White Eagle said. "It would be best if you waited until the rising of the sun. You will need plenty of rest after all you have been through today."

"We will be ready," Nate signed, then cocked his head when he heard the drumming of hooves from outside. Moments later the animal halted close to the entrance, footsteps sounded, and in came its rider. He smiled at the familiar figure and said in English, "Hello, Shakespeare."

The mountain man grinned and nodded. "Has White Eagle told you what he has in mind?"

"Yes."

"Figured as much. That's why I rode right over," Shakespeare said, then switched to sign language. "Greetings, Wind In The Grass and Flower Woman. I am honored to be in your lodge." He glanced at the chief. "And greetings again to you, White Eagle."

"Please, sit down," Wind In The Grass signed.

"Another time, perhaps," Shakespeare signed. "I can not stay long." He squatted beside the cooking fire. "I knew White Eagle was coming here to ask you to go with me to check on the Blackfeet. Have you both agreed?"

"Of course," Wind In The Grass replied.

Nate let a bob of his chin be his answer.

"I figured you would," Shakespeare said, "which is why I wanted to let you know right away that we will be leaving after dark."

Wind In The Grass appeared uneasy at the news. "Tonight?" he asked.

"Yes," Shakespeare said, and lifted his right arm to point at an angle toward the east, approximately twelve inches above an imaginary horizon. "When the moon is that high."

Nate could tell from the expressions on the Flatheads that none of them were very fond of the idea, and he knew the reason. Many Indians, as Shakespeare had taught him, rarely traveled at night; most of those in the Rockies and those dwelling on the plains farther east ventured abroad only between dawn and sunset. There were notable exceptions to the general rule, such as war parties who occasionally took advantage of the night to take enemies by surprise, and the dreaded Apaches who lived far to the southwest and reportedly preferred traveling after the sun went down rather than during the day.

"I will be ready," Wind In The Grass signed.

"Why not wait until morning?" White Eagle asked. "Riding at night is very dangerous. A man can not see as well, and the grizzlies, the long tailed cats, and the wolves are everywhere."

"We have a better chance of spotting the Blackfeet from a distance after dark," Shakespeare noted, and vented a reassuring chuckle. "I know what I'm doing. Trust me."

"I would never doubt you, Carcajou," White Eagle said. "I know you have the welfare of our people at heart."

"Thank you," Shakespeare said, standing and gazing at Nate and Wind In The Grass. "I just wanted to let you know ahead of time so the two of you can get some sleep before we leave."

"Appreciate it," Nate said.

"I will see both of you later," Shakespeare signed, and departed hastily.

Nate figured his friend was going to see Blue Water Woman, and he realized he should tell Shakespeare about the argument with Bad Face. But as he put his hands down to push to his feet, he heard Shakespeare's mount hurry off. Shrugging, he relaxed, certain Blue Water Woman would inform Shakespeare herself.

"I must also be going," White Eagle noted, rising. He stepped over to the infant first and spoke a few words in the Flathead language that made Wind In The Grass and Flower Woman smiled broadly, and then departed.

No sooner was the chief gone than Flower Woman

impulsively moved over to Wind In The Grass and tenderly stroked his cheek. "Do you see?," she signed. "Now you are accounted a true warrior. By tomorrow the whole village will know White Eagle paid us a visit. We will no longer be shunned by our own people."

"And we owe it all to Grizzly Killer," Wind In The Grass stated, affectionately placing his hand on Nate's arm.

Flower Woman gazed fondly at Nate. "I will feed you until you burst."

"Thank you," Nate signed. "But we should not overeat if we are riding out after the Blackfeet tonight."

"Oh. Yes. I did not think," Flower Woman commented sheepishly, and turned to the fire to begin her preparations.

Nate felt Wind In The Grass give him a squeeze, and then the warrior went over to Roaring Mountain. The sight of the family happily engaged in mundane activities prompted him to think yet again of Winona. He wondered what she was doing.

Many miles to the south, outside of a sturdy cabin overlooking a serene lake teeming with waterfowl and fish, stood a beautiful Indian woman in a beaded buckskin dress, her dark hair flowing down to her hips. She placed both hands on the mound that had once been her flat stomach and felt movement as the infant growing within kicked.

She smiled, at peace with herself. It would be a boy. She just knew it. And she would be the proudest woman alive when the child came forth into the world, proud because she had honored her husband in one of the highest ways any woman could honor the man she loved; by giving him the sacred gift of a new life, a child to carry on in the footsteps of the parents, to keep the family alive for generations to come.

Her mouth curling downward, she faced northward. Where are you, my husband? she mused. He had said that he would be back after two sleeps at the most. Did he decide to stay with his friend a while longer, perhaps to talk over whatever had been bothering him?

She knew he had been troubled, although he would not come right out and tell her the reason. She had not pried, not made a nuisance of herself by intruding on his private thoughts. Deep down, though, she worried, worried greatly.

What if he was losing interest in her?

The thought sparked intense terror. She often speculated on how much he missed his family back in New York City, wherever that was, and whether he felt any inclination to return to them. He'd tried several times to explain about the place where he had been born and spent most of his life, and once had even drawn a picture on a board with a piece of charcoal to show her how to get there. Even so, New York City seemed unreal to her, an alien place filled with strange people who lived incomprehensible lives, spending their days and nights devoted to the making of the strange paper and metal they worshipped above all else. According to her beloved, very few people in the entire city bothered to make a diligent effort to live in harmony with the Everywhere Spirit.

How could such a thing be? she had often asked herself. How could any people hope to flourish if they denied the source of all that existed? The stories he had told her seemed too incredible to be true, yet she knew he never lied. Stories about lodges made of stone, towering high in the air. Stories about mighty metal animals called steam engines that were expected to one day do the work of horses. And stories about people who were always on the go, from dawn to dusk, never giving themselves a moment's rest.

In a way, the white race reminded her of ants. As a young girl, she had spent many an idle hour observing an ant hill, watching the tiny creatures go about their lives, always in motion, always working, working, working, never taking time to enjoy the fruits of their labor.

Was it possible her husband missed such a distressing life? Did he secretly pine to go back? It would explain his unusual moody behavior of late. And she had to be honest; she knew of many Indian women who had taken white men as husbands, and in most of the cases the men had left the women after only a year or so to head east and never returned.

What if the same fate befell her?

She anxiously bit her lower lip and lightly smacked her right palm against her thigh. This was not the way for the wife of the mighty Grizzly Killer to act. She must not give in to her fear. To do so insulted him, insulted their love. He had been true to her from the first day they met, and in the depth of her soul she felt he would remain true until the day they died.

Turning, she walked toward the south end of the cabin where the pen holding their horses was situated. If she kept busy, she wouldn't have time for such foolish thoughts. She hummed, trying to cheer herself up, and rounded the corner.

The eight animals were idly munching on grass she had fed them earlier. A few gazed at her, then resumed eating.

Satisfied, she retraced her steps to the front door and just reached it when a tremendous commotion erupted at the lake. She pivoted, her eyes narrowing, seeking the source.

Every bird on the lake and in its immediate vicinity had taken wing. Ducks, geese, gulls, and others were flapping into the sky, voicing a chorus of distinct quacks and cries.

She saw nothing to account for the peculiar behavior, which worried her. There might be a predator abroad, perhaps a panther or a grizzly. If so, she couldn't afford to take any risks. She entered the cabin, then closed and locked the door. To the right, leaning against the wall, was a loaded flintlock. She patted the barrel, reassured by its feel, remembering the lessons her husband had given her in how to shoot the cumbersome gun and how pleased he'd been when one afternoon she'd consistently hit a circle he had carved in a tree from a distance of thirty yards. He had laughed and hugged her and kissed her until her lips had been sore.

Oh Nate, she wondered, where are you?

Chapter Fifteen

Nate opened his eyes to find Wind In The Grass shaking his left shoulder. He promptly sat up, yawned, and gazed at the entrance. The flap had been tied up, and through the opening could be seen part of the star filled heavens.

"It is time," Wind In The Grass signed.

"Did you get any sleep?" Nate asked.

"I tried," the young warrior said.

Placing a hand on the Hawken at his side, Nate rose. His mind felt sluggish, and he almost regretted taking the nap. He'd felt better several hours ago when he'd laid down on his blanket. But he'd needed the rest if he hoped to be fully alert once the hunt for the Blackfeet began. Turning, he saw Flower Woman at the back of the lodge, tenderly cradling Roaring Mountain in her arms, rocking the infant back and forth. "I should saddle my horse," he signed, and took his leave, giving Wind In The Grass time in private to say good-bye.

The cool air invigorated him as he stepped outside. His nostrils registered the sweet scent of burning wood, principally pine, and he inhaled deeply. Leaning his rifle against the lodge, he saddled the stallion. Then he double-checked to be certain all of his guns were loaded.

Wind In The Grass emerged, appearing rather downcast, and set about preparing his own horse.

"Is anything wrong?" Nate signed when the warrior glanced in his direction.

"Flower Woman is not very happy about my going."

"You can stay if you want," Nate suggested. "No one would hold it against you. Why risk your life when you have a young son and a wife to provide for?"

"You have a wife too," Wind In The Grass noted. "Yet I see you are all ready to go." He paused and sighed. "No, I gave my word, and I will accompany Carcajou and you."

Nate sympathized with the warrior's obvious inner turmoil since he felt the same way about having left Winona to help Shakespeare. Life sometimes required the making of hard decisions and compelled a man to do something he otherwise would never do, such as leaving one's family to venture into the jaws of danger. At such times the only thing a man could do was pray those jaws never snapped shut.

They both looked up as a white horse approached from the south.

"Well, look at you two eager beavers," Shakespeare declared in English, and chuckled as he halted near their mounts. "Are you ready to go?"

"I am," Nate said.

The mountain man addressed Wind In The Grass in the Flathead language, and the young warrior went into the lodge, stepping out a minute later with a parfleche in his left hand, a bow in his right.

"We'll head for Still Lake," Shakespeare told Nate. "If those vermin are still camped in the vicinity, we should be able to spot their campfire a long ways off. Then we'll sneak up on the devils and give them a taste of their own medicine."

"Suits me," Nate said, anxious to get underway. He wanted to bring up the subject of Blue Water Woman and ascertain his mentor's plans concerning Standing Bear. In a lithe motion he swung into the saddle and gripped the reins in his left hand, listening to Shakespeare explain their plan to Wind In The Grass.

The warrior was securing the parfleche to his stallion's back. He stopped to address McNair for a minute, then completed his work.

"What was that all about?" Nate inquired, using English.

"Wind In The Grass isn't too partial to the notion of fighting the Blackfeet when there are only three of us," Shakespeare translated. "And it's not that he's afraid. He's simply being practical and realistically weighing the odds."

"None of the Flatheads are too keen on tangling with the Blackfeet," Nate noted.

"Who can blame them? The Blackfeet have terrorized every tribe in the northern Rockies, the plains east of the mountains, and southern Canada for more years than most folks can recollect. They have more hunting territory under their control than any three tribes combined. As you well know, they're natural scrappers. They'll fight until they drop."

"I'm surprised they haven't conquered the entire Rocky Mountain region by now."

"If they ever take to the horse as heartily as most of the others tribes have, they will," Shakespeare predicted. "But they still insist on conducting their raids on foot, which limits their range and the speed of their attacks."

Wind In The Grass climbed onto his war stallion and signed, "I am ready, my friends."

Nate gazed up at the full moon as Shakespeare headed north, then fell in behind his mentor. And so it begins, he reflected, hoping the Blackfeet would be long gone when they arrived at the lake. The last thing he wanted was to tangle with those tenacious savages again. But as things now stood, he didn't have any choice.

Winona tensed, her hands frozen above the buckskins pants she had been sewing for Nate, her ears straining to catch another sound. She was positive she had heard a faint, guttural snarl, and waited for it to be repeated. Most likely it had been a prowling bobcat or a lynx, perhaps even a panther, which was little cause for alarm. None of the big cats ever came close to the cabin, undoubtedly because of the human scent.

Still, she worried about the horses. A panther, or even a lynx if it was starving, might decide to make one of the animals its next meal. And with her husband gone, the duty of protecting the animals fell on her shoulders. She listened for the horses to begin whinnying, a sure sign that something was lurking nearby, but there wasn't a peep out of them.

She resumed working on the pants, a present she would give Nate when he returned. If she kept herself busy, she had reasoned, she would be less prone to miss him and less likely to let her imagination run wild, conjuring up vivid images of all the sundry horrible fates that could befall her beloved. The heavy thread she was using, made from buffalo tendons, had to be unwound a bit further, so she lifted the stick that served as her spool and began slowly twirling it.

Just then, from the south, several of the horses neighed loudly.

She was out of the chair the next instant, scarcely

breathing as the animals continued to whinny. They were quite agitated and making a considerable racket. There was no doubt that something lurked outside. Placing the pants, the thread and the bone needle on the chair, she crossed silently to the window. A deerhide flap had been tacked over the opening for use in keeping out insects in the summer and the cold wind in the winter. Now she unfastened the bottom of the flap and rolled it up several inches, then bent at the waist and peered into the murky darkness beyond.

Something growled.

An involuntary chill rippled down her spine. She gripped the bottom sill so hard her knuckles turned white, then chided herself for losing control. Be calm, Winona, she told herself. It was just a wild animal, and she had seen countless wild animals during her life.

As with most women in her tribe, she had killed scores of rabbits, grouse, ducks, and other small game for her family's cooking pot. But the taking of larger game had been the sole province of the men. Only warriors were permitted to go on buffalo hunts or after deer and elk, and only warriors killed the occasional bear or panther. She hoped the creature out there wasn't one of the big predators.

Winona stared at the surrounding forest, trying to detect movement. All she saw were shadowy trees and gloomy undergrowth, nothing to give a hint of whatever it might be. Girding herself, she stepped to the door and picked up the flintlock.

All the horses were neighing now, creating a din that could be heard for half a mile.

She had to go out. There was a slim chance Utes might be camped in the area, and if they heard the horses they would be sure to investigate in the morning. She must quiet them immediately.

Holding the rifle firmly in her left hand, she opened

the door halfway and listened. From the commotion, the horses were milling around inside the pen in fearful confusion. She disliked the idea of stepping out there where the creature prowling about could see her better than she could see it.

An idea occurred to her, and she moved to the stone fireplace Nate's uncle had constructed when building the cabin. The fire crackled noisily, eating at the broken branches she had gathered earlier in the day. Taking hold of one end of a thick, short limb untouched by the flames, she carefully pulled it out and held the torch aloft. The light wouldn't last long, but perhaps it would scare off her unwanted visitor.

Feeling braver, Winona went straight outside, turned right, and stopped. She raised the torch as high as she could, scanning the vegetation, her heart beating wildly, ready to bolt inside should the creature turn out to be a huge grizzly.

One of the horses vented a particularly high-pitched whinny.

Figuring the prowler must be near the pen, Winona hastened to the end of the cabin, the flickering flames dancing as if alive and casting their glowing radiance out to a distance of about eight feet. She halted again, extending the torch toward the animals, and saw them moving in a nervous circle, packed together for mutual protection.

There was no sign of whatever skulked in the woods.

Suddenly all the horses stopped and swung to the south, their nostrils flaring, their ears pricked, their collective attention riveted on the thick brush.

Winona heard something moving, heard a twig snap and another feral growl, and her body was instantly transformed into a block of ice. She stood still, her lips parted, afraid to take a breath. A large bush off to her left moved as if shaken by an invisible hand. Gulping, she swung the torch toward it and the shaking ceased.

The thing uttered a fierce snarl.

She knew it must be watching her and backed up until her back touched the log wall. Now, if the creature attacked, it wouldn't be able to come at her from the rear. One handed, she pointed the heavy flintlock at the bush, wondering how she was going to fire and hold the torch at the same time.

The horses had quieted down, comforted by her presence. They were all gazing toward the same bush, completely motionless, standing as if sculpted from clay.

Winona held the torch out and slowly moved it back and forth. The circle of light barely went half the distance to the forest, not illuminating the bush at all, and she realized she must get closer if she hoped to identify the creature. She hesitated, though, thinking of the new life within her, of the consequences to the baby should she become gravely injured. Nate might come back to find them both dead.

But she couldn't just stand there.

She edged forward, taking little steps, the rifle barrel swaying with each pace. Using her thumb, she cocked the hammer to set the trigger. Moments later she saw something.

Eyes. A pair of close-set, beady eyes were reflecting the torch light, gleaming reddish against the backdrop of foliage, fixed balefully on her.

Winona stopped. The eyes were too small and too low to the ground to be those of a bear or a panther. Her mind raced as she attempted to deduce its identity. Could it be a bobcat? she wondered, and dismissed the idea because the eyes weren't the proper shape.

The animal moved, gliding a few feet to its right, never once taking its eyes off her, and halted.

She noticed it had an odd, flowing sort of gait, and a

vague memory blossomed at the back of her mind, convincing her she should know what it was. Not wanting to provoke it, she remained rooted to the spot, moving only the torch so she could keep track of the beast's red orbs.

Again the thing moved, a few cautious steps, and its eyes rose several inches as if it had elevated its head.

Relief seeped into Winona. The creature clearly wasn't more than two feet high at the front shoulders, and she was confident she could dispatch the animal with a single shot if it should attack. To her surprise, the thing appeared about to do just that by moving a few feet toward her and giving voice to a growl that would have done justice to an enraged grizzly.

She saw more of it now, observing a heavyset body held close to the ground, apparently dark brown in hue and covered with the densest of fur. There also seemed to be a rather short tail. Those beady eyes blazed at her without once blinking. The breeze briefly shifted then, and she smelled the faintest of foul odors.

Then she knew. Her fear resurfaced, stronger than before, as she cried out "No!" in Shoshone. Her voice had a surprising effect; the creature started, whirled, and ran into the woods, its passage marked by much crashing of the undergrowth.

Winona was safe for now, but she still felt weak at the knees. The thing she had encountered was far worse than any grizzly or panther, far deadlier than any other animal. Its voracious appetite and tenacity were legendary among all the tribes, and few were the warriors who had ever bested one in battle. Elusive, fearless, and the most powerful animal in existence for its size, the mere mention of its name inspired utter dread.

Such was the reputation of the wolverine.

Chapter Sixteen

The moon was well past its zenith when Shakespeare led them to the top of a hill and reined up. "This is as far as we go on horseback," he announced, first in English, then in the Flathead tongue.

Nate didn't need to ask why. Visible a quarter of a mile away, resembling a large, pale mirror, shimmering with reflected moonlight, was Still Lake. Dismounting, he tied the reins to a nearby tree and faced his companions.

Shakespeare was scanning the area around the water. "I don't see any campfires, but we'll play it safe anyway. Slow and quiet is the way we'll do this." He started forward.

Doing the same, Nate looked over his shoulder at their Flathead friend. Wind In The Grass had not uttered a word since departing the village. He imagined the warrior was thinking about Flower Woman and Roaring Mountain, troubled by the prospect of never seeing them again. And Nate couldn't blame him one bit.

They flitted down the hill like ghosts through a cemetery, their footfalls virtually silent as was the forest all around them.

Nate didn't like the quiet one bit. There should be animal sounds, he mused, the many snarls and growls and squeals that regularly arose from the wilderness during those hours when many of the predators were abroad. But there was nothing save the wind rustling in the trees to even hint at the existence of life in the inky realm. Oddly, the wolves and coyotes were also silent and had been for some time.

Shakespeare demonstrated an uncanny knack for seeing in the dark, leading them around thorny thickets, over logs, and around other obstacles with the agility and fluid motion of a twenty year old. Every now and then he paused to listen and sniff.

What did he think he would smell? Nate wondered, grinning. Sometimes his mentor displayed eccentric behavior he found almost comical. Maybe the reason could be attributed to Shakespeare having lived for so many years in the wild among the animals. Anyone who lived with wild creatures long enough, Nate reflected, might well take on some of their mannerisms after a while.

Several times Nate glanced to his rear to verify Wind In The Grass still followed. The Flathead was exceptionally stealthy, his moccasin covered feet flowing effortlessly over the ground, his head cocked, an arrow notched to his bow string.

Nate held himself bent at the waist, his finger caressing the Hawken's trigger, treading in Shakespeare's footsteps. The lake grew nearer by the minute, but there were still no campfires in evidence. Even if the Blackfeet had retired to their forts hours ago, there should still be enough smoldering embers to mark the locations of those fires. But a shroud of black covered the landscape.

Shakespeare stopped more frequently now, glancing right and left. Suddenly he pressed a hand over his nose and mouth and motioned for them to do the same.

Not understanding, Nate hesitated, and a moment later the awful stench hit him with the force of a physical blow, making him gag and almost stagger backwards. He clamped a hand over the lower part of his face, barely inhaling, and gazed past his mentor to behold the source of the revolting stench.

A rotting corpse lay a dozen feet away.

They went around it. Nate was unable to take his eyes from the grisly legacy of the battle. He guessed it had been a Flathead. Stripped of all clothes and weapons, the body had suffered a fate typical of those who fell during Indian warfare. Most of the hair was gone, taken by a Blackfoot no doubt. The face had been mutilated, the nose and lips sliced off and the eyes gouged out. Both arms had been chopped off at the elbows and the legs below the ankles. Animals had been at the flesh, tearing off strips of skin to get at the juicy meat underneath. The gory remains disgusted him, and he felt bile rise in his gorge. He swallowed hard, refusing to be sick.

As they continued, they encountered more bodies, all in similar ghastly condition. The Blackfeet had butchered the fallen Flatheads just as the Flatheads had previously butchered the fallen Utes.

By breathing shallowly, Nate was able to avoid inhaling most of the odor. Still, his stomach was queasy by the time they came to the tree line. Before them were the forts, dark and apparently empty. He crouched behind a tree and studied the structures.

Shakespeare came over and squatted, then gestured for Wind In The Grass to join them. "I'm fixing to swing around to the west and come up on the forts from the rear. The two of you sit tight until I give you a signal."

"I'll go with you," Nate proposed out of concern for his friend's safety.

"I need you to cover the entrances in case there is someone inside, which I doubt," Shakespeare whispered. He spoke to Wind In The Grass for half a minute, then hastened off, vanishing in the undergrowth.

Nate trained the Hawken on the forts and impatiently waited for the mountain man to reappear. A stray cloud passed in front of the moon, plunging the landscape into total gloom, and he could barely see the end of his barrel. He glanced at the cloud, trying to will it to go faster, fearful Shakespeare would be attacked and he wouldn't be able to help because he couldn't see targets to shoot. Thankfully, the cloud drifted eastward before too long.

Focusing on the forts, Nate was surprised to see McNair was already there, creeping from the forest like a stalking panther. He steadied the rifle and cocked the hammer.

Wind In The Grass took a stride forward, elevated the bow, and partially drew back the string.

Moving rapidly, Shakespeare entered the first structure. He promptly emerged and went to the second, then the third. Finally he came out and waved.

Glad the Blackfeet were gone, Nate rose and hurried over.

"The varmints have skedaddled," Shakespeare declared, sounding disappointed. "They must be well on their way back to their own country with all their booty."

"White Eagle will be glad to hear the news," Nate said, letting the hammer down. He lowered the rifle, turned, and stared out over the tranquil lake, feeling extremely fatigued, the nap not having refreshed him as much as he had hoped. Now they could return to the village and get some real rest. A pinpoint of flickering light in the distance, at the base of a mountain range approximately four miles off, arrested his attention. "What's that?" he asked, knowing the answer but hoping he was wrong.

His companions turned.

"It's a campfire," Shakespeare said.

Nate's elation immediately evaporated. "The Blackfeet, you reckon?"

"Maybe," Shakespeare replied. "Maybe other Indians. Or it could be white men, for all we know." He walked toward the forest. "There's only one way to find out."

Disappointment turned to resentment as Nate hastened to their horses. With each passing hour his conscience bothered him more and more. He wanted to return to Winona, and it angered him that yet another delay barred his departure. There was nothing to prevent him from simply riding homeward whenever he wished—except his devotion to Shakespeare, and he couldn't bring himself to desert his best friend—yet. But if things didn't come to a head soon, if the Blackfeet hadn't truly left and if Shakespeare didn't resolve his dispute with Standing Bear, he would be forced to make a most distasteful decision, to chose between his beloved wife and his mentor.

Winona came awake with a start and sat bolt upright in bed, her mind racing as she struggled to become fully alert. Something had awakened her, but what? She glanced around, listening intently.

All appeared to be in the order. A single charred log still glowed reddish-orange in the fireplace; otherwise, the interior was plunged in darkness. A faint breeze stirred the flap covering the window. Outside, silence ruled. Not even the horses were stirring.

So what could it have been?

She swung her legs around and touched her bare feet to the floor. The cool air from the window faintly fanned her left cheek while the heat from the fireplace warmed her right. Perhaps, she reasoned, a dream had been responsible for interrupting her slumber, although for the life of her she couldn't recall having dreamed anything since falling asleep.

Very unusual.

Winona grinned at her foolishness and went to lie back down. Then, from near the door, came a loud scratching noise repeated three times.

An animal was clawing at the cabin!

She knew who the culprit must be, and a paralysis sparked by sheer fear glued her to the bed. The loaded rifle was propped against the wall near the entrance, but it might as well be on the next mountain. She was simply too scared to go get it.

A growl broke the silence and the animal renewed its assault, its claws tearing into the wood with rhythmic precision as first one paw, and then the other, ripped in vertical strokes.

The wolverine had returned.

Taking a breath, Winona compelled her body to stand. Perhaps the glutton, as many called the beasts, had never left. Perhaps it had been lurking in the woods, waiting for her to go to sleep, for the lights to go out and quiet to descend, before approaching the cabin.

She took a few tentative steps toward the rifle. Staring at the front of the cabin, she realized the creature wasn't trying to claw its way through the wall; it was concentrating on the weaker door. How did it know to do that? she wondered. Then she figured it had observed her come inside earlier and its rudimentary brain had compared the open doorway to the open holes of the burrows of some of its victims.

Wolverines would eat anything they could find and slay. They were known to prefer carrion, but the most knowledgeable Shoshone hunters also claimed wolverines would eat birds, squirrels, badgers, and a host of smaller game. They had also been known to kill deer, elk, and moose bogged down in heavy snow. Hunters had witnessed encounters between wolverines and grizzlies in which the wolverines drove the mighty bears from their kills and claimed the carcasses as their own. Wolverines would even readily fight the big cats.

Winona was most worried about another aspect to wolverine lore. Many times wolverines had raided lodges or cabins temporarily vacated by their owners and consumed every edible morsel within while systematically destroying every possession. It seemed this particular wolverine entertained a similar intention.

What was she to do?

She girded herself and tiptoed to the rifle, watching the door tremble as the beast clawed at the bottom. Once her hands closed on the weapon she felt somewhat better. Moving back a few paces, she pointed the flintlock at the door.

The wolverine stopped clawing.

Had it heard her? Winona reflected. Loud sniffing ensued, arising from the narrow crack between the floor and the door. She took another step backward, aware it was trying to pick up her scent.

Voicing a growl that would have done justice to the largest grizzly that ever lived, the wolverine tore into the door with extra vigor.

Winona swallowed hard. The thing knew she was there, and her intuition told her the wolverine wasn't all that interested in the contents of the cabin. It wanted her.

The door shook violently now. Occasionally the tips of a few claws would jut under the bottom, trying to get a firm purchase.

Desperate to drive the beast off, Winona shouted as loud as she could in Shoshone. "Go away, destroyer! Leave this place in peace!"

The clawing ceased.

Winona waited, her body tingling in anxious anticipation, hoping the yell had driven the monster off. The time dragged by and nothing happened. Encouraged, she crept to the door and pressed her right ear to the upper half.

In an explosion of fury the wolverine attacked the door once more, its paws pumping in a frenzy, its lethal claws biting into the wood like ten slender tomahawks, slowly chopping the stout door to bits.

Caught off guard, Winona jumped backwards, her limbs quivering in fright. She closed her eyes, directing her concentration inward, striving to control her surging emotions. This was no way for a Shoshone woman to behave, she berated herself. Shoshone women were raised to be worthy of the men they married and to be a credit to their people. Her behavior so far had been almost cowardly, and it was time she lived up to the standards of her tribe and the teachings instilled in her from childhood by her mother, her grandmother, and other women who had lived to ripe years and knew the way of wisdom all women should follow.

Kneeling, Winona cocked the flintlock and placed the end of the barrel within a hand's width of the door, aligning it with where she felt the wolverine stood. For all she knew, she might miss or merely wound the beast, which would only increase its rage and place her life in graver jeopardy, but she had to try something before it got through the door. Once the wolverine broke inside, she would be easy prey.

She willed her arms to hold steady, glanced at shadowy claws that materialized under the door, took a breath as Nate had taught her, and squeezed the trigger.

Chapter Seventeen

Nate hauled on the reins and brought his stallion to a stop. He glanced around in confusion, bothered by an acute sensation of imminent danger, but all he saw was Stygian forest. The feeling intensified, filling him with inexplicable dread, and he raised the Hawken halfway to his shoulder in case it should be needed.

"What's wrong?" Shakespeare asked. He had halted a dozen feet ahead and was gazing back in perplexity.

"I'm not sure," Nate replied.

"Did you see something?"

"No."

"Did you hear something?"

"No."

"Did you *smell* something?"

"Of course not."

"Then why in the world are you all set to shoot anything that moves?" Shakespeare asked in exasperation.

"I don't rightly know," Nate admitted, unable to

find anything menacing them. "I have a strange feeling, is all."

"Oh?" Shakespeare said, and surveyed the woodland. "What kind of feeling?"

"I don't rightly know."

The mountain man made a puffing sound. "If anyone ever accuses you of being a fount of information, tell them they're off their rocker."

As suddenly as the strange feeling came over Nate, it dissipated. He slowly lowered the Hawken and commented, "I'm sorry. I just don't know what to make of it."

"Maybe it was supernatural," Shakespeare suggested with a straight face.

"You've been in the saddle too long," Nate responded. "All the bouncing up and down has addled your brain."

"There are more things in heaven and earth, Horatio, than are dreamt of in your philosophy," Shakespeare quoted, and then altered his voice to a crackling whine. "Double, double toil and trouble, fire burn and cauldron bubble."

"Is that supposed to mean you're quite serious?"

"Quite, and rather eloquently too, if I do say so myself," Shakespeare said, leaning toward him. "Do you still have the feeling?"

"No, it's gone."

"And so are we unless it should return," Shakespeare said, and continued toward their destination.

Picking up the reins, Nate rode onward. The campfire still blazed and was now less than half a mile distant, leading him to question the wisdom of drawing any closer on horseback. They were in thick forest, hemmed in by underbrush, causing their animals to make more noise than he believed prudent.

Several hundred yards farther on, Shakespeare

lifted his arm to signify they should rein up.

Nate gladly did so, then secured the stallion to a tree. He studied the campfire, which was now glowing dully as if burning itself out. With Shakespeare on his right and Wind In The Grass on his left, he advanced warily. As the distance narrowed, it became apparent the camp was situated at the base of a steep cliff, hidden among a cluster of enormous boulders. Through a narrow crack between two of them the fire could be seen.

He realized he'd been lucky in spotting it. Whoever was in there had gone to great lengths to conceal their presence. If not for some of the firelight reflecting off the boulders and intensifying the illumination, he would never have seen the campfire.

The forest ended seventy-five yards away, and a grassy stretch of open land spread out before them.

Shakespeare stopped at the tree line and squatted. "If they've posted a guard, we'll never make it across."

"Do we wait until daylight?" Nate asked.

"Might be our best bet," Shakespeare said.

Wind In The Grass spoke up, conversing with the mountain man at length. Then he placed his bow on the ground, unslung his quiver, and drew his knife. Easing to his hands and knees, he quickly crawled into the high grass and was swallowed by the darkness.

Nate almost reached out a hand to stop him, but he guessed where his host was going and knew there was nothing he could say that would change the warrior's mind. "Is he doing what I think he's doing?" he whispered.

"Yep. He volunteered to sneak over there and see who it is," Shakespeare said.

"What can we do?"

Shakespeare sank onto his buttocks and rested his

rifle across his thighs. "Sit here and twiddle our thumbs until he gets back."

If he gets back, Nate reflected.

At the booming discharge of the flintlock the wolverine emitted a tremendous, raspy snarl, and Winona heard it thrashing wildly about, its body smacking against the door over and over. She shoved to her feet and dashed to the table on which she had placed the ammunition pouch and powder horn Nate had given her. Reloading, due to her lack of proficiency, was a slow, meticulous process. She had to be careful not to put too much black powder into the rifle or she ran the risk of the barrel bursting. Breathing heavily from the excitement, she managed to complete the task and hurried to the door.

The thrashing and snarling had stopped.

She listened, but heard only the wind. Had she killed it? Squatting, she found the hole in the door made by the ball as it bored through the wood. She figured the beast was wounded at the very least, hopefully fatally. It might drag itself off to die, ending her problem.

Kneeling, Winona placed an eye to the hole and gazed out. She could see a narrow strip of ground in front of the door, and there was no sign of the wolverine. Which didn't mean all that much. The creature might be lurking nearby, waiting for her to emerge, craving vengeance.

She went to rise and grab the latch, then thought better of the idea. As long as she stayed in the cabin, she was safe. Once outside, she was in the wolverine's element. The beast's acute senses would give it a decided advantage over her, but only while night lingered. Once daylight arrived, she would be on an equal footing.

Moving to the right of the door, she sat down and

leaned her shoulder against the wall. She would wait until morning before venturing out. Perhaps the wolverine would be gone by then if it wasn't already dead.

Fatigued, she closed her eyes and felt the baby move, a tickling sensation that brought a smile to her sagging lips. The baby. Above all else she must not endanger the baby's life.

One of the horses neighed.

Winona's eyes snapped open and she straightened in consternation. If the beast went after their animals, she must protect them. Surely though, she hoped, a wounded wolverine would not risk entering a pen of terrified horses where it could be trampled to death if they went into a frenzy. But there was no predicting the behavior of such volatile beasts.

There were no other sounds from the pen.

She leaned against the wall again, relieved. Her thoughts drifted to Nate, and she prayed to the Everywhere Spirit that he would return soon. All would be well if only he would come home.

The great Grizzly Killer.

Winona grinned, thinking of how awkward he had been when first they met, afraid to touch her or kiss her, as if their romance had been so fragile it would shatter at the slightest expression of affection. She chuckled. Her darling husband had exhibited undeniable courage when battling the scourge of the Rockies, but he had also exhibited the timidity of a little rabbit during the early months of their acquaintance, which had made for a peculiar combination of personality traits. And he still hadn't completely overcome his awkwardness. In a way, she hoped he never did. There was a sparkling boyish quality about him she found appealing, a quality rarely found in grown Indian men who learned at an early age the cruel realities of life and matured accordingly. Perhaps Nate's background accounted for the difference. In any event, it hardly mattered. She loved him as he was.

Time passed.

Her eyelids drooped against her will and she found her mind tottering on the brink of sleep. Sweet sleep. She needed more rest recently than in days past, no doubt due to the baby. When Nate had broached the subject of visiting McNair, she'd almost protested because she knew she would not get as much sleep while he was gone. Dutifully, she'd suppressed the impulse and agreed going to see Shakespeare was a good idea. So, in a sense, she had only herself to blame for being alone now when she knew very well Nate would have stayed had she but voiced the slightest objection.

Love, she decided, made people do things they would never do otherwise. In the name of love they were more considerate, more tolerant, more compassionate. And more stubborn.

Winona's shoulders slumped as she drifted off, and her last thought before falling asleep was for her husband's safety.

"What's taking him so long?" Nate inquired, gazing at the boulders. The campfire had gone out an hour ago, plunging the base of the cliff into darkness.

"When sneaking up on Blackfeet, it's not very smart to advertise your presence," Shakespeare responded, his back propped against a tree. "Not unless you like the notion of going around bald the rest of your life."

"I know that."

"Then relax, Nate. Wind In The Grass knows what he's doing. He'll be back soon."

"Speaking of getting back, what are your plans once we return to the village?"

"To dazzle Blue Water Woman with my charm and handsome features, then get her drunk and trick her into marrying me."

Nate nearly laughed. "But she already wants you to be her man."

"I know," Shakespeare said. "If we were back in the civilized world, she'd be a prime candidate for admittance to one of those sanitariums."

"You're in an awfully good mood," Nate noted.

"Why shouldn't I be? One of the prettiest women alive wants to cuddle with my cold feet at night, which qualifies an old cuss like me as one of the luckiest men alive."

About to make a comment about Blue Water Woman's taste in men, Nate spied a vague figure rising out of the grass and brought his rifle to bear.

"It's Wind In The Grass," Shakespeare said.

The Flathead came up to them and sank to one knee, then addressed Shakespeare.

All Nate could do was listen in suspense while the pair discussed whatever the warrior had found. When, a minute later, there was a pause in the conversation, he looked at the mountain man and said, "Well?"

"There are four Blackfeet encamped at the bottom of that cliff, under a rock overhang. None of the four have horses, and none appeared to have any scalps. Wind In The Grass believes they stuck around because they failed to count coup during the battle and intend raiding the Flathead village. They probably came to this spot to camp because they felt the Flatheads might return to Still Lake in greater force."

"Just the four of them will tangle with the entire village?"

"It would be real easy for them to slip in at night, grab a few horses and maybe a woman or two, and

light out before the Flatheads knew what hit them,"
Shakespeare explained.

"So what do we do?" Nate asked. "Sneak on in
there and kill them while they sleep?"

"We could, but it wouldn't be the honorable thing
to do."

"What, then?"

"We wait here until daybreak, and when they show
their faces we stand up and challenge them to a fight."

"Just like that?" Nate said sarcastically. He would
much rather shoot them and be done with it. Fighting
for personal honor and glory was fine, but not when he
had a pregnant wife many miles away who needed him
at home.

"Unless you have a better way," Shakespeare said.

"No," Nate confessed.

"If you'd rather sit this out, we'll understand,"
Shakespeare remarked.

"Count me in," Nate said, and moved over to the
next tree. He propped the Hawken against the bole,
then sat with his forearms draped over his bent knees.
Melancholy set in, and he found himself feeling sorry
he had ever set off after McNair. All he could think of
was Winona, in the cabin alone, easy prey for any wild
animal that might catch her outside or any hostile
Indians who stumbled on their remote valley.

Days ago, when he'd found Shakespeare's cabin in
such disarray, his obligation to his friend had seemed
so clear-cut, so absolute. Now, he perceived he'd made
a major mistake. He should have gone home to his
wife. By virtue of having taken him as her mate for the
rest of her born days, she deserved his unstinting
devotion.

Loyalty to friends was all well and good, but when
he got down to the crux of the matter, to the morality
of his act, he now knew with granite certainty that a

husband should always—*always*—be loyal first and foremost to his wife. All other obligations were secondary.

Nate gazed at the myriad stars sparkling in the firmament and imagined Winona snug in their bed, sleeping peacefully, as safe as could be. He hoped.

Chapter Eighteen

The screech of a jay brought Winona out of her slumber. She sat up, saw the sunlight streaming in the gap below the window flap, and beamed. Daylight. Now she could check on her nocturnal visitor. Rising, she almost toppled over before discovering both of her legs had also fallen asleep during the night. She leaned on the wall for support, feeling a tingling sensation in both limbs, then shook them to fully restore the circulation.

Once satisfied her legs were back to normal, she gripped the rifle and cautiously opened the door a crack. The bright light made her blink, compelling her to wait until she could see clearly before pulling the door all the way open and stepping into the brisk morning air.

She saw the blood right away, a large dark crimson puddle to the left of the doorway, congealed into an irregular mass from which a few blades of brown grass protruded. So she had hit the beast! She scanned the ground in front of the cabin but saw neither the wolverine nor any more patches of blood.

Encouraged, confident the animal was somewhere off in the brush dying in private as most animals preferred to do, Winona moved to the south and stared at the horse pen. The animals were fine, standing at ease, a few nibbling on bits of feed left over from yesterday.

The danger had passed.

In the brilliant sunshine her fears of the night before seemed childish, more the result of the stress she was under and an overactive imagination than any threat the wolverine had posed. Why had she let herself become so distraught when the beast could never get inside to harm her?

Winona laughed, spun on her heels, and walked back into the cabin to begin her daily routine. Now if only her husband would get back, everything would be perfect.

On the way inside she paused to stare once more at the puddle. The amount of blood convinced her the wolverine was most certainly dead or very close to it.

Most certainly.

Nate didn't sleep all night. As the sun crowned the eastern horizon he took hold of the Hawken and stood. Shakespeare and Wind In The Grass were already on their feet and advancing into the field. He moved between them and lightly touched the stock to his shoulder.

"Wind In The Grass wants to be the one to challenge them," Shakespeare said. "We'll follow his lead."

Nate nodded. If the young warrior could count coup and take scalps, particularly Blackfeet scalps, it would elevate his status as a warrior immeasurably. The

Flathead had proven his courage and reliability by bringing the horses during the battle at the lake; now, Wind In The Grass would go one step farther, would join the ranks of those privileged warriors who had counted coup on their most dreaded enemies. Either that, or he would die trying.

They advanced twenty yards, spreading out, their weapons ready.

Nate scanned the huge boulders, his thumb glued to the hammer. Suddenly he saw movement and halted. Four buckskin clad warriors walked into view, all young, all armed with bows and knives and tomahawks, all conversing animatedly, perhaps about their plans for raiding the village.

The tallest of the Blackfeet gazed out over the grassy tract and halted, barking words to his fellow warriors. Every one stopped, their features betraying their astonishment. Arrows were hastily yanked from quivers.

Wind In The Grass walked ten more feet. He hefted his bow and hailed them in a mocking tone.

"What's he saying?" Nate asked.

Shakespeare snorted. "He's telling them he wants to learn whether the Blackfeet are as brave as everyone says, or whether they are all cowards who only attack from ambush or fight women and children."

The tall Blackfoot shouted a reply.

"He just told Wind In The Grass his mother was suckled by a mongrel and his father was afraid of his own shadow," Shakespeare translated.

At a gesture from the tall warrior, the Blackfeet started toward them.

"When will they get to fighting?" Nate asked, every nerve on edge, wishing they would conclude the fight instead of wasting time by shouting insults back and forth.

"Be patient," Shakespeare said. "Indians aren't always in a godforsaken rush like most white men. They take their time and do things right. After the challenges are out of the way, you'll have all the bloodshed you can handle."

Wind In The Grass and the tall Blackfoot exchanged further insults. All the while, the four Blackfeet came nearer and nearer, negating any range advantage the two Hawkens possessed.

Nate cocked his rifle, his palms feeling clammy, sweat breaking out on his brow. He concentrated on the warrior directly across from him, watching the man's hands. To his rear a loud fluttering and chirping occurred as a flock of birds took panicky wing from the forest. He thought little of it. Maybe an animal had spooked them, he reasoned.

Suddenly Wind In The Grass vented a fluttering shriek, his personal war cry, and whipped his bow up.

The Blackfeet reacted instantly, elevating their own bows.

At last! Nate took a bead on his target, held the barrel rigid, and fired, the Hawken blasting and bucking in his hands. The warrior had his bow string all the way back when the ball took him in the mouth, twirled him around where he stood, and dropped him in a heap.

Then everything happened incredibly fast. Nate glimpsed three shafts streaking toward them, heard Shakespeare's rifle crack and saw a second Blackfoot fall, and pivoted to avoid the shaft whizzing at his chest. To his amazement, another arrow flashed out of nowhere first, narrowly missing his torso. It came from behind them!

The arrow fired by the Blackfoot flew past a fraction of a second later and Nate glanced at the tree line, not knowing what to expect but certainly not expecting to find Standing Bear and Bad Face, each nocking arrows to their bow strings. In a rush of insight he realized the awful truth. The duo had trailed them from the village and had chosen this most vulnerable of moments to strike, while their backs were turned and they were preoccupied, to eliminate Standing Bear's rival and achieve their vengeance for the insults Nate had handed them. Conveniently, the deaths would be attributed to the Blackfeet. "Shakespeare! Wind In The Grass!" he bellowed, aware the Flathead wouldn't be able to understand but hoping Wind In The Grass would look anyway. "Behind us!"

He began reloading, trying to look every which way at once, appalled by the sight in each direction. One of the Blackfeet was still alive and charging toward them. Shakespeare had seen Standing Bear and Bad Face and was frantically feeding black powder into his rifle. And as he glanced at Wind In The Grass, the young warrior was hit squarely between the shoulder blades by an arrow from the rear.

Nate dropped to his knees, giving his adversaries less of a profile to aim at, and crammed a ball and patch into the rifle. Looking up, he saw his newfound friend pitch into the grass. The Blackfoot was coming on strong, another shaft ready to fly. So were Standing Bear and Bad Face.

Shakespeare's Hawken spoke, and Standing Bear's malevolent face developed a new hole in the center of the forehead. The Flathead tripped over his own feet and toppled.

Leaving two foes, Bad Face and the sole remaining Blackfoot.

Nate raised his rifle, about to fire when Shakespeare cried out in pain and he shifted to see his mentor going down, an arrow sticking from the grizzled mountain man's chest.

Shakespeare!

Livid rage brought Nate to his feet, whirling as he stood, the Hawken tucked tight to his right shoulder. The bead settled on the Blackfoot's head and he squeezed off the shot. Not even bothering to verify the result, he whirled again, letting go of the Hawken to claw at both flintlocks, the patter of Bad Face's moccasins in his ears.

The hateful Flathead was eight yards away, an arrow drawn back to his cheek, grinning in triumph. Nate was a blur. He extended and cocked the pistols, his blood boiling as he fired both at the same instant Bad Face loosed the shaft. His twin balls cored the Flathead's chest, lifting Bad Face from his feet and hurling him to the ground. Nate felt something tug at his hair, and then the fight was over as abruptly as it had begun. He was the only one standing, shrouded by acrid gunsmoke.

For a moment he stood there, dazed by the savagery and the toll. He thought of Shakespeare and turned, shocked to discover the mountain man sitting up and glaring at the arrow in his body. "Shakespeare!" he cried, running over. "How bad is it?"

"It tickles like hell."

"Tickles?" Nate repeated in disbelief.

Shakespeare nodded and twisted to afford a clear view. The arrow had actually struck him on the right side of his chest, penetrating at an angle through the flesh covering the ribs. The barbed point, coated with blood, protruded four or five inches from the back of his buckskin shirt, about level with his shoulder blade. "Give me a hand," he said, gripping the feathered end of the shaft with both hands.

"What do you want me to do?" Nate asked.

"We can't leave this in," Shakespeare said, his features flushed. Unexpectedly, he tensed and exerted pressure on the arrow, snapping it off close to his body, gritting his teeth to keep from calling out. The effort weakened him and he sagged.

"You should have let me do that," Nate chided him, tucking the pistols under his belt. He squatted and placed a hand on Shakespeare's shoulder.

"Pull out the other half," the mountain man directed.

"Now?"

"We could wait for spring, but I might not last that long," Shakespeare said, mustering a grin. "Do it, please. The sooner it's out, the sooner we can clean and cauterize the hole."

Frowning distastefully, Nate moved behind him and gingerly grasped the arrow below the point, the blood coating his palms. He feared his hands would be too slippery to maintain a firm purchase, but when he gave the shaft a sharp wrench, it slid right out.

Shakespeare gasped and arched his back, then exhaled loudly and said, "Thanks. You'd better check on Wind In The Grass and the bastards we fought before we finish up with me."

"Be right back," Nate promised, and sprinted toward their Flathead friend, dreading what he would find.

The arrow had transfixed Wind In The Grass from back to front, evidently puncturing the heart. A pool of blood rimmed the warrior's body, spreading outward. His eyes were open, lifelessly fixed on the grass that had been his namesake.

Profound sadness formed a lump in Nate's throat. Why had Standing Bear and Bad Face gone after Wind In The Grass? he wondered, and reached an obvious conclusion; they hadn't wanted any witnesses. He thought of Flower Woman and Roaring Mountain and tears moistened his eyes.

Not now! he chided himself, gazing out over the field at the bodies dotting the ground. He must make certain all of their enemies were dead. Quickly reloading the flintlocks, he went from corpse to corpse. Not a flicker of life among them.

"Wind In The Grass?" Shakespeare inquired as he walked back.

Nate simply shook his head.

"Damn. That's a shame," Shakespeare said morosely, his hand pressed over the blood stain on his shirt.

"What will happen to his wife and son?"

"Flower Woman is a fine woman. Most likely another warrior will take her into his lodge and raise the boy as his own. Don't worry. Indian women are tough. They know all about making do."

Making do? Yes, maybe that was the best way to describe the life of someone who had lost the person they loved most in all creation. Nate headed for the woods. "Don't move. I'll have a fire started in no time."

He set about collecting broken limbs, preoccupied with thoughts of life and death, love and emptiness, happiness and sorrow, and Winona. Of all the worst possible fates that could befall him, being deprived of her company for the rest of his life would be the ultimate injustice. She had become as much a part of him as the air he breathed and the water he drank. Her love was more priceless than all the gold ever mined and the most expensive diamonds ever produced.

Unbidden, memories of New York filled his mind. He recalled married friends who had often neglected their wives and families to go off with their chums, carousing or gambling to all hours. Back then, he'd admired their independence and laughed at their antics. Now, he saw them for what they had been.

Soon he had enough limbs and hastened to Shakespeare's side. "How are you holding up?"

The mountain man was sitting quietly, staring at a distant majestic mountain. "Just fine. How about you?"

"Me? I wasn't hit," Nate said, depositing the branches at his feet.

"No, but I saw the look on your face a while ago. Were you thinking about Winona?"

Nate glanced at him in surprise. "Do you read thoughts now?"

Shakespeare shook his head. "I would be thinking of her if I was in your shoes. As soon as I'm patched up, head for home."

"First I'll drop you off at the village," Nate said. "Blue Water Woman should have you as fit as a fiddle in no time. Bring her for a visit when you can. I'm sure Winona will be delighted to have the company."

"I bet she will," Shakespeare agreed. "The poor woman must be bored to death sitting around that cabin with nothing to do but talk to you."

Chapter Nineteen

Her husband was on his way home!

Winona stood on the west shore of the lake, an empty bucket in her left hand, and gazed northward. She couldn't explain exactly how she knew, but she knew. In her bones she felt she would soon be holding her man in her arms once again, and she was ecstatic. The baby reacted to her joy by giving her a good, solid kick.

She knelt at the water's edge and dipped in the bucket. Since the incident with the wolverine two days ago, the tranquility of her life at their humble cabin had been undisturbed. She had finished sewing the pants for Nate and was trying to decide what to make him next. A new hat would be nice. The one he occasionally wore had been taken from a dead Blackfoot warrior named Mad Dog, the same warrior who was directly responsible for the deaths of her mother and father. She disliked seeing it on her husband's head; it brought back too many acutely painful memories. If she made him a new one, they could get rid of Mad Dog's.

Nate had caught hundreds of beaver during the last trapping season, and the pelts were now safely cached out behind the cabin. He intended to take them to the next rendezvous and sell them for the highest dollar they could command, but she knew he wouldn't mind if she took a few to make the hat.

Using both hands, she lifted the almost full bucket from the cold lake and stood. Nearby floated a flock of ducks, eyeing her hungrily. Sometimes she brought them food and they would gather within an arm's length of her legs to quack incessantly in the hope of getting a morsel. "Not today, little ones," she told them, grinning, and headed for the cabin.

Soon darkness would descend. Half of the sun had already disappeared, and the lengthening shadows of early evening were spreading out over more and more ground, shrouding the undergrowth in gloom.

Winona hummed as she retraced her steps. The horses had been fed, the cabin cleaned, and she had a fresh supply of water to last through the night. She looked forward to relaxing and getting a good night's sleep.

Once inside she locked the door, placed the bucket on the table, and went to the window. A little air would be delightful, she reasoned, and rolled the flap all the way up, securing it with the strips of rawhide tacked to the top.

She busied herself making supper, boiling a grouse she had killed with an accurately aimed stone that very morning. After pouring more water into the big pot above the fire, she stirred the meat and herbs she had mixed together before going to the lake. The tantalizing aroma made her mouth water.

Winona pulled the chair closer to the fireplace and

took a seat, glad to be off her feet. Her stamina wasn't what it used to be, a condition that would remedy itself after the baby was born. She placed her hands on her tummy, waiting for the infant to squirm, and closed her eyes. Lassitude pervaded her body. The soft crackling of the fire, the light bubbling of the water, and the faint breeze stroking her hair lulled her into dreamland.

Moments later she opened her eyes. Or so she believed until she noticed the fire had diminished considerably. Even so, the room was much darker than it should be during daylight hours. Twisting, she gazed out the window and was startled to see night had claimed the land while she slept. How long had she been out?

She rose and inspected the cooking pot. Half of the water in it had evaporated, indicating she had been asleep for hours. Chuckling, she went to the door and reached for the latch. An armful of branches would have the fire roaring again in no time.

From the horse pen there suddenly arose a series of frightened whinnies as first one animal, then another, expressed building fear.

Winona hesitated, her intuition blaring a warning in her brain. "It can not be," she said softly, and then felt her blood become icy as a chilling, all too familiar snarl came from outside.

The wolverine was back.

She scooped the flintlock into her hands and backed up a few paces. Some creatures, it seemed, were too persistent for their own good. Once it began tearing at the door, she'd fire another ball into its stocky body. This time, perhaps, she would end the threat once and for all.

Seconds later the wolverine obliged her by slashing at the door in a frenzy, growling the whole time. The door trembled but held.

Winona inched closer. She knelt and lowered her right eye to the hole made by the ball the other night. Through it she glimpsed the animal's furry form in perpetual motion as its claws raked deep grooves in the wood.

The wolverine stopped. She could see a shoulder—or was it a leg?—until the beast shifted position. One of its beady eyes appeared at the other end of the hole, balefully regarding her, and she recoiled in surprise.

Snarling, the wolverine renewed its attempt to get inside.

She leveled the rifle, holding the barrel at the height she estimated the beast's head would be, and braced herself to fire. From the din the wolverine created, it sounded as if the door was being reduced to kindling. If she didn't shoot soon, the bloodthirsty killer might get inside.

Winona fired, putting a hole inches to the left of the previous one. The blast hurt her ears, the pungent gunsmoke stung her eyes and nostrils. On its heels came absolute quiet as both the wolverine and the horses fell silent. She pushed to her feet and moved toward the table to reload.

Had she done it? Was the beast dead?

She picked up the powder horn, her eyes on the door, unable to detect any movement beyond. Out of the corner of her left eye, however, she did register motion and heard a thud. She pivoted to find the source and nearly dropped the powder horn as consternation gripped her soul.

Framed in the window, its shoulders partly through, its front legs dangling over the sill, was the living embodiment of primal ferocity. Exercising agility that rivaled a mountain lion's, the wolverine had leaped to the window and was now clinging fast. The moment she saw it, the beast growled and began pumping its rear legs to get a firmer purchase so it could push inside.

Winona knew she must stop it at all costs. If she could knock it off the sill and fasten the flap, she'd gain the time she needed to reload the flintlock. Placing the powder horn on the table, she dashed toward the window, firming her hold on the rifle and lifting it overhead to use as a club.

The wolverine went into a frenzy, snapping and snarling as it eased its body higher, close to gaining entry.

In three strides Winona was there and driving the rifle's stock into the beast's forehead. The wolverine recoiled but didn't lose its grip. She smashed it again, narrowly missing having her forearms torn open.

More of the glutton squeezed inside.

No! Winona mentally shrieked, and swung the rifle overhand like a club, the stock crunching into the wolverine's face. Blood sprayed from above its right eye, but it never flagged. If anything, its rear legs worked harder.

She realized the skull was simply too thick to damage and ran to the table. Another shot was her only hope. She started reloading, glancing countless times at the window as her fingers flew.

The wolverine had half of its body over the sill and was striving to get a purchase with its rear legs. Blood seeped from the gash above its eye and saliva dribbled from its open mouth. Its tapered teeth glistened in the firelight.

Winona fed the powder into the flintlock and went to put in the ball and patch. The futility of her act hit home. In moments the thing would be inside, well before she could get the gun loaded, and she would be completely at its mercy. She spun, casting about for something to use as a weapon. On a peg above the bed hung her knife, but she would have to cross the room to reach it and by then the wolverine would gain entry. Much closer was the fireplace.

In desperation she tossed the flintlock onto the table and dashed over, stooping so she could grab the unlit end of a burning branch and yank it from the fire. She whirled, horrified to see the wolverine's haunches were almost through. Holding the firebrand out from her body, she charged.

The wolverine, intent on the floor below as it went to jump, looked up upon hearing her footfalls.

Winona voiced an inarticulate cry of rage and rammed the firebrand into its left eye, the flames searing the orb and scorching the hair on contact. Hissing, the wolverine recoiled, and she promptly speared the firebrand into the other eye. The smell of burning flesh filled the air.

With a violent jerk of its hips, the wolverine tore loose of the window and dropped to the floor. Its vision blurred by the searing flames, it tried to focus while snarling its defiance and swinging its front paws.

Winona barely jumped back in time. The wolverine somehow pinpointed her position and closed in, snapping at her legs. Again she evaded those razor teeth, but in doing so she tripped and fell onto her back directly in its path. The impact jarred her body, making the baby kick.

The baby!

She grit her teeth, determined to defend the infant with her last breath, and scrambled to her knees. The wolverine opened its mouth wide and sprang. In a sheer reflex action, she drove the firebrand into the beast's mouth, driving the branch in as far as it would go, and then frantically threw herself to the rear to avoid the wolverine's claws.

The glutton went berserk, thrashing and spinning as it tried to pry the branch from its mouth, its claws unable to get a grip. Blood cascaded over its lips.

Gagging and sputtering, the wolverine smacked into the wall and halted, its side heaving, shaking its head vigorously.

Winona was afraid it would attack again. While it wouldn't be able to bite her, those wicked claws could tear her to ribbons. She backed up until she bumped into something, and glancing over her shoulder she saw the chair she had sat in. Pivoting, she grabbed the arms, then faced the wheezing predator, just as the wolverine mustered its strength and bounded across the floor toward her. She swung the chair with all her might at the very instant the beast sprang.

The big black stallion was flecked with sweat when Nate reached the top of a rise to the north of his cabin and broke into a broad smile. Home, at last! He'd ridden like a madman to reach Winona, pushing the stallion to its limits, and in ten minutes he would be hugging her tight.

He goaded the stallion down the rise, and once he hit level ground broke into a gallop again. No smoke wafted from the chimney, which struck him as odd. Normally, Winona liked to keep a fire going on chilly days and the February thaw was about over. The temperature last night had dipped into the low twenties, at least, and not warmed much during the day.

Anxiety gnawed at his mind like a beaver on a tree, bringing all of his worries to the forefront. What if something had happened to her? he speculated, and felt a twinge of terror.

Please, no.

He threaded among the trees at a rash speed, angling at the front of the cabin, and he was still a couple of dozen yards off when he noticed the door didn't seem quite right. It took him a few seconds to realize the reason, and when he saw the distinct claw marks and the deep grooves in the wood he felt lightheaded.

Something had tried to get in.

The stallion was still in motion when Nate vaulted out of the saddle, the Hawken clenched in his right hand, and sprinted madly to the door. He hesitated when his fingers touched the latch, fearful of what he might find within. Swallowing hard, he threw the door wide and leaped inside.

All appeared in order, but the cabin was empty. The bed had been made, the chairs neatly arranged around the table, and leaning against the wall was her flint-lock.

Where was *she?*

Confused, he took a step, then heard light laughter to his rear.

"Welcome home, husband."

Nate spun, rejoicing at the sight of his beloved standing in the doorway, her eyes aglow with affection, an impish grin creasing her full lips, her hands held behind her back. He reached her in two long strides and swept her into his arms, choked with emotion at their reunion. "Winona," he said breathlessly.

"It is nice of you to remember my name," she responded playfully. "You were gone so long, I thought you might have forgotten."

"Never," Nate stated, and tenderly kissed her. "I never stopped thinking about you for a minute."

"How is Shakespeare?" Winona asked, trying to maintain a casual conversation with moisture rimming her eyes and her voice quavering.

"He's taking a Flathead woman as his wife," Nate disclosed, "just as soon as he mends. A Blackfoot arrow caught him in the side."

"You fought the Blackfeet?"

"A couple of times," Nate said. "I'll tell you all about it later." He nodded at the door. "First tell me what happened here. Why is that door in the shape it's in?"

Winona grinned. "Mice."

"Be serious."

"Big mice."

"Why won't you tell me?" Nate inquired. "What are you trying to hide?"

"Nothing," Winona said. "But I know you. I know how upset you can become over things. I will tell you after you have had a chance to rest and eat."

Knowing better than to buck her when she had made her mind up, Nate sighed and touched her belly. "How is our baby?"

"Fine. He kicks all the time now."

Nate beamed. "I can hardly wait."

"Me too," Winona said, and gave him an ardent kiss that lingered on and on. At last she drew her head back and said, "I have a surprise for you."

"What kind of surprise?"

"A gift."

"When do I get it?"

In response, Winona brought her hands from behind her back and held out the hat she had worked on every waking moment since the chair had saved her life. "Here."

"Well, I'll be," Nate said, delighted. He leaned the Hawken against the wall and took her present, running his fingers through the soft, dark brown fur. "You've done a marvelous job," he complimented her, wishing he'd had the foresight to bring her something.

Winona brightened. "Thank you. I worked very hard to make it the best hat I have ever made."

"It's not beaver," Nate commented, examining the

fur carefully, his brow creasing in contemplation. "In fact, it's not like any other fur I've seen close up. What exactly is this made of?"

"Carcajou."

"Carca—," Nate began, and glanced down at the door. He blanched, his mouth going slack, and then embraced her. For the longest time they simply stood there, cheek to cheek, each aware of the other's heart pounding rapidly, oblivious to the world around them. He finally broke the silence by saying, ever so softly, "Never again."

DEATH HUNT

Dedicated to
Judy, Joshua, and Shane.

Chapter One

"Do you reckon we have everything we'll need?" asked the muscular young man in buckskins.

The lovely Indian woman to whom the question had been addressed looked at their packhorse, her features barely concealing her keen amusement. "We have enough supplies to last a year, husband," she said and grinned. "Any more and that horse will keel over." She glanced at him. "That is the right expression, yes? Keel over?"

"It's the right one, Winona," the man responded a bit testily.

Ever sensitive to his moods, Winona moved closer and affectionately reached up to caress his cheek. "I am sorry if I hurt your feelings, Nate."

Nineteen-year-old Nathaniel King softened under the loving gaze of her dark eyes. He shrugged his broad shoulders and gestured at the assortment of parfleches, saddlebags, and other supplies piled high on the pack animal. "I'm taking so much because of the condition you're in. Who knows what we'll need along the way? It will take seven or eight days to reach the village, maybe longer."

Winona glanced down at the highly prominent bulge in her beaded buckskin dress, then pressed both palms to her swollen belly. "There is no need to worry. Our son will not be ready to enter this world for fifteen or twenty sleeps yet."

Nate put his hands on his hips and regarded her critically, extreme anxiety mirrored in his penetrating green eyes. In addition to his buckskins, he also wore moccasins and a brown leather belt. Wedged under the belt, one on either side of the large buckle, were two flintlock pistols, and suspended in a sheath on his left hip was a big butcher knife. Angled across his chest were a powder horn and a bullet pouch. "You can't say for certain when the baby will come, and I'd rather not take any chances. What if you go into childbirth before we find the village? We'll wind up stranded in the middle of nowhere until you're back on your feet. That could take days."

"What nonsense," Winona said lightheartedly, as she smoothed the flowing raven tresses that fell to her hips. "I will be able to ride the day after our son is born. There will be little delay."

A sigh of exasperation hissed from between Nate's lips. He simply couldn't understand his wife's cavalier attitude; she seemed to view giving birth in the same manner as she did eating and sleeping, as a bodily function that would pretty much take care of itself and wasn't any cause for concern. "If I had any sense, I would have taken you to St. Louis to have the baby," he said.

Blinking in surprise, Winona stared eastward, out over the verdant valley in which their sturdy cabin was situated, and watched a flight of ducks come in for a landing on the aquamarine surface of the tranquil lake a stone's throw away. The mere thought of traveling to one of the strange cities Nate had told her about sent a chill of apprehension rippling down her spine. Much of what he had described was incomprehensible—vast tracts of land covered in haphazard fashion with countless stone and wood lodges separated by narrow passages called streets, all swarming with the ceaseless activities of more people than there were blades of grass. To her, to a Shoshone woman accustomed to the orderly, quiet life of an Indian village, the sprawling cities of the whites seemed to be the embodiment of insanity, at odds with the way of Nature and the Great Medicine. "Why would you have taken me there?" she wondered.

"Because a woman should have the best medical help available when she gives birth," Nate said, turning to his black stallion. He began checking the cinch. "This is 1829, after all. It's not like we live in the Dark Ages. A modern doctor would make sure everything came out just fine."

Winona grinned. "Everything will come out just fine without a doctor. Women have been having babies since the dawn of time and human beings have not died out yet."

Nate glanced at her. "I wish you would take this seriously. You don't know how worried I am."

"Yes, I do," Winona assured him. "And I know you worry because you love me." She felt the baby kick and beamed. "But you worry too much, husband."

Finishing with the cinch, Nate walked into the cabin. He knew better than to debate the issue. They had been through it again and again with the same result. She simply refused to become in the least bit anxious about the birth. Fine and dandy, he reflected. At least he'd been able to talk her into visiting her relatives at a Shoshone village far to the north where there would be other women who could lend a hand just in case something did go wrong. Although, when he thought about it, she had agreed a bit too readily, as if she had wanted to visit her kin all along and was merely using his anxiety as an excuse to go. How typical, he thought. Women were the most devious creatures on God's green earth. They always got their way, no matter what their men might prefer. Why was that? Why did men always fall for feminine ploys? It certainly couldn't be because the men weren't as smart.

He retrieved his Hawken from the large table on which he had placed it an hour earlier after loading it. The feel of the heavy rifle snug against his palm heartened him slightly. The trip would take eight or nine days, perhaps more. They were bound to run into contrary critters and maybe a few hostiles. The Hawken would come in handy; next to the horses, it was the most indispensable item they were taking.

Nate gazed around the interior, making sure they had packed everything he wanted to lug along, then went outside and closed the door behind him. The morning sun hung above the snow-crowned peaks rimming the eastern horizon, and there was a cool nip to the early April air.

Winona had already mounted the mare she would ride and held the lead to the pack animal.

"I'll take that," Nate said, walking toward her.

"I am not helpless," Winona said, giving the lead a tug as she brought her mare around to face due north.

"But you're pregnant," Nate objected.

"You are an observant man, husband," Winona said and snickered.

Annoyed, Nate mounted his stallion and moved out, passing her. "I don't see why you must be so stubborn. I'm only trying to help." He headed for a gap in the mountains, thinking about the route they must take, remembering where water existed and planning his stops accordingly. A person could go without food, if need be, for weeks, but anyone who went without water for more than three or four days stood a good chance of perishing. So, like the Indians, he would camp each night near water and start each morning refreshed and revitalized.

"Do all white men act like you do when their women are heavy with child?" Winona inquired.

"Most, I guess," Nate said, wondering what she was leading up to. "Why?"

"I would expect it."

Nate glanced over his shoulder. "Oh?"

"From the stories you have told me and those I heard when I was younger, I know white men treat their women very strangely. You treat them like dolls."

"Dolls?"

"Yes," Winona said in her precise English. She had spent months mastering the language, and now she took great pride in pronouncing every word distinctly. "Among my people it is a custom for mothers and other relatives to make dolls for the little girls to play with. I had three dolls when I was a child, all from my mother. She even made clothes for them to wear and built a small lodge for them to live in."

"I don't see the connection," Nate said.

"I treated my dolls very carefully because I was afraid they would break," Winona elaborated. "Every day I dressed them in their fine clothes and had them do all the things real women would do, but I never let them get dirty or was rough with them."

"I still don't see the point."

"Don't you?" Winona responded. "White men treat their women just like I treated my dolls. You keep them in great lodges and dress them in fancy clothes. You let them rear the children and take care of the lodge, but you never let them do any of the work the men do. You act as if they will break if they do anything a man does."

"That's not necessarily true," Nate said. "And you're a fine one to criticize the way white men live. When was the last time you went on a buffalo hunt?"

"I never have and you know it."

"And why not?" Nate asked and promptly answered his own question. "Because Indian men don't let their women hunt big game or go on a raid or do most of the things men do." He paused. "I guess when you get right down to it, Indian men aren't much different from white men."

"In some respects they are much alike," Winona agreed wistfully.

"Does that upset you?"

"I always wanted to go buffalo hunting or be part of a war party," Winona said. "But I did not complain when my father told me I could not. My father loved me very much, and it was my duty as his daughter to obey his wishes."

Nate looked at her and detected a tinge of melancholy in her expression. "Tell you what," he said impulsively. "After the baby is born, the two of us will go after buffalo."

"You would do that for me?"

"Of course."

Winona brightened, then burst into laughter.

"What is so funny?" Nate asked.

"Who will watch our baby while we are off chasing buffalo?"

"I don't know. I hadn't thought of that," Nate admitted. "Maybe we'll have to wait until the baby is old enough to tag along."

They fell silent, Nate pleased with himself for having made such a considerate offer. But the more he thought about it, the more convinced he became that he'd made a rash mistake. What if Winona was injured, or worse? Hunting buffalo was a tricky, extremely dangerous task. Many warriors died each year doing so. Next to being slain in battle, more Indian men died from hunting the shaggy brutes than from any other cause. Since Winona had no experience at it, she would be at even greater risk. Perhaps, Nate concluded, he should come up with a reason for her to not do it. Something logical, something devious. And if that failed, maybe she'd agree to go after elk or deer instead.

He scanned the surrounding landscape, alert for movement or noise. They were crossing a boulder-strewn field between tracts of dense woodland. Chipmunks chattered at them or darted off at their approach. Far overhead, to the west, sailed a large red hawk, its wings virtually motionless as it glided on the air currents seeking prey. In the brush to the east a black-tailed buck appeared and watched them for a minute before bounding away in great leaps.

Nate inhaled and smiled. This was the life! He could hardly believe that only a year earlier he'd left New York City to join his Uncle Zeke in St. Louis and, through a series of unexpected events, had found himself joining the slim ranks of those hardy trappers and adventurous mountain men who chose to dwell in the Rocky Mountains. He had, as the saying went, "gone native," and he didn't regret the decision one bit.

Only out here, in the unspoiled wilderness where men could roam as they pleased and live as they wanted, was there true freedom. His Uncle Zeke had promised him a share in the greatest treasure any man could ever find, and Nate had to admit his uncle had been right. Freedom was more precious than all the money in the world, than all the gold and gems in existence.

Thinking of Zeke brought to mind his father and

mother, and Nate felt a twinge of guilt at having left them so abruptly with no more than a note of farewell. Did they miss him? Did they wonder if he was alive or dead? He speculated on the wisdom of contacting them, perhaps sending a letter back east with the next person he met who was heading that way. At least they would know he was all right.

They would also probably despise him for what he had done. After all, his father had refused to allow Zeke's name to be mentioned in their house after Zeke ventured beyond the frontier and never came back. That had been a decade before Nate left New York. To think that his father had nurtured such keen resentment for over ten years made him see his father in a whole new light. Zeke had been his father's brother. How could a man hate his own brother?

Nate shook his head to dispel the bothersome thoughts and skirted a boulder the size of a pony. It was too late to have regrets, he figured. He'd made the decision to leave New York on his own, and he would have to live with the consequences for the rest of his life.

Twisting, Nate gazed fondly at Winona, who gave him a smile. If he had not headed west, he would never have met his wife, and he considered her the best thing that had ever happened to him. She brought genuine happiness into his life, helped him to smile when he was depressed and to confront hardships squarely. For her, he would do anything. And he didn't give a damn whether his folks would approve of the marriage or not.

There came a time, he reflected, when every man and woman must strike off on their own, must leave the nest just like little birds eventually left theirs to take up the responsibilities of adults. Well, he'd simply gone a lot farther from his nest than most did, and the rewards justified the deed.

Nate saw Winona passing a cluster of small rocks on her left. He spied a flash of movement near a rock tilted upward at an angle and figured her horse had spooked a chipmunk. But then he saw a sinuous shape glide into the open and coil for a strike. The next moment, as he realized with horror what it was, he heard the distinct rattling of its tail.

Chapter Two

Rattlesnake!

The word peeled like the loud clanging of a fire bell in Nate's mind, and he reined the stallion around to bring his Hawken into play.

Startled by the rattler's buzzing, Winona's mare started to rear up, its nostrils flaring, whinnying in alarm. Winona yanked on the reins, trying to turn her mount to the right away from the deadly reptile.

A terrifying mental image of Winona being thrown filled Nate with fear. If she went down, they might well lose the baby! He whipped the Hawken to his shoulder and took a hasty bead on the rattler's head. Its forked red tongue was flicking out and in, its tail vibrating vigorously. He cocked the hammer, held the barrel as steady as he could, and squeezed off the shot.

At the booming report, a cloud of smoke burst from the rifle as the lead streaked true to the mark, the ball hitting the rattler between the eyes and coring the brain. The snake flipped onto its side and thrashed wildly, blood and brains oozing from the thumb-sized hole in its shattered cranium.

Nate hardly gave the rattler a second glance. His wife was still striving mightily to bring the mare under control while holding onto the lead to the packhorse, which was trying to jerk free. He goaded the stallion to her side and leaned over to grip the mare's bridle. "Whoa, there. Calm down. Calm down," he said in a soothing tone.

The mare—the same horse he had ridden all the way from New York to the Rockies and then presented to Winona because the animal was normally supremely gentle and obedient—reacted to his voice by standing still and bobbing its head, its eyes wide, still afraid but compliant.

Winona turned her attention to the pack animal, hauling on the lead with both hands and speaking to the horse in Shoshone. "The snake is dead, silly one. Be still."

It took all of ten seconds, but the packhorse stopped trying to bolt and stood as quietly as the mare.

Nate looked down at the motionless snake, then at his wife. "Are you all right?" he asked in her native tongue. He had spent as many hours trying to master Shoshone as she had mastering English, but he was not half as proficient at her language as she was at his.

"I am fine," Winona said and placed a hand on her belly.

"Are you sure? What about the baby?"

"Our son kicked to let me know we disturbed his nap," Winona replied, grinning.

Nate let go of the mare, moved closer, and placed a hand on her shoulder to draw her face near to his. He gave her a tender look, glad she was unharmed, thinking of how she always took everything in stride, how she seldom became agitated or anxious. He wished he had a smidgen of her self-possession. She was gazing at him with a puzzled expression. Nate chuckled, then planted a passionate kiss full on her soft lips before she knew what he was going to do.

When he pulled back, Winona stared at him in surprise. "Why did you do that?"

"My heart overflowed with love," Nate answered in Shoshone and climbed down. Having learned many months ago that a man in the wilderness must always keep his rifle loaded because trouble had a habit of popping up when least expected, he quickly reloaded the Hawken. First he placed the butt on the ground, then he poured the proper amount of black powder from his powder horn into the palm of his hand, knowing by sight exactly how much to use. He carefully poured the powder down the barrel, then took a ball and a patch from his ammunition pouch. Wrapping the ball in the patch, he wedged both into the end of the barrel with his thumb. Next he pulled the ramrod free, then pushed the ball all the way down.

"Do you want to save the snake for a meal later?" Winona asked. "I can wrap it in a blanket and skin it when we stop."

Nate glanced at the dead reptile. Although rattle-snake meat was highly extolled by many of the trappers, the mere thought of eating one made him slightly queasy. If he had been without food for a spell, he'd tear into a rattler with relish. But given a choice, he'd rather eat rabbit or venison or *anything* that didn't slither to get around. "I'll bag us something else," he promised her and slid the ramrod into its housing under the rifle barrel. Swinging into the saddle, he grasped the reins and headed northward again.

Soon they were at the gap, riding between towering cliffs on either side, the path steeped in deep shadow, the wind whistling shrilly past them.

Nate craned his neck, staring at huge boulders perched precariously on the rims of both cliffs, dreading what might occur should one suddenly come crashing down. He recalled a tale he'd heard about a trapper who was leading a pack string down a winding mountain trail when a ten-ton boulder swept down out of nowhere and slammed the man and his horse right over the edge. The trapper's friend, who witnessed the freak accident, went down to see if there was anything he could do and reportedly found the trapper crushed to a pulp, unrecognizable. A shudder rippled through Nate at the memory.

He breathed deeply in relief when they were in the valley beyond, delighted at the warm sunshine and the chirping of birds in the forest to their left. A narrow stream, fed by a spring high in the mountains, meandered across a grassy meadow before them, and he stuck to the bank, watching to see if there were any fish in the water.

"May I ask you a question, husband?" Winona spoke up.

Nate recognized a formal tone in her voice, a tone she used only when she felt she might be prying into his personal feelings and was reluctant to broach whatever subject she had in mind. "Ask away," he said.

"Do you think of Adeline often?"

"I should have known," Nate muttered and chided himself for ever having mentioned Adeline to Winona.

The daughter of one of the wealthiest men in New York City, Adeline Van Buren had been the epitome of beauty and charm and could have taken her pick of any man she wanted for her husband. To Nate's unending astonishment, she had chosen him. They'd met at one of those boring social functions the upper crust so delighted in putting on, and an immediate attraction had led to their avowed intent to marry. In retrospect, Nate knew his love for her had been more in the order of awed devotion; he'd practically worshipped her. He'd placed her on a pedestal a mile high and had constantly reminded himself that he was the luckiest mortal alive simply because he was so unworthy of her affection. All she had to do was snap her fingers and he was at her beck and call.

How strange, he reflected. Back then he'd believed he was truly in love. Now, with the benefit of hindsight, he saw how foolish and immature he'd truly been. Comparing his love for Adeline to his love for Winona was like comparing night and day. He loved Winona as she was and related to her as an equal instead of as a supplicant before a goddess.

When he'd departed New York to go join his Uncle Zeke, he'd written Adeline a letter in which he'd promised to return one day with a great fortune. He'd wanted to be able to support her in the same lavish fashion her father always had; it was the main reason he'd left everything behind to venture west.

Had she found someone else by now? Nate wondered. Most likely. Suitors would have lined up for blocks once word of her eligibility spread. No doubt her father hated Nate. But that couldn't be helped and didn't bother him all that much because he had never been fond of her father anyway.

Should he write her another letter? No, he decided. She must resent the way he had gone off and left her; sending a letter would only spark bitter emotions. It was best for him to forget about her and get on with his life, which was hard to do with Winona bringing Adeline up at least once a week.

"Do you think of her?" Winona repeated when he failed to answer right away.

"No."

"Then why did you take so long to say so?"

Nate glanced back. "When will you get it through your pretty head that you are the only woman I care for? If I still loved Adeline, I wouldn't have married you, now would I?"

"I have heard about white men who take Indian women as wives for a winter or two, then leave them to go back to families the Indian women never knew they had."

"Do you think I could ever do such a thing?"

Winona locked her eyes on his as if trying to peer into the depths of his soul. "No," she admitted softly. "You are a good man."

"And you are the one I want to start a family with," Nate said. "You and our children will be all the family I need. I'll be your husband for as long as you want me."

Her mouth curled upward. "Then you will be my husband forever."

"Now that we've settled the matter for the twentieth time, do you suppose we can drop it for good?"

"I am sorry if I upset you."

"You didn't."

They pressed onward in awkward silence. By midday both had forgotten the discussion, and they chatted and laughed while taking a break beside a spring situated at the base of a bald mountain.

Sunset found them many miles farther along, in dense woodland. Nate scoured the terrain ahead, seeking a small lake he'd stumbled on previously. He was certain the lake must be close by, and a quarter of a mile later his hunch was confirmed when they emerged from the trees and discovered the serene body of water before them.

"I'll tend to the horses, start a fire, and go find us something to eat," Nate proposed as he rode to the water's edge and dismounted.

"And what should I do while you are taking care of everything else?" Winona asked.

"Rest," Nate said. "You must be tired after being in the saddle all day."

Winona sighed. "When will you learn? I am all right.

You go hunt while I take care of the horses and the fire."

Knowing a protest would cause an argument, Nate resigned himself to the inevitable and headed toward the forest 40 yards to the south. Twilight shrouded the landscape, bathing everything in a shade of gray. He glanced back to see his wife watering their animals, then peered at the trees and detected a flicker of movement out of the corner of his left eye. Halting, he looked and spotted a large jackrabbit bounding for the shelter of the vegetation. It was moving slowly, covering only five feet at a hop. On every fourth or fifth leap it would jump several feet into the air, giving itself a better view of him and the surrounding ground.

Nate pressed the Hawken to his right shoulder, recalling information imparted by Shakespeare McNair, the gray-haired mountain man who was his best friend and mentor. "If you spook a rabbit," Shakespeare had said, "stand stock-still and get ready. They usually stop after going a short ways and look back to see if they're being chased."

He hoped his friend was right. If he could bag the jackrabbit, it would save a lot of time and effort. Taking careful aim, he tracked the rabbit's course. After only four more bounds it abruptly stopped and stared at him.

Now!

Nate squeezed off the shot and saw the jackrabbit flip into the air, then slam into the ground hard and commence flopping around. He ran toward it, drawing his butcher knife, preferring to save his twin flintlocks for an emergency.

The ball had struck the hapless rabbit in the neck, and it now lay still on its side, blood gushing out, its eyes flared in panic.

Swiftly, Nate stooped over and plunged the blade

into the yielding body, putting the animal out of its misery with one stab by piercing the heart. The jackrabbit quivered for a bit, uttered a low squeal, and died. Watching it expire, Nate thought of the rabbits he'd raised as a child back in New York and felt a twinge of guilt. "Sorry, bunny," he said softly. "But I have two mouths to feed besides my own."

He yanked the knife free, wiped the blade clean on the rabbit's fur, and slid the weapon into its sheath. Grasping the rabbit by the rear legs, he stood and carried his trophy toward the lake. He guessed its weight to be nine or ten pounds, which would more than suffice to feed them.

Winona had turned at the crack of the shot and was waiting for him, smiling proudly. "That did not take long," she said as he drew closer.

"I was lucky," Nate replied. He dropped the rabbit on the grass and began reloading.

"I will skin it as soon as I have the fire started," Winona said and headed for the trees.

"Where do you think you're going?"

"To get firewood."

Nate gazed at the gloomy woods and changed his mind about objecting. "Let me take care of fetching branches while you hobble the horses and get the rabbit ready," he suggested. "To his surprise, she halted, glanced at the forest, and came back.

"All right. But please be careful. I have a feeling."

"What kind of feeling?" Nate asked.

"It is difficult to describe. A feeling all is not well."

Nate surveyed the countryside but saw no sign of danger. "I'll take care," he promised, hoping his wife's intuition was wrong. After loading the rifle, he hastened off, eager to gather the wood they would need before night fell. A cool breeze from the northwest stirred his hair. He was almost to the forest when the air was rent by an eerie, drawn-out howl arising on the far side of the lake. Nate stopped in mid-stride. Seconds later another howl sounded, then a third and a fourth. An icy hand seemed to gouge into Nate's stomach and twist his innards as he swung around in alarm.

A wolf pack was abroad!

Chapter Three

Nate had a decision to make. Should he keep going or go back to Winona? He didn't like the notion of leaving her alone with wolves in the vicinity. Although wolves rarely attacked humans, he knew from bitter experience that a pack would do so if the wolves were hungry enough. A few months ago he'd nearly lost his life in such an incident. He weighed the need for a fire against his guess that the wolves were still a quarter of a mile away and kept going. A roaring fire would keep most animals at bay. Once he had their campfire blazing, the pack would leave them alone.

Finding enough broken limbs was easy. Nature's tantrums and old age had scattered scores on the forest floor. Nate swiftly collected enough to fill both arms and hastened back to the lake. As he neared the horses, the wolves howled once more. Winona was busy at work on the jackrabbit. "Did you hear that?" he asked anxiously.

"How could I not?"

"They might be coming in this direction," Nate said, selecting a spot to start the fire. He deposited the branches and straightened. From the continued howling, he deduced the pack was moving slowly along the west shore. His stallion whinnied and tried to stamp the ground with a front hoof but the hobble prevented its leg from lifting very high.

Nate stepped to the big horse and opened his possibles bag, which hung from the saddle horn. He rummaged inside and found his tinderbox, then set about starting a fire as he continued listening for the approaching pack. They were yipping as well as howling, and he marveled at the noise they were making.

It took the better part of a minute to ignite the kindling, and then another minute to fan the tiny flames with his breath until they rose over six inches high. He fed small pieces of dry wood to the fire and soon had the campfire roaring in all its comforting glory.

The wolves promptly fell silent.

Nate stood, the tinderbox in his left hand, the Hawken in his right, and looked at his wife. "If those wolves should attack, stay behind me."

"I do not think they will," Winona said, removing the last fold of skin from the butchered rabbit. "They are talking to the moon is all."

The moon? Nate gazed eastward and was surprised to behold a radiant full moon perched above the horizon. Shakespeare had once divulged that wolves and coyotes voiced their plaintive cries much more frequently on moonlit nights than they did on nights when the moon was absent. Why, no one knew.

He replaced the tinderbox in the possibles bag and scanned the southwest corner of the lake, wondering if the wolves would come very close or be intimidated by the fire. He saw several inky shapes flitting over the ground and swept the rifle to his shoulder. A second later the shapes halted and seemed to be regarding the campsite intently. A huge wolf advanced much closer, the firelight dancing in its eyes, making them glow a reddish hue.

Winona had also seen the pack. "Throw him the rabbit skin," she said.

"What?" Nate responded, surprised by the suggestion.

"That big one is the leader of the pack. As a token of good will, take him the skin and a little meat."

"And leave you here alone? Not on your life," Nate said.

"Trust me. My people have been dealing with wolves for more winters than anyone can count. If you do not want to do it, I will."

"No," Nate said, moving to her side. He stared at the motionless pack, counting six lupine forms, and envisioned the consequences should Winona go out there and be wrong about the wolves' intentions. "I'll handle it."

Winona picked up the skin and a handful of meat. "Here. Go out a ways and put this on the ground."

Nate took the rabbit parts in his left hand, feeling the meat squish against his palm and blood seep between his fingers. Dismayed but striving hard not to show it, he advanced toward the predators with his left arm extended. What if they detected the smell of fresh blood and came for him? he wondered. There was no way he could down them all before they reached him and ripped him to ribbons.

The wolves promptly backed away, warily keeping their distance, not taking their eyes off him. Last to back off was the leader, and he only went a dozen yards before stopping.

Nate walked to the spot where he believed the big wolf had stood and squatted to put down his offering.

Loath to touch the rifle with his gore-covered hand, he wiped his left palm on his pants before rising and backpedaling to the fire. He scarcely breathed while waiting to see what the pack would do.

The leader of the pack cautiously moved forward. When it came to the rabbit parts, the wolf sniffed loudly, then swallowed the morsels in three gulps.

"What if he wants more?" Nate asked.

"That is the whole idea," Winona said.

"Mind explaining it to me?"

Winona spoke softly. "By giving him the rabbit skin, we have whetted his appetite. Now he is hungry for more meat and he will lead his pack off to find it."

"Or attack us."

"Why must you always expect the worst?"

"Experience," Nate said. "If anything can go wrong, it usually will."

Suddenly the big wolf wheeled and loped off into the enveloping darkness, the other wolves right behind him. They disappeared without another sound.

Nate expelled a breath, then chuckled. "Your little trick worked." He paused. "You don't happen to have one that works on grizzly bears, do you?"

"No."

"Too bad. The way I keep running into them, I could use an ace up my sleeve."

The next several hours were spent enjoyably. Nate unsaddled their horses and removed the packs from their pack animal while Winona roasted tasty portions of jackrabbit by imbedding slender forked branches on either side of the fire and impaling the meat on a straight stick supported by the forks. By the time Nate finished with the horses, the tantalizing aroma of their impending meal filled the air and made his stomach growl with hunger.

They savored the food, slaking their thirst with cold water from the lake. A multitude of twinkling stars covered the heavens, and they saw several shooting stars while they ate.

Afterwards, Nate spread blankets on the ground and stacked limbs near the fire so he would have a ready source of fuel to use during the night whenever the fire started to die out. They reclined side-by-side and he pulled another blanket over the two of them. "This is nice," he said.

Winona nodded and kissed him on the cheek, and they cuddled together for a while, whispering as they discussed plans for their future and their hopes for the child soon to be born. More fatigued by the arduous traveling than she was willing to admit, Winona fell asleep first, nestled in Nate's arms. He beamed happily, pulled the blanket higher, and drifted asleep thinking that he must be the luckiest man on the planet.

Dawn etched the horizon with a rosy hue when Nate awoke and sat up. As always when in the wilderness, he made a quick survey of their camp to ensure all was in order. The horses had not wandered very far, due to the hobbles, and were munching on the dew-covered grass. A fish jumped in the lake, splashing down loudly and causing concentric circles to ripple outward from the impact point. Off to the east were several deer eyeing the camp. Apparently they had been on their way to the lake for their morning drink, but were now reluctant to approach.

Nate stretched, inhaling the crisp, invigorating mountain air. He slid out from under the blanket, being careful not to disturb Winona, and attended to his toilet. Then he collected the horses, saddled the stallion and the mare, and got the pack animal ready to go. He heard a rustling noise as he completed the job and turned to find Winona sitting up and gazing around in annoyance. "Good morning, honey."

"I slept too long," Winona said. "The sun is already

rising. You should have woken me up."

"You needed the extra rest," Nate said, going over and squatting by her side.

"A person should never sleep past sunrise. It makes them lazy," Winona stated, running a hand through her hair.

"My, aren't you the grump this morning?" Nate quipped and kissed her.

"Grump? What is that? I do not remember hearing that word before."

"A grump is someone who is always in a bad mood. They always look at the bad side of things."

Winona seemed shocked. "Am I truly a grump?"

"Not in the least," Nate assured her, grinning. "I was only making a joke."

"You should work more on your sense of humor," Winona admonished him.

"Yes, dear," Nate said dutifully and kissed her again. He gave her a hand as she began to climb out from under the blanket, gazing in awe at her huge belly. "What do you want for breakfast?"

"Nothing."

"Not a thing? We have jerky and bread in our supplies. Why not start the day with a full meal?"

"Because my stomach is not feeling well," Winona said, straightening with a frown.

Nate didn't like the sound of that. Her bouts of morning sickness had ended months ago. This new feeling might have been brought on by all the riding they had done, and he berated himself for being a fool, for lugging her scores of miles across the Rockies in her present condition. She should be back in the cabin, snug in their bed, and he told her as much.

"Nonsense," Winona replied. "A woman who lies around all the time becomes weak and no good as a wife. It is too late to turn back, anyway. I am looking forward to seeing my aunt and her family."

The reminder prompted Nate to nod. In his concern he'd almost forgotten the reason for the trip; he certainly didn't want his wife giving birth by herself. "All right. I'll finish packing everything and we'll be ready to go when you are."

In ten minutes they were heading northward again, journeying through virgin wilderness overflowing with game. Nate used the time to improve his Shoshone so he would make a favorable impression on Winona's tribe. She enjoyed giving the lessons, her patience inexhaustible, correcting him repeatedly and laughing at some of his grammatical blunders.

At midday they stopped briefly, then went on.

During the afternoon, as they were crossing a ridge that barred their path, Nate reined up in surprise at the sight of smoke curling above the trees half a mile to the west. "Look," he said.

Winona did and said, "A campfire."

"Might be Indians," Nate said.

"It could be white men. Trappers, maybe."

"I'm not about to risk finding out," Nate said, goading the stallion down the opposite side. "If it's Utes, they'll kill us, take my hair, and mutilate you. We keep going."

"Yes, husband."

Nate picked up the pace and was glad when they had put a few more miles behind them. His safest bet was to avoid all other parties they saw until they reached their destination. If they should be seen by hostiles, they would not be able to outrun enemy warriors with Winona in the family way. "Lie low and live longer," Shakespeare had once advised Nate concerning travel in hostile country, and he intended to follow the advice to the letter.

Evening found them by a small spring at the base of a rocky escarpment, and Nate halted for the night. Despite his usual protests, Winona insisted on taking care of their animals. He went into the forest to bag their supper and was fortunate in spying several large, plump mountain grouse in a thicket. By bracing the barrel of the Hawken against a tree trunk and taking careful aim, he shot the biggest of the bunch and proudly took the kill back to their camp.

Unlike the previous night, there were no nocturnal visitors. They ate their meal in peace and were soon tucked under their blankets, admiring the magnificent celestial display. Slumber claimed them and they slept until dawn in each other's arms.

And so it went.

For the next four days they made steady progress. Game was abundant and they ate their fill each night. Twice they spotted grizzly bears, but fortunately the fierce beasts were at a distance and didn't charge them. They saw no sign of other humans, Indians or whites.

On the afternoon of the seventh day, as they were skirting a mountain that towered over ten thousand feet above them, Winona unexpectedly reined up. "We must stop for a while," she announced.

Nate stopped, then turned the stallion. He noticed her features were drawn, her eye betraying great fatigue. "We'll rest for as long as you want," he said, sliding down.

"I am sorry," Winona said wearily. "The trip has been harder on me than I figured it would be. I am slowing us down."

"Nonsense," Nate said, leaning the Hawken against a nearby boulder. He reached up and lifted her to the ground. "You've held up fine. And by tomorrow we should be at the lake where your people are supposed to be camped at this time of year. You can lie down for days if you want."

Winona sagged against him, her cheek on his chest.

"I am sorry to be such a burden."

"Don't be silly," Nate said and stroked her hair. "You're the best wife a man could ever want."

Smiling, Winona looked up at him. "There are times when you are the most wonderful man I have ever known." She kissed his chin. "And then there are times when you are the most hardheaded man who ever lived."

"Which am I now?" Nate asked, grinning.

Winona opened her mouth to reply, her gaze straying past him, and suddenly she involuntarily stiffened and gasped.

Nate let go of her and spun, spying the source of her alarm immediately. Thirty yards off, sitting astride a fine brown stallion and watching them intently, was a lone warrior.

Chapter Four

Nate scooped up the rifle and pressed the stock to his right shoulder, about to take a bead on the man when he realized the warrior wasn't making any threatening moves. The man simply sat there, studying them.

"He is a Dakota, but I do not know which tribe," Winona said. "The French call his people the *Nadowessioux*."

Nate had heard the term before. Some of the trappers had taken to referring to the Dakota people by an abbreviated version of the French word: the Sioux. "I thought the Sioux live far to the east of here, on the plains," Nate said, noting the warrior appeared to be in his thirties and wore buckskins leggings and moccasins, but no shirt. The man carried a shield bearing the red emblem of a bird of prey on his left forearm and a lance in his right hand. A bow and a quiver full of arrows were slung over his back.

"They do," Winona confirmed. "They seldom come into the mountains."

Nate glanced right and left, seeking other warriors, certain the man was a member of a war party in the region on a raid. But he spied no one else. Perhaps, he reasoned, the others were lying in ambush.

The Sioux abruptly started toward them.

Not about to let the warrior get close enough to hurl the lance, but unwilling to fire unless provoked, Nate sighted his rifle squarely on the man's muscular chest. Instantly, the warrior reined up. Nate lowered the Hawken a few inches, debating whether to try sign language to communicate. To do so, he would have to lower the Hawken all the way, delaying his reaction time should the Sioux charge.

The warrior glanced at both of them, then placed his lance across his legs and lifted his hands. "I will not harm you," he signed.

"Should I trust him?" Nate asked, relying on Winona's superior knowledge of Indian ways to guide him.

"Not yet," Winona said.

Nate saw the warrior was awaiting a reply. He shifted and extended the Hawken toward his wife. "Here. Keep me covered while I talk to him."

"If he tries to lift his lance, he is dead," Winona promised, grasping the rifle and taking deliberate aim. Under Nate's tutelage she had learned to be a fair shot and could down small game at over 50 yards consistently.

Loosening the flintlocks under his belt, Nate advanced ten feet and addressed the Sioux in the universal language of the Indian tribes inhabiting western North America. From Canada to Mexico, from the Mississippi River to the Pacific Ocean, practically every tribe used sign language, with minor variations in different areas. And since their spoken tongues were so diverse, sign had long since become the accepted means of communication when people from far-flung tribes met. "What do you want?" Nate asked.

"I am Red Hawk of the Oglala Dakotas. I would talk with you," the warrior answered.

Was it a ruse? Nate wondered. There was only one way to find out. He beckoned for the man to approach, saying, "You may approach, but be warned our guns are loaded and we will shoot at the first sign of hostility."

"I come in peace," Red Hawk said and rode forward.

Nate held his hands near his flintlocks. If it was a trap, he'd take as many of the Sioux with him as he could. Fleeing was out of the question with Winona in the condition she was in. A sustained flight over the rough terrain might kill her and the baby.

The Dakota appeared at ease and made no threatening gestures as he narrowed the gap.

Nate noticed symbols painted in red on the warrior's horse. Six horizontal lines had been etched on its neck, and on its flank was the likeness of a human hand. "What are those marks?" he asked Winona.

"The lines mean he has counted coup six times," she said. "The hand means at least one of his enemies was killed in hand combat, either with a knife, a tomahawk, or a war club."

"Oh?" Nate said, edging his fingers a tad closer to his pistols. He still saw no sign of any other Dakotas, which mystified him. It was inconceivable that the warrior was alone.

Red Hawk halted ten feet out and extended his hands to demonstrate they were empty. "How are you known?" he inquired.

"I am Grizzly Killer," Nate responded, feeling grateful to the Cheyenne warrior who had initially bestowed the name on him. At times like this it had a nice ring to it. "This is my wife, Winona."

"A Shoshone," Red Hawk signed, nodding politely at

her. "My people have fought the Shoshones a few times. They are brave fighters."

Nate decided to be blunt. "Where is the rest of your war party?" he inquired, gazing around.

"I am alone," Red Hawk said, frowning.

Skeptical of the claim, Nate said, "It is very dangerous for a lone Dakota in this territory. The Utes, the Blackfeet, the Crows, and perhaps even the Shoshones would kill you on sight."

"I know," Red Hawk signed. "But it is just as dangerous for me east of the mountains where the Arapahos, the Cheyennes, the Pawnees, and my own people would do the same."

"Your own people?" Nate repeated, adding the hand signal for a question. "I do not understand."

"I am an outcast."

The revelation surprised Nate. He'd heard that certain tribes would cast out members if various customs or taboos were violated, but the offense had to be extreme to justify such a severe punishment. He speculated on whether it would be polite to request the details.

"If you are willing, I would like to ride with you for a while," Red Hawk said.

"We travel by ourselves," Nate quickly replied, unwilling to let the warrior go along and thereby possibly put Winona's life in jeopardy.

"Please," Red Hawk said. "I have given you my word that I will do you no harm." He paused. "I have not talked with anyone in many sleeps. It would be nice to have the company of other people again, if only for a little while."

Nate hesitated. He believed the man was being sincere, but his innate wariness compelled him to balk at the notion. A tactful way of getting the Dakota to move on occurred to him, and he signed, "We are very near a large Shoshone village. Should the Shoshone warriors find us, they might slay you."

"I no longer care," Red Hawk answered. "At least I will not be alone when I die."

About to make a frank refusal, Nate felt Winona press flush with his back and heard her whisper in his ear.

"It is all right, husband. I think you can trust this man."

"Very well," Nate signed. "You may accompany us. But you must ride at my side the whole time."

"I understand," Red Hawk said, "and agree."

Nate took the Hawken from Winona. "Do you still want to rest for a spell?"

"No. Let us move on. I am eager to reach the village."

Casting repeated glances at the Dakota, Nate assisted his wife in mounting the mare, then swung onto the stallion. They moved out, the warrior falling in beside Nate's horse. Up close, he observed that Red Hawk appeared to be much younger than he had estimated.

"I thank you for this privilege," the Sioux signed, his face conveying genuine gratitude.

Nate got the impression his newfound acquaintance was literally starved for human companionship. "Do you happen to speak any of the Shoshone tongue or the language of the white men?"

"No."

"No matter. We will get by with sign language."

"You use it very well," Red Hawk noted, "better than any white man I have ever met. Most of the traders and trappers I have known learn just enough to get by."

They moved out into a wide valley, riding northward across a verdant meadow. A raven flew past them, uttering its raucous cry at their intrusion into its domain.

"These mountains stir the spirit," Red Hawk said.

"My people prefer the plains, where most·of the buffalo roam. But now I think these mountains would be a fine place to live."

"There are plenty of remote valleys, far from any tribe, where you could set up a lodge and live happily. Most of the time it is quite pleasant in the high country, but The Long Night Moon, the Snow Moon, and the Hunger Moon can be bitterly cold and it is sometimes hard to find game then," Nate signed, referring to the harshest months of the year—December, January, and February.

"I doubt I will ever have a home again," Red Hawk said. "My fate is to wander the land until I die."

The warrior wore a melancholy expression as his hands moved, and Nate experienced a twinge of pity although he hardly knew the man. He tried to imagine what the life of an outcast was like—always on the go, considered an enemy by his own tribe and every other tribes besides, unable to go near any village without risking the loss of his life, banished to a lonely existence with the sole prospect for the future being eventual death. He tried to cheer the man up by pointing at the coup stripes and signing, "You must be a brave warrior to have counted so many coup."

"Four were earned in one battle when the Blackfeet raided our village and tried to steal our horses," Red Hawk responded, gesturing crisply in a matter-of-fact fashion. "I killed one of them with my knife after he had stabbed me." He touched an inch-long scar on his lower right side.

"The Blackfeet do not die easily," Nate signed by way of a compliment. "Your people must have been very proud of you."

A shadow clouded Red Hawk's features. "Yes, they were. My wife was the proudest one of all."

"You have a family?"

"I had a wife once, and we often talked of having

children. Now I will never have either."

What did that mean? Nate mused, but he didn't pry. He scanned the meadow, where the grass grew as high as their horses' bellies, and spied a butterfly flitting to the southwest.

"I have thought of going north into the land you call Canada," Red Hawk said. "Have you ever been there?"

"Not yet," Nate signed. "One of these days I will get around to it. For now, I am kept busy providing for us and trapping. If all goes well, by the Blood Moon I will have many pelts I can trade or sell for much money."

Red Hawk pursed his lips. "I have noticed white men are very fond of money. Why is that?"

"A person cannot survive for long in the white world without it," Nate explained. "Whites use money to buy food and clothes and horses and weapons."

"I do not see the sense in such a strange way of living. Why should whites pay money for food when they can hunt for it or grow their own?"

"Some whites do grow food, and they provide enough for those who do not grow it to live," Nate signed. "Those who do not grow food pay money to those who do for the food they need."

"And why do whites pay money for clothes when making clothes is so easy? All they have to do is go out and kill a buffalo or a deer, work the hide until it is soft and can be sewn together, and they will have clothes that last many years," Red Hawk said.

"Many whites, mainly those who live in the big towns and cities, do not know how to hunt. They have never shot an animal in their life."

Red Hawk looked at Nate in amazement. "How can such a thing be?"

"They buy the clothing they need," Nate said.

"And their weapons too, you said?"

"Yes," Nate affirmed. "Although in many of the cities back in the East men have no need for them."

"They go around unarmed?"

"Yes."

"I have never heard of such a thing," Red Hawk signed, shaking his head in disbelief. "Your people are lucky to still be alive."

Nate smiled, idly gazing out over the high grass. The stallion suddenly raised its head and sniffed loudly, then snorted.

"Now I understand why your people love money so much," Red Hawk remarked. "They would die without it."

Again the stallion snorted and looked to the right and the left, as if seeking something. Nate surveyed the meadow but saw nothing to explain his mount's peculiar behavior. The big horse was acting as if a predator was in the area. Perhaps, he reasoned, the wind had carried the scent of a prowling panther or some such animal.

Winona's mare also snorted and balked, and she had to goad it forward with her knees.

"Something is wrong," Red Hawk signed. His own war-horse began behaving skittishly.

What could it be? Nate wondered. Abruptly, the grass ended at the rim of a huge depression and he had to rein up sharply to avoid going over the edge. He looked down into the bottom of the eight-foot-deep hole and felt the hairs at the nape of his neck tingle. For there, lying on her side on the bottom, sound asleep, was an enormous female grizzly. He knew it was a female because lying beside her, flush with her massive form, were two young cubs likewise asleep. All three had probably gorged themselves recently and were sleeping off the stupor brought on by their filled bellies.

Nate heard a gasp and glanced to his right to find Winona staring at the beasts in horror. He'd heard of trappers who had stumbled on sleeping grizzlies and lived to tell about it by quietly hastening elsewhere before the fierce bears could awaken. Consequently, he motioned for Winona and Red Hawk to move away from the rim, but no sooner had he done so than Red Hawk's horse whinnied loudly and the female grizzly opened her eyes.

Chapter Five

The instant the she-bear laid eyes on the riders above her, she scrambled to her feet and vented a horrid roar that exposed her large, razor-edged teeth.

"Run!" Nate shouted in English, forgetting in the intense excitement of the perilous moment that Red Hawk wouldn't be able to understand the words. He saw Winona cut to the right to go around the depression and did the same, staying behind her to cover her should the grizzly pursue them.

Red Hawk was going around on the other side.

Startled into wakefulness by their mother's roar, the two cubs were on their feet and bawling in terror. The mother rumbled deep in her chest and surged out of the hole, her powerful muscles rippling under her golden-brown coat of fur. She paused on the rim and glanced both ways, apparently undecided about which way she should go.

Nate hoped the she-bear would let them depart in

peace even though his past dealings with grizzlies had convinced him they would go after anything that moved. Females with cubs were especially dangerous; they would even attack other grizzlies who presumed to get too close to their offspring. This one proved to be typical of the breed.

The mother bear uttered another mighty roar and charged after Nate and Winona.

Could they outrun the beast? Nate wondered. The mare and the pack animal were going all out and his stallion was right on their heels. If he wanted, he could make the stallion go even faster and easily escape, but he would never desert Winona. He glanced back, watching the she-bear run, marveling that such a huge creature could move so rapidly.

Out of the corner of Nate's eye he saw Red Hawk turn his war-horse and gallop toward the depression housing the cubs. The Sioux gave the grizzly a wide berth. Amazed, Nate saw the she-bear slow, her attention diverted to the warrior for a few seconds. What in the world was the man trying to do? he mused. But his thoughts were interrupted when the bear came swiftly toward him and his wife again.

Red Hawk was almost to the hole when he stopped and started whooping at the top of his lungs, waving his lance overhead.

The she-bear twisted her head, saw the warrior in close proximity to her offspring, and suddenly forgot all about chasing Nate and Winona. Spinning, the grizzly raced to save her cubs.

"Get out of there!" Nate shouted in Shoshone, afraid the warrior was about to sacrifice himself so they could escape safely. He saw the she-bear draw closer and closer to the hole, and just when he thought Red Hawk would surely die, when the bear was within four or five bounds of the Sioux's mount, Red Hawk angled the horse to the west and took off like a bolt of lightning.

The she-bear reached the depression and stopped at the rim, glaring about her in primal fury. She took a few steps after Red Hawk, then halted. Growling hideously, she lumbered ponderously to the hole and vanished from view.

Once she was gone, Red Hawk swung northward again.

"Hold up," Nate shouted to Winona and brought the stallion to a halt beside her, within a few dozen yards of a tract of woodland. "Are you all right?" he asked.

Winona took a breath and put a hand on her belly. "I feel a little sick, but otherwise I am fine."

"We should find a spot for you to rest a spell."

"No. Please," Winona said. "We are close to the village. I just know it. If we stop, we might not get there until tomorrow and I would rather spend tonight in a warm lodge than sleep on the cold ground."

Nate could rarely refuse her anything. Her pleading tone, combined with the silent appeal mirrored in her eyes, made him go against his better judgment and say, "If that's what you want, we'll keep going. But if you feel any pain, any discomfort at all, you're to let me know and we'll take a break. Fair enough?"

"Yes," Winona said, smiling gratefully.

Pounding hooves brought Nate around to face the Dakota as Red Hawk rejoined them. "That was a very brave thing you did," he signed.

"My horse can fly like the wind. I was in no real danger," Red Hawk responded, giving his mount a pat on the neck.

"I know better," Nate said, "and I thank you for risking your life so that we might get away. I hope one day I can repay the favor."

"There is no need," Red Hawk signed.

They resumed their journey, the incident with the grizzly largely forgotten, just another happenstance in the daily lives of those accustomed to living in the harsh wilderness and coping with the occasionally savage wildlife. After traveling for over an hour, a high hill appeared in their path.

"I know that hill," Winona said to Nate. "It is near Clear Lake where my people will be camped."

Nate picked up the pace, eager to get his wife out of the saddle and resting on soft robes. When they reached the hill he spied a game trail winding up the slope and took it, riding all the way to the top where a magnificent vista of the surrounding countryside unfolded before his appreciative gaze. He beamed happily upon spying a large body of water a mile and a half off to the northwest. Even at such a distance the sprawling collection of lodges rimming its shores was visible although they appeared to be little more than tiny peaked cones, with thin columns of smoke spiraling skyward above them.

"The village," Winona said, smiling.

Red Hawk glanced at Nate. "It is time I rode on by myself. Thank you for your company," he signed. "Should we ever meet again, I will remember you as a friend."

"Wait," Nate impulsively signed. He didn't like the idea of the Dakota wandering aimlessly over the Rockies, with nowhere to call home, the war-horse his sole companion.

About to turn his horse, Red Hawk paused.

"Come with us to the Shoshone village," Nate said. "I will ask Winona's aunt to put you up with us."

"You are kind," Red Hawk said, "but her people and my people have never been on friendly terms. As you mentioned before, they might kill me on sight. It is best if I leave you now."

Nate looked at Winona, hoping she would speak up

and try to persuade the Dakota to stay, but she said nothing. In exasperation he watched Red Hawk ride off to the southwest. "This isn't right," he said. "Why didn't you say something?"

"You know why. If he went with us, nothing I could say or do would stop my people from doing him harm."

Frowning, Nate started down the opposite side of the hill. Sometimes, he reasoned, life could be extremely unfair. Red Hawk had impressed him as being a fine person, yet the warrior had been banished to a lonely life of quiet desperation. What could the Dakota have done to deserve such a fate?

At the base of the hill they entered a maze of pine trees, threading among the conifers until they came to a wide field. A doe, feeding near the tree line to the east, bounded into the underbrush.

Winona rode on her husband's right side. She studied his features, as ever sensitive to his moods, and said, "You are upset."

"Only because I wanted to help Red Hawk," Nate responded wistfully. "Surely there must be a tribe somewhere that would take him in? He doesn't deserve to be an outcast the rest of his life."

"How do we know what he deserves?" Winona said. "We have no idea why he was made an outcast. Perhaps he committed a horrible deed."

"Maybe," Nate said. But somehow he doubted such was the case. In any event, the issue hardly mattered now that they had parted company with the warrior. He focused on the village ahead, feeling a twinge of nervousness at the prospect of being among the Shoshones again. Not that they would mistreat him. They were always courteous and kind. There just was an unnerving aspect to being the sole white person among hundreds of Indians. He couldn't help but see himself as an outsider. "What's the name of your aunt again?" he inquired to take his mind off entering the village.

"Morning Dove," Winona said. "Her husband is named Spotted Bull. They have a son, Touch The Clouds, who has a wife and two children of his own. And they have a daughter called Willow Woman who once had a husband named Brown Leaf. She lives with them now."

"What happened to her husband?" Nate asked. "Did they go their separate ways?" He knew that many tribes indulged in lax marriage practices. Among the Shoshones a man could simply tell his wife to leave. Among the Cheyennes, a woman could divorce her husband merely by moving back in with her parents.

"No," Winona said sadly. "Brown Leaf was killed on a buffalo hunt." She paused, then said meaningfully, "On a surround."

"A what?" Nate asked.

"A surround is the greatest of all buffalo hunts," Winona elaborated. "The warriors close in on a buffalo herd from opposite directions, driving the animals into a large circle. Then the warriors charge from all sides and slay as many as they can. The buffalo fight fiercely, using their horns to rip open men and horses. More warriors are killed in surrounds than in any other kind of hunt."

Nate could see why. He'd hunted a few buffalo and had learned to respect their formidable size and nature. A full-grown bull stood six feet tall at the shoulders, weighed about two thousand pounds, and possessed wicked curved horns capable of tearing into a horse and rider with the same ease a knife sliced into butter. "You'll never catch me going on a surround," he said.

"I am most happy to hear that," Winona said. "I would dislike losing you so early in our marriage."

Nate looked at her and saw she was grinning.

Suddenly, from off to the left, arose loud whoops. He faced in that direction and discovered seven riders galloping toward them, Shoshone warriors who were shouting and waving their weapons overhead. He reined up and gripped the Hawken in both hands.

"Look who is in the lead," Winona said.

Studying the foremost Shoshone, Nate smiled when he recognized the tall, lanky form of Drags The Rope, a young warrior he had met months ago. He relaxed and waved, glad to see his friend again.

All seven of the riders were young warriors, all dressed in buckskin shirts or no shirts at all and buckskin leggings. All were well armed with bows, war clubs or tomahawks, and lances.

"Greetings, Drags The Rope," Nate called out in their language as they approached.

The tall warrior blinked in surprise as he brought his horse to a stop. "Grizzly Killer!" he exclaimed in English. "You have learned our tongue much well."

"Thank you," Nate said, recalling that a mountaineer known as Trapper Pete had taught Drags The Rope a little English over six years earlier and now the warrior liked to converse in it every chance he got. "I've had an exceptional teacher," he said and indicated Winona.

One of the other young warriors, a stocky youth who wore a perpetual smile, inquired in Shoshone, "Have you killed any grizzlies since last you were with us, Grizzly Killer?"

"Just two," Nate answered.

The warriors exchanged amazed expressions and Drags The Rope laughed.

"*Only* two?" the tall man said in his own language. "Some of us go our whole lives without killing one. If you keep going at this rate, there will be none left in these mountains in a few years."

The others erupted in hearty mirth.

Nate smiled with them. One of the Indian traits he most admired was their keen sense of humor. Even in adverse circumstances they invariably found humor. Indians, he had learned, were rarely as grimly somber as many whites often were, and their refreshing, naturally joyful attitude appealed to him. He often wished he could develop a similar outlook on life.

Drags The Rope glanced at Winona. "Soon you will be a father," he said.

"Very soon," Nate agreed, keeping his voice level so he wouldn't betray his anxiety over the impending birth. "How about you? Have you taken a wife yet?"

"No," Drags The Rope said. "Soon, I hope. I have been walking under the robe with Singing Bird, and I believe she will agree to be my wife before the next moon."

"I'm happy for you," Nate said, recollecting his own courtship with Winona. A common romantic practice among several tribes was that of permitting courting couples to stand under a buffalo robe and whisper sweet words to each other, or the young lovers might be allowed to go for short moonlit strolls while wrapped in the same robe and, if they were lucky, they would be able to sneak a few kisses. Heavy fondling, however, was strictly frowned upon, viewed as an insult to the girl that could get the prospective suitor in a lot of trouble if she complained. Fortunately, few girls did.

"If you are here when she says yes, you will be welcome to my lodge for the celebration," Drags The Rope said.

"You honor me."

Drags The Rope gestured to the southwest. "We are on our way to hunt deer or elk. Would you like to come along?"

"Another time, perhaps," Nate said. "We must get

settled in. It's been a long ride and Winona is very tired."

"Later then, my friend," Drags The Rope said and led the small band off at a gallop. They screeched and shouted in wild abandon, hot-blooded youths eager for adventure.

Nate watched them depart, remembering how it was to be reckless and without a care in the world. Then he looked at Winona, at the bulge in her dress, and swallowed hard. Even though he was not yet 20, those days were over for him forever. Now he had responsibilities, and he must face up to them as best he knew how. Squaring his shoulders, he headed toward the village.

Chapter Six

The Shoshone encampment presented a fascinating spectacle. Three hundred and sixty lodges were spread out to the east and south of Clear Lake. Varying in size depending on the wealth of the owners, all the lodges were made of meticulously dressed buffalo skins. Children scurried among them, the boys conducting foot races, shooting small bows, or playing games while the girls played with dolls or assisted their mothers. Women were everywhere, engaged in the many tasks required of them, from cooking to preparing rawhide to drying meat and repairing torn lodge skins. The men, for the most part, were either talking in groups, tending to their horses, or else gambling with buffalo-bone dice.

The Shoshone clan to which Winona belonged had adopted many of the ways of the Plains tribes, the Cheyennes, the Arapahoes, and the Dakotas. There were other Shoshones who still lived much as had their ancestors, subsisting primarily on fish, roots, berries, and seeds. This second branch of the Shoshone people lived farther west and rarely ventured after buffalo, which had become the focus for the eastern Shoshones' very existence. They depended on the great brutes for the food they ate, the clothes they wore, and for the lodges that kept them warm at night.

Curious glances were cast in Nate's direction as he approached the village with Winona at his side. Such a large number of lodges meant that numerous smaller bands, usually composed of those with family ties to one another, had gotten together for a mass reunion, an event that transpired only two or three times a year. Because it was difficult to find enough game to keep so many mouths fed, most of the time Indians preferred to travel in smaller bands.

"Any idea where we'll find your aunt's lodge?" Nate asked.

"None at all," Winona answered. "We will have to ask around until we find someone who knows."

An elderly warrior with white hair came toward them, walking with a slight limp. "Welcome, white man," he said to Nate in Shoshone. His gaze strayed to Winona. "Have you come to join our gathering?"

"Yes," Nate replied, halting. "Do you happen to know where we might find the lodge belonging to Spotted Bull?"

The warrior seemed surprised at Nate's fluency. "Yes, I do. I have known him for years," he said, pointing to the north. "It is near the lake within a stone's throw of where we stand."

"Thank you," Nate said and headed off. What luck! He noticed a few boys were trailing behind, studying him and whispering among themselves. White men elicited as much curiousity among Indians as Indians did among whites.

"At last," Winona said. "I am excited about seeing my aunt again. She is a sweet woman."

Nate didn't bother mentioning the profound relief he felt at having Winona among her kin again. Now she would have help when the baby came and he could breathe a lot easier. He surveyed the lodges nearest the lake. They formed an uneven line, each separated by 20 or 25 yards from its neighbor. The third one bore the painted likeness of a great bull buffalo with light-colored spots on its back. "Let me guess. That must be the one we want," he said.

"You are learning," Winona said with a smile.

As they neared the entrance an attractive woman in her early to mid-twenties emerged from the lodge carrying an empty parfleche in her left hand. She looked up, saw Winona, and uttered a squeal of delight. "Cousin! Is it really you?"

"Willow Woman," Winona declared happily and rode up to her relative before dismounting.

Nate reined up. He leaned on the saddle horn and idly watched the women exchange heartfelt greetings. The commotion brought two other people out of the lodge, a woman in her fifties and a slim warrior sporting streaks of gray in his hair, who then greeted Winona with as much enthusiasm as Willow Woman had. The words were flying so thick and fast that Nate had a hard time keeping abreast of the discussion. Finally Winona turned to him.

"I almost forgot. This is my husband, Grizzly Killer," she said sheepishly. Then she indicated the man and the older woman. "This is Spotted Bull and Morning Dove."

"I am honored to meet both of you," Nate said, sliding down. He realized a half-dozen Shoshones, on their way southward, had stopped to observe the pleasantries and he began to feel as if he was being examined under a magnifying glass. To his surprise, Spotted Bull stepped forward and squeezed his shoulders.

"I am the one who is honored," the warrior said. "I have heard much about you." He gazed past Nate. "Since you do not have a lodge, I insist that you stay with us for as long as you like."

"We are grateful," Nate said. "My wife needs to rest after our long trip."

Spotted Bull glanced at the three women, who were chatting away, and grinned. "She will be occupied for a while. If I know women, and after fifty-six winters I know them as well as a man can, she will rest when she is ready. Come, I will help you unpack your horses and show you where to tie them."

Although Nate would rather have insisted that Winona lie down, he couldn't bring himself to make an issue of it when she was so happy at being reunited with her relatives. With Spotted Bull's assistance he removed their belongings from the pack animal, unsaddled both mounts, and took everything into the lodge. Nate grabbed the three hobbles he had made from rope out of a pack, then Spotted Bull helped him lead his horses around to the rear of the lodge where nine others were grazing contentedly.

"You may leave your horses with mine," Spotted Bull said. "There is plenty of grass and water here."

"How long have you been at this spot?" Nate asked as he hobbled his stallion.

"Twenty sleeps," Spotted Bull said and looked out over the village. "It is a good gathering this year. I have seen friends I have not talked to in many winters."

Nate went about hobbling the mare and the pack-horse, and when he straightened he saw a bemused expression on the warrior's face. "Did I do something funny?"

"Do your horses wander off often?" Spotted Bull asked and pointed at the hobble on the mare.

"I don't give them the chance."

Spotted Bull gestured at his own animals, none of

which were hobbled or ground-hitched. "I train them to always stay near my lodge. Horses are a lot like children. They must be taught the proper way of doing things, and when they have been they usually turn out all right."

Nate admired the fine animals the warrior owned. He knew how highly Indians valued their horses, especially their war-horses, the mounts warriors invariably rode while raiding or hunting. Such steeds had to be fearless, fast, and responsive to the slightest pressure from the warriors. "Surely one must stray off every now and then," Nate said.

"Unfortunately, yes."

"What do you then? Beat it?"

Spotted Bull recoiled in shock. "I would never beat an animal. Such cruelty is unnecessary."

"Then what do you do when a horse won't behave?"

An impish grin curled the warrior's mouth. "I eat it." He turned and headed back.

Wondering if the Shoshone was joshing, Nate followed, tucking the Hawken in the crook of his left elbow. The women had gone inside. Approaching from the south was the same white-haired warrior who had supplied directions to the lodge.

"Here comes my friend, Lame Elk," Spotted Bull said.

"He told us where to find you," Nate said.

"Lame Elk and I have been on many hunts together. He saved me from a charging buffalo once. I had wounded it with my lance, and it turned on me and knocked my horse down before I could get away. I was pinned under my animal, helpless, and the buffalo moved in to gore me. That was when Lame Elk rode right up to it and buried his lance in the buffalo's chest."

"Friends like that are rare."

Spotted Bull glanced at him. "True, Grizzly Killer,

and worth more than the best war-horse that ever lived."

The elderly warrior reached them and was warmly greeted by Spotted Bull, who then made the formal introductions.

"It occurred to me who you must be after you had ridden off," Lame Elk said to Nate. "I have heard stories about you, and I thought I would come to learn if they are true."

"What kind of stories?" Nate asked.

"They say you are different from most whites, that you have the soul of an Indian in a white man's body. They say you kill grizzlies like most men kill ants. And they say you have slain more Blackfeet than anyone else," Lame Elk said.

"Whoever made these claims must have been hit on the head with a war club first," Nate joked.

Both Shoshones laughed.

"You are not vain," Lame Elk said. "That is good. There is too much vanity in the younger warriors these days. All they think of is wearing the best buckskin and riding the best horses. They must have a new lodge every year or so, even when their old one has not yet worn out. In my day things were different. A man was measured by his courage, not by his wealth. If a man had the smallest lodge in the village but was the bravest fighter in the tribe, he became a top man, maybe even a chief. Now a man would rather have twenty horses than have counted twenty coup, and those who have many possessions look down their noses at those who do not."

Spotted Bull grinned. "You exaggerate again, old friend."

"Do I?" Lame Elk asked.

Nate didn't think so. When first learning about Indian culture, he had been surprised that there actually were rich and poor Indians and that the gulf between them could be considerable. Certain chiefs and other wealthy warriors might own hundreds of horses, have two or three wives, and have a lodge large enough to accommodate 30 people at once. By contrast, there were warriors who only owned two or three horses, had one wife, and lived in a small lodge that threatened to fall over with the next strong gust of wind. In many respects Indians and whites were more alike than they realized or would admit. "If your people aren't careful, Lame Elk," he said, "they will become more and more like the whites until there is no difference between the two."

"If that ever happens, my people will deserve their fate," the elderly warrior said. "They will have lost the guidance of the Everywhere Spirit and be adrift in the world."

Nate detected melancholy in the old man's eyes. He thought about the reference to the Everywhere Spirit. Some Indians referred to God as the Great Medicine or Great Mystery. Others called the Supreme Deity the Great Spirit. All the terms meant the same thing, as far as he could determine. And he'd been amazed to discover how truly religious the Indians were. In their own way, Indians were generally even more spiritual than the majority of whites. Ironically, back in the States most folks regarded the Indians as heathens or pagans.

"Come inside and we will smoke the pipe," Spotted Bull said and stood aside to let them enter his lodge first.

Nate went in through the open flap. To his left, huddled together in animated conversation, were Winona, Willow Woman, and Morning Dove. Recalling the proper tepee etiquette, he stood to the right and waited for Spotted Bull to indicate where he should sit. As Shakespeare had told him, there were certain formal rules of conduct visitors to any lodge must follow. Not to do so was considered rude, an insult to the host.

The two men entered, and Spotted Bull asked that Nate sit in the seat of honor which was at the rear of the lodge and to the left of the spot where Spotted Bull normally took his seat. Lame Elk was asked to sit on Spotted Bull's right.

Nate leaned the Hawken against the wall, then sank down cross-legged as was the custom for Indian men. Women were strictly forbidden from doing so because they might inadvertently expose their upper legs or private parts; they must sit on their heels or kneel at all times when in mixed company.

"Bring my best pipe and the kinnikinnick," Spotted Bull said to his wife.

Morning Dove dutifully opened a parflache and took out an exquisitely adorned pipe and a buckskin pouch. She brought them over and placed them in front of her husband, then rejoined Winona and Willow Woman.

Nate got a good look at the pipe as Spotted Bull started filling the intricately carved buffalo-shaped bowl. Indians took great stock in their pipes. A fine one like his host's would be worth at least one horse or several buffalo robes in trade. It was decorated with brown horsehair, which hung over two dozen glass beads, four silk ribbons, and bands of wool. Nate figured it was Spotted Bull's best pipe, one reserved specifically for special occasions. Most warriors owned at least two: one for everyday use and one for ceremonial purposes.

Whichever pipe was used, smoking was considered a solemn ritual. Indians smoked to ratify personal pledges, to formalize agreements between tribes, to communicate with the spirit world, and to display a token of friendship. When a warrior invited someone into his lodge to smoke with him, it meant the warrior had only the friendliest of intentions and could be counted on to be as good as his word.

Spotted Bull wore an intent expression as he packed the mixture of tobacco and willow bark into the bowl. This mixture, known as kinnikinnick, varied from tribe to tribe and even between individuals. Because the wild tobacco Indians harvested was exceptionally strong, they often added other ingredients for balance. Bearberries, sumac leaves, and willow bark were all favorites.

Having tamped the contents of the bowl down to his satisfaction, Spotted Bull moved to the fire and retrieved a burning brand. He lit the kinnikinnick, puffing heavily as wreaths of smoke floated toward the ventilation opening at the top of the conical lodge. When at last he had the pipe going to his satisfaction, he took his seat and offered it to Nate. "Here, Grizzly Killer. As my guest of honor, you go first."

"Thank you," Nate said, taking the long pipe in both hands. He'd only smoked a few times, and he hoped he wouldn't embarrass himself by coughing or hacking. As he touched the stem to his lips, Spotted Bull made a comment that caused him to forget all about such a minor matter.

"There is something I would like to discuss with you as we smoke. How would you like to go on a surround with us?"

Chapter Seven

"After buffalo?" Nate asked, stunned by the proposal.

Lame Elk snickered. "We rarely surround rabbits," he said, his eyes twinkling.

"The hunt is still being planned," Spotted Bull said. "It might be four or five sleeps before the hunters leave. Would you like to go?"

Nate became aware of Winona staring at him. All the women had ceased chatting. He lowered the pipestem a fraction and tried to keep his voice steady as he answered. "Will the hunters be traveling all the way to the plains?"

"Yes," Spotted Bull confirmed. "The trip there for us will take about three sleeps. There is no telling how long the surround will take because there is no way of predicting how many buffalo will be slain and how long it will take to butcher them."

"Which means I would be away from my wife for quite a while," Nate observed.

"Is that a problem?" Spotted Bull asked and then glanced at Winona. A knowing smile brightened his face. "Oh. I am sorry. I almost forgot about the birth. This will be your first child, and a husband should be with his wife at such a time."

Relief washed over Nate. He had a legitimate excuse to bow out of the surround, and after all the terrible tales he'd heard about the practice he wasn't inclined to jeopardize his life with Winona due to deliver any day now. "I will give it some thought," he said, "but I will be honest and tell you that under the circumstances I believe my place is with Winona."

Lame Elk snorted. "Our young warriors do the same thing. They refuse to go hunting or raiding while their wives are heavy with child. Back in my time things were different. When a woman was ready to have a baby, she just walked into the woods, squatted, and out it dropped. She never made any fuss about it, and she never asked her husband to stay around and hold her hand."

"Behave yourself," Spotted Bull said and grinned at Nate. "You must overlook his words sometimes. In his advanced years he has become as testy as a rattlesnake."

"I have not," Lame Elk said. "All I'm doing is dispensing the wisdom of my years, and you should have the courtesy to listen without criticizing me."

Nate chuckled. He could tell the two friends enjoyed needling one another. "How many warriors will go on the surround?" he asked out of curiosity.

"Twenty-five or thirty," Spotted Bull said. "I will be leading them."

Morning Dove interjected a remark. "You need not go, husband. The younger warriors can manage quite well without you."

"We have already talked this over several times," Spotted Bull reminded her. "I have not been on a surround in many winters and I want to do it one more time."

"You can go off and kill a buffalo any time you want," Morning Dove said. "Leave the surrounds to the young men."

Spotted Bull frowned. "Why must you keep making an issue of my age? I can still ride with the best of them and shoot an arrow as straight as anyone in the village. My war-horse is experienced and quick on its feet. You need not concern yourself over my safety."

Although Nate felt inclined to agree with Morning Dove, he knew it would be considered bad manners if he were to involve himself in their personal dispute. The worry in her eyes was as plain as the nose on her face, and he didn't blame her one bit. Surrounds were too dangerous for a man of Spotted Bull's advanced years, and he wondered what the warrior was trying to prove by going on one.

"Excuse me, Grizzly Killer," Lame Elk said. "Are you planning to keep that pipe or will you smoke sometime today and let us share also?"

"Sorry," Nate said and self-consciously took a puff, drawing the smoke down into his lungs and then exhaling loudly. He suppressed a strong impulse to cough and handed the pipe back to his host.

Spotted Bull took the pipe without comment and gave it to Lame Elk, who smiled and puffed vigorously.

The women began conversing in low tones.

"So tell me," Spotted Bull said, looking at Nate, "did you happen to see any sign of Blackfeet on your way here?"

"No. Have there been any reported in this area?"

"Five sleeps ago a party of hunters came across signs that a small band of Blackfeet were roaming the country north of our village. Since then no one has seen a thing."

Bitter memories of Nate's previous conflicts with

the bloodthirsty Blackfeet filled his mind. Of all the tribes in the northern and central Rockies, the Blackfeet were the most feared and with good reason. They killed whites on sight and made relentless war on practically every other tribe. The Blackfeet exhibited the same unbridled ferocity as the Comanches, who dwelt far to the south, and the Apaches, who lived a great distance to the southwest. But of the three, the Blackfeet were widely regarded as the worst.

"I doubt a small band would dare bother a village this size," Spotted Bull was saying. "Even Blackfeet are not that crazy."

"There is no telling where they are concerned," Nate said.

"True, Grizzly Killer," Lame Elk interjected, exhaling a cloud of smoke. "The Blackfeet have always regarded themselves as the best fighters in existence. In order to prove this, all they do is fight, fight, fight. They don't care if they are outnumbered. And they are not afraid to die. Why, once when I was a boy I witnessed a battle between sixty of our warriors and twelve Blackfeet who came too near our camp and were spotted. Although the Blackfeet were surrounded, they formed into a wedge and attacked our warriors like rabid wolves. I was amazed by what I saw."

"Were all the Blackfeet slain?"

"Not at first. Five were only wounded," Lame Elk related. "Our men let the women beat on them for a while, and then our warriors gouged out their eyes, cut off their tongues and noses, and hacked their bodies into tiny bits. Other boys and I picked up some of the body parts and threw them at each other. Later the pieces were fed to the camp dogs." He smiled wistfully. "It was a grand time for everyone."

Nate glanced at Winona. Her parents had been

killed by Blackfeet, and he didn't want to upset her by discussing the Blackfeet further and possibly sparking sad recollections of the event. "Are there any other white men here?" he asked to change the topic.

"Three trappers visited us six sleeps ago," Spotted Bull answered. "They only stayed for one night and then went off to lay their traps for beaver."

Nate nodded. If not for the pregnancy, he would be out doing the same thing himself. The more pelts he could collect before the annual rendezvous, the more money and trade goods he would reap as his reward.

"One of the trappers told us there is a large Flathead village fifteen sleeps to the northwest of here," Spotted Bull said.

Right away Nate thought of his mentor, Shakespeare. The last time he'd seen McNair had been at a Flathead village where his friend had married a Flathead woman, Indian fashion. He wondered if Shakespeare was still there, or if the newlyweds had gone to Shakespeare's cabin, which was located not all that far from Nate's own. He decided to stop and see them on the way home.

"We are not very concerned about the Flatheads," Spotted Bull said. "They leave us alone and we leave them alone. Why should we waste energy fighting them when there are always plenty of Blackfeet and Utes to fight?"

"The Flatheads are fine people," Nate said. "I lived with them for a short while recently. They treated me courteously."

Lame Elk leaned forward to gaze at him. "I have heard that Flathead women are as beautiful as our own. Is this true?"

Suddenly Winona, Morning Dove, and Willow Woman stopped talking and fixed their attention on Nate, waiting expectantly to hear the answer he would give.

Resisting an urge to snicker, Nate said, "It's true the Flathead women are quite lovely, but they cannot begin to compare to Shoshone women. In all my travels I've never seen women anywhere who are as beautiful as yours."

"I thought as much," Lame Elk said.

All three women smiled and went back to talking.

"Grizzly Killer is wise beyond his years," Spotted Bull said softly, a grin touching his lips.

Nate moved his head a bit closer to his host and whispered, "Marriage does that to a man. I would rather face a horde of enraged Blackfeet than one angry wife."

Spotted Bull chuckled. "The Blackfeet would treat you better," he said.

Laughing, Nate nodded and bestowed a loving look on Winona when she gazed in his direction.

Lame Elk took another puff and said in all earnestness, "Women have always been a mystery to me. When I was a young man I thought I knew all there was to know about them. Then I took a beautiful woman as my wife and discovered everything I thought was wrong. So I changed my thinking and took a second woman into my lodge. It was most confusing. Everything I had learned from the first woman did little to help me understand the second woman." He paused, his forehead creased in deep contemplation. "Finally I decided men are not meant to understand women. I do not know why this should be unless the Everywhere Spirit has a strange sense of humor."

"Women are like the spirit realm," Spotted Bull said. "They are one of the two great mysteries in life."

Nate noticed that the women were staring at them again so he promptly changed the subject. "Does every Shoshone believe in the Everywhere Spirit?"

Spotted Bull and Lame Elk glanced at him. "Of

course," the former said. "Why do you ask?"

"Because a while ago I was thinking about the fact that Indian people as a whole are more spiritual than my own people," Nate said.

"I have noticed this," Lame Elk said. "White people do not seem to know about spirit things. They do not let the Everywhere Spirit guide their lives. They do not even know they have a spirit center. This, too, is most perplexing. I do not see how the whites can hope to prosper unless they drastically change their ways."

"I am sorry to say it, but I agree," Spotted Bull said to Nate. "Your people are more puzzling than women. Whites treat the land as if they own it, and they take more from the land than they give to it. This is terribly wrong." He scratched his chin. "Look at what has happened to the beaver. In the few winters that white trappers have been taking pelts, more beavers have been killed than in all the winters that have gone before all the way back to the beginning of all things. Why do whites have such little regard for the natural order of the world?"

"I honestly do not know," Nate replied.

"Well I do," Lame Elk said. "I have given the matter much thought and I believe the problem is that whites do not go around barefoot enough."

Nate blinked, uncertain if he'd heard correctly. "I don't follow you."

"I was told that most white men wear heavy boots and white women wear odd shoes all the time. The trappers and a few others wear moccasins. But except for white children, hardly any whites ever go around barefoot," Lame Elk said. "How do your people expect to stay in touch with Nature if they fail to take a walk in the grass every now and then? We must feel the earth under our naked feet if we are to fully appreciate our ties to the natural order of things."

"I never thought of it in quite that way," Nate said.

Just then, from off to the south, arose the clamor of many voices and the sound of a general commotion. Footsteps pounded outside the lodge entrance and a male voice called out, "Spotted Bull, this is Fox Tail. May I speak to you?"

"Enter," Spotted Bull said.

A young warrior poked his head inside. "I thought you would like to know. A hunting party has just returned, and they have captured an enemy of our people."

"Where are they now?" Spotted Bull asked, rising.

"On the south shore of the lake near Chief Broken Paw's lodge," the young warrior said. "Now, if you will excuse me, I must inform others."

"Thank you for telling us," Spotted Bull said.

The young warrior backed out and raced off.

"This is great news," Lame Elk said. "Things were getting too boring around here. Now we will have some excitement. Maybe we will get to torture this enemy before he dies." He laid down the pipe and pushed himself up to his feet. "Let us go see what is happening."

Spotted Bull looked at Nate. "Would you like to come along?"

"I certainly would," Nate said, rising and grabbing the Hawken. He winked at Winona and trailed the two men outside where the bright light made him squint. They turned southward, joining scores of other Shoshones, mostly men but also a few women who had heard the news and were eager to glimpse the prisoner for themselves.

By the time Nate and his new friends arrived at the chief's huge lodge, over 100 Shoshones already ringed the lodge entrance where the chief, the hunting party, and the captive now stood. Nate had to stand on tiptoe to see the members of the hunting party, and he was surprised to spot Drags The Rope among them. Then the ranks of spectators in front of him momentarily parted and he got a good look at the prisoner. His blood ran cold at the sight.

It was Red Hawk.

Chapter Eight

The Dakota warrior stood with his shoulders squared and his head held erect and proud, radiating defiance from every pore. His wrists had been bound with thick strips of leather behind his back. His chest and arms bore scratch marks, indicating he had been involved in a fight, and a jagged tear now marred his leggings from his left knee to his ankle. All of his weapons had been confiscated. His brown stallion was off to the left with the mounts belonging to the hunting party.

Drags The Rope was engaged in earnest conversation with an elderly warrior who wore a crown of eagle feathers.

Some of the Shoshones were taunting the Sioux, insulting his tribe and lineage or casting aspersions on his manhood. A few bold children dashed up to him and threw sticks at his face and torso.

Nate didn't know what to do. During the brief time he'd been with Red Hawk, he'd grown to like him. He didn't want to see anything happen to the outcast. But he worried that if he dared to speak up the Shoshones might hold it against him. He bided his time and moved closer, trying to hear the discussion between Drags The Rope and Chief Broken Paw.

"—climbed a ridge to spot game and saw him watering his horse at a stream," Drags The Rope was saying. "White Lynx, Man Afraid, and I sneaked down and surprised him while he was seated on the bank, deep in thought. He never heard us coming. Once we laid our hands on him, he put up a great struggle. The others had to come help us subdue him."

The Chief glanced at their prisoner. "I know you are an Oglala. Do you speak our tongue?"

Red Hawk made no reply.

"Very well," Broken Paw said and switched to sign language. "We will untie you so you can speak in sign. If you try to get away, we will cut your feet off." He nodded at Drags The Rope.

A knife flashed in the sunlight and the leather strips binding the Sioux fell to the grass. He began rubbing his wrists while glaring at his captors.

"Now tell us your name," Broken Paw said.

"Red Hawk."

"Where is the rest of your war party? Were you sent ahead to spy on our village? How many Dakotas are with you?" Broken Paw asked, his hands flying.

"I am alone."

The chief frowned. "Do you take me for a fool, Oglala? You would have me believe that you came all the way from the Dakota hunting grounds alone?"

"I speak the truth," Red Hawk said. "I am not here on a raid. All I want is to be left in peace."

Many in the crowd started whispering, and from the baleful glances they cast at the captive it became apparent to Nate that Red Hawk would be extremely lucky to live out the hour.

A husky Shoshone standing near Drags The Rope

suddenly raised a war club overhead and bellowed for all to hear. "There is only one way to deal with this Oglala dog! I say we treat him as his kind would treat us!"

There were cries of assent from a number of spectators, and a few men clamored for the Sioux's scalp.

Nate realized the Shoshones were gradually working themselves into a killing frame of mind. No matter what Red Hawk said, the Shoshones wouldn't believe him. He hefted the Hawken, debating what to do. As an adopted member of the tribe he was welcome to speak up at formal gatherings, but he didn't know what to say.

Broken Paw gestured for silence and faced the prisoner again. "If you are not here on a raid, then why are you in our territory?"

"I am passing through," Red Hawk said. "I did not know I was close to your village until a short while before your warriors jumped me, and I was heading away from here when they did."

"Even if your words are true," Broken Paw signed, "our people and yours have fought a number of times in the past. We have no treaty with the Oglalas. This makes you our enemy."

Red Hawk sighed. "I know."

"As our enemy, you know the treatment you will receive," Broken Paw said. "The same treatment your people would give one of us if the situation was reversed."

Suddenly the husky warrior gave Red Hawk a brutal shove that knocked the Dakota to his knees, then waved his war club in the air and whooped wildly. "I say we stake this dog out and try our luck with lances."

"I agree, White Lynx!" one of the watching warriors called out. "He will look like a porcupine when we are done."

Nate glanced at Spotted Bull and Lame Elk, both of

whom were solemnly observing the proceedings. He doubted either would help him if he dared to intervene.

White Lynx took hold of Red Hawk's hair and jerked savagely. "Who will help me stake him out?"

Several men eagerly started forward.

Horrified at the prospect of Red Hawk being killed, Nate gripped the Hawken in both hands and gulped. It was now or never. He might not be able to influence the outcome, but at least he could live with his conscience if he knew he'd tried his best to assist the Dakota. His every nerve tingling, he took several strides past the ring of Shoshones and shouted at the top of his lungs. "No!"

Total silence abruptly engulfed the Shoshones. Amazed expressions were turned in the frontiersman's direction and a murmur rippled among the crowd.

Broken Paw pivoted, betraying surprise when he laid eyes on Nate. "And who are you, white man? I do not believe we have ever met."

"I am known as Grizzly Killer," Nate said formally. "I am married to Black Kettle's daughter, Winona." He became aware that Spotted Bull and Lame Elk were standing at his side.

"Yes. I have heard of you," Broken Paw said, stepping forward. He gestured at Red Hawk. "Why do you seek to protect this man?"

"I know him," Nate declared and listened to even more whispering break out among the spectators.

"How is this possible?" Broken Paw asked in surprise.

"My wife and I met him earlier. He saved us from a grizzly," Nate said and launched into a brief recital of the encounter. He concluded his story by saying, "You should believe him when he says he is alone. He is an outcast."

"Oh?" Broken Paw said, glancing at the captive, his

eyebrows arched. "That would explain a lot."

"He made no attempt to harm us," Nate said, hoping to convince the chief to spare the Dakota's life. "Yet had he wanted to, he could easily have ambushed us."

White Lynx let go of Red Hawk's long hair and stalked toward Nate. "What difference does that make, white eyes? The Oglala is still our enemy and everyone knows what we must do to him."

"Why not let him live?" Nate asked.

"So that he might sneak back here in the dead of night and murder some of us in our sleep?" White Lynx rejoined in contempt. "No. I say we kill him now."

"It is customary for us to slay enemies of our people," Broken Paw agreed. "If we were to let this one go, it would show us to be weak."

"Not at all," Nate said. "It would show that you have wisdom and compassion. The true mark of a warrior is knowing when to kill and when not to kill."

"What do you know about being a warrior, white man?" White Lynx asked.

"My name is Grizzly Killer," Nate said.

"So I have heard, but it does not impress me as it does so many others," White Lynx said. "To me you are nothing but a white man, and a white man has no business interfering in tribal matters."

"That is no way to talk," Broken Paw said. "You know that Grizzly Killer has every right to speak as he wishes. By taking Winona as his wife, he has become a part of our tribe."

White Lynx sneered. "Next we will be admitting Blackfeet and Kiowas." He jabbed a thumb at Nate while addressing the chief. "What does he know of our ways? No matter what you say, he is not a Shoshone."

"I can speak for myself," Nate said before Broken

Paw could answer. "It's true I wasn't born into the tribe, but I admire and respect the Shoshone way of living more than I do the way of the white man. My heart is the heart of an Indian."

A snort burst from White Lynx. "You are touched in the head, white man. Only an Indian knows the heart of an Indian."

Nate's anger flared. He'd tolerated all of the insults and belligerence he could stomach. "And only a fool takes a human life, white or Indian, without just cause. To kill the Dakota just because he is from a different tribe is something the Blackfeet would do, and I thought the Shoshones were better than the Blackfeet."

White Lynx bristled, hefting his war club. "Are you calling me a fool?"

Broken Paw looked from one to the other. "Enough of this bickering," he said sternly. "We should behave as reasonable men."

"What is there to be reasonable about?" White Lynx demanded. "I say we kill the Dakota now. Let Grizzly Killer go hide in a lodge if he is afraid to watch."

Struggling to restrain himself, Nate said, "And I say killing the Dakota is bad medicine. Spare him instead."

"Both of you have good points," Broken Paw said diplomatically. "This is a grave issue that should not be decided by one man alone. We will call a council and discuss what is best to do."

"A council? Why waste the time over such a trifle?" White Lynx asked.

"Since when is the taking of any life a trifle?" Broken Paw said. "No, we will let the Dakota live until after we hold a council tonight."

"Then let me have him until then," White Lynx said, leering. "I will give him the treatment he deserves."

The chief hesitated, then said emphatically, "No. The Oglala will be in Grizzly Killer's custody until after the council meeting."

"You pick this white eyes over me?" White Lynx snapped.

Unruffled, Broken Paw said, "Grizzly Killer is the one who has spoken in the Oglala's defense. It is only fitting that he look after the prisoner."

White Lynx glared at Nate. "I will remember this," he said and abruptly stormed off into the crowd, shouldering his way through, oblivious to the reproach of those he bumped aside.

Nate was elated at the temporary reprieve he'd obtained for the Sioux. He motioned for Red Hawk to join him.

"While I admire what you have done," Broken Paw said, "and might even agree with you, there is something you should know."

"What?"

"You are responsible for this man," Broken Paw said. "If he escapes, you will be punished. If he kills or hurts anyone, you will be held accountable. Your fate is as much in his hands as his is in yours." He paused. "Are you certain you want to go through with this?"

Red Hawk reached them and halted. He gave Nate a grateful smile.

"I'm certain," Nate said.

"Very well. Just remember you have been warned," Broken Paw said and walked toward his lodge.

Now that the issue had been decided, the hunting party and the spectators began to disperse. Many conversed in low tones.

Nate watched them go. Within an hour the argument would be the talk of the tribe. He looked at Spotted Bull, who was staring at him strangely. "With your permission, I will keep Red Hawk in your lodge until tonight. I promise to keep an eye on him the whole time."

"It is against my better judgment, but I trust you," Spotted Bull said. "Very well. This Oglala may stay with us. I will go on ahead and inform the women so it doesn't come as a shock." He moved off, Lame Elk at his side.

Nate drew his knife, stepped behind the Dakota, and carefully sliced the leather strips in half. When they fell to the ground he slid the knife back into its sheath and tucked the Hawken under his left arm to leave his hands free for signing.

Red Hawk turned. "Thank you, Grizzly Killer, for speaking in my behalf."

"Perhaps one day you can return the favor," Nate signed and started toward Spotted Bull's lodge. "Come with me." He was conscious of the stares of the Shoshones who had not yet left, a few openly hostile. Not everyone agreed with Broken Paw's decision.

"As much as I would like to do you a kindness," Red Hawk signed, "I doubt I will live long enough to be able to pay you back."

"You do not know that for certain. There is to be a council. White Lynx might not get his way. The council meeting will be conducted by the older warriors and they are not as bloodthirsty as he is."

"I hope you are right," Red Hawk said. "Although there have been many times since I became an outcast that I wished I were dead, now that I face the prospect I find death is not so appealing any more."

Nate glanced at the Dakota, curiosity eating at him. "Do you mind if I ask you a personal question?" he signed.

"I can imagine what it is."

"If you think I am prying into your personal affairs, I won't insist on an answer."

Red Hawk sighed, then moved his hands slowly. "You want to ask me the reason my people cast me out."

"If you care to tell me."

"After what you have done for me, it is only fitting that you know," Red Hawk said, a melancholy shadow darkening his features. "I am an outcast because I murdered an unarmed member of my tribe."

Chapter Nine

The revelation upset Nate although it came as no great surprise. Banishment from a tribe was a severe practice adopted as a last resort. Only the gravest of offenses could result in a warrior being made an outcast. It was rarely done. He knew of only two other instances, and both of those, like this one, involved murder.

The truth of the matter was that Indians seldom killed fellow tribal members. They would go off and raid another tribe and kill with reckless abandon, but once back in their own village they were expected to keep a lid on their tempers no matter what the provocation might be.

All tribes preferred to settle personal disputes in a civil matter. The Indians dwelling on the plains east of the Rockies even had what were known as soldier societies who policed the encampments and punished those who broke tribal custom. Violators would be judged according to the seriousness of the offense, the reason for the violation, and the culprit's attitude. Punishments ranged from light, such as having an ear cut off the offender's war-horse, to severe, such as beating the offender so badly he could barely stand.

Knowing all this, Nate had surmised that Red Hawk's offense must have been extreme, but he hadn't pegged the Dakota as a wanton murderer. And now, looking into the warrior's troubled eyes and recalling how Red Hawk had deliberately risked his life to save Winona and him from the grizzly bear, Nate figured there must be more to the story. "Want to talk about it?" he asked.

"There is nothing to say. I was guilty. My punishment was just."

Nate reluctantly decided to drop the subject. Further questions would be a rude breach of Indian etiquette and might offend Red Hawk. He heard voices upraised in anger and looked up to see Spotted Bull and White Lynx arguing. Lame Elk stood to one side, while behind White Lynx were two other warriors.

"—none of your concern," Spotted Bull was saying. "And I will not stand by and let you insult him."

"I never thought you would side with a white man against your own people," White Lynx said.

Nate was almost to them. Suddenly one of the other warriors saw him and whispered a word in warning to White Lynx, who looked over Spotted Bull's shoulder and smirked.

"And here he is now. We were just talking about you."

"So I gathered," Nate said coldly. "If you have something to say about me, say it to my face." He paused. "That is, if you are man enough."

White Lynx flushed scarlet and glowered. "No one can accuse me of being a coward. I have counted twelve coup, two on Blackfeet. Ten scalps hang in my lodge. And I have led five successful raids."

Despite himself, Nate was impressed. Twelve coup was quite a feat, above average for a man White Lynx's age. Even more remarkable were the five successful raids. It meant that the raiding parties had not lost a single warrior, and losses of one or two men on a raid were not uncommon. White Lynx, therefore, for all his fiery temperament, was a competent, brave warrior who must enjoy considerable esteem in his tribe. Nate kept his features composed and said, "Then tell me what you were talking about."

"I was telling Spotted Bull that he makes a mistake in letting you stay with him," White Lynx said. "Even though you took one of our women for your wife, you do not have the best interests of our people at heart. You are like some other white men I have known. You think you know better than we do how we should live our lives."

Nate was about to protest when he realized that the Shoshone, in a sense, was right. He'd known his fair share of trappers and traders who tended to look down their noses at the Indians and regarded all tribes with paternal contempt. There were many whites with very firm and drastic opinions on how to deal with the Indians, not the least of whom was President Andrew Jackson. "Old Hickory"—as Jackson was widely known because he had been as tough as hickory during his illustrious military career—felt it was the inalienable right of the federal government to do whatever might be necessary to subjugate the Indian tribes and force the Indians to live wherever the government saw fit to place them. Already thousands of Indians had been compelled to move west of the Mississippi, with countless numbers dying along the way. In the midst of his thoughts, Nate suddenly realized over half a minute had gone by and the Shoshones were regarding him expectantly.

"Why do you not speak?" White Lynx asked.

"I was thinking about your words," Nate said. "And I agree with you to a point."

"You do?" White Lynx said in surprise.

"Yes. Many whites do believe they know more about things than your people do," Nate said, "but I have learned they are wrong. And the reason I objected to killing Red Hawk has nothing to do with such an attitude. I do not think any life should be taken lightly, even the life of an enemy. The man who does so is no better than the bear I have been named after."

The speech appeared to have a positive impact on the two warriors with White Lynx. They exchanged looks and one of them said softly, "His words are true, I think."

White Lynx cocked his head and examined Nate as if under a microscope. "Perhaps I have misjudged you a little, but I still feel we are making a mistake by not killing this Oglala right away. And tonight I will argue at the council to have him put to death."

"What if the council decides against you?" Nate asked.

"Then I will abide by their wishes," White Lynx said, his tone implying he would rather not. He abruptly turned around and walked off without another word, his friends in tow.

Nate looked at Spotted Bull. "I am sorry for any problems this will cause you."

"There may be a few like White Lynx who will think badly of me for a time, but most of the tribe will understand," Spotted Bull said, leading the way northward.

"I hope so," Nate replied. He glanced at Red Hawk to make certain the Sioux was following, then surveyed the encampment. The situation accented his odd feeling of being an outsider, and he began to wish he'd stayed back in the cabin. Then he thought of Winona. "I forgot to bring this up earlier, but I have been told that your tribe uses midwives to assist women in having babies."

"This is so," Spotted Bull said.

"Can you recommend a good one?" Nate asked. Behind him Lame Elk gave a little laugh.

"Your wife can pick a midwife on her own. Having babies is something women do very well. Men should not concern themselves with such matters."

"I am concerned for Winona's safety and health," Nate said defensively. "What is wrong with that?"

"You have much to learn about men and women," Lame Elk said. "There are certain things only women are meant to do and other things only men are meant to do. Since there has never been a single man who has given birth, so far as I am aware, it is best for men to let women take care of dropping babies. They know how to do it. We do not. It is as simple as that, and that is why it is unwise for a man to meddle in the affairs of women and for women to meddle in our affairs."

Spotted Bull chuckled. "You are talking in circles again."

"No, you are listening in circles," the elderly Shoshone said.

Nate was about to press for more information on the midwives when a shriek of sheer terror sounded to the east. Immediately Spotted Bull turned and ran to investigate. "Come," Nate signed to Red Hawk and followed.

Other Shoshones were hastening toward the person who had screamed, a young woman standing at the very edge of the encampment with her face buried in her hands. She sobbed hysterically.

Nate slowed as he neared her. Several women and men were already there, trying to comfort her and asking about the reason for the scream. They spoke swiftly, almost too fast for Nate to understand. Then the terrified woman answered, and he was able to get the gist of her statement.

Her child had been crying, and to teach it a lesson she had taken the infant out past the last row of lodges in the village and hung the child's cradleboard on a bush. This was a widespread Indian custom. Crying was not permitted because the wailing could give away the position of a camp to enemies who might be in the area. Consequently, when babies cried too long or too loud they were taken out and hidden in the brush. When the infants calmed down, their mothers retrieved them. It seldom took more than two or three times for even the most stubborn child to learn that crying wasn't tolerated and to refrain from doing so.

Now this woman had done the same thing, but when she heard her baby stop wailing and went to get it, the child and the cradleboard were gone and imprinted in the soil near the bush were the large tracks of a mountain lion.

As the distraught mother concluded her narrative, warriors hastened off to grab their weapons and other women tried to comfort her.

Nate saw Spotted Bull race away, then faced eastward. He already had his Hawken. If he hurried, he'd reach the scene first and possibly find the big cat if it was still in the area, before a group of excited warriors arrived to scare it off. He broke into a run, the rifle clutched in his right hand, and quickly left the crowd behind. Winding among the lodges, he soon came to the perimeter. Only then did he become aware of the soft pad of footsteps to his rear, and he stopped to look over his left shoulder.

Red Hawk was trailing along, ten feet back.

"Stay here," Nate signed. "A mountain lion has taken a child and I must try to save it."

The Oglala halted and scanned the terrain ahead. "I will stay with you," he signed.

"But you are unarmed."

"I will not stay in the village without you," Red Hawk said. "What does it matter whether I face a mountain lion or White Lynx?"

Reluctantly, Nate resumed running. Had there been more time he would have argued the point, but every second wasted now was crucial. There was a slim chance the infant was still alive. Mountain lions often took their prey into thickets or crevasses where the meat could be consumed in peace and quiet, and if he could locate the cat swiftly then the baby stood a chance. If not, he didn't like to think about the consequences.

A narrow field bordered the village on the east. Beyond the field lay rugged woodland.

As Nate sprinted across the field he spied a tall bush off to the left, beside a small boulder. The bush had thick limbs, ideal for supporting a cradleboard. On a hunch he ran to the bush and examined the ground around it, but he saw nothing until Red Hawk gave his arm a nudge.

The Sioux pointed at a circle of barren earth next to his moccasins.

Goose bumps broke out over Nate's skin as he laid eyes on the immense paw print. He'd seen panther tracks before, distinctive by their large size, their four toes, and a complete absence of claw marks. In this case the print measured approximately four inches in length and four-and-a-half inches in width, exceptionally big even for a mountain lion. He guessed that the print was of a front foot because the front feet were normally larger than the rear feet. Even so, they were after a giant feline.

Red Hawk pointed to the southeast, the direction the print was slanted, and led the way.

Nate was about to object, but changed his mind. Undoubtedly the Oglala was a much better tracker. He would rely on Red Hawk's skill and stay alert enough to protect his newfound friend should they run into trouble.

They entered the forest and found more tracks in a small clearing. Red Hawk picked up the pace, reading the signs faster than seemed humanly possible. Predictably, the big cat had stuck to the open ground in its haste to put distance between itself and the village.

Nate constantly scoured the vegetation before them, hoping to glimpse the predator and its tiny burden. Since they had not found the cradleboard yet, he figured the panther must have the board in its mouth. An image of the cat's long teeth impaling the infant brought a shudder to his spine, and he shook his head to dispel it.

Cradleboards were universally used by Indians. Consisting essentially of a wooden frame over which a soft pouch was sewn, the ingenuous device was used to transport an infant everywhere. It could be slung on the mother's back, hung on a horse, strapped to a travois, or simply carried when the tribe was on the march. And when not being used to convey the baby, the cradleboard could be leaned against any convenient support, such as the wall of a lodge. At all times the baby was kept upright. The cradleboards varied widely in size and construction. Those of wealthy parents were often gaily painted and adorned with beads or horse hair. Those owned by poorer parents usually were little more than a bare skin stretched over the wood frame.

Nate realized the prints were leading toward a dense thicket, and he hoped the cat might be within the tangle of vegetation. Instead, the tracks skirted the thicket on the right and continued southeastward, perhaps in the direction of the mountain lion's den. Doubt assailed him, and he wondered if they were wasting their time, if the lion was already feasting on the child.

Then, from not more than a dozen yards in front of them, there came a low, raspy snarl.

Chapter Ten

The dense undergrowth prevented Nate from spotting the big cat. He tucked the Hawken to his shoulder to be ready in case it should charge out at them and quickly stepped abreast of Red Hawk to be in a better position to defend him. The trees ahead thinned out, and there appeared to be a clearing on the other side of a wide strip of waist-high weeds. Maybe, he reasoned, the mountain lion had stopped there to eat.

Red Hawk motioned for Nate to stop and went to move into the weeds.

Nate gripped the Oglala's arm and held him in place. When Red Hawk looked at him questioningly, he used one hand to indicate he was going to take the lead. With his other hand, Nate parted the weeds quietly, his nerves on the raw edge, his eyes darting right and left. Seven yards into the strip he noticed a break in the vegetation a few more yards in front of him. Puzzled, he warily stepped forward until he could see that the break was actually a drop-off, the top of an earthen bank that blocked from his view whatever lay below.

Exercising extreme caution, Nate moved closer to the rim of the bank. He heard a guttural cough, then the distinct whine of an infant. The baby was down there! Eager to save the child, he dashed forward and took in the scene 12 feet below.

The mountain lion stood in the middle of a secluded gully. At its huge feet rested the cradleboard, and the child inside was crying softly and waving its arms about, its small fingers jutting out of the opening at the top. The lion was eyeing the baby hungrily and might tear into it at any moment.

Nate took a hasty bead on the cat's head, hoping to end the menace with one shot, but in his eagerness he took another half step forward to be sure of not missing. He began to steady his rifle when he felt his left foot slip out from under him. Startled, he realized he was going over the bank, and the next second he plummeted feet first toward the ground below. Although Nate fell only 12 feet, the landing jarred his feet and legs, pitching him off balance so that he wound up on his stinging knees, the rifle clutched firmly in both hands. The cougar crouched and regarded him coldly.

He started to bring the Hawken to bear again when the big cat suddenly came toward him, walking slowly, its pads making no noise whatsoever. Only six feet separated them, and at such close range, staring into the depths of the mountain lion's eerie, slanted eyes, he froze. He wanted to shoot, to slay the beast, but try as he might his mind refused to function, refused to relay the mental message to his arms and hands.

The mountain lion came within two feet and halted. It regarded him intently, as if trying to make up its mind whether he qualified as dinner.

Now that the cat was so close, Nate couldn't fully extend the rifle to fire. He would have to level the gun from the waist and shoot. At such short range the odds of missing were remote, which bolstered his confidence. He girded himself, then swept into motion, whipping the Hawken barrel up as his thumb cocked the hammer. In the blink of an eye the muzzle was trained on the panther and his finger curled around the trigger. The blast caused the powerful rifle to buck in his hands and discharged a small cloud of gunsmoke.

Unfortunately, at the very instant he fired, the mountain lion leaped to one side, perhaps goaded by a primordial instinct that told it the gun was dangerous. The ball missed by a fraction and the lion vented an enraged roar, then pounced.

Nate was knocked onto his back by the heavy beast, the Hawken wedged between them. Inadvertently, the rifle saved his life, because the first swipe of the cat's razor-tipped claws was accidentally deflected by the Hawken. The panther snapped at Nate's face, and he narrowly evaded its raking teeth by twisting his head to the right. Frantic, he heaved, striving to throw the creature off him, but the huge lion weighed upwards of 300 pounds and it barely budged despite Nate's efforts. A paw struck his left shoulder a glancing blow, ripping open his buckskin shirt and slicing into his soft flesh. He squirmed and thrashed in a desperate bid for freedom, staring into the glaring orbs of his feline adversary, orbs that promised imminent death.

Unexpectedly, there came a whoop and something hit the mountain lion's left side. The cat bounded off Nate and whirled, temporarily forgetting about him to confront another attacker.

Nate scrambled to his feet, astounded to see Red Hawk beside the cradleboard, rocks held in each hand. He realized the Oglala had saved his life by throwing a rock at the panther, and he hoped to return the favor before the mountain lion sprang. Letting the rifle fall, he grabbed at his twin flintlocks, a hand closing on each one. But he was too late.

The cat hissed and leaped.

Red Hawk hurled both stones simultaneously even as he ducked low. Struck in the face, the mountain lion involuntarily jerked to the right, ruining the angle of its jump. It landed a yard shy of its intended victim and crouched, snarling savagely.

Nate wanted to shoot but couldn't. The cat was between Red Hawk and him, and there was the chance a ball would pass completely through the feline and hit the Sioux—or worse, the child. So he darted to the left to get a better shot.

Red Hawk was also in motion. He pivoted, clutched the cradleboard to his chest, and took off for the opposite side of the gully.

The lion roared and began to pursue him.

Finally Nate had the angle he wanted. He brought both flintlocks up, the hammers clicking as he cocked them, and squeezed both triggers at the same time. The smoothbore single-shot .55 caliber guns boomed louder than any rifle.

Two balls caught the big cat behind the left shoulder and bored deep into its body. It went down, rolling over and over, growling horribly, then stood upright with its face distorted in feral hatred. Blood oozed from the wounds, staining the beast's tawny hide a dark crimson.

Red Hawk reached the sheer gully wall and paused, seeking a way out. The child bawled in abject fright.

The mountain lion moved toward the Oglala and the baby.

There was no time for Nate to reload his pistols; he tossed them aside and drew his butcher knife, then ran to intercept the panther. A knife was no match for the cat's claws, but he would rather sell his life dearly than let the predator slay the infant. He vented a whoop that would have done justice to the fiercest Blackfoot who ever lived, trying to draw the cat's attention.

But the mountain lion ignored him. Instead, it crouched and coiled its mighty muscles for another leap at Red Hawk.

"No!" Nate shouted, afraid all his effort would be in vain. Then, from his rear, arose a series of low twangs, one after the other, at least a dozen in swift succession, and he heard a buzzing noise as slender shafts streaked past him to thud into the panther.

One moment the big cat was about to spring. The next, a dozen shafts protruded from its body and it was flipping wildly about, trying to tear out the offending arrows. It succeeded in breaking off two of them, but was unable to remove the barbed points imbedded in its sleek form. In a berserk fury it became a whirlwind of motion until, abruptly, it stiffened, vented a scream that sounded remarkably like that of a terrified woman, and collapsed on its side.

Yells of delight broke out behind Nate, and he turned to find over 20 Shoshone warriors spread out along the top of the earthen bank. Prominent among them were Spotted Bull and White Lynx, both holding bows. The warriors were all smiles, and those who had shot arrows were being clapped on the back and congratulated for a job well done. Nate slid his knife into its sheath, then faced the Oglala.

Red Hawk was walking toward him, the cradleboard nestled snugly in the crook of his left arm.

"Is the child all right?" Nate signed.

The Oglala held out the cradleboard so Nate could see for himself that the infant was unharmed and had stopped crying. There were teeth marks in the top of the cradleboard above the baby's hair, where the wood frame flared out to serve as a wide backrest for the child's head. Apparently the mountain lion had bitten into the cradleboard at just that one spot, its teeth missing the infant by less than an inch, when it carried the child to the gully.

Up close, Nate realized the baby was a little girl. He smiled and touched his finger to the child's cheek. She grinned, demonstrating the innate resilience of children to bounce back quickly from emotional distress. Where a minute earlier she had been crying, she now cooed happily. It made him think of the child Winona would soon deliver, and he longed to hold his own son or daughter in his arms.

"Is the baby hurt?" Spotted Bull called down.

Nate glanced around and shook his head out of force of habit. "No," he said. "She's fine, thanks to Red Hawk."

"I know," Spotted Bull said and bestowed a friendly smile on the Oglala. "We saw what he did."

Several of the warriors were moving south along the top of the gully, seeking an easy way down. They found a spot a dozen yards to the south where part of the bank had buckled, creating a gradual incline to the bottom. Yelling to the others, they descended.

Nate retrieved his pistols and wedged them under his belt. He was bending to pick up the Hawken when the Shoshones swarmed around him and Red Hawk, boisterously expressing their gratitude for saving the infant's life.

Suddenly White Lynx stepped in front of the Sioux and everyone else fell silent. He slung the bow over his left shoulder and coughed.

Red Hawk stood his ground, his features composed, the baby resting quietly in his arm.

Nate stared at the stocky Shoshone, wishing his guns were loaded. He wouldn't put it past White Lynx to start more trouble, and he wasn't about to let the man harass Red Hawk after what the Oglala had done.

"I arrived in time to see you try to save the child," White Lynx signed. He reached out, placed his right hand on Red Hawk's shoulder for a moment, and signed, "You are a good man, Dakota. I was wrong about you. Tonight I will say as much to the council and tell them of your deed."

Everyone else visibly relaxed.

White Lynx took Red Hawk by the arm and started to usher him from the gully when a lean warrior bounded up to the group and shoved his way through to the center. He was out of breath, his expression one of intense anxiety.

"My daughter?" he said.

Even though Red Hawk couldn't understand the words, he took one look at the man's face and extended the cradleboard toward him.

The newcomer took it and stared lovingly at the child. "You are safe," he said softly, almost choking on the words.

"Grizzly Killer and the Dakota saved her," White Lynx said. "Where were you, Tall Grass, when your daughter needed you the most?"

"I went to visit a friend on the other side of the village," the father said, leaning down to touch his nose to the little girl's. "I came as soon as someone told me."

"You should go show Clay Woman that your child is fine," Spotted Bull said. "She will be worried sick until you do."

"Yes, you are right," Tall Grass said absently and began to leave. He paused and gazed at Nate and Red Hawk. "Thank you," he said and his eyes brimmed with moisture. "I am forever in your debt." Then he spun around and hastened off.

The rest of the Shoshones started back. Four of them

picked up the mountain lion and brought up the rear. Nate fell in beside Red Hawk.

"It was too bad your clever trick did not work," the Dakota signed as they went up the incline.

"What trick was that?" Nate asked.

"I saw how you let the mountain lion get so close that you could not miss. I thought for sure you would kill it, but they can be very fast when they want to be."

"I noticed," Nate signed. He debated whether to admit the truth, to inform Red Hawk that he had frozen at a crucial moment, but decided against doing so. It was a personal matter, and he would deal with it in his own good time. Freezing when confronted with danger was not an uncommon experience. Any man might do so at one time or another. But if he did it again, if he found himself succumbing to inordinate fear on a regular basis, then he would have cause to worry greatly.

A large crowd of men, women, and children awaited the return of those who had hastened out to rescue the infant. The father became the center of attention as he and the mother tenderly clasped the child and received the heartfelt sympathies of their many friends and acquaintances. Averting the tragedy had put everyone in a good mood.

Nate received countless compliments, as did Red Hawk. Word of their battle with the mountain lion spread rapidly among the Shoshones, embellished, no doubt, in the telling, and Nate started to feel slightly embarrassed by the unwarranted attention. In one respect, though, he was delighted. Red Hawk had become the toast of the tribe, and not one Shoshone so much as gave him a hostile stare. It gave Nate cause to hope that all talk of killing the Sioux had died with the mountain lion.

After 20 minutes the Shoshones began to disperse. Spotted Bull led Nate and Red Hawk toward his lodge.

They covered only 30 yards when they saw Willow Woman hurrying in their direction.

"Grizzly Killer! You must come quickly!"

Alarmed, thinking that something must have happened to Winona or the baby, Nate ran to meet the young woman. "What is it?" he asked urgently.

"It is your wife. She is about to give birth."

Chapter Eleven

Give birth? Nate shook his head and said, "You must be mistaken. I left Winona a little while ago and she was fine. And the baby isn't due for fifteen sleeps or so yet."

"She is ready to have it now," Willow Woman said. "She sent me to find you because she knows you want to be with her when it happens."

Nate gazed northward in amazement, stunned by the realization that the blessed event he had been acutely dreading might actually be upon him.

"Sometimes babies drop early," Willow Woman said and motioned for him to get going. "Hurry. She can not hold it in forever."

"Hold it in?" Nate said and took off for the lodge as if a slavering grizzly was on his heels. In his mind's eye he conjured up an image of his wife gritting her teeth and clamping her legs together so the baby wouldn't pop out before he arrived. Surprised Shoshones glanced at him as he passed, but he ignored them. All he could think of was reaching his wife's side.

He half expected to find a small crowd gathered in front of Spotted Bull's lodge, or at the very least a few of the village women, but there was no one. It must be because most of the Shoshones had gone to see about Tall Grass's daughter, he reasoned, and covered the final 20 yards with the speed of a bounding antelope. The flap was open so he didn't bother with the social amenity of announcing his presence. He simply barged inside, then halted in astonishment.

Winona and Morning Dove were seated on the left side of the lodge, chatting. Neither appeared in the least bit agitated about the impending birth. They casually glanced up as he entered, and Winona smiled.

"I am glad you are here," she said.

Nate darted to her side. "Willow Woman told me you're about to have the baby."

"True," Winona said calmly.

"You can't be," Nate said, thinking that perhaps they had played a joke on him.

Winona's brow knit and she regarded him curiously. "I think I would know better than you."

"But why are you just sitting here? Where are the midwives? Shouldn't you be lying down? Shouldn't Morning Dove be boiling water?" Nate asked.

"Oh," Winona said in English and smiled. Then she changed to her own tongue again. "I have no need of a midwife. Morning Dove will prepare water for my cleansing while I am away. And I am sitting here waiting for you because walking would only hasten the birth."

Nate leaned over and studied her belly. "Are you certain now is the time?"

"Yes. The pains are very close now."

"Pains?" Nate said, aghast.

"Women experience regular pains before childbirth," Winona patiently explained. "Contractions deep inside."

"How soon will the baby be born?"

"As soon as you take me into the forest," Winona said and held up her right hand. "Please help me up."

"The forest?" Nate said. "Why can't you have it right here so Morning Dove can assist if necessary?"

"That is not our way. I am a grown woman and will drop the baby myself."

"But—" Nate began to protest, petrified at the idea of what might happen should he take her into the woods alone and a problem should arise.

"I have no time to discuss this," Winona said. "The pains are very close." She wagged her right hand. "Please help me up."

Swallowing hard, Nate dutifully complied, first leaning the Hawken against the lodge wall and then carefully lifting her to her feet. She immediately walked toward the entrance.

"Wait a minute," Nate said. "Shouldn't we take a medicine bag along or some blankets or a water bag or something?"

Winona sighed and stepped to a large buffalo robe that had been folded neatly and placed near the entrance. "This is all I will need. Please bring it."

"But—" Nate said, then hastened to the robe when she turned and walked out without waiting for him to finish. He started to follow, realized he had forgotten the Hawken, and dashed back to retrieve it. Morning Dove was looking at him as if he might be touched in the head. He grinned to show her he had everything under control, then whirled and ran outside, nearly colliding with Willow Woman, who had chosen that moment to return. "Sorry," he said and took off after his wife.

Winona was already ten yards to the east.

"Not so fast," Nate admonished her in English. "My guns aren't loaded. What if we run into a grizzly?"

"You can load them later," Winona said and walked

faster. Her mouth compressed into a thin line.

"Are you all right?" Nate asked anxiously, sticking close to her left side.

"As well as can be expected," Winona assured him in a strained tone. She abruptly grabbed hold of his arm for support. "I hope I have not waited too long, but I knew how much you wanted to be with me."

"I appreciate it," Nate said, almost wishing she had given birth while he was off fighting the mountain lion. His pulse raced, his mind whirled, and he couldn't seem to concentrate. He had never felt so nervous in all his born days. Whoever claimed having a child was easy had never known the torture a prospective father went through.

Winona picked up the pace, making a beeline through the lodges until they were out of the village. Then she headed for dense woodland.

Nate suspiciously scanned the wall of vegetation, dreading there might be hostile Indians out there, or maybe the mate of the panther he'd slain, or who knew what.

"We must find a sapling," Winona said.

"Why?" Nate asked, his attention focused on a bush that was shaking slightly. He gripped the hilt of his knife, then relaxed when a sparrow flew out of the bush.

"You will see," Winona told him. She placed both hands on her abdomen and grimaced. "We must hurry, husband, or I will have the baby right here."

Oh, Lord! Nate thought, and looked right and left as they entered the forest, seeking the type of tree she needed. But all the trees he saw were much older with thick trunks.

"Oh, my," Winona said softly. "Our baby is eager to enter this world."

Wait! Nate wanted to shout. For the love of God, please wait! He spied a sapling off to the left approximately 30 yards and steered Winona toward it. "There's one," he said. "Hang on. We're almost there."

"My legs are drenched," she said.

"Drenched? What do you mean by drenched?" Nate asked, fearing that she had accidentally urinated and the baby would be soiled.

"I will explain later," Winona said.

His heart pounding, Nate got her to the tree. She promptly gripped it with both hands, then glanced at him.

"Are you certain you want to see this?"

"Of course. I'm your husband. My place is right here with you," Nate assured her, although deep down he was terror-stricken. He recalled viewing the birth of a colt when he was eight or nine; he had nearly fainted from the sight. If he passed out on Winona, he'd never be able to hold his head high again.

"Please give me the robe."

"Here," Nate said, handing it to her. "Is there anything else I can do?"

"Not at the moment," Winona said, letting go of the sapling. She took the robe and spread it on the ground at the base of the tree, and as she unfolded it a small knife that had been wrapped inside rolled out.

"What's the knife for?" Nate inquired.

"You will see," Winona said, picking up the weapon and placing it at the edge of the robe. Then she raised her dress, pulling it above her waist, exposing her sleek thighs and her expanded belly.

Embarrassment assailed Nate. He glanced around, fearful of someone spotting them and beholding his wife's private parts. All he saw was a small finch flitting about in the trees, which reminded him that larger animals might well be prowling in the area. "I'm going to load my guns," he said.

Winona said nothing. She squatted and seized hold of the tree again, her knees outspread, her features etched in intense concentration, her bottom positioned over the soft robe.

Nate yanked the ramrod out of the Hawken, glad for the diversion. It gave him an excuse to take his mind and his eyes off the matter at hand. Working methodically, he measured out the proper amount of powder, fed it down the barrel, then wrapped a ball in a patch and rammed both into the rifle. Unable to take his eyes off Winona for very long, every 15 or 20 seconds he would glance at her. She continued to squat there, her chin bowed, her cheeks flushed. After a bit she commenced breathing loudly and regularly.

Why was she doing that? Nate wondered. He leaned the rifle against a nearby tree so he could load both flintlocks. The snap of a twig to his rear brought him around in alarm, but the cause turned out to be a chipmunk that took one look at him and fled as if a demon was on its heels. He swiftly finished with the two pistols and wedged them under his belt.

Winona gasped.

Nate faced her and saw her legs trembling, her bosom heaving as she began breathing even harder. Fascinated, he moved closer to be there if she needed him but she paid no attention. He wished he had asked more questions about the birth process. How long would it take? Did babies start crawling right away or did it take an hour or so for them to coordinate the movement of their limbs, as it did with certain farm animals? There was so much he didn't know and he regretted his ignorance.

Winona hunkered lower, her breaths loud enough now to be heard for yards. Her face was red and sweat beaded her brow.

"Anything I can do yet?" Nate asked on the off chance there might be. To his surprise, she ignored him. Feeling like a bump on a log, he surveyed the woods once more. Now there were three finches in a tree a few yards to the north. They were sitting quietly, staring at Winona as if equally fascinated by what was going on.

The breeze became stronger, stirring the leaves.

Nate rested his hands on the pistols and stepped nearer to Winona. He saw the muscles on her arms and legs quivering, saw her abdomen tightening, and realized she was straining with all of her might. The robe under her legs was wet, and a tangy scent unlike any he'd ever smelled tingled in his nostrils. To his great concern, Winona's breathing became even deeper.

A minute passed.

Two.

Five.

"Would you like some water?" Nate asked, anxious to do something. He began to doubt the wisdom of being by her side. What could he possibly accomplish that she couldn't? Maybe Lame Elk had been right. Giving birth should be a strictly feminine affair.

Again Winona made no comment, although she did look up for a few seconds and revealed her taut face and neck. Then she tucked her chin low and breathed with a rhythmic cadence.

Nate shifted uneasily, bothered by her silence. Was she mad at him, or was it simply hard for her to speak when she was focusing her entire energy on the birth? He gazed at her legs, then stiffened when he spied a dark object suspended from between them.

The baby!

He took a half-step and dropped to one knee. Sure enough, the top of a tiny head had poked out of the womb. The head was crowned with slick black hair, and the infant's face was as red as his Mackinaw coat. He couldn't determine if the baby's eyes were open yet or not, so he simply waved and beamed.

Suddenly voices sounded, coming from the direction of the village.

Spinning, Nate scanned the forest. He recognized the voices as female, and before long he spied three Shoshone women walking eastward, small baskets in their arms. Probably going to find herbs or roots, he guessed; by his estimation, the trio would pass within 15 feet of Winona. He stood and moved to intercept them.

One of the women spotted him and whispered to her companions. All three halted.

"Hello," Nate said, smiling to show he was friendly. He nodded at Winona. "My wife is having a baby. We need our privacy for the time being. Would you mind going well around us?"

The three Shoshones gazed past him, then talked excitedly. Finally, the shortest woman spoke. "Is your wife having a problem?"

"No. She is fine so far."

"Why are you here?"

"To do whatever I can," Nate said and became annoyed when they grinned and resumed whispering. "We really need to be by ourselves," he said and was grateful when they angled to the southeast and melted into the vegetation. They were bound to relate the encounter to their friends and relatives, and before long it would be common knowledge in the village. He might become the laughingstock of the tribe. But who cared? he asked himself. Winona was more important than idle gossip.

He heard Winona begin breathing in a nosier fashion, like a horse that had run five miles nonstop, and turned back in time to see the baby's head appear. Entranced, he edged closer. That was when he registered movement at the periphery of his vision and glanced to the north to discover the coyote.

Chapter Twelve

Nate jerked both flintlocks out and trained them on the slinking beast. He knew that coyotes sometimes hung around the outskirts of Indian villages in the hope of obtaining food. They would eat practically anything, and when butchered animal carcasses were tossed into the weeds, as often happened, the coyotes were there to gulp down whatever remained. And when the lodges were struck and a village moved on, coyotes frequently checked the campsite for edible scraps left behind or deliberately dumped.

This one happened to be a large male. It was wending through the undergrowth, fixedly gazing at Winona. Fifteen yards off the coyote halted.

Nate had never heard of coyotes attacking people and he was at a loss to explain the beast's behavior. With Winona preoccupied and unable to protect herself, he didn't want the coyote anywhere in the area. Wagging the pistols, he dashed toward it in an attempt to scare it off, not harm it.

The coyote held its ground for all of two seconds, then wheeled and sped off, its bushy tail held level with its body.

Stopping, Nate waited until the beast was gone before sticking the flintlocks under his brown belt and returning to his wife. Her entire body trembled from her supreme exertion. He moved to the left a bit for a better view of the baby and squatted.

The infant's head, neck, and a trace of its shoulders were out of Winona's womb, suspended just above the soft buffalo robe which was drenched by her fluids. The baby's eyes were closed, and it breathed shallowly.

Nate studied his offspring intently, mesmerized. He hadn't realized how small the child would be. Everything about it was tiny: tiny nose, tiny mouth, tiny ears, tiny hands, tiny fingers. It seemed so fragile that he was amazed it could survive the ordeal. His heart went out to the little treasure and joy filled him. Soon, if nothing went wrong, he would be a proud father, and he couldn't wait to hold the baby in his arms.

Was it a boy or a girl? He leaned forward, unable to determine the sex from the countenance or the small amount of hair. Winona was grunting, her eyes shut tight, oblivious to the world around her. He wanted to touch her, to let her know he was right there, but he was afraid the innocent gesture might break her concentration. A slight squishing noise drew his eyes to the baby, who had emerged a hair farther. The shoulders appeared to be wedged fast.

Winona began panting and rested her forehead on her forearm. Sweat coated her face and dripped from her legs. She spoke, the words almost inaudible, getting a word or two out between each pant. "Are you still here, husband?"

"No, I went to the lodge. Lame Elk and I are sitting around talking about the good old days," Nate said, grinning. "Need you ask?"

"Thank you."

"For what?"

"For you."

"I don't understand. What did I do?"

"How is the baby?"

"Fine, as near as I can tell," Nate said.

Nate glanced at the quietly resting infant. He wondered if Winona was aware that most of the baby was still up inside her. "Uh, dearest, there's something you should know."

"What?"

"The baby isn't all the way out yet."

"I know."

"You do? Then why have you stopped?" Nate asked. He blinked in bewilderment when she lifted her head and gave him a look capable of withering a plant at ten paces.

Winona sighed, adjusted her grip on the sapling, and strained.

Cocking his head, Nate watched the rest of the birth. Her thighs quivered and more fluid came out as the baby's shoulders slowly eased nearly all the way from her womb. She halted again, inhaling and gathering her strength, and when next she applied herself she wheezed mightily. He heard a plop as the shoulders finally slipped free, and he saw the infant slide onto the robe on its back.

It was a boy!

The word rang in Nate's head like the clanging of the church bell on a bright Sunday morning back in New York City. He almost laughed aloud in delight at the sight of the baby. In every respect the child was an exquisite copy of himself, although he noted definite traces of Winona's ancestry in the boy's face. He was amazed at how fragile and vulnerable newborn infants were, even more so than the colt he'd seen being born, and he pondered how dependent the child would be on Winona and him during his first few years of life.

What was that? Nate wondered when, to his surprise, he noticed a rope-like cord extending from the baby's stomach up into Winona. Then he realized it was the umbilical cord. Fortunately, the cord wasn't wrapped around the infant's neck, as occasionally happened. If it had been, his child might have emerged from the womb dead or been strangled during birth. Nate shuddered at the thought.

He emerged from his revery and realized that Winona wasn't done.

He listened to her grunt as she worked her stomach and leg muscles anew. The umbilical cord inched a bit lower, then stopped descending. Her whole body shook, yet still the cord hung in place. To him, it seemed as if it was taking her longer to drop the cord than the baby.

"Nate?"

"It's a boy," he told her proudly.

"A boy?" Winona asked. "The Great Medicine has been kind to us. The next time, though, I want a girl." She suddenly groaned.

Nate glanced up, saw his wife looking at him, and was shocked at the utter exhaustion he read in her drooping eyes and the deep lines in her face. "Yes?"

"I need your help."

"You do?" Nate said, confounded by the request. What in the world could he do to assist at this stage of the birth? A disturbing possibility occurred to him and his gaze dropped to between her legs.

"Pull it out."

"Me?"

"It is stuck."

"Me?"

"Is our son sitting up yet?"

"No."

"Then it must be you," Winona said wearily. "I am

tired, Nate. So tired. Please. We can go back once it is done and I can rest."

"I'd rather not."

"Is the great Grizzly Killer afraid?"

"Scared to death," Nate said and reluctantly bent forward, his hair brushing her leg as he tentatively reached under her to gently grasp the spongy umbilical cord. Her sweet scent engulfed him. Queasiness flooded through him and he clamped his mouth shut to prevent the contents of his stomach from mixing with the puddle of blood and other fluid already soaking into the robe. The touch of the cord brought gooseflesh to every square inch of his skin.

"Pull slowly," Winona cautioned. "Do not break it."

"Lord, help me," Nate said, and did as she wanted, terrified of making a mistake and snapping the cord in half. If the afterbirth didn't come out, she might sicken and die. It had happened to other women, which was why doctors took such careful pains to guarantee every last bit was removed.

"Slowly," Winona said again.

As if pulling on the delicate stem of a flower, Nate gently applied enough force to draw the cord slowly lower. Inch by gradual inch, it came out. Suddenly the cord stopped. Deep inside her the afterbirth had encountered an obstruction or was somehow snagged. He tugged lightly, but the cord wouldn't budge.

"What has happened?" Winona asked.

"I don't rightly know," Nate said, feeling sweat form under his arms. "It's stuck again. Maybe I should run to the village and get Morning Dove or Willow Woman."

"And leave our son and me here alone?"

Nate frowned at his stupidity. "No, I guess not."

"Keep trying. I trust you."

"Thanks," Nate said, wishing he trusted his own ability half as much as she did. He lay on his stomach and reached higher, grasping the cord just below her body, his fingers brushing against her as he pulled once more. The added leverage helped. Abruptly, the umbilical cord eased out and brought with it the rest of the afterbirth, falling clear of her body onto his right hand. He brought his arm out from under her and stared in horrified astonishment at the eerie mass clinging to his flesh. For a few moments he felt dizzy and worried he might humiliate himself by fainting.

"It's out, isn't it?" Winona asked.

Nate went to answer but his mouth was completely dry. The best he could do was imitate a tree frog.

"What?" Winona said. "Can you see the afterbirth? Is it out?"

"It's out," Nate managed to say.

"Are you all right?"

"Never better," Nate fibbed and placed the afterbirth on the robe. He rose, his knees unsteady, and mechanically brushed dirt and bits of grass from his buckskins.

Winona, her features contorted, painfully straightened until her knees audibly popped. As she moved haltingly to one side, her dress fell down around her ankles. She gazed down at the baby, happiness replacing her discomfort. "Our son," she said with pride.

"Want me to carry him back?" Nate said.

"There is something I must do first," Winona said and sank to her knees beside the baby. She caressed its cheeks and head, cooing tenderly in Shoshone, then traced a finger around the umbilical cord where it was attached to the child's abdomen.

Mystified, Nate watched her examine the cord. All was explained the instant she picked up the small knife she had brought along. "Are you fixing to cut the cord?" he asked.

"Unless you would rather do it?"

"Go ahead," Nate said and casually placed a hand

over his mouth to be on the safe side. The vertigo struck him again when she started to slice and he had to turn away to suppress another bout of sickness. His whole body shuddered. He didn't dare risk a peek as she finished her task. A minute went by.

"Here. You can hold him now."

Nate turned, relieved to see that she had swaddled their son in a clean corner of the buffalo robe. The rest of the robe dangled underneath. He took the bundle in his arms, amazed at how dainty the child was, and felt unbridled love course through his being for his wife and the new pride of their life. At that moment, in that time and place, in that heartbeat of eternity, his love was pure and absolute, bordering on reverence. Was this how every new father felt?

Using the tree for support, Winona stood. "We must hurry," she said. "He must be bathed and wrapped in a clean blanket before he becomes sick."

"Lean on me," Nate told her. She put her left hand on his shoulder and took a step that any self-respecting snail could have beaten. "You were magnificent," he complimented her, staying by her side as she walked westward.

Winona beamed. "So were you. I am glad you insisted on being there. If you had not been, I would never have gotten the afterbirth out."

"You'll be fine once you've rested," Nate said and twisted his head to peck her on the cheek. "I've never seen anyone work so hard at anything. You must want to sleep around the clock."

"No, although you would think that would be the case," Winona said. "My strength is returning quickly. By tomorrow I will be up and about as if nothing had happened."

"Don't push yourself," Nate cautioned and glanced at the baby. Something about the child was different, and it wasn't until the infant blinked that he realized his son's eyes were open. "Look," he exclaimed. "His eyes are brown."

Winona stared affectionately at their offspring and rested her head on Nate's broad shoulder. "We must select a name for him."

"So soon?"

"It is the custom of my people to pick a name before a sleep has gone by," Winona said, then tilted her head upward. "I did not think to ask. Do you want to give him a Shoshone name or a white man's name?"

"Why not both?"

"A fine idea," Winona said. "Then he will be at home in both worlds." She straightened and surveyed the forest around them, a shadow creeping over her face. "I see nothing worth naming a son after, not even an animal."

"Too bad you weren't paying attention while you were giving birth," Nate said. "A coyote tried to sneak up on you but I chased the critter off."

"A coyote?"

"Yep. One of the biggest male coyotes I've ever laid eyes on," Nate confirmed.

"It is an omen."

"What?"

Winona laughed and squeezed his arm in her gaiety. "A sign from the Everywhere Spirit. Don't you see, husband? We are supposed to name our son Sneaking Coyote."

Nate snorted. "Like hell we will."

"I beg your pardon?"

"No son of mine is going around with a name that implies he skulks about like a thief in the night," Nate said. "I don't mind the Coyote part, but the first half has to go." He pondered for a minute. "How about Stalking Coyote? It has a ring to it, just like a warrior's name should."

"Stalking Coyote," Winona repeated, rolling the

words on her tongue. "Yes, I like it very much. But what about his other name?"

"It goes without saying that his last name will be King," Nate noted. "As for his first name, there is one I've been partial to ever since I was a boy."

"What is it?"

"Orville."

Winona scrunched up her nose as if she'd inhaled a bitter odor. "Orville?"

"Yes. What's wrong with it?"

"It is difficult to describe. The best I can do is say it offends my ears. Perhaps you should pick another name."

"I've always liked Orville."

"Please. I agreed to change when you were upset."

"True," Nate said, racking his brain for another name worthy of being bestowed on their son. Finally the perfect choice occurred to him. "I have another suggestion. It was the name of my great-great-grandfather, and I like it almost as much as I do Orville."

"What is this one?" Winona asked uncertainly.

"Zachary."

"I like it," Winona said without hesitation. "Zachary King is a fine name."

"Then we're agreed," Nate said and lifted their child higher so he could lightly kiss the boy on the forehead. "Zachary King and Stalking Coyote it is. Now let's go introduce you to your mother's people."

"Yours also, husband."

Chapter Thirteen

The next three days were some of the happiest of Nate's entire life. He basked in the profound happiness of having a new son, and took great comfort in the steady string of well-wishers who stopped by Spotted Bull's lodge to relay their congratulations and kind regards. The Shoshones revered all life, as did most Indian tribes, and they took particular delight in newborns. They saw spirit omens in everything, and infants, especially male infants, were regarded as confirmation of the Everywhere Spirit's blessing.

The birth of Stalking Coyote, following as it did so closely on the heels of the incident with the mountain lion, convinced the Shoshones that Nate was a man who brought good fortune on himself and others. Several prominent warriors told him outright that he possessed great medicine, and he basked in their esteem and good will.

To make matters complete, Nate was elated when the council decided to let Red Hawk stay at the village for as long as he wanted. The leaders of the tribe had decided that any man willing to risk his life to save a Shoshone child was a true friend of their people. Spotted Bull insisted on permitting Red Hawk to stay with him.

So on the fourth day Nate sat outside of the lodge, feeling the warmth of the morning sun on his face, and counted himself fortunate at the way things had worked out. He had a new son, a new friend, and a new appreciation of the Shoshones. After their marvelous display of friendship, he felt more at home among them than he ever had before. He heard footsteps, and around the corner came his host and the Oglala. "How do you like your new horses?" he inquired using sign.

"They are fine animals," Red Hawk replied in kind and looked at Spotted Bull. "I appreciate your generosity, but I will never be able to give you a gift of equal value."

"A gift should never be given with thought of a reward," Spotted Bull said. "And you will need horses if you hope to have your own lodge."

"What is this?" Nate asked.

Red Hawk took a seat. "I cannot stay in Spotted Bull's lodge forever. It would be unfair to his family." He gazed out over the lake. "I have been giving the matter much thought, and I have decided to live among the Shoshones until my breath fades away on the wind. They have accepted me without question. They have given me the chance to start my life over. To do that, I need my own lodge. Only then can I hope to acquire a wife."

"A lodge will be easy to make once you have enough buffalo hides and poles," Nate said.

"A man can get poles any time," Red Hawk signed. "Buffalo hides take longer to collect. First enough buffalo must be slain, and hunting them down one or two at a time could take two moons or more."

"I know," Nate said. Buffalo tended to take flight at the first sight or scent of humans. Once a hunter loosed an arrow or fired a shot, the rest of any given herd would pound off into the distance as fast as their heavy legs would take them. So when a man needed to kill more than one, he had to take companions along and hope each was lucky; or he could spend weeks stalking any buffalo he spied, but this method was a tedious and not infrequently futile exercise. Because even if the hunt did score a hit, there was no guarantee the buffalo would fall. Buffalo were exceptionally hardy animals, almost as hard to kill as grizzlies. There had been verified instances where a buffalo bristling with a dozen arrows or pierced by five to ten balls had fled and eluded the hapless men after it.

Nate didn't envy Red Hawk his task. Slaying buffalo was only the first step in going about making a lodge. Depending on the projected size of the structure, a dozen or more large hides might be required and each one had to be meticulously skinned from the carcass, then diligently prepared to make it waterproof yet resilient.

"I know of a way you can obtain all the hides you might need at one time," Spotted Bull signed.

"How?" Red Hawk asked.

"Join us in a surround."

In all the excitement of the past few days, Nate had completely forgotten about the planned surround. The reminder jarred him. He felt certain that Spotted Bull would again ask him to go along, and this time he couldn't plead his son's birth as an excuse. He still didn't want to participate in the hunt. Unfortunately, since surrounds were considered tests of bravery and skill, any man who repeatedly refused to go on one stood the risk of having his manhood questioned. If he was to decline graciously again, he must have a legitimate excuse for not going. He listened attentively to their conversation.

"I have been on surrounds before," Red Hawk said. "They are grisly business. Many of your warriors might die."

"We are aware of the risks," Spotted Bull said. "The Oglalas are not the only people who know how to properly hunt buffalo."

"When are you leaving?" Red Hawk asked.

"In two or three sleeps."

Red Hawk reflected for a moment. "All right. I will go with you. Perhaps, if I am lucky, I will kill many buffalo and my lodge will be completed that much sooner."

"We will be glad to have you ride with us," Spotted Bull said. "And I would not worry much about the danger. So many good omens have taken place in the past few days that every warrior in our village is confident this will be the best surround we have ever taken part in."

"I pray you are right," Red Hawk said.

Spotted Bull glanced at Nate. "The hunt would go all that much better if the man many believe carries good fortune on his shoulders would come with us."

An icy finger stabbed into Nate's chest. He knew the Shoshone was referring to him, and he deliberately stared at a snowcapped mountain situated north of the encampment to give the false impression that he wasn't paying attention.

"Grizzly Killer?" Spotted Bull said aloud.

Nate's heart sank. He couldn't avoid the inevitable. "Yes?" he answered, facing his host.

"Now that your son has been born, would you agree to accompany myself and the other warriors who are going on the surround? We would be very honored," Spotted Bull signed.

Nate suppressed an automatic impulse to frown. There was no way out. If he declined, by nightfall every man in the tribe would know. He would be the main topic of discussion around every lodge fire, with everyone in the village speculating on the reason for his refusal. They might doubt his bravery, or they might mistakenly believe that he knew something they didn't, that he had experienced a dire premonition and expected the hunting party to meet with disaster. They would take the refusal as a bad omen. His future relations with the tribe could be severely jeopardized by his answer, and he disliked being put on the spot. He tried not to let his resentment show as he replied, "I would be delighted to go with you."

Spotted Bull grinned. "This is great news. Excuse me while I go inform the others who are going." He headed off at a brisk clip, saying over his shoulder, "I would not be surprised if more warriors decided to go once they learn you will be along."

Nate plastered a phony smile on his face until the Shoshone was out of sight. He glanced at Red Hawk and found the Oglala studying him critically. "You have something to say?" Nate signed.

"If you do not want to go, why not tell Spotted Bull the truth?"

"Is it that obvious?" Nate asked.

"To me," Red Hawk signed. "Even though I have not known you long, I feel as if I know you as well as I do my own brother."

"You have a brother?"

"Two. Both married with children."

"Do you miss them?"

"Of course," Red Hawk signed. "We were always in each other's company. In our childhood we played, rode horses, and practiced with weapons together. When we became grown men we hunted, went on raids, and even took our brides at the same time so we could be married together." He smiled wistfully. "I miss them most of all."

"Maybe one day you will see them again," Nate said.

"If I do, they would be forced to slay me. An outcast who tries to return is always put to death. They could not spare me because we are related."

Nate felt a burning curiosity to inquire about the specific details behind his friend's expulsion, but he wisely refrained. "I am glad things have worked out for you here," he said. "You have a new home. The Shoshones accept you as one of their own, so your wandering days are over."

"And I owe it all to you," Red Hawk signed.

From inside the lodge arose light feminine laughter. Nate glanced at the closed flap and mulled over how best to inform Winona of his upcoming departure. The direct approach would only upset her. He had to exercise tact.

Red Hawk stood. "I am going to take another walk around the village," he signed. "After being alone for so long, I find that I like to mingle with people more than I ever did." He surveyed the village, his eyes alight with contentment. "These are my people now, and I must get to know them like I know my own."

"Enjoy yourself," Nate said and watched the warrior stroll away. He shoved to his feet, stepped to the lodge, and slapped the flap. "It's me," he called out in English. "Are all of you decent?"

"What a silly question," Winona said. "Shoshone women are not like the Otos. We do not sit around naked in our lodges. Come in, husband."

Nate entered. His wife sat to the left, cradling little Zachary King in her arms. The baby had been bundled in a blanket, leaving only the top of his head visible. Morning Dove was busy at the cooking pot, while

Willow Woman was sorting through a parflache in the far corner. He walked over and sat down next to Winona. "How is our son?"

"Sleeping soundly," Winona said and parted the blanket to reveal Zachary's tranquil features. She tenderly stroked the infant's rounded chin. "Would you care to hold him?"

"He looks comfortable right where he is," Nate said, glad they could speak English and not be understood by the other women. "I don't want to wake him up." He leaned closer, proudly examining their son's face, and said softly, "Stalking Coyote is in perfect health, isn't he?"

"Yes," Winona said. "We have been blessed with a fine son. He hasn't cried once yet."

"When they're this age," Nate said, "taking care of them is easy. One parent can do it with no problem."

Winona regarded him thoughtfully for a full 15 seconds before she asked, "What are you getting at?"

"I have something to tell you," Nate said, refusing to meet her probing gaze. He should have known she would realize he was beating around the bush. Now he must come right out with it. The thought of deserting her so soon after their son had been born racked him with guilt. At least, he rationalized, she would be among relatives and friends, so it wasn't the same as when he occasionally left her alone at their cabin to go off trapping or whatever.

Winona waited expectantly.

"Spotted Bull asked me to go on the surround," Nate said.

"What did you tell him?"

"What could I tell him?" Nate asked, finally looking at her. "I told him I would go."

Anxiety lined Winona's countenance. "I do not like it," she said flatly. "You have never been on a surround before. It's not fair that they should want you to go when our son was born just a few days ago."

"I agree, but there's nothing I can do."

Winona placed a hand on his shoulder. "You can let him know you have changed your mind. Wait until tomorrow and tell him you had a bad dream while you slept. Tell him that you saw yourself being gored. He will understand."

"I would be lying," Nate said. "And I have already given my word. There is no way out. When the warriors leave on the great hunt, I'll be with them."

"And if something happens to you? What will I do then?"

"Take good care of our son," Nate said and felt her fingers dig into him. He placed a hand on hers and patted it. "Don't worry. I'm not about to make you a widow after all the trouble you went through."

"No man can predict his time," Winona said.

"You sure know how to cheer a man up," Nate said, trying to make light of the situation, hoping to bring a smile to her lips. Instead, she scowled.

"I am not trying to cheer you up. I am trying to convince you that you are taking your life in your hands if you go," Winona said earnestly. "I lost a cousin and two close friends to surrounds when I was a girl, and I have never forgotten the way their bodies looked after the buffalo were done with them."

"I can imagine," Nate said. He touched her cheek and kissed her. "Mark my words, dearest. If it's humanly possible, I will return."

Refusing to be comforted, Winona held their son to her bosom and said sadly, "Words are no match for buffalo horns."

Chapter Fourteen

Two days later 41 riders rode eastward from Clear Lake. Forty were in exuberant spirits, talking and laughing and singing, while one rode in somber silence at the head of the band wishing he was somewhere else. Most of the villagers turned out for the departure, with the women waving and smiling and the children dashing playfully around the mounted men.

Nate would never forget the haunted aspect to Winona's eyes as she bid him farewell. He got the impression she never expected to see him again, although she had never come right out and said so. For the better part of 48 hours she had moped around the lodge, her usual cheerful disposition replaced by moody preoccupation with the surround.

And she hadn't been the only one.

Nate had noticed both Morning Dove and Willow Woman become unusually taciturn the closer it grew to the appointed time for leaving. Morning Dove's attitude he could comprehend; she was concerned about Spotted Bull. But Willow Woman's melancholy had puzzled him at first. He'd attributed her feelings to her affection for her father, although at times she seemed even more upset than her mother. Then he'd seen Willow Woman and Red Hawk strolling along the lake, their shoulders occasionally brushing together as they chatted amiably, the one always glancing at the other when the other wasn't looking, and he could have slapped himself for being such a dunderhead.

Afterwards, he noticed other things. Such as how Willow Woman had taken to doting over Red Hawk, giving him extra portions at meal times and preparing his bedding at night. She was even sewing a pair of leggings for him. And once, when Nate unexpectedly entered the lodge, he caught them kissing. No one else had been there at the time, and he had quickly backed out.

The only one Nate told about his discovery was Winona, and she had actually grinned and asked why it had taken so long for him to see the obvious. Apparently everyone else in the lodge knew of the budding romance, which had Spotted Bull's blessing. The Shoshone had taken Red Hawk under his wing and regarded him as a second son.

The first son, Touch The Clouds, showed up at the lodge the day before the 40 warriors were to leave for the surround. He had been off hunting elk with friends and consequently learned of the encounter with the mountain lion after his return. He'd immediately gone to his father's lodge to pay his respects to the famous Grizzly Killer and the Oglala.

Of all the men Nate had ever met, Touch The Clouds was the biggest. A veritable giant, standing close to seven feet tall and endowed with a powerful physique, Touch The Clouds appeared capable of fighting a grizzly with his bare hands and emerging triumphant.

When he entered a lodge he had to squeeze through the entrance, and if he was to straighten too quickly, he often bumped his head. When he rode his warhorse, it was as if he rode a pony even though his splendid black stallion was larger than any other horse in the camp. His war club was three times the size of those carried by his fellow warriors, and his bow could shoot twice as far. His lance resembled a lodge pole. All in all, it was no wonder that Touch The Clouds was widely regarded as the single bravest warrior in the Shoshone nation although he had yet to count as many coup as some of the older men.

Now Nate rode between the giant on his left and Spotted Bull on his right. Behind them came Red Hawk, White Lynx, and Drags The Rope. The rest of the hunters were clustered in groups and strung out over 50 yards to the rear.

"Where should we seek the herds, father?" Touch The Clouds asked.

Spotted Bull, as befitted his status as the leader of the hunters, was responsible for making the major decisions pertaining to their course of travel and the sites they would select as their nightly camps. He scratched his chin, his brow knit in thought. "I told Broken Paw that we would head toward the Greasy Grass River country. Buffalo are always plentiful there at this time of the year."

"So are the Arapaho, Cheyenne, and Crow," Touch The Clouds said.

"We will stay to the west of their usual hunting grounds," Spotted Bull said. "If the Everywhere Spirit smiles on us, we will not run into them. And once the rest of our people have established a village in the foothills, there will be so many of us that the Arapahos, Cheyennes, and Crows dare not attack."

Nate tensed and glanced at him. "What is this about the rest of your people?"

"Surely someone told you," Spotted Bull said. "Those we left behind will strike camp tomorrow morning, and within six or seven sleeps they will have set up a new village near the area where we will be hunting."

"Everyone will come there?"

"Of course."

Flabbergasted, Nate stared straight ahead. No one had bothered to mention the entire village would move to be closer to the surround. Winona had not said a word, either because she'd believed he would object to her being in close proximity to hostile territory or because, like the rest of her tribe, she had taken it for granted that he would know the whole tribe would relocate.

"Why are you so surprised?" Spotted Bull asked.

"No one bothered to tell me," Nate said lamely.

"Who do you think will butcher the buffalo we slay?" Touch The Clouds said. "Warriors don't do the work of women. By moving the village to the foothills, the women will be near at hand when the surround is over and can skin the animals on the spot."

"We go ahead of the main camp because such a large number of people often scares the buffalo away," Spotted Bull said. "We will find a herd the proper size and keep watch over it until the village is in place. If the buffalo wander, we will keep track of where they go." He paused. "A surround must be well thought out or it will fail."

"So I see," Nate said. He made a mental note to have a long talk with Winona once they were reunited.

"I hope to take fifteen buffalo, at least," Touch The Clouds said. "I can use a new lodge."

"The one you have now is only two winters old," Spotted Bull said.

"And already it shows signs of wear and has been repaired in several spots," Touch The Clouds said.

Spotted Bull looked at Nate. "Perhaps Lame Elk was right," he said, his eyes twinkling.

Nate politely smiled, his mind not on their discussion. All he could think of was the fact that they were going to enter the hunting grounds traditionally used by the tribes who dwelled on the Plains, and how the Arapahos and others were bound to resent the intrusion. He wasn't as optimistic as Spotted Bull; if something could go wrong, it invariably did. Which meant the Shoshones might find themselves embroiled in tribal warfare with one of the powerful nations inhabiting the region adjacent to the Greasy Grass River. He didn't like the idea one bit.

"I will be content with one buffalo," Spotted Bull said. "I have it in my heart to give Morning Dove a new robe as a gift, and the wife of a friend has agreed to make it if I supply the hide." He grinned. "Morning Dove will be very surprised."

"You're going on a surround for just one robe?" Nate asked in disbelief.

"It is part of my plan."

"I do not understand."

"If I were to go off hunting buffalo by myself, Morning Dove might guess that I intend to give her a new robe," Spotted Bull said. "This way, she will have no idea. It would never occur to her that I would go on a surround just to obtain a single hide."

"Nor anyone else," Nate said dryly.

"I am proud of you, father," Touch The Clouds said. "It is a kind gesture. I hope my wife and I are still as much in love when we are your age."

"Never take your wife for granted," Spotted Bull said, "never let her take you for granted, and your marriage will last until you are both gray-haired and ready to depart this world."

Nate absently bobbed his chin in agreement. He'd never discussed marriage with a warrior before and found the insights fascinating. "I agree with you. But there are other factors that go into making a successful marriage."

"True," Spotted Bull said. "Loyalty, a calm tongue, and a sense of humor."

"A sense of humor?"

"People who cannot laugh at their own mistakes take themselves far too seriously to be able to get along well with others. Life was meant for laughing."

"Never thought of it that way."

"I think loyalty is the most important," Touch The Clouds said. "Without loyalty, a couple will quickly drift apart. If the man's eyes stray to other women and the wife's to other men, they might as well not get married."

"Their eyes would not stray if they would remember that the true beauty of a person is not found on the outside, but deep inside. When I was a young married man and I found myself looking at another pretty woman, thinking of how nice it would be to lie with her under my robe, I always reminded myself that I already had a woman who kept me warm at night and she did not mind touching my cold feet."

Nate laughed heartily. For the next several hours he conversed with the Shoshones about everything from proper hunting techniques to ways to determine changes in the weather. At midday Spotted Bull called a halt on the bank of a stream and the warriors watered their mounts. Drags The Rope walked up to Nate as he was checking the cinch on his saddle.

"This will be a fine hunt, my friend. I had a dream last night that I killed nine buffalo."

"I am eager to find the herd," Nate said, neglecting to mention that he was also eager to get the surround over with so he could spend time with Winona and Zachary.

"If I do well, it will greatly impress Singing Bird,"

Drags The Rope said. "She will gladly give her word to marry me." He paused. "I have wanted to ask you about Shakespeare. I thought the two of you were inseparable. Where is he?"

"He went and got himself married to a Flathead woman. I haven't seen him in a while, but when this is over I intend to swing by his cabin and see if he's back home yet."

Drags The Rope smirked. "Shakespeare too. I guess the saying is true."

"What saying?"

"A warrior is never too old to be stung by a bee while collecting honey."

Soon they were back on their horses and heading ever eastward, wending among stark, towering peaks that seemed to touch the pillowy white clouds floating far overhead. They traversed lush valleys, crossed grassy meadows, and skirted high ridges. The Rocky Mountain wildlife, as always, was abundant, and they spotted scores of deer and elk, as well as smaller game such as rabbits, squirrels, and chipmunks.

By the end of the first day Nate began to thoroughly enjoy himself. Or at least, he tried to. But every time he let himself get into the spirit of things, guilt at being away from his family would spoil his good mood. He kept thinking of Winona, who undoubtedly was miserable, pining for him back at the village, and he couldn't bring himself to be happy when he knew she wasn't. Then he would become involved in a lively discussion and forget all about her until he had a spare moment to reflect and realized his oversight, at which point he would be racked with guilt again.

Since he wasn't selected to pull sentry duty, Nate slept soundly the whole night through, exhausted more by his emotional turmoil than the many hours in the saddle. He was roused out of slumber the next morning by Drags The Rope, and together they shuffled to the stream to drink and splash frigid water on their faces. It was the part of traveling that Nate liked the least. There was something about being transformed into gooseflesh the first thing in the morning that smacked of outright torture.

After a breakfast of jerked venison and pemmican, the Shoshones resumed their journey. Nate noticed that the warriors were not quite as lighthearted as the day before. Indeed, the closer they drew to prime buffalo country, which also happened to be the hunting grounds of their many enemies, the more subdued the Shoshones became. By the afternoon of the second day, Spotted Bull had selected four men to ride half a mile ahead of the main group. He was taking no chances.

Nate got to know other warriors quite well. There was Little Beaver, who stood only an inch over five feet but could shoot an arrow with uncanny precision. There was Worm, who had lost his left ear and half of his face to a grizzly. And there was Lone Wolf, who had three wives and was considering taking another.

From his talks, Nate learned that about half of the Shoshone men had more than one wife. The shortage of warriors was the main reason; there simply weren't enough men to go around. Many of the men, though, such as Spotted Bull, disliked the idea of having two or three wives and steadfastly refused to do so. Which pleased Lone Wolf no end, because then there were more women to go around to those warriors who wanted them.

That afternoon, as they ascended a low hill, Lone Wolf turned to Nate in all earnestness and said, "You should take another wife or two for your own. You will be a happier man if you do."

"You think so?" Nate said, suppressing a grin.

"Most definitely," Lone Wolf said. "Think of the benefits. Your lodge will always be clean and kept in perfect condition. The women will compete with each other to see who can make you the best food. And at night, there will always be at least one who is in the mood for love." He grinned. "I could never go back to having one wife now that I know the joys of having three."

"You are a braver man than I am," Nate said.

"What do—" Lone Wolf began, then stopped speaking and reined up sharply.

Nate automatically did the same. He saw that Spotted Bull had halted and was peering intently to the northwest.

Not a quarter of a mile away was another large band of Indians.

Chapter Fifteen

All the Shoshones came to a stop.

Nate shielded his eyes from the bright sun with his left hand, trying to identify the other party. They were too far off for him to note much detail except that they were on foot. He hoped—he prayed—they weren't Blackfeet.

"Bloods," Touch The Clouds said.

"Twenty-four of them," Drags The Rope added.

The news caused Nate's pulse to quicken. The Bloods were allies of the Blackfeet, who enjoyed a fierce reputation in their own right. He'd tangled with them once before and barely escaped with his hide.

"They have seen us," Spotted Bull said.

The Bloods were aligned in the formation they typically used when a war party was on the march. They stood in a single file arranged in the shape of a crescent with the central arc out in front of the curved arms. They were crossing the open slope of a mountain; in another minute, they would have been into dense forest.

"Our scouts missed seeing them," Touch The Clouds said.

"They were probably not in sight when our scouts went over this hill," Spotted Bull said. He twisted to scan the rest of the Shoshones, his face alight with excitement. "This is an opportunity we cannot let pass. We outnumber them, and we have horses. They will not be able to run away. I say we attack them and take as many scalps as we can."

"Yes!" Touch The Clouds said, hefting his huge lance.

Nate looked at the others, hoping a voice of reason would be raised. But the warriors all vented whoops of joy at the prospect of bloody battle. Wildly waving their weapons in the air, they worked themselves into a fever pitch. He wondered whether he should object, reminding them that they were after buffalo hides, not scalps.

With a strident shriek, Spotted Bull urged his horse down the hill, leading the charge. The rest of the Shoshones fell in behind him, forming a screeching mass of bloodthirsty riders each anxious to claim the first coup.

Nate found himself left behind. He goaded the stallion into a run, trailing the rest by ten yards or more, firming his grip on the Hawken. The ground was rough, dotted with fallen trees and lined with shallow gullies. He had to concentrate exclusively on avoiding all obstacles and keeping the Shoshones in sight, and before he knew it they were almost to the mountain slope. He looked up to find that the Bloods had disappeared into the trees, where they would be able to give a good account of themselves, and he dreaded a slaughter if the Shoshones rode into a hail of arrows.

Spotted Bull apparently had the same thought. He

angled into the forest well below the spot where the Bloods had been and promptly slowed. The other warriors fanned out, forming a skirmish line, staying on their horses so they could see farther even though it made them better targets.

Nate caught up with them shortly after they spread out. He took up a position near Red Hawk, who had stayed with the Shoshones every step of the way. Before them lay thick undergrowth and tall trees. Underfoot lay a carpet of pine needles and matted vegetation. A deathly silence shrouded the wilderness.

Nate wondered if the Bloods would employ a tactic invariably resorted to by the Blackfeet when they were on the defensive. When pressed, the Blackfeet would hastily erect conical forts constructed from long tree limbs, then wage their fight from inside such crude shelters. The forts were proof against arrows and lances, but they were of little protection against guns. Once a group of trappers had surrounded a fort occupied by ten Blackfeet and slain all but one simply by shooting into the center of the structure.

Something moved up ahead.

Leaning low over the pommel to minimize his silhouette, Nate scoured the forest. Since the Bloods hadn't had the time to erect forts, they would try to spring an ambush at any moment, and Nate didn't intend to be on the receiving end of one of their barbed shafts.

Spotted Bull and Touch The Clouds had pulled slightly in front of the others. The giant held his lance poised to throw.

Suddenly harsh cries rent the stillness, and the Bloods swarmed from concealment in a frenzy of swirling tomahawks and war clubs. Several employed bows with lethal effect.

In the opening moments of the battle Nate saw three Shoshones go down, and then the band retaliated with vigor, bearing down on their enemies and fighting man to man, many leaping from their horses and forsaking their height advantage to get in close. He marveled that few of the Shoshones used their bows, but then recalled that it was considered far braver for a warrior to kill with a club or a tomahawk than to kill from a distance with an arrow. The highest coup always went to those who slew their foes in personal combat.

The next moment reflection became impossible. A beefy Blood dashed toward him, a war club uplifted to strike. Nate felt no compunction about killing from a distance; the Blood was still 12 feet away when he took a hasty bead and fired, his ball coring the man's brain and flipping the warrior onto his back.

He wrenched on the reins, bringing his stallion to a halt behind a pine tree, and grabbed his powder horn to reload. To his right was Red Hawk, still mounted and trying to pierce a Blood with his lance. The Blood pranced just out of range, waving a tomahawk and taunting the Oglala to try harder.

Nate spied another Blood, armed with a war club, closing on Red Hawk from the rear. He quickly drew his right flintlock, extended the pistol, and when the Blood drew back an arm to smash the war club against Red Hawk's spine, he fired. Lead and smoke spurted from the pistol at the sharp report, and a hole blossomed in the center of the Blood's chest. The warrior clutched at the wound, screamed, and pitched onto his face.

All around Nate was a whirling melee of savage combatants. The Bloods, for the most part, were naked from the waist up and had their faces painted for war. Otherwise, Nate would have had a difficult time telling the two factions apart.

He constantly glanced right and left, his body tingling in expectation of being hit by an arrow, as he hurriedly reloaded the flintlock, then the rifle. When under pressure he could load any of his weapons in under 30 seconds. This time he did the two in under forty.

The Shoshones were keeping the Bloods busy. Outnumbered, the Bloods fought valiantly, refusing to give up. Bodies dotted the ground, some twitching and convulsing. A horse was down on its side, accidentally struck in the neck by an arrow.

Nate tried to keep track of his friends, but the task was hopeless. He'd lost sight of Spotted Bull and Touch The Clouds. Drags The Rope was off somewhere to the west. Red Hawk had dispatched the prancing Blood and was now after another.

A strident chorus of whoops and yells filled the woods, mixed intermittently with the death wail of a dying warrior. Bedlam and unbridled brutality reigned throughout the forest.

Wedging the reloaded pistol under his belt, Nate rode forward, prepared to aid Shoshones in trouble, but not intending to become actively involved unless put upon. Almost immediately, he was. A lean Blood, a tomahawk in one hand and a bloody scalp in the other, bounded at him with the feline grace of a lynx about to spring on its prey.

Nate didn't have time to aim. He simply pointed the Hawken in the Blood's direction and hastily fired, the rifle recoiling as it boomed. The ball smash into the warrior's forehead. Then the Blood stumbled forward, propelled by his momentum, and thudded to the earth at the stallion's feet.

An arrow streaked out of nowhere and smacked into a nearby tree.

To the right a Shoshone and a Blood were grappling on the ground, locked in a grim clash to the death.

Nate kept going. If he stayed in one spot, he practically invited the Bloods to use him as a pincushion. He drew his pistol again and twisted this way and that, trying to see every which way at once. The short hairs at the nape of his neck prickled, but he resisted an urge to wheel his horse and race to safety.

The stallion abruptly shied, and Nate looked down to see a dead Shoshone in their path. Jerking on the reins, he skirted the corpse. From the sound of the conflict, it appeared the battle was drifting to the northwest. Perhaps the Bloods had finally realized they couldn't win and were retreating.

A rider appeared, coming slowly toward him, swaying on his animal, his arms limp at his sides.

Nate moved to help the man. He was almost to the warrior's side before he recognized Little Beaver and saw the feathered end of an arrow sticking out of the base of the Shoshone's throat. "Little Beaver!" he said and drew alongside the warrior just as his injured friend started to fall. With a rifle and the reins in one hand and a pistol in the other, there was little Nate could do other than throw out an arm in an attempt stop the Shoshone from toppling. He managed to brace his right forearm against the warrior's shoulder, checking the fall.

Little Beaver's eyes were closed. They suddenly fluttered and opened, and he looked at Nate. "Grizzly Killer?" he said softly. "I am so cold." As he spoke, blood spurted from the corners of his mouth.

"I will help you," Nate said and went to slip the pistol under his belt.

"Tell my wife I was thinking of her," Little Beaver said and keeled over backwards, a protracted breath fluttering from his lips.

"No!" Nate cried and tried to clutch the warrior's hand. He missed, and the next moment Little Beaver dropped to the pine needles and lay still. Furious, Nate scanned the area for a Blood he could shoot only to find there were no other men in sight, Bloods or

Shoshones. He kneed his stallion forward, alert for adversaries, and covered 20 yards without seeing a soul. Then he came to a wide clearing and discovered six Bloods lying sprawled in the positions their bodies had assumed when death claimed them. He halted to get his bearings.

To the northwest arose a few shouts. Otherwise, the battle seemed to have wound down.

Was it truly over? Nate reflected hopefully. Another mounted warrior materialized in the trees across the clearing. It was Spotted Bull, riding proudly, a bloody tomahawk in his right hand, his bow and arrows slung over his back, untouched.

"Hello, Grizzly Killer," the Shoshone said and smiled. "It was a good fight."

Nate said nothing. He would have much rather avoided the bloodshed.

"Touch The Clouds and the others are chasing the few Bloods still alive back toward their own territory," Spotted Bull said. "They will be fortunate if one of them survives to tell of their great defeat."

"Your own people will be quite proud," Nate said politely.

"There will be much rejoicing," Spotted Bull agreed. He stopped next to one of the dead Bloods and dismounted. "This one is mine. How many did you slay?"

Nate had to think before he answered. "Three."

"Truly you are a mighty fighter," Spotted Bull said. "I only killed two myself." He stuck the tomahawk under the leather cord supporting his pants and drew his butcher knife. "You should take their scalps right away, while the flesh is still warm and soft and easy to slice."

"I will," Nate said, and turned the stallion. He'd witnessed enough scalp taking to last him a lifetime and had no desire to watch Spotted Bull take another.

Back into the trees he went, pondering what to do about the trophies he had earned. If he didn't take the hair of the men he'd shot, the Shoshones would wonder about his manhood. Every warrior was expected to take scalps and keep them as mementos of his prowess in battle. Not to do so was a serious breach of the unwritten warrior code of conduct to which every Shoshone male subscribed.

He came to the spot where the third Blood he'd shot still lay and stared down at the body, torn between his responsibilities as an adopted Shoshone and his repugnance at the thought of scalping a corpse. He'd taken a few scalps himself in the past, but he still couldn't accept the practice as necessary or desirable. Of the few Indian customs that he viewed as truly barbaric, scalping was the worst.

Voices sounded, and he knew the rest of the Shoshones were on their way back. They would soon be there, and would no doubt inquire as to why he wasn't taking the scalps to which he was entitled. They would surely laugh if they found that the great Grizzly Killer was afraid to take a little hair.

Nate swung down, stuck the pistol under his belt again, and carefully placed the rifle on the ground. He drew his knife, knelt, seized the Blood's long hair in his free hand, and inserted the tip of the blade under the skin at the top of the man's forehead. Blood seeped out, and he had to gird himself before he could make the first precise incision. He cut methodically, separating enough of the scalp from the head that the rest could be lifted in a quick motion once the knife had completed its grisly handiwork. Gore spattered onto his leggings and moccasins as the prize dangled in his grip, and he thought for a second that he might be sick.

One down, two to go.

He went to each of his remaining victims and appropriated their hair, and as he finished with the last

Blood the Shoshones drifted back. He cut off a strip of fringe from his buckskin shirt and used it to tie the scalps to his saddle horn, where the air would soon have them dry and ready for storage in his saddlebags.

Red Hawk rode up. "This day has made me proud that the Shoshones have accepted me into their tribe," he signed. "They are brave warriors, as brave as any Oglala who ever lived."

"That they are," Nate said.

Red Hawk nodded at the scalps. "You killed three. So did I. This has been a great day for both of us."

"I'll never forget it."

"There is only one thing I regret," Red Hawk said.

"What?"

"That there were not more Bloods. I would have been glad to kill three or four more."

"There will be other days."

The Oglala smiled. "That is what I like about you, Grizzly Killer. You always look at the good side of things."

Chapter Sixteen

The Shoshones lost seven warriors, which was not considered a high price to pay for the hair of 21 Bloods. Spotted Bull held a council to decide what to do with the bodies of their fallen friends. Ordinarily, Shoshone warriors could expect elaborate burials. But when they died on raids or while out hunting far from their village, they were frequently committed to the earth at the first convenient spot. In this case, since the hunting party had traveled less than two sleeps from the village, and since the entire village was on the march and had narrowed the distance even farther, it was unanimously decided to have six warriors take the bodies back. This left 28, including Nate, to go on in search of the buffalo.

Spotted Bull pointed out that it meant their fellow tribesmen would stop for a day to properly dispatch the fallen to the spirit realm. So it would be at least one sleep longer before the members of the hunting party saw their loved ones again. The delay, he stressed, couldn't be helped. None of the warriors complained.

Nate would have liked to be one of those taking the bodies back so he could see Winona and Zachary. But he wasn't asked and didn't think it proper to volunteer his services when he had specifically been invited along as a guest of honor. He helped drape the deceased over their war-horses, then stood enviously watching the six warriors lead the animals off.

The band mounted up and resumed their trek eastward. Hours later, almost at nightfall, they came to a pond and Spotted Bull called a halt. Several warriors went off after game while the rest started fires and tended the horses.

Nate assisted Red Hawk in watering a number of animals, and as he worked, he reflected. On the long ride to the pond he had listened to the warriors proudly relating their exploits during the battle, and he found himself speculating on why he couldn't enter into the spirit of things, why slaying enemies sometimes bothered him so much. He'd lost track of the number of men he'd killed since taking up residence in the Rockies. Some, such as the many Blackfeet he'd slain, didn't upset him in the least. Others, like the Bloods, did. But he couldn't figure out why.

"Is something wrong, Grizzly Killer?" Red Hawk signed.

Nate realized the warrior was studying him intently. He was about to lie, to sign everything was fine, when he changed his mind. "Does killing men ever bother you?" he asked.

The Oglala's eyes narrowed. "Yes," he answered without hesitation.

"It does?"

"A warrior would have to possess a heart of stone not to be affected by the taking of another life. When I was a child, I was taught to have deep reverence for all living things, and especially for those things I kill. If I shoot a deer, I always give thanks to the Everywhere Spirit for the gift of the life I had taken."

"But a man isn't a deer."

"True. I killed my first man, a member of a Cheyenne raiding party who was trying to steal some of our horses, when I was only twelve winters old. For the longest time the deed upset me, and I would have terrible dreams of the man lying in the dust with my arrow in his eye socket and raising his arm to point an accusing finger at me. Finally, when I was older, I went off on a vision quest, and the vision I saw cured me of the terrible dreams forever."

Nate knew of such quests, of how young Indian men and women would go off by themselves to remote spots and fast or commit self-torture in the hope of being visited by a supernatural being who would become the personal guardian spirit of that youth for the remainder of his or her days. The guardian instructed the seeker in proper behavior and in how to perform rituals that would foster health and happiness. "What happened?" he asked.

Red Hawk gazed into the distance. "I saw many strange and wondrous things, but one of the most amazing was the great fiery vulture."

"A vulture?"

"Yes. I saw a field, and on it lay many dead warriors. Then the vulture appeared, flying out of the sun to swoop down and land in the middle of all those dead men. As I watched, the bird began eating their flesh, wolfing it down in huge gulps. As soon as it was done with one body, it would turn to the next. And so it went, on and on, until the vulture had eaten every last warrior."

"And then?" Nate said when the Oglala stopped.

"The vulture kept looking for more bodies to eat, but there were none. It looked and looked, becoming more and more desperate, running this way and that, until finally it grew weak and collapsed from lack of food," Red Hawk said. "I wondered why it did not just fly back up into the sun, but visions are like that. They are not always logical."

Nate didn't see the significance of the vision, but he refused to offend his friend by saying so.

"I thought about it for a long time, and then the meaning became clear."

"It did?"

"Men are meant to die. All men do, sooner or later. Whether they die in their blankets at an old age or die in battle while young, their destiny is all the same. We are all food for the vultures. If men were to stop dying, it would upset the natural order of things."

"But how did this help you get over being upset when you killed another person?"

"Don't you see? Men have been killing each other since the dawn of time. It is natural for men to kill, as natural as eating or sleeping or loving a woman. Yes, slaying another man bothers me, but only if I forget to keep in mind that when I kill I am doing one of the things I was created to do," Red Hawk signed and stared expectantly at Nate. "Do you understand?"

"Yes," Nate replied, although in all truth he didn't. He refused to accept the tenet that men were natural-born killers, predators no different from the grizzly and the mountain lion. There had to be more to humanity. There had to.

"You still appear troubled," Red Hawk said.

"I am," Nate said. "You see, when I was young, I was taught that a man should never kill. Never. It is one of the ten great laws of my people."

"Really?" Red Hawk asked in surprise. "Why is it, then, that so few white men I know follow it?"

"Because my people love to have laws they can break."

"That makes no sense."

"Few things do in this world," Nate muttered, then signed clearly, "I was taught that when a man kills and violates the great law, he displeases the Everywhere Spirit. He will end up in—" Nate paused, trying to find a comparable sign for the concept of Hell. There was none.

"End up where?"

"In a place where people are made to suffer for all time, where they burn in flames that never go out and their cries of agony are never answered."

"Your people truly believe this?"

"Many do."

"The more I learn about your people, the less I understand them. How can mature men hold such a belief when everyone knows that in the spirit world there is no pain or suffering?"

Nate was tempted to point out that a belief in Hell was no stranger than believing in the spiritual significance of visions that included bizarre apparitions such as the fiery vulture, but he held his tongue. What difference did it make? They could discuss the issue until winter, and it would not alter his confusion over killing. Maybe one day he'd find the answer he sought. Until then, he would simply live his life as best he knew how, kill only when put upon, and pray he didn't jeopardize the status of his eternal soul in the bargain. To conclude their talk, he signed, "There is no explaining the things people will believe in." Then he devoted his attention to watering more horses.

The men who had gone out hunting returned with a black-tailed buck, and in due course the aroma of roasting meat wafted on the sluggish breeze. In good spirits, the Shoshones talked and joked until late.

Nate ate his fill, then idly listened to the conversations while thinking about Winona and their son. After the surround—provided he survived—he would take them back to their cabin, and he planned to stop at

Shakespeare's en route. Maybe he would be able to prevail on his mentor to come for a visit. Winona would enjoy having Shakespeare's wife for company, and he could avail himself of the grizzled mountaineer's wisdom. He spent the hours until midnight reviewing the varied and hair-raising adventures that had befallen him since journeying west of the Mississippi River. At last, he wrapped up his introspection by marveling that he had lived as long as he had.

The odds were against him in the long run.

It was common knowledge that few of the white men who entered the uncharted wilderness to take up the trapping trade lasted very long at their new profession. Most perished within two years. Those who lasted three or more were considered old-timers. And rare men like Shakespeare, who had lasted decades, were living legends, widely respected for their store of valuable knowledge as well as their unwavering persistence and iron fortitude.

Nate well knew the risks. But he wasn't about to give up a way of life that totally satisfied every craving of his inner nature. Since coming to the mountains he had found true freedom, genuine peace of mind, and more adventure than most men underwent in their entire lifetimes. Despite the chronic dangers, he felt at home in the Rockies. The wilderness wasn't so much a harsh taskmaster as an instructive tutor. If he kept his wits about him and avoided becoming food for a wandering grizzly or losing his hair to hostiles, he stood one day to be as Shakespeare now was—the epitome of the natural man, rugged and independent and, above all, wise.

There were worse fates.

The next morning the chirping of sparrows brought Nate out of heavy sleep half an hour before sunrise. He sat up, stretched, and noticed he was the first one up except for the sentry. The fire was still going strong. He rose, grabbed the Hawken, and walked into the brush to relieve himself.

All around him the wild creatures were stirring, brought to life by the faint rays of light rimming the eastern horizon. Birds broke into song. The insects buzzed.

Once done, he strolled back to the camp and took a handful of jerky from his saddlebags, then knelt by the fire and ate, enjoying the pungent odor of the burning wood and the warmth on his exposed skin. A few of the Shoshones were snoring. He surveyed the camp, seeing the dozens of buckskin-clad figures with their bows and lances close at hand in case of an emergency. For a fleeting interval he lost all sense of time and place. He had the illusion of being cast back into a primitive era before the coming of the white man to the shores of North America, of being stripped of every last vestige of civilization, of being primitive and in harmony with Nature. He felt as if he was as much a part of the wild as the trees and the beasts. Then Touch The Clouds snorted and sat up and the moment was ruined.

"Grizzly Killer! You are awake early."

"Good morning," Nate said.

The giant yawned and gazed at the gradually brightening sky. "By tonight we should be close to the big buffalo herds. I can hardly wait."

"I am looking forward to finding them also," Nate said to hold up his end of the conversation, and he abruptly realized he really *was* anticipating the upcoming hunt with keen relish. He didn't know of any other white man, not even Shakespeare, who had been on a surround. That thought brought a tingle to his spine. Think of it, he told himself. The first white man ever to do such a thing. The more he thought about it, the more excited he became.

It was not long before all of the Shoshones were up

and prepared to depart. Again Spotted Bull took the lead, and Nate fell in on the warrior's right. During the morning hours little was said. At midday they halted briefly at a stream, then went on. Spotted Bull began relating tales from his youth, and for hours Nate listened in fascination to accounts of how it was in the Rockies long before the arrival of the white man. The Indians had lived much as they did now, as they had for more years than anyone could count. They roamed where they pleased, accountable to no one. Tribe had fought tribe. Warriors had married maidens and reared children. The cycle of life went on as it ever had. For the first time in his life, Nate viewed his own existence as a tiny drop in the river of history. He seemed so small and insignificant when compared to the unfolding tapestry of infinity.

The terrain changed as the day progressed. There were fewer high mountains and more hills. By the afternoon they were in the midst of the foothills bordering the Rockies, and occasionally they glimpsed the plains beyond.

Suppressed excitement animated the Shoshones the closer they drew to their destination. When, a few hours before dark, the scouts raced back to announce that the grasslands were right up ahead, the band broke into whoops of delight and urged their mounts into a mass gallop.

Nate whooped with the loudest of them and waved his Hawken overhead. Although he had once crossed the plains to reach the Rockies, he had forgotten how vast the flatlands were, but was vividly reminded when the hunting party emerged from between two hills and halted at the edge of a sea of waving grass that stretched eastward as far as the eye could see.

"We have arrived," Spotted Bull said and nodded in satisfaction. "Tomorrow the hunt begins."

Chapter Seventeen

Nate could barely sleep. Many of the warriors were the same way, tossing and turning in their blankets and muttering to themselves at their inability to rein in their surging emotions. He was lying on his back, his head propped on his hands, when dawn broke, and he leaped to his feet as soon as the first warrior did.

Few were interested in breakfast. Spotted Bull divided the band into four groups with instructions to fan out in different directions in search of a large herd.

Nate found himself in a group with Touch The Clouds, Red Hawk, Drags The Rope, Worm, Lone Wolf, and a warrior named Eagle Claw. He suspected that Spotted Bull deliberately placed him with men he knew well, out of kindness, no doubt, and was grateful for the consideration.

Touch The Clouds led them northward along the fringe of the forest. After an hour a few dark dots appeared to the northeast, and the giant promptly halted.

"Buffalo," he said.

"Do we try and get closer?" Nate asked.

"Not yet," Touch The Clouds said. "We do not want to spook them. They would run back to their herd and might in turn spook the whole bunch." He paused. "Have you ever seen buffalo stampede?"

"No."

"They do not stop for anything until they have totally worn themselves out. We would end up chasing them for a day and a night. I would rather keep the herd close to the foothills to make it easier on our women when the time comes to butcher those we slay."

"I understand."

"We will swing around them and seek the rest," Touch The Clouds said and started off.

Nate anxiously scanned the prairie for more dots. He counted five to the northeast; that was all. There were low hills a few miles past the quintet, and he wondered if the main body might be concealed on the opposite side.

Touch The Clouds angled away from the forest, making a loop to the north of the five beasts, and headed toward those hills.

A warm breeze fanned Nate's face as he rode, stirring his long hair, reminding him of the scalps he had tied to his saddle horn the day before. They were still there, swaying with the rolling gait of the stallion. He touched them, running his fingers through the soft strands and feeling the consistency of the skin at the base of each trophy. They were dry. Later he would stuff them into his saddlebags, and when he got back to the cabin, he would add them to the string of those he had previously taken.

When Touch The Clouds neared the first hill, he slowed and raised an arm to indicate caution. Hunching low over his mount, he advanced.

Nate imitated the giant's example. He held the rifle

low at his side to prevent the sun from glinting off the metal and advertising his presence. Although he hoped to find more buffalo over the crest, he knew that strays often wandered miles from any given herd and that he shouldn't be surprised to find the plain beyond empty.

It wasn't.

Nate came to the top a few steps behind the giant, then halted in dumfounded astonishment at the spectacle of a veritable shaggy carpet of grunting, sniffing brutes that extended for countless miles into the distance. There were thousands and thousands of buffalo—perhaps hundreds of thousands. He heard someone gasp, then realized he had been the one.

Once before Nate had seen a herd, when on his way from St. Louis to the Rockies with his Uncle Zeke. That herd had seemed immense at the time, but it paled into inconsequential puniness when compared with the herd now spread out before his wide eyes. It gave him the willies to see so many enormous beasts congregated together, and he shuddered to think what would happen should they suddenly stampede in his direction. Winona would never find all the tiny pieces.

The males were magnificent, standing over six feet high at the shoulders and weighing about 2000 pounds. The females were only slightly smaller. Both possessed scruffy beards, shaggy manes, and a dark-brown hue. Wicked black horns forked out from their huge heads, with a spread of a yard from horn tip to horn tip. Large humps on their backs, above the shoulders, contained fat that Indians rated a delicacy. The tongue of a buffalo was given the same distinction.

Nate tried to recall everything his uncle had told him about the brutes. They had poor eyesight, but compensated with a sharp sense of smell. They were fierce when provoked and could rip a man or a horse wide open with a single swipe of their horns. Not very intelligent, they would let themselves be driven off of cliffs or run in circles, which would make it possible for the Indians to use the surround as a hunting tactic.

Nate also recollected being told that their skulls were almost impervious to a ball or an arrow. The bone covering the brain was massive and thick. To slay one of the beasts, a hunter must go for the lungs or the heart. "Aim just behind the last rib," Uncle Zeke had advised.

Easier said than done.

Once a buffalo was in motion, racing along as rapidly as a horse, trying to get a bead on the proper spot to hit was a damned difficult task. And even if a hit was scored, there was no guarantee the buffalo would go down. It might keep going for miles, or it might turn on its attacker and charge. As Nate well knew, there were few sights as fearsome as that of having a 2000-pound enraged behemoth barreling straight at you.

He saw several bulls glance up at the top of the hill and tensed. But they simply stared for a bit, then resumed grazing, their large teeth chomping the grass to bits. There were a few calves among the adults, distinguished by their reddish coats. In another month there would be many more. May was the month when most of the females delivered their young.

Touch The Clouds turned his horse, motioned for them to follow, and went to the bottom of the hill. Once there he straightened and beamed. "My father will be very pleased. We have found the main herd. Now two of us must stay here and keep watch while the rest of us go tell my father and the others."

"I'll stay," Nate said impulsively.

Red Hawk lifted his hands to address them in sign. "I wish I spoke your tongue so I could know what is happening."

Nate translated, and the Oglala promptly offered to stay with him.

"Very well," Touch The Clouds said. "Keep out of

sight. If the herd moves, trail them. We will set up a camp at the point where we first came out of the forest. By evening I will send two men to relieve you." He scanned the prairie on all sides. "And stay alert for warriors from other tribes."

"You can count on that," Nate said, then watched the giant lead the rest to the southwest. Drags The Rope waved and Nate waved back. In minutes he was alone with Red Hawk, just two more dots in the limitless expanse of grassland.

"We can take turns lying at the top of the hill," the Oglala signed. "That way if the herd begins to move, we will know right away."

"I will take the first turn," Nate said and slid down from his horse. He handed the reins to his friend and padded up the slope until his head was just below the rim. Flattening, he crawled forward until he could view the herd in all its primeval glory. He made himself comfortable, placing the Hawken at his side and resting his chin on his forearms.

The buffalo were engaged in the varied activities of their species; standing idly, feeding on the lush grass, swatting flies from their thick flanks with swipes of their long, thin tails, or rolling in wallows. The bulls created the latter by gouging their horns in the earth until they had turned over a large circle of sod. Once the soil was exposed to their satisfaction, they would urinate on the dirt, turning the exposed area into mud. Then they would lie down and roll over and over, caking their coats with a muddy layer that temporarily kept insect pests from bothering them.

Nate's initial excitement subsided. As he observed the buffalo over the next few hours, he came to realize his uncle had been absolutely right. They were dumb brutes, nothing more. The mystique they had held for him evaporated in the light of knowledge that they were little different from ordinary cattle. Although they were bigger and stronger and inherently wild, their temperament and behavior were much like their domesticated bovine cousins.

Only once in the time he spent on the hill did anything of significance occur. There was a commotion among the buffalo to his north, and he looked to see a pack of eight white wolves warily approaching the herd.

Immediately, a line of bulls formed at the perimeter while the cows and calves moved deeper into the multitude. The bulls planted their hooves, lowered their heads, and bellowed their warnings to the intruders.

Nate had heard tell that buffalo did not fear any predators except man. He now saw this demonstrated as the wolves halted and contemplated the wall of sinew and the dozens of horns confronting them. One of the wolves yipped, and the entire pack swung to the northwest and loped off toward the foothills. The bulls soon went about their business as if nothing had happened.

Later, as Nate began to doze, he heard light footsteps behind him and looked over his shoulder.

Red Hawk was creeping to the rim. "It is my turn," he signed.

"Have fun," Nate said and went down the hill to the horses. The Oglala had ground-hitched them and they were standing still in the warm sunlight, swatting their tails or flicking an ear every now and then to ward off bugs. He reclined on his back nearby, put his head in his hands, and passed the time thinking about Winona and Zachary.

It was odd, he reflected, that every time he thought about his son he did so using the boy's English name. But Zachary was part Shoshone, and the Indians would always call him Stalking Coyote. It made sense, therefore, for Winona and him to use the boy's Indian name most of the time. He would have to constantly remind himself of that. Old habits were difficult to break.

The afternoon dragged on. Nate dozed some more. Several times he sat up and scoured the prairie for sign of hostiles, but all he saw were a few wolves in the distance and hawks high in the sky. He was relieved when he finally heard horses approaching from the southwest and stood up to discover Drags The Rope and Worm returning.

"Greetings again, Grizzly Killer," Drags The Rope said when they stopped. He grinned. "Did you scare the buffalo off?"

"I tried," Nate said. "Fired my rifle a few times and shouted my head off, but they just looked at me as if I was crazy."

The Shoshones laughed and dismounted.

"Spotted Bull has set up camp," Drags The Rope said and indicated their back trail with a bob of his head. "Ride just a little ways and you will see the smoke from their fire."

Nate rotated, intending to fetch Red Hawk, but the Oglala was already walking toward them. He stepped to the stallion and took hold of its reins. "Try to stay awake," Nate said. "Watching over buffalo has got to be the most boring job a man can have."

"Once our people get here, it will become more exciting than you can imagine," Drags The Rope said.

Nate swung onto his horse. That was the problem, he mused. He could imagine what would happen, and the prospect chilled him to the marrow. But—and the good Lord preserve him—it also thrilled him, and he anticipated the surround with intense expectation. Was he a fool? Or was he merely becoming more like his Indian friends every day?

He waited until Red Hawk mounted, then headed for the camp, looking forward to a hot meal. After traveling 100 yards, the Oglala nudged his arm to get his attention.

"Grizzly Killer, there is something I would like to tell you," Red Hawk signed solemnly.

Nate waited.

"It is about the reason I was cast out of my tribe."

Surprised, Nate responded, "There is no need. Your personal affairs are your own."

"There is a need," Red Hawk said. "I would like you to know, just in case."

"In case what?"

The warrior ignored the question. "I told you that I killed an unarmed man. I did not explain why." He paused, his features shifting, registering profound inner torment. "I was married to a lovely woman, the prettiest in our tribe. Her name is Raven Woman. She and I planned to have many children. I wanted nothing more than to please her and prosper."

Nate said nothing when the Oglala stopped. He had a feeling he knew why Red Hawk was unburdening himself, and he didn't like it at all.

"Our life together was happy until another warrior, High Backed Bear, took an interest in her. He was wealthy. He owned hundreds of horses and already had two wives. But he was not satisfied with what he had."

The ending of the story became obvious. Nate bowed his head in sympathy.

"He took to visiting my wife while I was away. I had no idea until a friend confided in me. When I confronted her, she told me that she loved High Backed Bear and wanted to live in his lodge," Red Hawk said, his hands moving slowly. "Under our law, I should have let her go. I could have thrown her away publicly, and she would then have been free to go to High Backed Bear. No one would have blamed me." He stopped and sighed. "But I was a fool. I would not let her go. So she told me she was going to leave me and go live with her parents."

Nate nodded knowingly. An Indian woman could divorce her husband simply by packing up her things and moving back in with her father and mother. Had Raven Woman done so, Red Hawk would have had no grounds for interfering in her desire to live with High Backed Bear.

"She piled her belongings outside our lodge. Her father and brother came to help carry them. So did High Backed Bear," Red Hawk signed. "I should have ignored him and let them go their way in peace. But he looked at me as she was walking off, looked at me and laughed, and something inside of me snapped. Before I knew what I was doing, I had my tomahawk in my hand and attacked. He tried to back away, but I was too fast."

The Oglala let his hands slump, his story concluded.

"Thank you for telling me," Nate signed. "If it is any consolation, I might have done the same thing if it had happened to me."

"I pray it never does. When a wife does such a terrible thing, it twists a man's insides apart. My heart would not stop weeping."

"You should try to put the past behind you," Nate said in an attempt to cheer his friend up. "You have a second chance on life now. Willow Woman would make a fine wife."

"I know," Red Hawk signed, the corners of his mouth twitching upward. "I plan to ask her after the surround. All I have to do is survive."

That makes two of us, Nate thought.

That makes two of us.

Chapter Eighteen

It took six days for the rest of the Shoshones to arrive at the edge of the foothills. All that time, working in rotation, Spotted Bull's band kept watch over the enormous herd. Two men at a time, day and night, rain or shine, hot or cold, were always close to the buffalo. The herd drifted slowly eastward, and at the end of the six days had gone a distance of 14 miles. With the green grass in abundant supply, the mighty brutes were in no hurry to go elsewhere.

Nate alternated between bothersome boredom when on watch at the herd and avid interest in getting to know the Shoshones better during those hours spent at camp or while out hunting. He spent a lot of time, in particular, in the company of Drags The Rope and Worm. The three of them took it upon themselves to teach Red Hawk the Shoshone language, and Nate was amazed at how readily the Oglala learned it.

Despite the boredom, the time passed quickly. He

was elated when on the afternoon of the seventh day several warriors arrived at the camp to inform Spotted Bull that the lodges were set up not far to the west. A rider was sent to tell the two men on herd duty, and then all the warriors hastened to the encampment.

Nate rode at the head of the band beside Spotted Bull, scarcely able to contain his excitement. The wives of the members of the hunting party were gathered on the east side of the village to greet their husbands, and he spotted Winona the moment the band emerged from the trees. She spied him and dashed forward, Stalking Coyote cradled in her arms, snug in a blanket.

Oblivious to everyone else, Nate reined up, jumped to the ground, and ran to meet her. "I missed you," he said and embraced her, being careful not to squeeze the baby between them. For the longest while they merely stood there, their cheeks touching, their breath soft.

"I missed you too," Winona said. "When I heard about the Bloods, I was afraid for your life."

"Didn't the men who brought the bodies back let you know I was alive?"

"Yes. I still worried."

"I'm here now. There's nothing to worry about."

"Yes, there is."

Nate didn't bother to ask her what that might be. He knew. "How is our son?" he asked to change the subject.

"Take a look," Winona said, stepping back and parting the blanket so he could see their son's face. Stalking Coyote was awake and staring at the world in innocent wonder.

"My son," Nate said and kissed the boy on the forehead. A shadow suddenly fell over them, and he glanced up. Touch The Clouds was a few feet away, astride his huge mount.

The giant beamed. "Tomorrow is the big day, Grizzly Killer," he said, hefting his lance. "My father wants everyone ready to leave at first light."

"I will be set to go," Nate said and felt Winona's fingers dig into his arm. Touch The Clouds moved off, and Nate gazed into his wife's eyes.

Neither said a word.

Dawn bathed the eastern half of the sky in a rosy glow. The Shoshone camp was astir before first light, with the warriors who were going on the surround tending to their horses and triple-checking their weapons while the women of the village sharpened their knives and prepared for the work they would do once the men were done.

Winona gave Nate a kiss that might have lingered until noon had he not gently pushed away and climbed on his horse. He nodded once, then rode off without a backward glance.

Spotted Bull and 34 warriors were waiting near the forest. No one spoke as Nate joined them, and in a body they swung eastward, making for the prairie, each man a study in somber contemplation.

Nate scarcely noticed the birds in the trees or the cool morning breeze. His mind seemed to be detached from his body, as if it floated above his head and observed the proceedings with detachment. This can't really be happening, he told himself, and yet it was. He would soon be risking life and limb, not to mention his future with the most beautiful woman in the world. Any sane person would bow out, but he rode on.

Spotted Bull picked up the pace when they reached the prairie, and the 14 miles to the herd were covered in grim silence. The two men on watch were concealed in a thin stand of trees a quarter mile from the unsuspecting beasts. Spotted Bull rode into the stand and did not bother to climb down. He moved to the east edge of the stand where he could study the position of the buffalo.

Nate did the same. He noticed a small section of the herd, comprising 300 or 400 animals, was grazing a few hundred yards north of the main body, separated from the rest by a series of low knolls.

Spotted Bull pointed at the small group. "They are the ones we will kill," he said. "Half of you will go with me. The rest will go with my son." He paused and swept over them with a meaningful gaze. "All of you know what to do."

"Except me," Nate said.

"We are going to approach the buffalo from two sides and drive them ahead of us," Spotted Bull said. "Once they are running at full speed, we will try to turn the leaders in upon the rest. If it works, we will slay many." He mustered a smile. "Stick close to me, my friend. You will do fine."

In another minute the band was divided and Touch The Clouds led his men from the stand, heading to the north to get on the far side of the herd. Once there they stopped and the giant waved his lance overhead. Spotted Bull then led Nate and the rest toward the knolls.

Nate figured out the strategy right away. If Spotted Bull could gain the knolls before the buffalo to the north knew what was happening, then the small section would be effectively cut off from the main body and caught between Spotted Bull's men and his son's. Simple, but perfect. Nate tightened his grip on the Hawken and stayed near Spotted Bull at the head of their group, trying to keep his surging emotions in check. His pulse was racing faster than the stallion.

Many of the buffalo on both sides looked up as the Shoshones approached, the bulls adopting their characteristic defiant stance, but they made no attempt to flee. Confident in their might and their numbers for the moment, they held their ground.

Spotted Bull was virtually flying across the plain, and Nate was hard pressed to stay even with the aged warrior. He flowed with the rhythm of the stallion, bent at the waist with his head almost touching the horse's rippling neck. The pounding of many hooves behind him sounded like the distant rumble of thunder.

Nate glanced off to the left, to the north, and saw Touch The Clouds and his men in motion, paralleling Spotted Bull. Both bands were rapidly narrowing the gap, and he wondered how much longer the small section of buffalo would stand firm. The answer came seconds later, at the selfsame instant his group attained the knolls.

Erupting into motion, the buffalo wheeled and fled, and since there were now Shoshones between them and the main herd to the south and more Shoshones to the north, they had no choice but to sprint generally eastward, a few of the biggest bulls taking the lead. Dust swirled skyward from under their driving hooves.

Spotted Bull began whooping wildly and all the Shoshones with him took up the chorus.

Nate did likewise. Gazing out over the rushing beasts, he noticed that Touch The Clouds and the warriors with him were not making any noise. Why not? he wondered, and then the reason occurred to him. Spotted Bull was trying to drive the small section away from the main herd. If Touch The Clouds and those with him were to start making as much noise as the men with Spotted Bull, the buffalo might turn to the south in a frantic effort to regain the safety of the larger body.

As it was, the ploy worked. The hundreds of buffalo in the small section angled to the northeast, at least a third of the small herd well ahead of the pursuing Shoshones on both sides.

A minute elapsed, the race continuing. Nate inhaled dust and tasted it in his mouth. To his consternation, Spotted Bull unexpectedly went faster. He followed suit, riding as he had never before ridden, keenly aware of the warriors to his rear and the stream of buffalo off to his left, not more than 15 yards away and drawing closer bit by bit as Spotted Bull slanted slowly toward them.

Nate risked a quick glance to his right to see if the main herd had moved and saw the whole great multitude in flight to the south. He couldn't afford to watch the spectacle; he had more pressing concerns. Clearly, Spotted Bull was trying to overtake the lead bulls in order to start driving them back into the small herd, and it would take every ounce of stamina and speed their horses possessed to accomplish the feat, not to mention superb skill on the part of the riders.

The 300 or more buffalo were still running hard, exhibiting the sterling endurance for which they were widely noted. Even the calves showed no sign of flagging. The bulls, ever more belligerent and naturally protective, were to the outside of the stampeding horde.

Nate screeched until his throat was raw, then screeched some more. He was pleased to see they were gaining on the herd leaders, but he dreaded what would occur once they caught up with the beasts. Turning such a swarm of massive brutes would be extremely dangerous. Now, more than ever, he understood why so many warriors lost their lives on a surround and why the women of the tribe became anxious at the mere mention of one.

He studied the buffalo, observing their peculiar gait, their bobbing heads, and their relatively short legs driving their enormous bodies, and he found himself wishing there were fewer of the brutes and more Shoshones participating in the chase.

After several more minutes, Nate was almost to the head of the herd. The din was deafening, a cacophony of pounding hooves, snorting brutes, and bleating, frightened calves. He repeatedly glanced at Spotted Bull, waiting for the warrior to cut in toward the lead bulls, knowing if he missed his cue he would overshoot the herd and make a prized fool of himself in the bargain.

Fortunately, Spotted Bull let everyone know his intent by bellowing at the top of his lungs, *"Now!"* Then, jerking on his mount's reins, the Indian galloped at the foremost bulls, yelling and waving like a madman.

Nate immediately performed the same maneuver, his stallion responding superbly, his breath catching in his throat as he galloped straight at the front row of buffalo. Panic seized him, and he thought for a moment that the beasts wouldn't turn, that they would plow into Spotted Bull and himself and probably the rest of the warriors, trampling every last man underfoot in the blink of an eye, reducing the hunters to so much pulp and crushed bone. He could see the lead bulls clearly, see their flared nostrils and their wide, dark eyes, see their sides heaving as they breathed, and see the curved horns that would rend him to pieces should anything go wrong.

Thankfully, no sooner did the hunting party turn than the foremost buffalo tried to flee to the north only to find their way blocked by Touch The Clouds and his men, who were cutting in from their side. Confused, trapped between the two groups of charging warriors, the lead bulls then did as the Shoshones were hoping: they abruptly turned back into the herd. Those following the leaders also turned inward, and the herd swirled in upon itself, in a state of utter confusion, many animals colliding, while a rising cloud of dust added immensely to the bedlam.

Nate saw Spotted Bull take aim with a bow and send a shaft into a bull. The brute staggered but stayed on its feet. A second arrow brought it down; it rolled forward and crashed into a cow. He glanced both ways and suddenly realized he was in the midst of the milling herd, surrounded by 2000-pound monsters, hemmed in with no way out.

Other warriors were in the same situation, and they were loosing arrows or employing lances to deadly effect, striving to slay as many buffalo as they could.

Nate glimpsed more Shoshones riding around the perimeter, trying to contain the disoriented beasts. Then he could not afford the luxury of simply observing; to stay alive he must kill and kill again. He whipped the Hawken to his right shoulder and took a bead on a huge bull nearby. At the sharp report, the bull crumpled onto its forelegs. Eager to finish it off, Nate reined up and started reloading. His fingers closed on the powder horn, and as he went to pour the proper amount of black powder into the palm of his left hand he happened to look to his right and saw another bull bearing down on his stallion with its head lowered, ready to gore and rip.

Chapter Nineteen

Nate hauled on the reins, turning the stallion to one side, and the bull went shooting past, its horn missing the horse by a hair. Expecting the bull to whirl and attack again, he rode behind a petrified cow to buy time to reload. To his amazement, the bull kept on going, ramming another bull instead, and the two took to fighting one another.

His fingers trembling, Nate poured out the powder. He wished he'd thought to ask for a lance. During the seconds he would be preoccupied with loading, he was a sitting target for any beast who spied him.

Be calm! he chided himself. Keep your hands steady! If he lost his nerve now, he was as good as dead. He didn't dare freeze up momentarily, as he'd done with the mountain lion. He must keep firing and riding and pray for the best.

Pandemonium reigned. The buffalo were caught in a muddled maze of their own devising, with animals dashing every which way and having nowhere to go because they were blocked by others of their kind or the Shoshones, who were whooping and killing in reckless abandon, in the grip of a primitive blood lust.

Nate got the Hawken reloaded and looked around for the bull he'd wounded. The animal was nowhere in sight, hidden by the ever thickening shroud of dust. Suddenly a buffalo bumped into his stallion's flank, and he goaded the horse forward but could only go a few feet so dense was the press of baffled brutes. Many buffalo were utterly confounded and stood there in helpless bewilderment, making no move to attack the Shoshones. Other animals, however, seemed to know instinctively just who to blame for their predicament and were charging the warriors as opportunities presented themselves.

Aiming hastily, Nate shot a cow. Reloading hurriedly, he shot another. His hands were a blur as he used the powder horn, reached into the ammunition pouch, and employed the ramrod. Move! Move! Move! he mentally shrieked. To slow down was to die.

He saw the bull he'd wounded and shot it, then moved a yard to reload yet again. The dust temporarily parted and he spotted Worm a dozen yards off, wedged in by buffalo and jabbing to the right and left with a lance. To his horror, an enormous bull lunged at Worm's horse, the curved horns slicing into the poor mount's stomach as easily as a sharp knife through butter. The war-horse threw back its head and neighed in terror, and then the buffalo slammed into it again and the horse went down.

Nate saw Worm leap clear, but now the Shoshone was afoot among the beasts, and Nate frantically kicked his stallion in an attempt to forge through the buffalo and reach the warrior. Worm speared a cow and she keeled over. The Shoshone rotated, his lance upraised for another cast.

Out of the pack came another bull, massive head down, hooves drumming forcefully.

"Worm!" Nate shouted in warning and gripped one of his pistols. The flintlocks wouldn't down a buffalo, but they might distract it. He started to yank the gun free.

Worm turned, saw the charging bull, and went to cast his lance. The bull reached him first, its broad forehead smacking into his chest and lifting him clean off the ground.

Nate distinctly heard the loud crack of Worm's ribs caving in. Blood spurted from the warrior's mouth, and then Worm fell in front of the bull and was lost to sight. Other beasts trampled him.

Appalled, Nate reloaded the Hawken, aimed at a nearby bull, and fired. He didn't know how long he could sustain such a hectic pace. His heart pounded in his chest and there was a roaring in his ears. Ignore it, he admonished himself. He had to ignore everything but the buffalo and shoot them until the rifle barrel became too hot to touch, and maybe he'd survive.

He downed another brute, then another, and lost track of the number he killed from there. Desperately, mechanically, he reloaded and fired, reloaded and fired, reloaded and fired. A small cloud of gunsmoke hovered above him, mixing with the dust. He shot and shot and shot until his hands were sore from shoving the ramrod home and his fingers were caked with grainy gunpowder. And still he shot some more.

Suddenly he noticed the buffalo had thinned out and he had extra space in which to turn the stallion. Either he had emerged from the center of the herd or the animals on the outer edge had fled, allowing those hemmed in the middle to flee. The dust was now so thick he could barely see ten feet in any direction. He spotted a dead horse to his right, but there was no sign of the rider. There were dead buffalo everywhere.

He skirted a convulsing cow and stopped when a Shoshone materialized out of the dust cloud like a ghost out of the fog. It was Spotted Bull, and the warrior smiled.

"Grizzly Killer! My wife will be pleased with her robe!"

Nate grinned, then stiffened when he spied a bull charging at Spotted Bull from the warrior's right side. "Look out!" he cried, goading the stallion forward to try to intercept the beast.

But the buffalo was lightning fast, and it was on Spotted Bull before the man could move his horse out of its path. The brute rammed into the mount, knocking the horse flat. But as the animal went down, Spotted Bull vaulted from its back, landed on his right shoulder, and rolled to his feet, his right hand sweeping an arrow from his quiver.

He never got the shaft off.

Uttering a roar of rage, Touch The Clouds galloped onto the scene, his huge lance held with the sharpened tip down, his muscular body braced for the impact. He never slowed, never deviated from his course, charging the bull as it tried to go after his father. The lance tore into the bull's side just shy of the ribs and sank in over a yard. The bull went berserk, thrashing and tugging to one side, trying to pull loose. Touch The Clouds held on firmly, his features flushed from the herculean exertion. He abruptly changed tactics, urging his horse to step forward, burying the lance farther.

The bull snorted, then went completely rigid and fell on its side with a pronounced thud.

Spotted Bull took two bounds and jumped up onto the back of Touch The Clouds's horse. The giant rode to the left, disappearing in the cloud.

Relieved that his friend was safe, Nate resumed

slaying buffalo, always alert for one that might come after him. He slew four, astounded that so many of the beasts simply stood there while he took their lives. If the Shoshones were having similar luck, he wouldn't be surprised if they decimated the herd.

He rode 15 yards after the fourth kill, seeking to add to his tally, and was surprised to find himself in the clear. There were no buffalo around. Reining up, he looked every which way, trying to see the rest of the herd. To his left the dust had thinned considerably and he saw a lone bull.

The animal wasn't alone.

There were nine wolves ringing the horned behemoth, each snapping and biting at its legs and belly, trying to cripple it and bring it down.

Nate was stunned to see them. He had no idea where they came from. The bull, despite having sustained serious wounds and bleeding profusely in a half-dozen spots, was giving an excellent account of itself. Even as Nate watched, those twin horns of destruction lifted a yowling wolf high into the air, splitting its side. He decided not to interfere in the battle. There were plenty of buffalo to go around, for both humans and wolves.

Turning, he scanned the prairie, or as much of it as was visible in the slowly dispersing dust. He discerned a large animal lying on its side not far off and moved toward it, thinking it might be a buffalo that needed to be put out of its misery. But when he drew close enough, he recognized the animal was a horse.

He stopped next to the mount, frowning at the sight of the nasty gashes in its side, gashes spurting a torrent of blood. A thin crimson trail led from the back of the horse into the dust cloud, leading Nate to surmise a wounded warrior had crawled off to escape the buffalo responsible for the attack.

Nate went around the horse and rode into the cloud,

hoping he could find the man and be of some assistance. Soon he distinguished the prone form of a Shoshone on the ground ahead. He hastened up to the body and, heedless of the danger, dropped to the earth. Kneeling, he gently gripped the warrior's shoulder and rolled the man over.

It wasn't a Shoshone.

Lying as still as a stone, his stomach torn to shreds, his intestines oozing out, was Red Hawk.

"No!" Nate screamed, dropping the Hawken and placing a hand on each side of the Oglala's head. "Not you!"

Red Hawk's eyelids fluttered, then snapped open. He grunted and blinked a few times before focusing on Nate. "Grizzly Killer," he said in Shoshone. "Happy you. Good thing."

"Do not talk," Nate admonished him, unable to stop moisture from filling his eyes. "I will wrap your stomach in my blanket and take you to the village."

Incredibly, Red Hawk grinned weakly. "No. Think not."

"Oh, God," Nate said in English, gaping in horror at the ruptured abdominal cavity. "Oh, sweet God."

"What?" Red Hawk asked, again using Shoshone.

"I do not want you to die," Nate said, choking on his words, swallowing hard when he was done.

"All die, Grizzly Killer," Red Hawk said. He coughed and grimaced.

"There must be something I can do," Nate said forlornly. Ineffable sorrow racked him, and he bit his lower lip to keep from crying.

"Remember me."

"I will," Nate promised. "Always."

Red Hawk coughed louder, and crimson drops formed at both corners of his mouth. "Not long," he breathed. His eyelids fluttered a second time. He wheezed, then regained full consciousness and stared intently at Nate. "One thing do me. Please."

"Anything. Anything at all."

"Tell Willow Woman—" Red Hawk began and stopped to groan and shiver. He took a deep breath and continued swiftly. "Tell Willow Woman I sorry. Love her much."

Nate tried to respond but his throat was strangely constricted.

"Please," Red Hawk said.

"I will," Nate croaked.

A serene expression came over Red Hawk's face and he smiled. "Thank you, friend. Thank you."

Nate felt the Oglala stiffen and saw Red Hawk's eyes go blank. "No!" he wailed and violently shook his friend's head, trying to shake the life back into him, shaking until his arms were so tired they could barely move. He belatedly realized what he was doing and ceased, aghast. A soul-wrenching sob tore from his lips and was carried on the sluggish breeze.

He heard a snort and grabbed the Hawken, his misery curtailed by the realization he might be in great peril. Surging upright, he spun and was astounded to see that the dust cloud had for the most part dispersed. He could see the prairie and the aftermath of the surround, and he could scarcely credit the testimony of his own eyes. It was as if Ares, the ancient Greek god of war had paid the earth a visit and waged battle with a horde of shaggy brutes. The prairie resembled a battlefield. No—it was a battlefield, and the soil in many places now bore a scarlet tinge. Scores of buffalo lay dying or dead, many in pools of blood. Dozens of wounded animals staggered in a vain attempt to run or stood with red rivulets pouring from their wounds. Here and there were fallen horses. And mingled among the animals were the bodies of five Shoshones.

Five Shoshones and one Oglala.

* * *

Three weeks later.

"I am sorry to see you go," Spotted Bull said sincerely. "We have enjoyed your company."

Nate, astride the stallion, hefted the Hawken and looked down at his host. Beside Spotted Bull stood Morning Dove, her fine new robe over her slender shoulders. A few feet to their rear, next to the lodge entrance, was Willow Woman. "We can never thank you enough for your kindness and hospitality," he said. "I hope you will permit us to return the favor one day by paying us a visit at our wooden lodge."

"We will," Spotted Bull promised. "I would like to see your unusual lodge for myself. Perhaps then I will understand why a man would build a lodge that must always stay in the same spot."

"Come whenever you want," Winona said. She sat on the mare, Stalking Coyote in a cradleboard strapped to her back. "Our home is your home."

Nate smiled, wheeled the stallion, and grasped the lead to their pack animal securely in his left hand. He rode southward, winding among the lodges, and didn't speak again until they had left the village a good distance behind. "At last," he said in English, glancing at Winona. "I like your kin and all, but we should have left a week or so ago."

"My aunt insisted that we stay a little longer. How could we refuse?"

"Are you upset that we're leaving now?" Nate asked. "We can turn around and go back, if you want."

Winona shook her head. "No. I am as eager to reach our cabin as you are."

"Are you certain?" Nate pressed her, well aware of her tendency to keep things that upset her to herself so she wouldn't in turn upset him.

"Yes," Winona said. "It is well we left now, before Willow Woman had a chance to talk to you."

"Willow Woman?" Nate said in surprise. "What did she want to talk to me about?"

"She wanted to ask you a question," Winona said, her tone betraying a degree of annoyance. "And I would rather not discuss it."

"Why not?"

"Because I have already decided what your answer to her would be," Winona said, gazing straight ahead.

"That's nice of you," Nate said, grinning. "Then there isn't any harm in telling me, is there?"

Winona looked at him and pursed her lips. "All right. I will let you know, only because you will pester me forever if I do not."

Nate waited.

"She was going to ask you if you would be interested in having two wives," Winona said in a rush.

Thinking that his wife was joking, Nate was about to laugh when he saw the anger in her eyes and knew she was serious. He also understood why she was so glad to be departing. Then, knowing full well he might have to spend a few nights sleeping on the floor when they got home, he asked a question of his own, struggling to stay composed. "What did you decide, anyway?"

WILDERNESS DOUBLE EDITION
DAVID THOMPSON

SAVE $$$!
The epic struggle for survival in America's untamed West.

Tomahawk Revenge. In 1828, few white men set foot west of the Mississippi River. Only tough mountain men like Nathaniel King have the strength and knowledge to carve out a life in that savage region. But when a war party of Blackfoot Indians kidnaps his friend Shakespeare McNair, Nathaniel finds his survival skills tested as never before. If King makes one mistake, neither he nor Shakespeare will live to tell the tale.

And in the same action–packed volume...

Black Powder Justice. When three vicious trappers ambush him and kidnap his pregnant wife, Winona, Nathaniel King faces the greatest challenge of his life. For if Nate doesn't rescue Winona and their unborn child, the life he has worked so hard to build will be worthless.

____4259-2 $4.99 US/$5.99 CAN

Dorchester Publishing Co., Inc.
65 Commerce Road
Stamford, CT 06902

Please add $1.75 for shipping and handling for the first book and

$.50 for each book thereafter. NY, NYC, PA and CT residents, please add appropriate sales tax. No cash, stamps, or C.O.D.s. All orders shipped within 6 weeks via postal service book rate. Canadian orders require $2.00 extra postage and must be paid in U.S. dollars through a U.S. banking facility.

Name _____
Address _____
City _____ State _____ Zip _____
I have enclosed $_____ in payment for the checked book(s).
Payment <u>must</u> accompany all orders. ❏ Please send a free catalog.

WILDERNESS

GIANT SPECIAL EDITION:
HAWKEN FURY
by David Thompson

Tough mountain men, proud Indians, and an America that was wild and free! It's twice the authentic frontier action and adventure during America's Black Powder Days!

AMERICA 1836

Although it took immense courage for frontiersmen like Nathaniel King to venture into the vast territories west of the Mississippi River, the freedom those bold adventures won in the unexplored region was worth the struggle.

THE HOME OF THE BRAVE

But when an old sweetheart from the East came searching for him, King learned that sometimes the deadliest foe could appear to be a trusted friend. And if he wasn't careful, the life he had worked so hard to build might be stolen from him and traded away for a few pieces of gold.

_3516-2 $4.50 US/$5.50 CAN

Dorchester Publishing Co., Inc.
65 Commerce Road
Stamford, CT 06902

Please add $1.75 for shipping and handling for the first book and $.50 for each book thereafter. NY, NYC, PA and CT residents, please add appropriate sales tax. No cash, stamps, or C.O.D.s. All orders shipped within 6 weeks via postal service book rate. Canadian orders require $2.00 extra postage and must be paid in U.S. dollars through a U.S. banking facility.

Name _____

Address _____

City _____ State _____ Zip _____

I have enclosed $_____ in payment for the checked book(s).

Payment **must** accompany all orders.□ Please send a free catalog.

WILDERNESS GIANT SPECIAL EDITION:

PRAIRIE BLOOD
David Thompson

The epic struggle for survival on America's frontier—in a Giant Special Edition!

While America is still a wild land, tough mountain men like Nathaniel King dare to venture into the majestic Rockies. And though he battles endlessly against savage enemies and hostile elements, his reward is a world unfettered by the corruption that grips the cities back east.

Then Nate's young son disappears, and the life he has struggled to build seems worthless. A desperate search is mounted to save Zach before he falls victim to untold perils. If the rugged pioneers are too late—and Zach hasn't learned the skills he needs to survive—all the freedom on the frontier won't save the boy.

_3679-7 $4.99

Dorchester Publishing Co., Inc.
65 Commerce Road
Stamford, CT 06902

Please add $1.75 for shipping and handling for the first book and $.50 for each book thereafter. NY, NYC, PA and CT residents, please add appropriate sales tax. No cash, stamps, or C.O.D.s. All orders shipped within 6 weeks via postal service book rate. Canadian orders require $2.00 extra postage and must be paid in U.S. dollars through a U.S. banking facility.

Name _____
Address _____
City _____ State _____ Zip _____
I have enclosed $_____ in payment for the checked book(s).
Payment <u>must</u> accompany all orders.☐ Please send a free catalog.

TWICE THE FRONTIER ACTION AND ADVENTURE IN ONE GIANT EDITION!

WILDERNESS

GIANT SPECIAL EDITION:
THE TRAIL WEST
David Thompson

Far from the teeming streets of civilization, rugged pioneers dare to carve a life out of the savage frontier, but few have a prayer of surviving there. Bravest among the frontiersmen is Nathaniel King—loyal friend, master trapper, and grizzly killer. Then a rich Easterner hires Nate to guide him to the virgin lands west of the Rockies, and he finds his life threatened by hostile Indians, greedy backshooters, and renegade settlers. If Nate fails to defeat those vicious enemies, he'll wind up buried beneath six feet of dirt.

—3938-9 $5.99 US/$7.99 CAN

Dorchester Publishing Co., Inc.
65 Commerce Road
Stamford, CT 06902

Please add $1.75 for shipping and handling for the first book and $.50 for each book thereafter. NY, NYC, PA and CT residents, please add appropriate sales tax. No cash, stamps, or C.O.D.s. All orders shipped within 6 weeks via postal service book rate. Canadian orders require $2.00 extra postage and must be paid in U.S. dollars through a U.S. banking facility.

Name_____
Address_____
City _____ State_____Zip_____
I have enclosed $_____in payment for the checked book(s).
Payment <u>must</u> accompany all orders.☐ Please send a free catalog.

ATTENTION WESTERN CUSTOMERS!

SPECIAL TOLL-FREE NUMBER
1-800-481-9191

Call Monday through Friday
12 noon to 10 p.m.
Eastern Time
Get a free catalogue,
join the Western Book Club,
and order books using your
Visa, MasterCard,
or Discover®

Leisure
Books